UNDERWORLD

Also by Shaun Clarke

The Exit Club

UNDERWORLD

Shaun Clarke

Hodder & Stoughton

Copyright © 1997 by Shaun Clarke

First published in Great Britain in 1997 by Hodder and Stoughton
A division of Hodder Headline PLC

The right of Shaun Clarke to be identified as the Author of
the Work has been asserted by him in accordance with the
Copyright, Designs and Patents Act 1988.

10 9 8 7 6 5 4 3 2 1

A CIP catalogue record for this title is available
from the British Library

ISBN 0 340 66063 5

Typeset by Palimpsest Book Production Limited,
Polmont, Stirlingshire
Printed and bound in Great Britain by
Mackays of Chatham PLC, Chatham, Kent

Hodder and Stoughton
A division of Hodder Headline PLC
338 Euston Road
London NW1 3BH

BELFAST, NORTHERN IRELAND

22 MARCH 1988

I t all began when it ended for Burton and it only took seconds.

The beginning of the end took longer, but he wasn't to know that when he sat in the armoured troop carrier, known locally as a 'pig', as it trundled along the upper Falls Road, its headlights beaming into early-morning darkness and a torrential rainfall. His fellow troopers were packed around him, silent, prepared, looking inhuman and fearsome in DPM clothing, steel helmets and GPVs, including ceramic contoured plates, fragmentation vests and protective groin panels. The 'snatch' teams in the other pigs, those here to take prisoners, looked just as frightening, Burton knew, in full riot gear, including helmets with chin straps, big boots, reinforced shields and truncheons.

We're like fucking extraterrestrials, Burton thought. *Even I wouldn't like to see me coming out of the darkness. And this shit's heavy as well.*

He meant the weapons and assault kit: the Heckler & Koch MP5 sub-machine guns, SA-80 assault rifles, Browning 9mm High Power handguns, affectionately known as 9-Millys, and sledgehammers for the smashing open of closed doors. They would know that the men coming at them meant business and that was a help.

He braced himself as the sirens started wailing and the pig made a sharp right turn into one of the streets picked for this cordon-and-search sweep. As the pig rumbled along the wet road and then ground to a halt, he heard the wailing of sirens, the noisy bawling of the troops in the armoured vehicles up ahead, already spilling out to cordon off the street, and the unmistakable *thwap-thwap* and roaring of an approaching Royal Marine Gazelle observation helicopter, now flying in low over the streets, its spotlights beaming down on the rooftops in wavering lines of dazzling light, illuminating the pouring rain.

Glancing at the other men bunched tightly around him, Burton saw two of his team members, troopers Robert 'Rob' McAllister and Tony 'Slim' Dalton, stiffen automatically and raise their MP5s from their knees, preparing to jump out. Rob was like a Rottweiler, small and broad, all solid muscle, plug-ugly and hot-tempered, always coiled and ready to spring, as he was right this instant. Slim was taller than him, but seemed wraithlike beside him, an undernourished, smooth-skinned matineé idol whose appearance belied his experience and hard, ruthless nature. Biggest of all was the team's fourth member, Corporal Winslow, fondly known as Big Bad Jake, built like an oak tree, absolutely fearless, and now holding his MP5 in one big fist, the thick handle of his sledgehammer in the other. Like Burton, none of these men were wearing their beige beret with badge; they were dressed like ordinary Army soldiers to ensure that they wouldn't stand out in the general mêlée. Their faces – or what could be seen of them between their helmets and chin-protectors – were white and deathlike in the light-flecked darkness. This was not a sign of fear. All three of them had been in Belfast and bandit country for many months, so Burton knew that he had no cause to doubt them if things became rough. Filled with confidence, feeling no fear at all, he prepared to lead his team out.

'*Go! Go! Go!*' he bawled.

The cold air rushed in as he jumped out into the pouring rain with his men close behind him. He was holding his MP5 in the crook of his left arm as the teenage boys known as 'dickers', those who watched out for the security forces, emerged from dark doorways and narrow, littered allies, where death and torture ruled, to hurl bottles, broken bricks and any other potentially wounding debris they could find close to hand. Lights were flickering on inside the houses and some front doors were opening even as British Army and Parachute Regiment troops – the 'greens' and the 'maroon machine' –

poured out of other pigs to race in opposite directions along the street, hammering on doors with the butts of their weapons and bawling aggressively for the residents to come out.

Many did so, looking dazed, some still in their underwear, hair-curlers in piled-up hair, feet bare or in slippers. The women were hauled onto the pavements and stood by their front windows. They were completely drenched within seconds, but the men and boys had it even worse: they were spun around and slammed face first into the walls, their legs spread, hands raised above their heads as the soldiers frisked them. Meanwhile, RUC officers wearing flak jackets, armed either with Ruger 5.56mm Mini-14 assault rifles or batons, had jumped out of their paddy wagons and surrounded the vehicles, waiting to receive the first of the prisoners. Bottles and other pieces of debris were smashing noisily around the soldiers, men were bawling, women were screaming, kids were crying, and the helicopter was now directly overhead, its roar almost deafening, the *thwap-thwapp*ing rotors creating a whirlwind that swept papers, empty beer cans and broken glass across the road and forced the soldiers to lean into the slipstream. It was a nightmarish bedlam.

'Follow me!' Burton bawled.

He knew just where he was going. The cordon-and-search sweep was taking in four parallel streets, ostensibly to pick up a whole bunch of IRA supporters for interrogation at the detention barracks at Castlereagh, but this was merely a cover for Burton's four-man SAS team. Their job was to recapture Dennis Flagherty, an escaped prisoner from Long Kesh, reported by a tout to be in hiding temporarily in the attic of PIRA leader Mick Hennessey's house, prior to being taken across the border to safety. Thus, while the other two hundred men of the SF were making a noisy, distracting show of searching the houses and arresting suspected terrorists in this and surrounding streets – bawling angrily, frisking the stunned male residents, firing rubber bullets at the debris-hurling touts, and throwing 'suspects' into the arms of the RUC officers standing by the paddy wagons – Burton raced along the pavement, through slashing, hissing rain, with his three men hot on his heels. He passed under light aluminium assault ladders raised against the walls to allow British Army snipers to clamber up to the rooftops, carrying their Lee Enfield .303 rifles in one hand, weaved between other soldiers and paratroopers even as they were dragging protesting men out onto the pavement, skirted around the RUC officers hammering suspects with their truncheons and roughly manhandling them up into the paddy wagons, and pushed drenched women and children aside until he finally reached Hennessey's house. The front door was closed and locked.

'Security forces!' Burton bawled. 'Open up!'

Not waiting for a response, knowing that none would be forthcoming, he stepped aside and pressed his back to the wall, his MP5 at the ready, while Corporal Winslow, covered by Rob and Slim, brutally smashed the door in with his sledgehammer. The hinges were torn screeching from the wooden frame and the door fell back into the hallway, light pouring out into darkness. Burton went in, crouched low, also covered by Rob and Slim, as the door was still slamming noisily onto the stairs with dust exploding around it.

He heard screaming, glanced left and saw a woman in the sitting room, Hennessey's wife, wrapped in a faded blue-and-white-striped dressing gown, her hands up to her pale, drawn face, her brown eyes wide with shock or rage. Her screaming stopped abruptly, there was silence, then she shrieked, 'You bastards!'

Ignoring her, Burton raced up the stairs, jumping over the fallen door, heading for the attic, followed by Corporal Winslow as Rob and Slim rushed into the kitchen to search and clear downstairs, where with luck they would also find Hennessey. Burton heard them bawling, the woman shrieking, chairs knocked over, crockery smashing, as he continued up the narrow stairs that were gloomily lit and poorly carpeted, hoping to take Flagherty alive but prepared for the worst.

Reaching the landing, he dropped low, swinging the MP5 left and right, expecting someone to burst out of a bedroom, firing a weapon. There was no sign of movement. Winslow rushed up behind him. 'Clear the bedrooms,' Burton told him, indicating the two doors on the left of the landing, 'while I check the attic.' Winslow nodded and dropped low, pressing himself against the wall, and was spinning around, bent over, to enter a bedroom as Burton grabbed a chair and stood on it, reaching up to the trapdoor of the attic. He was planning to open it slowly, very carefully, and call out for Hennessey to surrender. But he wasn't given the chance.

The trapdoor opened, jerked upwards from above, before Burton could touch it. A hand clutching a pistol materialized, the barrel wavering, searching for Burton, and he quickly threw himself off the chair as a single shot rang out.

The bullet ricocheted off the wall behind him, exploding plaster and brickwork, creating a cloud of dust as he swung his MP5 upwards, thinking only, *He's going to fight!* He fired automatically, a short, savage burst, moving the barrel left and right, sending a hail of bullets up through the trapdoor opening, then into the ceiling where the man above had to be kneeling. He heard a scream from up there. The pistol fell through the trapdoor and bounced off the linoleum floor as Winslow, still crouched low, raced from one bedroom into the next. Another shot rang out from in there.

Burton spun around on the balls of his feet as Winslow, struck violently by the bullet of his assailant, fell backwards through the door and landed, spreadeagled on his back, on the floor beside the fallen pistol. Even as the man above flopped across the attic trapdoor, one hand dangling down through it, his lifeless eyes staring down, Burton, seeing his dead friend, not able to take a chance, lobbed a stun grenade into the bedroom.

He waited for the explosion, heard unusually high-pitched screaming, and rushed in, crouched low, his MP5 at the ready, while the dazzling light of the 'flash-bang' was still filling the room.

He heard the click of a safety-catch, saw a man-sized shadow rising up through the smoke, and fired a short burst from his MP5, swinging it left to right.

The man was punched against the wall, his elbow smashing the window pane, as a small girl wearing wrinkled pyjamas rushed out past Burton, screaming hysterically, her hands covering her eyes, and fled, still screaming, down the stairs.

That was the end for him. Burton knew it on the instant. He scanned the smoke-filled room, his soul filled with dread and despair. As the smoke cleared, he saw Hennessey lying on his back, his chest covered in blood, his pistol lying by outstretched fingers, beside another girl, hardly more than ten years old, who had also been struck by the bullets and was as dead as her father.

Burton threw his weapon down. He picked the girl up in his arms. He wasn't weeping but his body was shuddering as he carried her down the stairs. He braced himself for more screaming, the bereaved mother's outcry of grief, and when the sound came, as he had known that it must, he knew that it would resound in his head for the rest of his life.

That's where it ended for him.

The rest started from that.

CHAPTER ONE

'Northern Ireland,' the man known only as 'The Secretary' said in a jaded tone of voice, followed by a sigh that spoke of weariness and cynicism in the same breath. 'At last we have all of our intelligence to hand and the full extent of the catastrophe is now self-evident. This problem is major.'

The Secretary, silver-haired and patrician, wearing an immaculate pinstripe suit with old school tie, his eyes of the clearest, coldest blue, was addressing a top-level crisis management team, known as COBR, pronounced 'cobra', representing the Cabinet Office Briefing Room. The meeting was taking place on 25 March 1998 in a basement in Whitehall, in a room whose deeply varnished wood panelling was bare except for the large portrait of the Queen dominating the wall directly behind the Secretary. The importance of the meeting could be gauged from the fact that while the Secretary was formally presiding over the meeting, the other men gathered around the conference table included Foreign Affairs ministers, representatives of MI5, the Commissioner of the Metropolitan Police, and the Commanding Officer of the Special Forces Group, based at the Duke of York's Barracks, Chelsea. Like the Secretary, whose age he matched, Brigadier Leonard Moorland was wearing a pinstripe suit and his old school tie.

'The on-and-off peace in Northern Ireland,' the Secretary continued while puffing contentedly on a Benson & Hedges cigarette, 'has brought in its wake an unprecedented crime wave. Indeed, Northern Ireland threatens to become the new Italy or Sicily, virtually controlled by the crime barons – all former paramilitaries – and we're going to have to do something about it before it gets completely out of hand.

Which is why this meeting has been convened. Now, to put us in the picture prior to our discussion, the Police Commissioner will give us the full facts.'

He turned to the only person in the room presently wearing a uniform: another silver-haired gentleman, though this one somewhat balding, wearing a Metropolitan Police uniform with a colourful string of ribbons and medals across the chest of his tunic. He was a large man with a flushed, decent face and an air of quiet authority.

'Bill?' the Secretary said, nodding.

'Yes, Mr Secretary.' The Police Commissioner, William Hargreaves, cleared his throat by coughing into his clenched fist. He glanced at the other men around the table, then looked down at his papers. 'The main problem,' he began, 'is that the peace initiative, though wavering, has put a lot of former paramilitaries in the province out of business. To keep themselves active, as well as in hard cash, these men have turned to organized crime. This we'd anticipated and tried to prepare for. What we didn't anticipate, however, was the sheer extent of it.'

'I've heard rumours,' Anthony Courtland-Smith, the senior Foreign Affairs minister, interjected, 'about crime on a large scale.'

'They weren't rumours,' the Police Commissioner replied. 'And the scale is appalling.'

'It's centralized?' Courtland-Smith asked impatiently.

'Yes,' the Police Commissioner replied.

'The IRA?'

'Exactly.' When Courtland-Smith nodded and then fell silent, the Police Commissioner studied his papers again before raising his eyes once more. 'In order to survive the cease-fire, the IRA has to keep its members busy. It also needs approximately nine million pounds a year to fund its daily commitments – mainly payments to the families of so-called *political* prisoners, subsidies to Sinn Fein, and cash for arms. With regard to this money, the IRA is having a particular problem because under the terms of the peace plan, tenuous though it may be, some of the organization's once-profitable rackets have been hit hard by new legislation as well as the successful work of C13.'

'Which is?' Courtland-Smith asked.

'The RUC's anti-racketeering squad.'

'Thank you. Please continue.'

The Police Commissioner nodded, sipped at his whisky, glanced distractedly at the modernist painting of the Queen, which he loathed, then lowered his gaze and went on. 'While Gerry Adams continues his interminable peace negotiations with our sceptical Prime Minister and an admiring American president, the IRA has been quietly realizing its long-term ambition: first, to seize control of Ireland's underworld; next, to become the dominant criminal force in the West – more powerful even than the Mafia. So the Secretary's allusion to Northern Ireland becoming like Italy, or even Sicily, isn't that far-fetched.'

'Thank you,' the Secretary murmured sardonically.

'What you're saying, then,' Brigadier Moorland interjected, 'is that the IRA, far from laying down their arms, are still highly active, albeit at purely criminal activities.'

'Yes,' the Police Commissioner replied. 'Instead of scaling down its operations, the IRA is still training new ASUs—'

'Pardon?' Courtland-Smith asked.

'Active service units.'

'Thank you.'

'Instead of scaling down its operations,' the Police Commissioner repeated, 'the IRA is still training new ASUs and continuing to acquire weapons from sources worldwide, including from other terrorist groups.'

'That confirms our intelligence,' said Daniel Edmondson, the MI5 representative, squinting through the cloud of smoke from his Havana cigar and toying with the glass of brandy in his free hand. 'And of course the Protestants – the UDA and so forth – are doing exactly the same thing, which doesn't help matters.'

'Your intelligence is correct,' the Commissioner told him. 'But we're more concerned with the IRA because they're bigger, more organized, and have close ties with Irish-American gangs in the US.'

'Damned right,' Edmondson said.

'The IRA has intensified, rather than reduced, its efforts to raise money through counterfeiting, extortion and fraud – and it's having even more success at that now than it had during the Troubles.'

'*How* successful?' Courtland-Smith asked. 'Do you have any reasonably accurate figures?'

The Police Commissioner nodded. 'One million pounds a year from fraud and extortion; two million from smuggling and video piracy; seven hundred and fifty thousand from taxis; five hundred thousand from fruit machines, and two hundred and fifty thousand from so-called charities and welfare groups. It's also earning a considerable income from armed robberies, which during the past year alone netted the organization two point eight million.'

Edmondson, the MI5 representative, whistled softly. Whether this was a sign of admiration or disbelief, no one could say.

'And those operations, the armed robberies,' Brigadier Moorland said, 'were carried out with military precision by a gang wielding AK-47 rifles.'

'Purchased from Russian gang lords,' the Police Commissioner responded. 'Now we have *them* to contend with as well.'

A silence lingering too long, too uneasily, was broken eventually by the Secretary. 'Let's not worry about the Russians for now,' he said. 'Let's stick to the IRA. What else are they up to?'

'Smuggling and buying drugs of all kinds,' the Police Commissioner told him. 'This problem is now rife in the streets of Dublin and Cork, as well as in Belfast. It's a real growth industry for the IRA. In fact, it may be their biggest. And, naturally, with all of these drugs floating about, we're having a *second* crime wave, this one caused by desperate drug addicts, mostly young people.'

The Secretary stared steadily at him for some time, letting his cigarette smoulder between his fingers. 'This could all be rather contentious,' he said finally. 'Do we have any proof?'

'Yes,' the Police Commissioner replied emphatically. 'According to a top Garda source, in the winter of 1994 the IRA tightened its hold on the Irish underworld by calling a so-called *non-voluntary* meeting of all Dublin's top criminal figures. We have it on the word of a reliable tout that the purpose of the meeting was to inform the crime bosses, with no holds barred, that the IRA could make them – and I quote – either rich or dead. Reportedly, that message got through and the Dublin underworld is now effectively under IRA control. Indeed, its major figures are threatened with death if they don't pay a regular levy to the IRA – so for that reason, not to mention increased profits, they do what they're told these days.'

'Which is?' Brigadier Moorland asked.

'The criminals are used to control the business, the IRA controls them, and both sides are presently making a lot of money. Since that *non-voluntary* meeting, the IRA's been offloading drinking clubs under the direction of some of its Northern Command Office finance officers. Social clubs, ostensibly owned as friendly societies for their members, are sold to businessmen in return for an over-the-counter payment to the members and an even bigger under-the-counter payment to the IRA – often as much as a hundred thousand pounds.'

Edmondson gave another low whistle.

'This profit to the IRA,' the Police Commissioner continued, 'is being ploughed back into ostensibly legitimate businesses, including taxi firms and building companies which, between them, are believed to net the organization about two point seven million a year. Also, Scotland Yard's presently monitoring a firm registered on the London Stock Exchange and thought to be used by the IRA to launder money and smuggle weapons. A lot of that money is moved across the border, to the Republic of Ireland.'

'That would make sense,' Edmondson said. 'Laws of disclosure are more lax there than here. They'll be well protected there.'

There was another brief silence while the men around the table smoked, sipped brandy or whisky, and contemplated uneasily the true enormity of what they were hearing.

'So why am I here?' Courtland-Smith asked. 'This would appear to be an internal affair – a straightforward local law-and-order job.'

'No, it's not,' the Police Commissioner said. 'According to FBI and British intelligence sources—' he paused to give the MI5 chief a nod of acknowledgement – 'IRA fundraising now stretches well outside Northern Ireland and one cell, the South Armagh Group, is believed to be responsible for most overseas racketeering. While the evidence isn't conclusive, it certainly seems possible that this particular group has been responsible for bank robberies in co-operation with Irish-American gangs in the United States, illegal exports from America of alcohol, tobacco and heavy equipment, and the smuggling of illegal immigrants through Canada and the US.'

'Have the great and the good in the White House, Washington DC been given this information?' Courtland-Smith asked.

'Yes,' the Secretary said.

'Yet the US President still shakes the hand of Sinn Fein.'

'He has the American electorate to think of – all those Irish politicians and policemen; the Catholic blue-collar workers. Our concerns are not his concerns.'

'Crime in America is surely his concern.'

'Not if it's likely to lose him votes. So we must assume that we'll receive little help from our American friend. Please continue, Bill.'

The Police Commissioner sucked his breath in and let it out slowly, as if sighing. 'We know that IRA bank accounts in the Channel Islands, the Isle of Man and New Jersey are conduits for hot money moved around the world. We also know that the IRA is responsible for the widespread circulation and sale of counterfeit currency. Indeed, regardless of the US President's continuing adulation of the so-called Irish freedom-fighters, American Customs have quietly informed us that an estimated twenty-five million dollars' worth of bogus currency is presently being circulated by their organizations.' He raised his eyes from his notes and glanced steadily, almost accusingly, at each of the men around the long table. 'In short,' he finished, 'the scope and reach of the IRA's operations have placed it in a position where it can now move in as the top layer of the Irish criminal underworld. It is our belief that if this isn't stopped, the IRA will end up as a criminal organization even bigger than the Mafia. This, we know, is its ultimate aim and it's getting there quickly.'

'In other words,' the Secretary added, looking steadily at each of the men around the table in turn, 'if peace fails yet again the IRA can return to war with vigour. If it lasts the IRA will tighten its profitable hold on the underworld and become the major criminal organization in the West.' He shook his head slowly from side to side in a negative gesture. 'Gentlemen, we simply cannot let that happen. We must put a stop to it.'

'How?' Courtland-Smith asked.

This blunt question raised a chorus of despairing sighs and led to the pouring of more drinks, the lighting-up of cigarettes and cigars. When the air was dense with smoke, the ice cubes rattling healthily, the Secretary leaned back in his chair beneath the painting of the Queen, and said, 'Put simply, we have to weed the garden. There's no other way.'

Most of the eyes around the table swivelled towards Brigadier Moorland before returning uneasily to the Secretary.

'Just how do we do that, Mr Secretary,' Courtland-Smith asked, 'when there are so many weeds in the garden?'

'Remove the biggest weeds,' the Secretary replied, 'and the rest will wither and die on the vine. Cut out the heart and leave a corpse. It's a surgical cleansing.'

'We're talking neutralization?' Edmondson asked on behalf of MI5.

'Yes,' the Secretary said.

'Is that why Brigadier Moorland is here?' the MI5 chief asked.

'Yes, that's correct.'

All eyes turned to Brigadier Moorland, who showed no sign of emotion. 'I'd assumed I was here for something,' he said, 'but I'm still in the dark.'

The Secretary nodded and smiled bleakly. 'This is a politically sensitive subject,' he explained. 'Because of the ongoing peace initiative, the Irish government can't be seen to be involved in anything that might be construed as an attack on the IRA.'

'And Stormont?' Courtland-Smith asked.

'The same. They're already walking a tightrope over there and dare not be part of any radical surgery with regard to their former enemy. They must continue their talks.'

'But surgery must be performed,' Edmondson said.

'Correct. Even were we to be given the offer of help from across the water, which we will not be, a full-scale war against the new crime barons would be unthinkable in the present circumstances. Our *modus operandi*, therefore, must be to cut off the head in a covert operation and step back while the main body collapses.'

'I take it,' Brigadier Moorland said, 'that you've narrowed the target down to a few, or perhaps even one, at the very top.'

'Six men,' the Secretary said.

That brief, quietly-spoken sentence sent an almost palpable shudder of shock and disquiet around the table, followed by more inhaling and exhaling of smoke and sipping of spirits. Eventually, when no one else had said a word, Edmondson said, 'That's a lot. Particularly in the present climate. A hit like that could backfire on us.'

'I know,' the Secretary replied. 'But it's the only route open. We have to neutralize all of them and ensure that the surgeons are not identified or, if they are, that they cannot be traced back to Whitehall.'

'A rogue operation,' Edmondson said.

'Precisely,' the Secretary said.

Again, all eyes turned to Brigadier Moorland, who smiled slightly, with a trace of cynicism, and said, 'The Special Forces Group.'

'That's why you're here, Leonard.'

'Can I narrow this down to the SAS?'

'You certainly can, Leonard.'

'Even an SAS operation could be traced back to here,' Brigadier Moorland said. 'We can't guarantee anonymity.'

'Every covert operation presents the risk of exposure,' the Secretary said. 'But if we send them in covertly, as civilians, with new identities, the risk will at least be minimized. The truth will only come out under torture and we can even ensure that it doesn't get that far.'

'Pardon?' Edmondson asked.

Brigadier Moorland turned his head to stare steadily at him. 'We can prepare them for the Exit Club,' he said, 'with cyanide tablets. They can take their own lives if they're caught and threatened with torture.'

His steady gaze was hard to meet. Edmondson lowered his eyes to the table, scratched his nose, looked uncomfortable.

'Oh,' he said, 'I see. I never thought . . .'

'It's not something we like to think about,' the Brigadier interjected, then moved his gaze on to the Police Commissioner. 'Which six?' he asked.

Without a word, the Police Commissioner pushed a manila folder along the table to the MI5 representative, who in turned slid it across to the brigadier. The latter opened it, studied it at length in total silence, then closed it again and looked up with his ageing though still handsome face expressionless.

'I know these men,' he said. 'All hard men. Widely experienced as youthful PIRA members, learned even more in Long Kesh, and emerged to become ASU leaders of considerable flair and ruthlessness. Not approving of the peace initiative, they formed an IRA splinter group that was responsible for the many vicious attacks on Protestants during the early days of the peace. They dropped out of sight when the peace continued, presumably because they couldn't damage it permanently. Now you tell me they're the crime lords of Belfast.'

'That's correct,' the Police Commissioner said.

'They're visible?'

'Yes. Living perfectly normal lives at their former addresses – the upper Falls, Turf Lodge and Andersonstown – but back with the IRA, very well protected, and quietly running a number of local gangs that interact with the criminals of Dublin. They're responsible for the rackets I've just informed you about. Each has his own turf, his own army, which is why we want rid of them. Cut off those six heads and the RUC can deal with the rest – including the criminal elements in the UDA – through the due process of law. But those six have to go first.'

'Do I have any restrictions?' Brigadier Moorland asked.

'Yes,' the Secretary said. 'We can't send in an army and we can't send in a gang. We want one man, one exceptional man, to do the whole job. Find that man for us, Leonard.'

'That won't be easy,' Brigadier Moorland said.

'Just find him,' the Secretary said.

'I will,' the Brigadier said.

CHAPTER TWO

B urton knew that if he attempted it at rush hour or very late at night, there would be too many people on the platform. He therefore entered Leicester Square Station at nine in the evening, well after the rush hour but before the late-night scramble for the final trains.

Taking the escalator down, he went straight to the Northern Line and was pleased to note that the few travellers were spread thinly along the platform. Wearing a windcheater, roll-neck pullover, blue denims and hush puppies, he did not stand out from those waiting for a train as he made his way along to the far end.

A drunkard in a state of considerable disarray, unshaven, hair uncombed, his eyes pink and watery, was lolling on a bench, drinking a can of Carlsberg Special, offering slurred threats to an imaginary enemy and only interrupting his monologue long enough to cough and make choking sounds, as if fighting the urge to throw up. Knowing that the drunkard's threatening presence would keep this area clear, Burton walked past him and positioned himself near the end wall, close to the edge of the platform. The drunkard looked up, saw him and bawled incoherent abuse. Burton pointed along the platform and the drunkard glanced automatically in that direction. By the time he looked back, Burton, unnoticed by anyone in the vicinity, had jumped down onto the track and disappeared into the tunnel. The drunkard blinked and rubbed his eyes and kept glancing around him, wondering if he had been hallucinating because Burton had vanished.

Burton made his way carefully into the long, dark tunnel, staying close to the curved, damp, soot-covered wall to his left, using a hand torch to illuminate the ground at his feet between the bottom of the wall and the steel tracks. The power cables were everywhere, coiled across each other like snakes, and he had to be careful not to touch them, as some would be damaged and have exposed live parts. Touch the wrong one and he would die. That was one way he could go here. The other was catching his foot under a railing and being trapped when a train came.

As quick a way as any, Burton thought. *A bit messy for those who pick up the pieces, but good enough for me. Maybe that's what I really want.*

He recognized the self-pity and tried to keep it down as he moved deeper into the tunnel, dimly lit here and there with overhead lights but mostly still too dark for comfort. Also, it was freezing cold, the air damp, filled with dust, and he could hear the constant movement of the rats that thrived here in great numbers. Those he could bear – he had faced much worse in the past – but he had to fight his helpless feelings of claustrophobia and disorientation. He'd had nightmares about bottomless wells and tunnels and spiralling darkness. He recalled them all too vividly, with unease, as he continued along the tunnel, following the thin beam of the torchlight. He checked the ground in front of him, the space between the railings, the wall beside him and the one at the other side, knowing the bomb could be anywhere.

Those bastards won't have made it easy, he thought. *I'll probably be here for hours – if I get out at all.*

The bomb was planted somewhere between here and Charing Cross Station, which was a lot of line to cover, particularly since he had to move so slowly, checking every inch of the tunnel while avoiding the dangers of damaged or exposed power cables and of oncoming trains.

Fuck, he thought. *Here's the first one.*

He felt it before he saw it. The first sign was the tremor that passed through the ground, coming up through his hush puppies, followed by a bass rumbling that seemed initially to emanate from the earth itself, the first throes of an earthquake, but then invaded the tunnel, coming from far ahead. Looking up, he saw the lights of the Tube train in the distance, bright eyes in the darkness, silvery striations beaming obliquely from both sides of a dark mass and shining back off the wet walls.

Instantly, he removed a couple of ear plugs from the pocket

of his jeans and jammed them into his ears. He then removed a pair of goggles from his jacket pocket and placed them over his eyes to protect them from the dust and gravel that the slipstream of the train would undoubtedly suck up and hurl at him. He pressed himself against the wall, wriggling carefully between the deadly power cables, and saw the glinting steel tracks vibrating as the train approached. Its bedlam could be heard even through his ear plugs as its lamps grew larger and filled the tunnel with a flickering, dazzling light. He was beaten by a fierce wind. The ground shook beneath his feet. The train raced straight towards him, growing enormous as it approached, seeming to touch the curved walls, making him fearful that there wouldn't be enough space between him and it to prevent him from being crushed or dragged away. He closed his eyes and sucked his breath in, pressing himself against the wet wall, and then the roaring filled his head despite the ear plugs and he felt the fierce slipstream tugging at him as the carriages raced past. He was slashed by flying gravel, choked in swirling dust, hammered by vibration and sound for what seemed like forever.

Suddenly, it was gone. He heard its roaring receding. He glanced right and saw the back of the train shrinking into the distance, then disappearing in darkness. Spitting dust from his mouth, rubbing it from his goggles, he heaved a sigh of relief and turned away and marched on along the tunnel.

Slow down, he thought. *This isn't a hike. Don't let the trains frighten you. Stay cool and keep looking.*

He obeyed his own commands, slowing down, advancing carefully, shining the beam of the torch left and right, trying to find the bomb. The dust was still swirling about him, reducing visibility even more, but eventually he left it behind him and could see a lot better.

Not easier, but better. It was still a difficult search. The walls of the tunnel were covered in cables – the bomb could be hidden there – and the floor, including the space between the tracks, was filled with rubble, including large stones and bricks, any one of which could have been the bomb, having the same general shape.

Another train came. Burton hugged the wall again, feeling the damp soaking into him, the shaking of the walls and ground, shivering with cold as the Tube train approached like some wrathful monster, its lights flaring out of the darkness, its roar filling the universe. Burton closed his eyes. Though wearing goggles, he kept his eyes closed. He heard the thundering of the wheels on the tracks even through his ear plugs. Again the dust swirled up to choke him, gravel showered up to sting him, and he felt the fierce tugging of the slipstream as the carriages raced past. He sucked his breath in, trying to make himself minute, dreading the thought of what would happen if the slightest protuberance on a carriage managed to touch him – it would tear him to shreds. He was crushed by noise and pressure, almost dragged off his feet, but managed to keep his balance until the last of the carriages had passed him and the turbulence settled down. When he opened his eyes, he saw the back of the last carriage disappearing in darkness. He released his breath in a sigh.

Don't trip, he thought as he started forward again, swinging his torch from left to right, scanning the walls and the rubble-strewn ground. *Watch out for naked cables and don't stumble onto the tracks. Where the hell is that bomb?*

He couldn't believe he was doing this. It was practically suicidal. He couldn't believe that they had asked him to do it, though he knew they had no choice. The world was changing every day, for the worse, not for the better, and terrorism was becoming more refined and absolutely ruthless. A bomb in the Underground. It had to happen sooner or later. When the next Tube train came along, as he watched it approaching, he saw the lack of space around it, the tunnel fitting it like a glove, and realized just how dreadful it would be if a bomb went off in here. The tunnel would cave in on the train, rubble would fill the space on both sides, the power cables would be torn apart and left exposed, spitting sparks, and those not killed by the explosion, by the mangling of the carriages, would either die from suffocation – all that smoke and dust in this enclosed space – or would be killed by the damaged power cables as they tried to make their way along the track, clambering desperately over the rubble in this terrible darkness. It would be a catastrophe.

Burton kept moving. Another two trains came through. In both instances, when the carriages thundered past him, he thought he might die. He wondered if he really cared and wasn't sure that he did. The past was still with him, even here in this hellish tunnel, and the thought crossed his mind that he could throw himself across the tracks and put an end to it. It had lasted that long, the recollection of that awful day, and he knew that he would think of it for as long as his lungs took in air. But he wouldn't do it – he knew that much. He had too much to live for. He had his wife and his kids, he had the Regiment, he had some kind of life. What he wanted was not oblivion, the Exit Club, but some form of redemption. He needed that pretty badly.

For Christ's sake, stop thinking about it. That's a form of self-pity. Think about the job, about the bomb, and then get the hell out of here. Where the hell have they hidden it?

He advanced along the tunnel. Another Tube train came and went. As it passed him, something flew up off the track and struck his left shoulder. The force of the blow punched him sideways and made him drop the torch, plunging him into almost total darkness and instant disorientation. He froze where he was standing, trying to get his senses back. He reached out for the wall, then just as quickly withdrew his hand in case he touched an exposed power cable. Breathing deeply, he bent his knees and lowered himself to the ground.

He spread his fingers to grope for the torch, then remembered that there were cables on the ground also and withdrew his hand again. Straining to see down through the darkness, he gradually adjusted to it and saw shadowy items of different shapes, mostly broken bricks. A rat scurried across his shoe and he recoiled instinctively, but then he heard a metallic rattling close to his right foot. The rat had bumped into the torch, making it roll a little, and he reached down, hoping the rat wouldn't bite him, then found the torch and picked it up.

He pressed the switch. The torch came back on. Relieved, he stood up and continued his advance along the tunnel, turning the beam of light left and right, up and down, searching for what might be a bomb in the soot-covered, cable-webbed black walls and on the ground beside and between the tracks. He was shivering with tension as well as cold when he finally saw it.

'Thank Christ for that,' he said.

His voice echoed sepulchrally in the tunnel's eerie temporary silence as he bent down to study the bomb that was, he saw instantly, taped to the wall behind a power cable. It was a crude, home-made job, like an IRA car bomb, with the packaged explosive and electric initiator taped to a brick-sized block of wood. It didn't look like much, but he knew that if such a bomb went off in here, particularly when a train was passing

– and it could be so timed with a remote-control button job –
the results would be utterly devastating.

'Smart buggers,' he whispered.

Briefly exhilarated, but still being very careful, he jammed
the handle of the torch in behind the power cables at an angle
that shed light on the bomb. He disconnected the device, which
took less than a minute, then removed a black plastic bag from
his pocket and placed the bomb into it. He didn't have to be
careful now. The bomb would not go off. Holding the bag
in his left hand, he grabbed the torch with the other and
tugged it out from behind the power cable. Then, feeling
pleased with himself, temporarily forgetting the past, his
haunting memories, his nightmares, he started along the
tunnel again, heading for the next Underground station, which
was Charing Cross.

It took forever to get there and more trains went through
the tunnel, each one forcing him to hug the wall again until
it had passed. He was cold and felt damp, choked with dust,
exhausted, still tense from having to be constantly on the
lookout for exposed power cables, bricks that could trip him,
overhead wires that could electrocute him, and areas where
the wall came too close to the tracks to protect him from the
oncoming trains. Also, as he walked on, stepping carefully over
obstructions, looking for light at the end of the tunnel, light
that would indicate the station, his exhilaration at finding
the bomb gradually dissipated and let his memories of the
past slip back in to encase him in ice.

You've got to forget it, he thought. *It's now well in the past.
You can't live the rest of your life with this guilt. You found the
bomb. You did your job. That's all that matters. All the rest is
bullshit.*

Yet it haunted him still.

Thankfully, after what seemed like hours, he saw the light
at the end of the tunnel and hurried towards it. He stopped
when he neared the station, pressing himself against the wall.
Removing the goggles, he was briefly dazzled by the brightly
lit, cavernous platform and had to repeatedly blink against it
until he got used to it. He put the goggles in one pocket, then
turned the torch off, placed it back into another pocket and
held the bag tightly, taking a deep breath, relieved. When
he glanced up, careful that no one could see him, he was
pleased to note that there were very few people at this end

of the platform. Nevertheless, he didn't move. The job wasn't finished yet. He had to get up there and out of the station without being noticed. He waited for the next train, watched it entering the station, slowing down gradually and looming larger as it came inexorably towards him as if it might not stop. In fact, it squealed to a halt, towering over him, its lights dazzling, and he heard the doors opening, people leaving and entering, then heard the doors closing and saw the train starting to move again, inching into the tunnel.

He pressed his back to the wall, moving sideways as the train passed. Reaching the end of the tunnel, he took a deep breath, then clambered up onto the platform before the passengers just entering for the next train could catch a glimpse of him. None of them did. There were no guards on the platform. The carriages slipped past him, their light flickering on and off him, as he dusted himself down with his free hand and then started walking.

He turned off the platform, just another face in the crowd, and took the escalators up to the exit, still carrying the plastic bag. He used his one-day pass to get through the exit gate and immediately saw Rob McAllister, small and broad, all solid muscle, plug-ugly, also wearing civilian clothing, grinning at him from where he was standing beside a newsagent's booth.

Burton walked towards him, stopped a few feet away, then grinned and threw the plastic bag at him. Rob, a former rugby player, reached out and expertly grabbed it, then straightened up again.

'Lucky it's not a real bomb,' he said, peeking into the plastic bag.

'Lucky you,' Burton said.

'I received a call from Hereford,' Rob told him as they walked together out of the station, into the bright lights of the West End. 'They've got something for you.'

'Lucky me,' Burton said.

CHAPTER THREE

Hegarty was breathing heavily with excitement when he dabbed aftershave lotion on his throat, admired himself in the mirror, then prepared to go out on the job. He was a big man, all fat, but he burned with restless energy and the face that he saw in the mirror was not the face others saw. It was a frightening face, self-satisfied and cruel, the grey eyes as cold as stones, the lips thick and lascivious. His nose was broken and flattened to a degree that made it look unnatural, and his visage, which was purple-veined from years of heavy drinking, was also scarred by the knuckledusters and knives of too many old fights. It was a face to frighten most of those who saw it, but Hegarty thought he was *masculine*.

'Sure yer the last of the real men,' he said, amusing himself by talking to himself. 'Now let's go out and prove it.'

Though now a wealthy man, he still lived in a small two-up, two-down terraced house in the upper Falls Road. He washed in the kitchen sink because the bathroom was too cold and he'd never thought to put in any heating. Hegarty was careful with money. He knew that those who spent it lost it. Satisfied, his skin tingling from the aftershave, he walked into the living room.

His wife was ironing the clothes on an ironing board placed in front of the electric fire: a fake coal fire fitted into the old tile fireplace. She was a deeply religious woman and the walls were covered with paintings of various Catholic saints and, of course, the Pope. She was also a fearful woman, fearful of Hegarty, though he viewed this as dependence upon him and took pride in how well he looked after her. Their sex had never been good, but they'd managed two children, both now in their early twenties and living in England, one in London, the other in Liverpool, having fled there to escape the lack of opportunities in Belfast during the Troubles. There were opportunities in Belfast now – plenty of them – though most of them were for the likes of Hegarty, with his particular talents. His children were soft but he was hard and he was proud of that fact.

'Where's m'coat?' he asked.

'Where you left it,' Maureen said.

'Where's that?'

Maureen nodded towards the armchair by the TV set. 'Over there,' she said.

Hegarty picked up the jacket of his plain grey suit and started putting it on, throwing his wife a crooked grin as he did so. 'Doin' a quare good job there, are you, luv?'

'As usual,' Maureen said, not looking up from what she was doing. She was a heavy woman – too heavy for his present liking – now grey-haired, matronly and suffering from varicose veins. She'd been a good wife, an *obedient* wife, but he had other interests now.

'I won't be back for dinner,' he told her. 'Puttin' in a good afternoon's work, then goin' out for some drinks with the fellas.'

'Sure that's grand,' she said.

Hegarty was in the building trade and had kept his business going, but that was only a front for the other things that kept him busy these days. Maureen knew what he was up to, but she said nothing, knowing from past experience that it was best to say as little as possible. She didn't approve, but she knew that she couldn't stop him, so she didn't ask questions and unburdened herself of guilt at confession. She trusted in God, not in her husband, and that got her through the days.

'Right, then,' Hegarty said, 'I'll be seein' ya.'

'Have a good day, luv.'

He left the house, relieved to get out as always, and made his way along the street, passing houses that had once been smashed up by the Prods, some boarded up for years, but were now looking lived-in again with good paint jobs, nice curtains. The peace had brought money pouring in from Brussels and the community had prospered, though not nearly as much as Hegarty and his friends, who were controlling the flow. As fast as the money was coming in, they were taking it out. The peace had been good to all of them.

It was a dark day in March, with a cold wind blowing, but the housewives and their unemployed husbands were out and about, the former sharing some crack – conversation – the latter lounging in gangs on the street corners, smoking and trying to work out just how much they could risk down in the bookie's. Hegarty liked that. Another source of income for him. He waved as he passed them, throwing that big, crooked grin, and they either waved back or nodded sombrely, all showing respect. They'd lose their fucking kneecaps if they didn't, so they all fell in line.

As Hegarty reached the bottom of the street and turned left into the Falls Road, busy as always, crammed with buses and taxis and pedestrians, lined with shops that no longer required reinforced steel windows, he recalled that day in 1968 when the Prods had come up from Sandy Row to smash the hell out of the street he lived in. That had been the start of it for him. He'd only been a kid then, barely into his teens, but he still felt the hatred he'd felt then for the Prods as they smashed the windows of the houses, broke the doors in with sledgehammers, and beat the shit out of men, women and children with lumps of wood, cricket bats or truncheons. Now Hegarty did the beating, using a baseball bat, and he didn't differentiate between Prods and Catholics, though he wouldn't touch a woman or a child. It was just a wee bit of business, like.

The first stop he made during this wet, dark afternoon was at his own company building, located about halfway down the Falls. A painted sign over a wide plate-glass window announced: WILLIAM HEGARTY & SONS – CONSTRUCTION. Hegarty was actually the son. He and his kid brother had inherited his father's business, but his father had died about nine years ago and the brother, Mick, had been shot on his doorstep by a UDA murder gang in June 1979, so now the business was all Hegarty's. The company was legitimate and, because of Hegarty, there was no problem in picking up lucrative contracts for the building of new homes financed by Brussels to encourage the peace plan; but Hegarty also used it as a cover for money earned from many other, less legal sources.

'Sure yer a quare sight for sore eyes,' he said to his receptionist, Mary Dogherty, when he entered and approached the wooden counter behind which she was sitting, tapping inexpertly at a computer keyboard on her desk, staring myopically through spectacles at the screen, and puffing on the cigarette dangling between her thin lips. She had the face of a rabbit – pointed chin, upturned nose, large brown eyes – but she also had big knockers and good legs, so Hegarty found her attractive. 'I get a rise just to see you,' he added. 'It puts lead in my pencil. Any news for me, darlin'?'

'Nothin' special,' Mary replied, looking up and blinking owlishly. 'The messages are all on yer desk, but it's just routine stuff.'

'Sure that's good to hear.' He opened the gate in the counter and walked through to the other side, squeezing Mary's bony shoulder as he passed, trying to send her a message. She didn't respond, being used to his sexist games. She just blew another cloud of ciggy smoke and went back to her work. Married, of course. A young husband and two kids, though the former would be no trouble to Hegarty if he decided to drop his bones on Mary and screw her to Kingdom Come. It was surprising what most men would agree to if he paid them a visit. A quiet word in the ear, like. They'd let you have their mothers, they would, and shake your hand when they left. Power could buy a man anything.

Hegarty shared his office with Joe Lynch, his bookkeeper, who sat at the other side of the single desk in the shabby room, chain-smoking and drinking endless cups of tea. Joe was all skin and bone, had a prominent Adam's apple, was balding rapidly at thirty-five years of age and, like Mary, wore spectacles. He aspired to be a gentleman and wore a pinstripe suit with tie, though the suit was crumpled and badly stained, the shoulders always covered with the dandruff that still fell from his thinning hair. The tie was an old school number that he'd picked up in the market in Petticoat Lane, London, when he'd been over there checking the books of some friends in that city. A bit of a wanker from way back – he had no woman in his life – but he'd kept the books for Hegarty for years and knew what he was doing.

'This place smells like a brothel,' Hegarty said, sniffing the dense cigarette smoke.

'I wouldn't know,' Joe replied.

'Not because yer against buyin' it,' Hegarty said, sitting down at his side of the desk and picking up the top letter of his correspondence. 'Yer just scared of the wimmen.'

'Sure I have m' own contentments, Mr Hegarty. Each man to his own, I say.'

'Ackay, that's true enough,' Hegarty said, mindful to keep his workers happy. 'So what shit have I got here?'

He scanned the various letters, found nothing of great importance, so put the correspondence aside and turned to more vital matters. 'Any gelt come in, Joe?'

'Aye. A nice fat cheque totalling nearly four hundred grand. Our under-the-counter payments for the past three months from the social clubs on our turf. Not bad goin', eh, boss?'

'Not bad,' Hegarty said. 'So how do we account for it this time?'

'It came from the Glenmare Social Club – all the clubs pooled their money – and it's down as payment for that construction work we did a few months back.'

The renovation of the Glenmare Social Club had cost less than £50,000, using stolen materials and cheap labour. The rest of the money was the under-the-counter profits payable by various social clubs to the six IRA splinter groups that had carved Belfast up between them over the past year or so. On the books, of course, it would look like legitimate income for Hegarty's firm. The other criminal groups would divvy in to pay the Inland Revenue demands, when they finally came, making everything legal and hunky dory.

'A nice wee earner, that one,' Hegarty said. 'So what else have we got?'

They went through the books together, totting up the 'donations' paid by, or still due from, drinking clubs, taxi firms, betting shops, video shops, pimps and kids selling drugs. Hegarty had his own turf and dealt with it on his own; the bigger stuff, the heavier earners, such as smuggling and money laundering, was dealt with at so-called 'Brigade meetings' held once a week. He was on his way to one now.

'I'll be off, then,' he said to Joe when they had finished checking the books and ascertained who hadn't coughed up. 'I'll drop in on a few binlids on my way there an' shake some gelt out of them.'

'Enjoy yerself,' Joe said.

Hegarty knew that he would. He liked a *hands-on* operation. Some of his cronies didn't approve, but he thought it wise to keep in training, back to grass roots as it were, letting the binlids see his mug when he kneed them in the groin or

smashed their teeth out or simply did their place over. It put
the fear of God into them, kept him in good shape – it was
better than exercise – and ensured that his nose was always
to the ground. He could sniff the wind there.

'Sure, I'm off now,' he said to Mary as he passed her on his
way out, squeezing her shoulder again but this time letting
his fingers spread out a bit more, inching down to the soft
outthrust of her breast. 'Can I have a quick one before I leave
or do I have t' stay upright?'

'Ha, ha,' Mary responded, used to his crude jokes so not
thinking for one second that he was serious. 'I'm a respectable married woman, don't you know, an' not given to other
men.'

'Sure doesn't that just excite me all the more?'

He left the office and did a tour of his own turf, trudging
through the pissing rain, past streets no longer blocked off
with British Army or RUC checkpoints, to drop in on betting
shops, video shops, pubs, drinking clubs and social clubs where
the owners had either not coughed up or hadn't coughed
up enough. These were the *binlids*: stupid gits who either
resented having to pay at all or, even worse, thought they
could fiddle their own books and fork over less than was due,
on a percentage basis, for 'protection' or as a 'contribution' to
IRA funds. The funds were supposed to be for the maintenance
of various charities and welfare groups relating to the families
of deceased or still-imprisoned political activists, but these
days most of the revenue went to line the pockets of the likes
of Hegarty. Knowing this, some of the binlids were resentful
and tried to resist, but Hegarty knew how to deal with the
dumb bastards. This was the *hands-on* part of his daily work
and it made him breathe deeply with pleasure, bringing out
the beast in him.

The heads of the other five gangs tended either to delegate
this part of the business to their minions or to take a couple
of hard men along with them; but Hegarty liked to do it all
by himself. It was the *hands-on* part that grabbed him –
break a few fingers here, punch a face there, maybe smash
a couple of chairs over a couple of tables or just sweep all
the bottles off the shelves along the back of the bar – create
pure devastation. Were this not enough, he would then insist
that the unlucky owner use Hegarty's construction company
to have the wrecked place fixed up at extortionate cost. Such

performances usually got the message across and the binlids coughed up.

Hegarty enjoyed himself that way for a couple of hours before taking himself off to the 6:00 p.m. Brigade meeting in a private room above a pub in the lower Falls Road. He arrived at the meeting only minutes after smashing a wooden chair over the head of Pat Sheehy, a rat-faced, fast-talking bookie, and then dragging him out to the back of his betting shop, where he'd shoved his battered head down the toilet bowl and flushed the blood off him, nearly choking him to death in the process. Now, as he entered the meeting room, where the other five gang leaders were already seated around the table, all drinking Guinness and smoking like trains, Hegarty was feeling good with himself and his pockets were stuffed with gelt.

'The last to arrive as always,' Neil Byrne said. 'Sure we can always depend on it.'

'Miss me, did ya?' Hegarty said. Grinning, he took his chair at the table, then removed the stacks of notes from his pockets, one after the other, and dramatically slammed them down on the table until they formed a nice pile in front of him. 'Doin' m' job as always,' he said. 'Beer money for all of us.'

'What the fuck's that?' Liam O'Shea asked.

'Bits and pieces held back from binlids who thought I wouldn't be onto 'em. They're all sufferin' for their sins right this minute and won't try it again.'

'A right fuckin' cowboy you are,' Michael Gallagher said, though he was quick enough to take the fistful of gelt that Hegarty shoved at him. 'Always out on yer own there.'

'It's my turf,' Hegarty told him, 'an' I do what I want *when* I want. So, boyos, what's the palaver about this evenin'?'

Neil Byrne sighed. 'Couple of problems,' he said.

'Like what?'

'Like fucking C13 using any excuse to roll up our carpets and look under them. Don't you read the newspapers?'

'I can read as much as you an' I can tell you that the anti-racketeering squad doesn't know fuckin' shite from shinola. They're just dealin' in hot air.'

'They know more than we want them to,' Shaun Keenan said. 'They're presently investigatin' the drug traffic between Belfast and Dublin and Cork. That's cause for a pause here.'

'Why pause? They'll just skate in a cold wind for years. They won't break any ice there.'

'I don't like it,' Patrick McCauley said. 'When you're dealin' in drugs you're on the surface – highly visible – and if C-fuckin'-thirteen starts squawkin' about it, it means they're gonna make a big do of it. I agree we should pause here.'

Hegarty was breathing deeply, feeling angry, his cheeks flushed. They were supposed to be hard men, the pick of the bunch, but without the umbrella of the IRA they were all out of sorts. They'd all been good in their time, fighting the Brits, strongly disciplined, but now that they were out on their own, they had their moments of doubt. This wasn't a local war anymore: it was crime on a large scale; and though they wanted it and were profiting by it, they sometimes thought they were in too deep.

Hegarty knew why. At first they had only planned to take control of Belfast by taking over the distribution and sale of pirated video films and drugs, by extracting 'protection' money or 'non-voluntary contributions' to so-called charities and welfare groups from taxi drivers, bookies and the owners of pubs and drinking or social clubs. But this local racketeering had been so successful during the uneasy peace that soon they had moved on to other things, reaching out beyond Belfast.

In fact, the political peace, while it lasted, had faced a tremendous number of adolescents, formerly kept busy by the IRA, with the prospect of long-term unemployment and boredom, which had encouraged the market for drugs to help them through the long days. When this illicit trade turned out to be lucrative, the six men gathered around this table, the hardest men in the old IRA, had joined forces to expand the business even more, eventually taking control of the established criminal elements of the city and also of Dublin, to create a drugs network that now covered the Republic's three major cities. With the professional criminals effectively under their control, and with Hegarty informally in charge of them, the new gang lords, ever mindful of the possibility of another war with the Brits, had then exploited the unemployed teenagers even more by enlisting many of them into new active service units (ASUs). They'd trained them with the weapons still withheld from the British government, and then sent them out to rob banks up and down the country, thus filling the gang lords' coffers even more and strengthening their hold over the criminals who had originally operated separately on both sides of the border. Now Hegarty and his five companions were the most powerful men in Ireland, north and south, though this had brought its own kind of problem: mainly in the shape of too much attention from the RUC's anti-racketeering squad, C13, as well as from Scotland Yard, London, and the Republic's Gardai. The heat was certainly starting to rise and some of these men were nervous.

Hegarty was disgusted with them. They were supposed to be partners, the six fucking tough Micks, but the others wanted to set limits on themselves and Hegarty didn't like that. There were no limits for him. He harboured no doubts or fears. He wanted to become the most powerful man in the Irish underworld and possibly even more than that. He saw the whole of Europe unrolling before him like a carpet for royalty. The other five knew it and certainly resented it, but so far, though they had often expressed their doubts, they had not resisted Hegarty's ambition. Hegarty knew why. They feared his deep breathing and his flushed cheeks and his hard, steady gaze. That made him the boss. They resented that as well, naturally, and would turn on him if they could, but he had another set of hard eyes in the back of his head and he always kept them wide open. No one sneaked up on him.

'Why pause?' he asked. 'Sure we've never had it so good in our fuckin' lives, so let's strike while the iron's hot. Fuck C13. They won't get far in Belfast. We've got this fuckin' city sewn up and those who could help the RUC aren't likely to talk. They fuckin' know better, don't they?'

'It's not just this city,' Neil Byrne said. He was the one least frightened of Hegarty. Joining the Provos when he was only seventeen, he had covered every base – door-step assassinations, ASU ambushes, sabotage, bank robberies – and completed his IRA education with two spells in Long Kesh. He'd been a hard-line Republican until the peace came. After that, feeling betrayed by Gerry Adams, he had teamed up with Hegarty and the others to turn their training to more profitable pursuits. Brown-haired and dark-eyed, rather handsome, lean and languid, he was almost, if not quite, as hard as Hegarty and often in conflict with him. He was the one to be watched the most.

'So what is it?' Hegarty asked.

'It's not just C13 we're up against,' Byrne said. 'Our drug

trade's been profitable, but it's also put us into the big time in ways that could be unhealthy. The authorities in Dublin are now claimin' that they have a major drug problem on their hands and they're determined to put a stop to it – that means the Gardai's Special Branch. Those bastards know that the drugs are being smuggled in through Cork and Dublin from Europe, so now they're liaising with the anti-drugs squads of London, Paris and Amsterdam. Also, given the fact that we're now responsible for swamping the United States with forged currency, the Brits in particular are worried that our activities are going to spread elswhere and that we could, in the end, become the biggest criminal organization in Europe – and they want to prevent that. In short, it's not just the RUC we have to worry about anymore. Pretty soon, we're going to have to deal with the whole fuckin' lot of them – on both sides of the border, in England, and even in Europe. So I say we should pause here.'

'An' I say yer a fuckin' ijit.' Hegarty was breathing deeply. 'We're already so big, we already control so much, it'd take a fuckin' army to break us – and even that mightn't work.'

'Ackay, that's true enough,' Liam O'Shea said. A butcher by trade and a killer by instinct, he had a scarred, badly twisted lower lip, eyes of the wildest blue, and the physique of a professional wrestler. 'Sure we fought a whole army for years an' they still couldn't beat us, so why worry now?'

'Right,' Michael Gallagher said, grinning and nodding his bald head, smiling out of a pink, babyish face that had never known the shadow of doubt. He had tortured and killed a few in his time but he lost no sleep over it. 'Sure we now control the criminal elements of every city in the twenty-six counties. Those criminals, in their turn, have a lot of Gardai and politicians in their pockets. Those greedy bastards in *their* turn will make sure we're protected. We fought the Brits for years and won the fight. We can do it again, like.'

'What about you?' Hegarty asked of Shaun Keenan, sitting beside his best friend, Neil Byrne, and looking just as thoughtful. Red-haired and pale-skinned, always calm, he took his time in replying.

'I think Neil has a point,' he said eventually, his green gaze steady but not really fixed on anyone, focused on the far distance. 'But I also think it's early days yet.' He had been educated at Trinity College, Dublin, and spoke just like an Englishman. 'Neil's right to express concern about how far we should take this, but I don't think that the Irish government – or the Brits, or the Europeans – can take too much action at the moment, given the ongoing peace initiative. Their hands are tied by that. If they took overt action, it could be interpreted as being detrimental to the peace, so they have to tread carefully.'

'What about *covert* action?' Byrne asked.

'I'm not sayin' they're not thinking about us; I'm just saying that their hands are tied. That means they'll have to move very slowly. I think we're safe for a long time.'

'Right,' Hegarty said. 'An' meanwhile we don't pause. In fact, we move quicker. By the time those fuckers get their act together, we'll be so strong *and* widespread, they won't even know where to start. Sure we'll have the whole place stitched up – and that may include Europe.'

'I think you're fuckin' mad,' Neil Byrne said.

'Mad enough to succeed. Any more business here?' They all glanced at each other and shook their heads. 'Right,' Hegarty said, pushing his chair back and standing up. 'I have to make tracks. I'm off to the Crown Liquor Saloon to have a yarn with some of our UDA friends.'

'Go in there too often,' Liam O'Shea said, 'and sooner or later you're gonna be carried out in a brass-handled casket. Those Prod bastards may be our friends now, but I wouldn't trust 'em to shine my shoes.'

'We're workin' together for the general good,' Hegarty said, snorting with cynical mirth. 'Sure they have their own interests now.'

'Some of the others in that bar mightn't know that,' Michael Gallagher said, 'so you'd best still be careful, like.'

'Ackay,' Hegarty said. 'I'll be seein' youse. Don't drop dead in my absence.'

He went down the narrow, crooked stairs, elbowed his way through the crowded, smoky bar and emerged onto the Falls Road, still busy in the early evening darkness with the street lamps turned on. Though the pavements were still wet, the rain had stopped falling. Hailing down a black taxi cab, he told the driver to take him to Great Victoria Street. Settling back into his seat, he looked out the window at the many people on the pavements, the brightly-lit shop windows, and was pleased to note that business

was booming in the absence of British soldiers and RUC
checkpoints.

The taxi reached the centre of town in minutes and was soon
stopping outside the mahogany and stained-glass doors of the
gaslit Victorian Crown Liquor Saloon which, only a couple
of years back, even Hegarty would not have dared enter.
Now, even though he wasn't welcome, he was reasonably
safe there.

He had paid off the cab driver and was turning away to
enter the pub when he stopped and glanced across the road,
at the entrance to the Europa Hotel. His attention had been
drawn by a woman who was just getting out of another cab
to enter the hotel. Though of medium height, she was wearing
high-heeled shoes and a long, elegant black overcoat that made
her seem taller than she was. Her hair, which was as black as
the coat, hung gleaming down the back of her spine, stopping
just above the waist. She was strikingly beautiful.

Hegarty watched her intently, breathing heavily, until she
had entered the hotel.

Some day I'll get my hands on that whore, he thought. *One
way or the other.*

Aroused and frustrated, feeling flushed, still breathing
heavily, he turned away and entered the pub for a bit of
crack with old enemies.

CHAPTER FOUR

All eyes in the Gallery Bar of the Europa Hotel turned to watch as the lady in the long black coat, with her long black hair gleaming, entered and made her way to the counter. Smiling at the barman, she removed her expensive leather bag from her shoulder, laid it on the counter, removed her black coat as she sat on a bat stool – the movement was sublime and seemed oddly like a striptease – and dropped it over the empty seat beside her. She was wearing a dress of deceptively simple elegance, made from black silk so fine and shiny that it appeared to ripple on every hollow and curve of her slim, full-breasted, perfect body. Its hemline was above the knees and it was held on with thin straps that emphasized the unblemished marble-white of her delicate shoulders. When she crossed her legs, which she did as she lit a cigarette, all the watching eyes widened. Her legs in the stiletto-heeled shoes were long and curvaceous.

'Evenin', Jim,' she said to the barman, her voice low and sensual, almost husky, sounding slightly sardonic. 'Set me up with the usual, thanks.'

'Still rainin'?' the barman asked.

'Rainin' shoemaker's knives, it was,' she replied, her accent pure Ulster but slightly softened. 'Though it's finally stopped, thank God.'

'He wouldn't want ya comin' in here like a drowned rat.'

'Just get my drink, Jim.'

'Aye, Teresa, I'll do that.'

Grinning, the barman turned away to mix the drink: a large Bushmills with ginger ale and ice. Exhaling a stream of smoke, Teresa glanced along the bar. The men on stools farther along were staring sideways at her, but they hastily turned their eyes away when they caught her bold, steady glance. Smiling, she glanced over her shoulder and saw that most of the men at the tables were also staring helplessly at her. The bar was full, so she should have a good evening, though it wouldn't be quite the same.

Christ, she thought, *I'm not sure that I want peace in Belfast. I might have to move on. Maybe London. Mayfair. I know enough to work there now.*

The present peace had its good side, but it certainly had its downside as well. Though the hotel had been bombed many times during the Troubles, this spacious, elegant bar had remained the best place in town to pick up good clients: journalists, photographers, media-hungry celebrities, politicians and, of course, high-ranking officers of the British Army and even the RUC. Now the clientele consisted mostly of pot-bellied businessmen, nervous tourists and local shysters, some of them former paramilitaries who had made a pile out of the Troubles and were making even more in the peace. Most of them, thank God, had money to burn. They paid and that was all that really mattered, but they weren't her ideal.

'Here ya are,' Jim said, placing the drink before her. Nodding, she opened her shoulder bag, withdrew two hundred pounds in £5 notes and laid them carefully down on the counter, covering them with her fine, pale hand to ensure that no one else would see them. Jim took the money – his cut from her earnings for letting her ply her trade here unbeknownst to the management – and expertly slid it to his own side of the counter. He turned to the till and rang up a fiver, deducted the cost of the drink and then brought her back the change from that one note. 'Here ya are, love. Enjoy.'

'I will,' Teresa said, leaving the change lying on the counter and sipping her drink. 'So what's new?' she asked.

'Nothin' grand, to be sure. Some bald heads in computers, some Yank tourists, and a few up from Dublin. There's a few on expense accounts.'

'The Yanks?'

'Two are travellin' alone, without their wives, and they're eager for action.'

'That sounds promising,' Teresa said.

'They're sittin' behind ya and starin' at ya,' Jim said, 'so ya just might get lucky.'

'Pass the word.'

'Ackay,' the barman said, 'I'll do that, all right.' His name was Jim Quaid. He had red hair, watery blue eyes and a pink, freckled face with pursed lips that often broke into a lopsided grin. Wearing a maroon jacket with black lapels and a maroon bow tie, he was a bit of a dandy who kept a keen eye on his bar and liked to talk to his customers, imparting local information to the men and flirting with the ladies. He was popular with the ladies and fancied Teresa, but he couldn't afford her. 'Judgin' by that little pile ya just slipped me,' he said, sounding happy, 'business has to be good.'

'You should know,' Teresa said. 'You see everything that goes on in here and fix me up with a few.'

'Sure that's only in here,' Jim said. 'I hear ya work the whole town.'

'A girl does what she has to do.'

Jim grinned again. 'Anyway, I have to take some drinks over to those two Yanks behind ya so I'll drop 'em the hint if they ask.'

'Only if they ask,' Teresa said.

'Ackay. Sure I know that.'

Though Jim helped fix her up and was handsomely rewarded for it, Teresa always reminded him that he wasn't to even hint to his customers that she was on the game. You never knew, after all, if they weren't there as plants from the Vice Squad. Instead, Jim only volunteered information to those who set the process in motion by asking about her, simply telling them that she was unattached and came in here often. Usually, they then responded by sidling up to the bar, engaging her in a bit of crack, and then asking if they could buy her a drink. She took over from there, sussing them out herself, gauging if they were on the level or not and, if they were, gently letting them know that she would charge. It had worked a treat so far.

'What are they drinking?' she asked.

'Bourbon on the rocks,' Jim replied as he fixed the two drinks.

'That's a good sign,' she said.

Jim placed the drinks on a tray and left the bar to carry them across to the two Yanks. The tables were normally served by black-jacketed, bow-tied waiters, but Jim liked to serve certain customers personally, checking them out and passing the word back to Teresa. She watched him at work. He was smiling broadly as he talked to the Yanks, giving them a bit of Irish blarney and getting them laughing. She saw the two Yanks glancing at her. Then one of them stared back at Jim, clearly asking about her. Teresa smiled and exhaled cigarette smoke. She was having another sip of her Bushmills when a local reporter, Frank Cooney, entered the bar and came up to stand beside her. He was a big man with a shock of silvery hair and a floridly handsome, cynical face. Glancing impatiently up and down the bar, he said, 'Is anyone serving here?'

'He's serving a couple of Yanks over there,' Teresa told him, nodding over her shoulder.

Cooney glanced across the room, then sighed and said, 'Bloody Yanks. Now that some kind of peace has come, they're flooding in to seek out their ancestors. Every American I've met seems to think he has Irish antecedents – Catholic, of course. No wonder they support the IRA. It makes me want to throw up. So how are you, gorgeous?'

'Not bad,' Teresa said.

'Business good?'

'What business?'

'Ha, ha. Sure we all know you're not *Saint* Teresa. The trade's good, I hope.'

'It's terrible the things that are said about a decent girl just because she's unattached.'

'My heart breaks for you, gorgeous. About time you got back,' he said to Jim when the latter returned to the bar and gave Teresa a wink. 'I'll have a large Jameson's on ice and be quick about it.'

'Right, Mister Cooney.'

As Jim was pouring Cooney's drink, the reporter lit a cigarette, coughed, exhaled and then said, 'You're a nice wee Catholic girl, Teresa. Do you go to confession?'

'No.'

'Not religious, then?'

'No.'

'Sure that's rare in a nice wee Catholic girl. What happened to you?'

'I saw what religion did to this country and that was enough for me.'

'Newtownards, wasn't it?'

'What?'

'Where you came from?'

'Aye. My parents moved there from here when I was young – to get away from the Troubles.'

To get away from a lot more than that, she thought, *but that's my business, shite-face.*

In truth, it still hurt to recall it. It would hurt her forever. She couldn't look back on what had happened to her without feeling terror. The Troubles were the least of it. What she recalled about the Troubles was bad, but the other was worse. She had come a long way since those days, but she still couldn't shake them off. Sooner or later, she would have to move on, putting more distance between herself and the past, letting time do the healing. She didn't know if she'd survive that long in this game, but she'd give it a go.

Cooney grinned at her. 'So how did a nice wee girl from Newtownards get on the game?'

'I'm talkin' to a reporter from the *Belfast Telegraph* and I'm not on the game. I'm in the bar of the Europa Hotel, so I'm *definitely* not on the game.'

Cooney chuckled and had a good swig of his whiskey, then puffed on his cigarette. 'All right,' he said, 'I get the message. I'll stop snoopin' right now.' He exhaled a cloud of smoke and squinted through it at the people seated around the tables behind him. 'Anything interestin' here, Jim,' he asked, 'apart from Yank tourists?'

'Nothin' for you,' Jim said.

Cooney sighed. 'Time was, you could pop in here any minute of the day and pick up a couple of good stories. Those were the days! Now it could be a bar in Milton Keynes for all the action there is.' He placed his clenched fist to his mouth and had a good burp. 'Though I see some familiar faces over there – Neil Reid, Glyn Foley and Jack Buckley – all former hard men with the UDA, now respectable businessmen, ho, ho. Sittin' there right as rain, drinkin' Guinness and probably talkin' about pirated videos and their take from fruit machines and the like. You can bet yer life on it.'

'Sure it gives them somethin' to do,' Teresa said, 'now that they've no Brits to fight.'

'I wouldn't mind that,' Cooney said, 'but those bastards are now working hand-in-glove with the hard men of the IRA. Things have changed around here, all right.' He finished off his whiskey with the second gulp and grinned again at Teresa. 'How's about a freebie,' he said, 'for the hard-workin' Press?'

'Get stuffed,' Teresa said.

Cooney laughed and squeezed her shoulder. 'Just wishful' thinkin',' he said. 'I think I'll go over an' say hallo to those bastards and see what I can dig up. Have a good evening, gorgeous.'

'You, too,' Teresa said. She waited until Cooney had crossed the room before saying to Jim, 'How were the Yanks?'

'They asked about you,' he replied. 'Wanted to know if you came here often. I said you did and they asked if you were unattached and I said I thought so. They asked if you were on the game. I said, sure I wouldn't know that. She just comes in regular-like, I said, and often leaves with a man. One of 'em's standin' up right now an' I think he'll talk to you. Here he comes now.'

Jim was cleaning some glasses as he talked to Teresa and he pretended to be having a normal conversation when the American approached the bar. 'So I was saying,' he said loudly, then deliberately cut himself short when the Yank reached the bar. 'Yes, sir? Another round of the same?'

'Yeah, right,' the Yank said. He was short and too fat, his belly shaped by hamburgers, and he had the kind of soft, flabby face that came to those with an easy life. He was wearing a black windcheater with white stitching, baggy brown corduroys, and black high-heeled leather boots to elevate his short stature. Grinning nervously, he watched Jim mix his drinks, but then he glanced sideways. 'Hi,' he said to Teresa.

She turned her head and gave him a million-dollar smile. 'Hi,' she said. 'How ya doin'?'

'Not bad,' he replied. 'Just touring around, having a good time. This is my first time in Belfast. It's a pretty nice city.'

'You expected something else?'

'Yeah. Something like Berlin, 1945. But it isn't like that at all. Can I buy you a drink?'

'Sure,' she said. 'Why not? What about your friend?'

That encouraged a cocky grin. 'He's okay, but he's a bit on the shy side. He'll be happy there on his own. Take his drink over to him,' he told Jim, 'and leave the lady's right here.' He stretched his hand out. 'Joe Donaghue.'

Teresa shook his hand, which was as soft as his face. 'Teresa Kiely,' she said.

'Nice to meet you, Teresa.'

'Same here.'

The next hour was taken up with the expected superficial conversation, during which he told her all about himself with the usual traveller's exaggerations thrown in. He was married, of course, with three kids and a satisfied wife back in Illinois. Not happy, Teresa noted, but *satisfied* and with no cause for complaints, presumably both in and out of bed. They'd had their problems, of course, some of which had been sexual, but he compensated by picking up a bit extra when he travelled for work. He did that a lot. A computer salesman, he had done most of Britain and Europe and the Far East, though this, he repeated, was his first time in Northern Ireland. His great grandparents came from here, naturally. Somewhere in the south, *naturally*. He had wanted to go down south and trace his roots, but he hadn't had time. He had only one more night in Belfast and then he was heading home, flying back via Heathrow. He wanted to go back with something to remember – an exceptional last night.

Teresa knew what he meant. She could make his night exceptional. She intended doing that very thing, but the Yank was still working up to it. He wanted to discuss the Troubles. All the Yanks did. And like all the Yanks, he was intensely romantic about it, confusing it, again as they all did, with the American War of Independence and viewing the IRA as freedom fighters, thinking them wonderful. Teresa nodded her head, agreeing, but thinking, *What a dumb shit*. She had her own recollections of the IRA and they were more down-to-earth. Nevertheless, she agreed. She kept her nightmares in the bottle. Though horror and grief welled up to flood her, she kept the smile on her face. When he said that he wished he'd been there, taking part in the valiant fight, she expressed her appreciation of his sentiments and then asked for another drink.

'My pleasure,' he said.

It was the customary beginning, the familiar preamble, but Teresa knew she had a client when, flushed with drink, he leaned closer to her, boldly looked her up and down, then said, 'That's one hell of a dress you're wearing, sweetheart. It just draws a man's gaze.'

'It's a pretty simple item,' she replied. 'Nothing much to it, really.'

'It's so simple, it makes you look naked.'

'Sure it saves you from usin' your imagination.'

'Yeah,' he said. 'Right.' Thus encouraged, he glanced back over his shoulder, checking his friend out. He saw that he'd disappeared from the bar, so turned back to grin nervously at her. 'Listen, sweetheart,' he said. 'I don't know quite how to approach this, but . . .'

'You want to go somewhere?' she asked.

'That's just what I was thinking.'

'Your room?'

'Well, yeah . . .' He was fingering his shirt collar. 'That sounds great to me. I just wondered . . . I mean, I don't really know if . . .'

'I charge,' Teresa said, putting him out of his agony. 'It depends on what you want. I charge by what you want and by the time, so it's all up to you.'

'Hell, right,' he said, having the decency to look almost embarrassed. 'I mean money's no object.' He paused as if doing his calculations. 'You're free for the whole evening?'

'Yes.'

'Terrific. All evening, then. Even longer if . . .'

'I have to know before midnight,' she told him. 'If you don't want me all night, I need the time to get ready and come back down here to find someone else.'

'Sure, Teresa, I understand. So let's say all night in advance. I mean, the money's no problem.'

She told him what she wanted. He blanched, but nodded assent. He was glancing nervously up and down the bar and she saw Jim's big grin.

'So how do we . . . ?'

'We just walk out together,' she told him, 'like any normal couple.'

'Well, I don't know about that, honey. I mean . . .'

Teresa sighed with impatience. 'What's your room number?' When he told her, she said, 'You leave now and I'll finish my drink and come up in half an hour.'

'Great,' he said. 'Terrific. I'll see you later, Teresa.'

He finished his drink, slid off the stool and hurried out of the bar. Teresa caught Jim's grin and she grinned back and then lit a cigarette. She took her time with the drink. She would turn up late and make him desperate. By the time she got there, he would be so relieved, so excited, he would pay what she demanded without argument and might even pay more.

God, she knew so much about men! She had learned it

the hard way. She had no single man in her life, but she knew those she slept with. She had never met a man she could fully trust because she knew men so well. They were a bottomless pit.

'Still here?' Frank Cooney asked. He had come up to stand beside her. 'Sure I thought ya were goin' to leave with that Yank. Now I'm real disappointed.'

'Fuck off, Frank,' she said.

'I'm on my way, gorgeous. The next time you're under someone think of me and you'll get through it easier.'

'Wishful thinking,' she said.

Cooney grinned and walked out. Teresa slipped off the stool. She put her overcoat on, slung the bag over her shoulder, waved to Jim and then left the bar. A lot of heads turned as she walked across the lobby to the elevator. She took it up to the fifth floor, hemmed in by three men who tried not to stare and failed, then she walked along the corridor to the Yank's room and knocked on the door. When he opened it, she saw with cynical amusement that he had divested himself of his clothing and was wearing a dressing gown.

He's too embarrassed to undress in front of me, she thought. *That means he's not dangerous. It's my night after all.*

'Welcome,' he said, trying for Cary Grant's light touch, though his smile was still nervous.

Teresa entered, brushing past him, and heard the door closing behind her as she reached the end of the bed. It was not a big room, but she saw that he had prepared: there was a bottle of champagne on the bedside cabinet and two sparkling glasses. She turned around to face him. He looked even fatter in the dressing gown than he had in his suit and his legs were webbed with varicose veins and altogether too hairy. He was smiling and his face was very flushed and she knew he was nervous.

'Thanks for ordering the champagne,' she said. 'I wasn't expecting that.'

'I thought you might like it.'

'So what do ya want?' Teresa asked, removing her overcoat and throwing it over the soft chair by the bed.

He took a deep breath and wiped the sweat from his brow with a shaking hand. Teresa thought him repulsive.

'I want you to strip that dress off . . . *very* slowly. That should do for starters.'

Teresa slid the strap off her right shoulder and offered a soft smile.

'I'll take it as slow as ya want,' she said. 'You pay for my time.'

He paid a lot for a little.

CHAPTER FIVE

'Today is April the first,' the Secretary said sardonically after reading the report placed before him and the others at another meeting of the top-level crisis management team, COBR, in the wood-panelled basement room in Whitehall. 'You surely must be joking.'

'No, Mr Secretary,' Brigadier Leonard Moorland said, his grey eyes unblinking. 'It's not an April Fool joke. This man is the best we have for the job, despite my own reservations.'

'In this particular instance, your reservations would appear to be well founded. We are talking about a soldier who was placed on trial for the shooting of a ten-year-old girl in Belfast in 1988.'

'And vindicated, Mr Secretary.'

'Vindicated or not, I don't think that a man with that behind him should be sent back to Belfast.'

'Burton,' the brigadier said, 'spent a total of two years in Belfast, mostly working undercover, and in the end he knew it better than anyone else. He knows the men we want, where they live and play, how they think and operate, and he pulled off some stunning stunts over there. For that reason, I concur with Lieutenant-Colonel Blackwell that he has to be first choice.'

'With all due respect to our present Commanding Officer of 22 SAS,' the MI5 representative, Daniel Edmondson, said, 'I have to say I'm bound to agree with the Secretary. We don't send into Belfast a man put on trial for killing a child there, albeit accidentally. If nothing else, he's bound to be known there and almost certainly he'll be on someone's hit list.'

Seated beside Brigadier Moorland, Lieutenant-Colonel Maurice Blackwell, just down for the day from the SAS base at Stirling Lines, Hereford, was wearing a pinstripe suit like all the others. A calm and thoughtful man, not easily goaded, he deliberately did not respond to Edmondson's statement.

'His is not a recognizable face,' Brigadier Moorland said. 'He never took part in overt operations – he always worked covertly – and officially he was never there at all. The man was practically invisible.'

'Not after the trial, surely,' Courtland-Smith, the senior Foreign Affairs Minister, said.

'Throughout the trial he was hidden behind a bamboo curtain and addressed only as Soldier "A". His identity was never revealed and it's not going to be.'

'He still killed a ten-year-old child,' Courtland-Smith said.

Brigadier Moorland was resolute. 'The jury concluded that the girl's death had been accidental and that Sergeant Burton could not have acted otherwise under the circumstances. For this reason, he was judged innocent of all charges and returned to the Regiment.'

The Secretary glanced down at his copy of the report on Sergeant Michael Burton, 22 SAS. He studied it in silence, then sighed, shook his head from side to side and looked up again. 'He also has a history of psychiatric treatment,' he said. 'I really don't think . . .'

'Not a history,' Brigadier Moorland interjected, being less patient than Lieutenant-Colonel Blackwell. 'He was referred to the psychiatric unit of the British Army for treatment of the trauma he had suffered after the accidental killing of the child. The trauma took the form of insomnia and nightmares, but he was only at the psychiatric unit for two weeks and then was deemed to be cured. This so-called psychiatric history has no bearing on his subsequent performance with the Regiment.'

'It says here,' the Secretary said, glancing down at the report again, 'that Sergeant Burton, at the time of his discharge, was still suffering from enormous guilt over his action and that the guilt would continue to haunt him until, in the words of the psychiatrist, he can atone for what he views as his sin or somehow – and I quote – *redeem* himself. That strikes me as unhealthy.'

'I agree,' the MI5 man, Edmondson, said.

'On the contrary,' Brigadier Moorland said, 'Sergeant Burton's sense of guilt has, if anything, turned him into an even better soldier and his performance since that unfortunate incident in Belfast has been no less than exemplary. We are talking about a remarkable soldier and I'll have that on the record of this meeting.'

This statement was followed by a brief silence as the men around the table puffed on cigarettes or cigars, sipped whisky or brandy, and, in some cases, studied the report placed in front of them. Eventually, breaking the silence, the Secretary said, 'I still have to be persuaded. I still have serious doubts.'

'Perhaps at this point,' Brigadier Moorland responded, 'Lieutenant-Colonel Blackwell should have his say with regard to this man. Maurice?'

Lieutenant-Colonel Blackwell nodded, then glanced down at his personal notes and commenced reading from them in a calm, authoritative tone of voice. 'Sergeant Burton transferred to 22 SAS from the Welsh Guards, passing the most rigorous Training and Selection course so far devised for the Regiment. That same year, 1982, he fought in the Falklands, taking an important role in the South Georgia operation. During the course of that operation, he was one of those who crashed into the Atlantic in a damaged Sea King helicopter. He spent four hours in the freezing sea, surviving physically and mentally, then took part in the strategically vital attack on Pebble Island. Upon the successful completion of that attack, he was transferred to East Falkland, inserting at San Carlos Waters, and from there he fought his way to Port Stanley, engaging en route in R&I patrols, sabotage and bloody fire fights. Though receiving a bullet wound in his left arm, he still managed to make his way to the port to link up with other members of the Regiment. Upon his return to England, he was awarded the Queen's Gallantry Medal.'

He paused to let his words sink in, but the Secretary, not easily swayed, slipped into the brief silence with, 'All very impressive, Lieutenant-Colonel, but that was all before Belfast.'

Blackwell nodded, then looked back down at his notes. 'Upon his return from the Falklands, Burton was promoted to corporal and transferred to the Training Wing, Hereford, as a DS. Unhappy with this role, he asked for further training and received it in the Killing House in—'

'Pardon?' Courtland-Smith asked.

'The CQB House, or Close-Quarter Battle House, of the Counter-Revolutionary Warfare Wing at Hereford.'

'Thank you,' Courtland-Smith said.

'There he received extensive training in counter-terrorist tactics. Impressed by his abilities in this field, his superiors sent him for even more extensive training with West Germany's GSG-9 anti-terrorist squad, Italy's NOCS, France's GIGN and Spain's GEO counter-terrorist units. Upon his return from Europe, he was posted to Belfast for covert operations with 14 Intelligence Group and proved himself to be one of the most able men ever to have operated in that particularly dangerous field. He remained in Belfast until the accidental shooting of the Catholic child, though it should be pointed out that even during that unfortunate incident he managed to eliminate two of the IRA's most wanted men, thus dealing the IRA a decisive blow.'

'And after that,' the Secretary said, refusing to let up, 'he was referred for psychiatric treatment and is known to be still suffering from extreme guilt. That, Lieutenant-Colonel, is the meat of the matter and that's what most concerns us here.'

'I appreciate that, Mr Secretary,' Blackwell responded, 'but I support Brigadier Moorland's contention that Burton's feelings of guilt have, if anything, turned him into an even better, more dedicated soldier. This man has the need to redeem himself and will go all out to do so.'

'So what has he been up to since Belfast 1988?'

'After his psychiatric treatment, he was returned to Hereford where again he became a DI with the CRW Wing. He was, of course, an exemplary DI in that particular area, adding the knowledge gained in Belfast to his already broad grasp of how terrorists operate. So good was he, indeed, that he was often called in to the Kremlin—'

'Pardon?' Courtland-Smith asked.

Lieutenant-Colonel Blackwell grinned. 'The Kremlin,' he repeated. 'That's our nickname for our Operations Planning and Intelligence cell at Stirling Lines.'

Courtland-Smith smiled back and nodded. 'Sorry for the interruption,' he said, 'but I'm not familiar with the esoteric language of the SAS. Please continue.'

'As I was saying, Burton was often called into the Kremlin to offer his opinion or give general advice with regard to particular problems or theories relating to CRW planning.

This, I should point out, is very rare for someone of his rank.'

'He was a sergeant by then?' William Hargreaves, the Commissioner for the Metropolitan Police, asked.

'No. He was only promoted to sergeant after his return from the Gulf War.'

'Impressive,' the Police Commissioner said.

'What did he do there?' the Secretary asked.

'He was part of the Pink Panther raiding teams – sorry, those are camouflaged, heavily-armed Land Rovers used for desert warfare.'

'They sound like fun,' Edmondson said.

'That, I assume,' the Secretary said, 'would depend upon one's idea of fun.'

'Quite,' Lieutenant-Colonel Blackwell said. 'Burton was in charge of a Pink Panther team charged with locating and taking out Saddam Hussein's mobile Scud launchers in the area known as Scud Alley, between Iraq and the border of Syria. This called for him and his four-man team to spend many days at a time in the desert, cut off from communication with the base camp, sleeping in OPs or shallow scrapes, and living off what we would normally deem to be barren land. Burton's team not only destroyed many mobile Scuds, but also knocked out Iraqi communication towers, ambushed Iraqi patrols, and brought back an invaluable wealth of intelligence. During his final patrol, his Pink Panther was destroyed in an Iraqi air attack and he and his men were compelled to hike across the desert to the Syrian border, without food and water, pursued all the way by the Iraqis. Only one of them made it the whole way back – and that one was Burton. He was emaciated and suffering from hypothermia, but he walked on his own two feet across the border and found safety there. Returned to England, he was awarded a Military Medal for exceptional bravery.'

'I'm even more impressed,' the Police Commissioner said.

'So what's he up to now?' Edmondson asked.

Lieutenant-Colonel Blackwell glanced at Brigadier Moorland and received a confirming nod.

'Sergeant Burton is back with the CRW Wing at Hereford.' Blackwell said, 'training for every conceivable kind of future terrorist threat.'

'Such as?' the Secretary asked. 'Can you be more specific?'

Lieutenant-Colonel Blackwell took a deep breath. 'The Kremlin has recently been concerned with the very real possibility that a terrorist group, either local or foreign, might plant a bomb in the London Underground. Because of this, we decided to plant fake bombs along the tunnels and send our men in to locate them and get them out without being noticed by the staff of the Underground or those waiting for trains. Burton, as usual, was the one most adept at doing this.'

The Commissioner of the Metropolitan Police looked aghast at the SAS CO. 'You've been planting fake bombs in the Tube without informing us or London Underground?'

'It was part of our intention to make it as real as possible,' Lieutenant-Colonel Blackwell said blandly. 'So far no one's been caught.'

'Which doesn't say much,' the MI5 man, Edmondson, said sardonically, 'for the security of London Underground.'

'I have to say,' the Police Commissioner began, his face flushed with anger, 'that I find this to be totally . . .'

'Let's stop right there,' the Secretary interjected. 'This isn't the time for infighting. If the Metropolitan Police wish to complain about the SAS, that's fine with me, though it will have to be at a later date. Right now, we have to decide if we use this Sergeant Burton or not.'

'Agreed,' Courtland-Smith said. 'We have to decide if Sergeant Burton is competent or if we need to look elsewhere. In my view, he sounds very competent indeed, so he has my vote at least. Anyone else?'

The rest were undecided, as the ensuing silence showed. The Secretary glanced down at his notes and then looked up again.

'I see that this man's married,' he said.

'Yes,' Lieutenant-Colonel Blackwell replied. 'With two children, a boy and a girl, ten and twelve years old respectively.'

'Any domestic problems?'

'No,' Blackwell said. 'As far as we can gather, Burton is devoted to his wife and children.'

'Indeed,' Brigadier Moorland added, 'according to the British Army psychiatric reports, Burton's accidental shooting of that unfortunate child in Belfast has, if anything, strengthened his bond to his own children. He will certainly have been making amends through his own children for what happened in Belfast.'

The Secretary leaned back in his chair, doodling with a ballpoint pen, the top of his silver-haired head blocking off the lower half of the modernist painting of the Queen that hung on the wall right behind him. He pursed his lips and thought for some time, then leaned forward again.

'So,' he said. 'Sergeant Michael Burton is thirty-four years of age, happily married and devoted to his children. He has received psychiatric treatment for the trauma caused by that unfortunate shooting in Belfast, still suffers guilt over it, but appears to be compensating for it by becoming an even better, even more dedicated soldier. His record as a soldier is exemplary, perhaps even remarkable, and he possesses an intimate knowledge of Belfast and the hard men, IRA and UDA, who are presently building a criminal empire there. It would seem to me, then, even given the doubts we all share, that this man is our best bet. Does anyone dispute this?'

He stared, one by one, at each of the men around the table and all of them, one after the other, shook their heads to say, 'No dispute.'

'Then I say we vote to send this man to Belfast.'

All hands were raised in Burton's favour and the motion was carried.

CHAPTER SIX

'Belfast?' Sergeant Burton said disbelievingly in the CO's office in the SAS base, Stirling Lines, Hereford. 'Me? I don't think so, boss.'

'Please sit down,' Lieutenant-Colonel Blackwell said, indicating the chair at the other side of his cluttered desk. 'Let's treat this meeting as a Chinese parliament,' he added, meaning that they were to have an informal conversation with no holds barred. 'Let's talk it through, Sergeant.'

Clearly surprised, even shocked, Burton sat in the wooden chair at the other side of the desk.

'If you wish to smoke, you may,' Lieutenant-Colonel Blackwell said.

'Thanks, boss,' Burton said, withdrawing a cigarette from the pack in the top pocket of his tunic, igniting it with a Zippo lighter and exhaling as if he really needed it. 'Belfast?' he asked again.

'Yes, Sergeant, Belfast. I appreciate that you imagined you would never have to go back there, particularly given the peace initiative, but the peace is not quite what it seems and we have a serious problem there.'

Burton's response to that was to inhale and blow out another stream of smoke. His gaze was steady but wary.

'Did you hear me, Sergeant?'

'Yes, boss, I heard you. There's a problem in Belfast.'

Realizing that Burton, a thoughtful man, was putting the ball back in his court, Blackwell sighed and sat back in his chair, clasping his hands under his chin, already knowing from the suspicion in Burton's grey gaze that this would not be easy.

'What kind of problem do you think we could have in

Belfast?' he asked, thereby hoping to arouse Burton's curiosity
and then draw him in.

Burton just shrugged. 'I can only assume that the peace
plan's breaking down and that some paramilitaries are up
to some mischief there. Whatever it is, boss, I don't need to
know because you can't send me back there.'

'I can,' Blackwell said. 'You've already been put forward for
this project and given the green light.'

Burton didn't try to hide his surprise. 'Even knowing
that . . . ?'

'Yes, Sergeant. Even knowing about what happened before.
They all agreed, when presented with the facts, that you're
the best man for this operation.' Burton's only response was
a sigh, though whether it was caused by nervousness or
despair Blackwell couldn't quite tell. 'Do you want to know
what it is?'

Burton was slow to respond, but eventually he said, 'No,
boss, I don't think so. I'm not the man for Belfast.'

'Yes, you are, Sergeant. You've swum under the surface in
Belfast more than anyone else. No one else knows it as well
as you do, so you're the logical choice.'

'I'm sorry, boss, but I don't want to go back there. I'm not
equipped for Belfast.'

'You mean emotionally?'

Burton shrugged. 'Yes, I guess so.'

Blackwell let the silence linger. He didn't want to rush this.
He studied Burton and saw an oddly handsome face, lean,
the cheekbones prominent, grey gaze steady under brown
hair, full lips that rarely smiled – the face of a resolute,
possibly ascetic man who had been close to death too many
times and did not take life lightly. He was certainly not the
kind of man to kill a child and easily forget it. He would need
some persuading.

'I hesitate to be so blunt,' Blackwell said, 'but I fear it can't be
avoided. I assume, since I know that you're a very committed
soldier, that your reluctance to go back to Belfast is due to
that incident.'

'That *incident*,' Burton said with soft sarcasm. 'That's a
polite way of putting it.'

'All right, Sergeant, let's take the wraps off it. You inadvert-
ently killed a child in Belfast and you're still troubled by it.'

'You *could* say that, boss.'

Blackwell noted the insolence, but decided to ignore it. This was a Chinese parliament, after all, and Burton could say as he pleased. Also, it was understandable that he should feel as he did – it was even a good sign. This was a man of integrity, a man with children of his own, and the killing of that child would have been worse for him than it might have been for others. Blackwell respected that – he was a father himself – but in this instance he needed Burton too much to let his sympathy show. This operation was too important to be botched and so it had to be Burton. What sending him back to Belfast might do to him could not be considered. He had to be persuaded to go, no matter what it might cost him. Blackwell didn't feel too good about this, but he had his own job to do.

'It wasn't your fault,' Blackwell said, 'and the trial proved that. You were exonerated and returned to the Regiment and have been with us ever since. It was an accident, Sergeant.'

'I know that,' Burton said. 'These things happen. But I still have to live with it. I can do that – my work hasn't been affected – but I still don't want to go back there. That's too close for comfort, boss.'

'Maybe,' Blackwell said, 'and then again, maybe not. Maybe going back there is what you need to burn it out of you finally. True, your work hasn't been affected by it – you certainly proved that in Iraq – but you're still troubled by it – your psychiatric report says so – and until you get it completely out of your system, you won't be able to trust yourself. Now isn't that true, Sergeant?'

It was a filthy trick, Blackwell knew, but it was all he could think of, though he didn't feel too proud of himself when he saw Burton's flashing eyes.

'Just what do you mean by that, boss?' he asked, his voice sounding harsh. 'Are you suggesting that what happened back there has turned me into a risk? If so, you've just contradicted yourself. As you said, I proved myself in Iraq. What I feel about what happened in Belfast hasn't impinged on my work. I'm still a good soldier – damned good – and that's all that should matter.'

Blackwell knew that this *was* all that mattered, but he needed to use Burton's anger, his pride, to get him to volunteer for the task. It wasn't a very pleasant hand to play but Blackwell had nothing else.

'I'm not disputing that you're an excellent soldier, Sergeant

– indeed, you're one of the best. I'm simply saying that until you fully exorcise that ghost – that horrendous accident in Belfast – you'll never completely trust yourself again and that could finally get to you. It could get to you anytime, anywhere, perhaps triggered by a similar situation, and if it does, it could endanger not only you but the men by your side.'

'I repeat, boss, that incident hasn't . . .'

But Blackwell cut him short. 'It's the fact that you're a damned good soldier, perhaps the best we have, that makes you secretly hate yourself for what you did. It was an accident, certainly, and in my view unavoidable, but you're a soldier who takes great pride in what he does and so you still blame yourself. My belief is that you'll continue to do so until, in your own eyes, you atone. You couldn't do that in Iraq and you can't do it playing anti-terrorist games in the tunnels of the London Underground. You *have* to go back to Belfast.'

Burton gazed steadily at him, controlling his anger, clearly thinking through what he had been told and not convinced of the truth in it.

'I don't need to atone for anything,' he said finally. 'I know it wasn't my fault.'

'It was unavoidable,' Blackwell said, feeling more ruthless by the minute, 'but you still blame yourself – and you do so *because* you're such a good soldier and take your pride from it. If another trooper had done it, you'd have been the first to excuse him. You'd have recognized that the man involved had no choice but to open fire the second he entered that room. But you're the best of the best, Sergeant, and you know it and that's your pride, and so you judge yourself more harshly than anyone else and refuse to excuse yourself.'

'Bullshit,' Burton said.

This was a favourite slang word with the SAS and Blackwell, not offended by it, pressed on with his attack.

'I know what you think, Sergeant. You think that you should have reacted quicker. In fact, you reacted as quickly as any man possibly could, but you still think that you weren't quick enough to see that poor child in the room before you squeezed the trigger. You think you could have neutralized Hennessey without including that child in your arc of fire. You think you failed at that instant.'

Burton exhaled a cloud of smoke, letting it out in a sigh,

squinting through it with his grey eyes too bright, betraying pain and resentment.

'Well, I did,' he said. 'I failed at that instant. I should have scanned the room before I squeezed the trigger and saw that the child was there. There's no excuse for that, boss.'

'Human fallibility, Sergeant.'

'That's no excuse in that kind of situation. I should have known better.'

'So you failed at that instant, a split second, and a child died because of it. It *was* human fallibility, Sergeant, but you still blame yourself and, given your nature, you'll continue to do so unless you make amends. I can't have you shouldering that burden for the rest of your life. Certainly not while you're serving with this Regiment where your guilt could cause damage. I say take this chance to atone and remove the guilt for all time. We'll all be better off, Sergeant.'

Burton studied his cigarette, which was only half smoked, then, agitated, he leaned across the desk and viciously stubbed it out in the ashtray. When he sat back again, his gaze was steady and now bright with anger.

'So how do I atone in Belfast?' he said. 'I'd just feel even worse there.'

'Initially, yes. But if you pull off this job, you'll do immeasurable good for Belfast and thus make amends for your sin – or what you feel is your sin. This isn't Iraq. It isn't the London Underground. You secretly feel that you *owe* Belfast, owe its citizens, owe that family, and if you manage to remove the blight of the city, you'll have paid back the debt. Deep down, that's what you want, Sergeant – to wipe the slate clean by somehow compensating for that incident. That's why you have to go back.'

Burton was silent for some time, taking this in, but he still had his doubts.

'There may be some truth in that, boss,' he said eventually, 'but that's not why you want me back there. The reason is the op, what needs doing, and it must be important. If that family's involved in any way, I don't want to know. I don't even want to see that house again. Not that house, not that street. I don't think I could take that.'

'That family has nothing to do with it,' Blackwell said, knowing that he was winning. 'You shot Hennessey and that was the end of it. We weren't interested in his family even then – and certainly they don't interest us now. Besides, this is nothing to do with the old IRA; it's a whole different ball game. But some of the original players are involved and that's where you come into it. We need your knowledge of the streets and of those men. That's why we need you.'

Burton reached into the top pocket of his tunic, withdrew another cigarette, took his time lighting it, then exhaled a thin stream of smoke and squinted through it at Blackwell.

'So what's the job?' he finally asked. 'Is the peace breaking down irrevocably?'

'No, the political peace isn't exactly breaking down – public sentiment is too strong for that – but some former paramilitaries are back on the streets and creating something even worse than the Troubles.'

'You mean organized crime.'

'Correct.'

'I read about it in the papers.'

'What you read wasn't the half of it. It's bad, Sergeant. Really bad. And if we don't put a stop to it right now, it's going to get worse.'

Blackwell explained the situation at great length, repeating almost verbatim what he had learned at that COBR meeting in Whitehall, leaving nothing out. When he had finished, Burton said: 'And this situation also prevails in Dublin?'

'Dublin and, to a lesser degree, Cork. With regard to the drug running, most of the drugs are coming in through Cork, though most of them end up in the streets of Belfast and Dublin.'

'And the paramilitaries in Belfast now control the gangsters of Dublin?'

'Correct.'

'So who's dealing with Dublin?'

'No one. It's the belief of MI5 and the Police Commissioner that if we can neutralize the six top men in Belfast, the gangs will fall into disarray and the Gardai, the RUC and the Metropolitan Police in London can between them take action against the others, including the known criminals of Dublin.' When Burton looked puzzled, Blackwell added: 'Apart from those six hard men, most of the gangs in Belfast are composed of second-rate former paramilitaries and unemployed youths. If we neutralize those six men in a covert operation, the rest will be rudderless and the RUC can gradually pick up the others on a variety of valid legal charges: illegal possession of firearms, extortion, intimidation, the use or sale of drugs, money laundering, tax evasion – you name it. The Gardai will do the same in Dublin and Cork; and the Metropolitan Police will swoop on cohorts in London who are, right now, being used to smuggle drugs from Europe to Cork, launder hot money and purchase more weapons. First, however, we have to get rid of those six hard men at the top.'

'Six,' Burton repeated. 'That's a lot.'

'We have to neutralize all of them.'

'Who are they?' Burton asked.

Realizing that he had his man ensnared, Blackwell pushed a manila folder across to him. Burton studied the folder for some time, his brow furrowed, his eyes gradually widening as he saw who he was up against. When he had finished reading, he closed the manila folder and pushed it back to Blackwell.

'You know those men?' Blackwell asked him.

'Of course,' Burton said. 'The worst of a bad bunch. All hard men. All clever. Fucking ruthless. They won't be easy to get at.'

'You can do it,' Blackwell said. 'I know you can. If you can't, no one can.'

Burton offered a slight, cynical grin that could not disguise the fact that he would find this challenge hard to resist, regardless of his personal feelings about returning to Belfast.

'What are my parameters?' he asked eventually, thereby letting Blackwell know that he was in.

Immensely relieved, Blackwell said, 'There aren't any. You'll have complete freedom – perhaps more than you'd like. By this I mean that you won't be able to communicate with us in any way, shape or form. If you need help, you'll have to find it in Belfast, either from touts or from your old 14 Intelligence Unit cronies, some of whom are still operating over there – but you can't turn to us. You'll be invisible. Officially, you won't exist. You'll be entirely alone there.'

'And if I'm caught?'

Blackwell did not hesitate. 'You mustn't talk under any circumstances – not even under torture. For that reason, it's imperative that you don't let them take you alive.'

Burton stared steadily at him. 'You mean I join the Exit Club?'

'You'll be given the necessary and carry them on you at all

times.' He didn't have to tell Burton that he was talking about cyanide capsules. Burton knew what the score was. He nodded to acknowledge this fact, then said, 'I can't do it entirely alone. I need two more men.'

'We'd rather you operated alone.'

'It can't be done.'

'All right, I'll accept that. But the men you pick will have to volunteer in the full knowledge of what I've just told you, including the possibility of the Exit Club.'

'They will,' Burton said.

'They're from the Regiment?'

'Yes.'

'Who are they?'

'Rob McAllister and Tony Dalton, both corporals, both with D Squadron.'

'Just a moment, Sergeant.' Blackwell turned sideways to punch his computer keyboard and bring up the details on each man. He studied the screen in silence, then turned back to Burton. 'Good men,' he said. 'I note they were both with you in Belfast.'

'Yes.'

'And actually with you at the time of the incident. Is that why you want them?'

'Not because of the incident. I want them because they trained under me and know how I work. They also know Belfast as well as I do – maybe not quite, but near enough. They're widely experienced, highly reliable and as tough as nails. *That*'s why I want them.'

Blackwell smiled. 'Point taken. But if they volunteer, they have to become invisible, exactly like you.'

'They will,' Burton said.

'Shall I approach them or will you?'

'I'll talk to them,' Burton said.

'Fine. You do that.'

Burton sat back in his chair, as if accepting the inevitable, and Blackwell knew that despite his personal doubts Burton now wanted to go. He was a man who could not live with guilt or doubt and he was out for a cure. Blackwell knew this and had used it adroitly, but it left a bad feeling. This mission, he knew, was highly dangerous and Burton might not come back. This was not a thought to offer Blackwell comfort, though he did feel relieved. At least Burton had a better chance than most and that was all that mattered here.

'So you're in?'

'Yes,' Burton said, 'I'm in. When do I start?'

'Take a fortnight's leave, attend to your wife and children, and quietly fix up your personal affairs. Don't tell your wife where you'll be going; just say it's a classified operation that might take some time. If you don't come back, or if you come back in a box, they'll be well taken care of. We'll brief you fully before insertion. That should take at least a week. New identification, of course, and two passports: British and Irish – or, to be more precise, one old British and one new EEC, though both in the same name. Money no object. The bank account will be in your new name. We suggest that you open other accounts when you're established there and spread the money around. The rest is up to you. No parameters, as I said. You can start as soon as you want once you've been briefed and kitted out. After that, it's all your choice. You pick the date and time. We don't even want to know how or when you plan to insert. We just want you to disappear.'

'Understood,' Burton said.

Blackwell nodded and grinned. 'Good. Now, please disappear, Sergeant.'

Burton pushed his chair back, stood up and leaned across Blackwell's desk. He stubbed out his cigarette in Blackwell's ashtray and then left the room.

Blackwell sighed with relief.

CHAPTER SEVEN

Punishment day. It was Hegarty's favourite day of the week. He rolled out of bed at eleven in the morning, feeling as fit as a fiddle even after his heavy night and thrilled by what was to come. Standing on the cold linoleum in the small but tidy bedroom, he could hear the TV set downstairs, turned on most of the day to keep Maureen distracted while she worked. Given that the kids had left home, she managed to keep herself pretty busy: ironing clothes, dusting the furniture, washing the floor and doorstep – Hegarty liked a clean house, though he wouldn't spend money on it – and generally pottering about one way or the other.

Hegarty slept in his underpants, which he changed every couple of days, so he just had to slip his trousers on over them, then put on his shoes and socks. He still used braces. He liked to feel loose down there. As he slipped the braces over his shoulders, he heard Maureen moving about and thought of the difference between her and that whore he had been with last night, after the pub. No varicose veins like Maureen. Not grey-haired and overweight. No, the whore had only been in her early twenties, with peroxide blonde hair, slim waist, big tits, and long, shapely pins. She had locked those pins around him as he thrashed about on top of her, but then, being crushed under his great weight, she had suggested that he let her sit astride him, which he had duly agreed to. Fucking marvellous, it was, seeing her arched above him, breasts outthrust, moving up and down, hips rolling, on his thrusting erection. Fucking fantastic. He'd come like a bomb exploding. He had never done that kind of thing with Maureen and now he knew what he'd been missing all these years. There was no looking back now.

Bare from the waist up, holding his shirt and tie in his hand, he made his way down the narrow stairs and into the living room. Crammed with religious paintings and ornaments, it looked like a bloody church, but Hegarty didn't really mind as Maureen gave a lot of her time to church activities and that kept her distracted. She was on her hands and knees right now, cleaning the floor with a wet cloth, and Hegarty left his footprints in the damp patches as he crossed to the kitchen.

'I've just cleaned that,' Maureen complained.

'Ya bloody ijit,' Hegarty said. 'Ya should've waited until I'd got up and was gone before you started that job.'

'Sure ya get up so late, I'd never get anythin' done.'

'Get organized,' Hegarty said.

He washed and shaved in the sink, splashed himself with a lot of aftershave, then put on his shirt and tie. Satisfied with what he saw in the mirror – that brutish, frightening face which he thought was merely masculine – he returned to the living room, tramping over the still-damp clean floor, and put on the jacket. Maureen, leaving the floor until he had left, was now smoking a cigarette.

'Ya shouldn't smoke them fags,' Hegarty said. 'They'll do yer lungs in.'

'Had a good night last night, did ya?' Maureen asked, sounding disgruntled.

'Ackay,' Hegarty replied without batting an eyelid. 'Did a round of the pubs, then finished up in the Glenmare Social Club where I stayed with the lads till three in the mornin', playin' billiards an' suchlike. Then hurried home to m'warm bed.'

'Staggered's more like it,' Maureen said. 'Don't you want any breakfast, then?'

'Naw. Sure I'm havin' an early business lunch in O'Donovan's pub. Another buildin' contractor. Has a bit of business to put my way, so I thought I'd talk to 'im. Then I'll make up for lost time in the office by workin' through this evenin'. Keep them all from complainin', like.'

'Yer never home these days,' Maureen complained. 'I never see ya at all.'

'I didn't get successful sittin' on my arse and watchin' TV with you. I did it by workin' night an' day and networkin' a lot.'

'What's networkin' mean?' Maureen asked. 'Sounds like one of them fancy newfangled words.'

Hegarty rolled his eyes. 'It means keepin' in contact with the people who can help ya out most. Do that and ya can't go too far wrong, so that's just what I do. Anyway, I've got to make tracks pretty quick. I'll see you some time tonight.'

'Aye,' Maureen said. 'Aren't I the lucky one?'

Hegarty left the house, relieved to get out as always, and made his way along the narrow street, greeting those he passed along the way, here a joke, there a handwave, sort of like Royalty, making sure they either loved you or feared you with no in-between. He was lord of his turf and he knew it and made sure that *they* knew it. So he did the odd favour – dropped a few quid to the needy, fixed up some unemployed dozer, helped some worthless shite shift his business up a step or two – and if that failed to work, if the bastards weren't grateful, he used a bit of muscle, greased and active, to put the fear of God into them. One way or the other, come rain or sunshine, he ruled his own turf like a king and had little aggro. In all truth, the peace had been a blessing to him and he couldn't deny it. It had brought him a new life.

Like that whore, for instance, he thought as he sank into the rear seat of a taxi, having told the dried-out wanker behind the wheel to take him to the Europa Hotel in what used to be the heart of Prod Land. *Even during the Troubles*, he thought, *when I ran my ASU, I never dreamt that I'd get my hands on a tart like that. And wasn't she a hot wee bitch?* Now that tart, working his turf, worked for him and so he had her for free. His horizons were broadening, like.

Not that everything was perfect. He realized this when he got out of the taxi at the Europa Hotel and recalled that other whore, Teresa Kiely, who had gone in there a few evenings ago, wearing the kind of clothes that only came with a great deal of expenditure. That whore worked her own turf – she seemed to think she was high-class, independent, in her own world – and she stuck to the centre of the city, which was mostly Prod Land. Hegarty knew little about her – apparently no one did – but the very sight of her made him want to come and he resented her for that. He resented her beauty, her independence, and, most of all, the fact that she was actually on the game and not under his control. Most of all, however, he resented the fact that she was an uncommonly beautiful whore and he hadn't had a piece of her, financially or otherwise. Sooner or later, he thought, as he paid the taxi driver and entered the hotel, he would have that haughty bitch on her knees. He would be nothing if he couldn't do that, so he would make sure he did it. That's what it meant to be king of your own turf: you had certain privileges.

Another privilege, he thought, was actually entering this hotel which was a far cry from O'Donovan's sleazy pub where Maureen thought he was going. A couple of years back, he couldn't have done this, but now he was doing business with the Prods and could go where he wanted. It was good to move upmarket, have new experiences, live in high style, and as he moved across the lobby to the lift, he felt pretty smart. The bellhops nodded at him, recognizing him, respecting him, and when he took the lift up to the suite hired for this meeting, he realized just how far he had come since his days as an ASU leader with the regular IRA. He relished the power he had gained since the Troubles had ended – he hadn't been that big in the organization. He liked to know that people feared and respected him, which they certainly did now. In fact, he liked it so much, he wanted more of it every day and had no thought of limiting himself. He would take this as far as humanly possible and let no one stop him. He would be the top dog.

Entering the large, luxury suite, he found three men already seated around the table, starting in on a cooked lunch and washing it down with lager or Guinness. The air was foul with the smoke from the cigar of the Yank, Luke Brady, who was seated opposite Neil Byrne and the latter's best friend, Shaun Keenan. The other three gang leaders had not been invited to this particular meeting.

'The last to arrive as always,' Byrne said sarcastically. 'Sure we can always depend on it.'

'Ya can depend on more than that if you don't shut yer trap,' Hegarty said, pulling up a chair. He had said it with a grin, as a joke, but he was secretly angry. Byrne was the one the least frightened of him, the one who argued the most. He was the one to be watched. 'Nice to see ya again,' Hegarty said to the Yank, stretching out his big hand. 'Ya had a good flight?'

'Not bad,' Brady said, standing to shake Hegarty's hand then sitting down again. 'Your lunch had just been put on the table. Help yourself to the drink.'

Hegarty tucked into his roast beef, which was standing in for breakfast, and conducted the conversation while he ate and drank. 'So what brings you to Ireland?' he asked of the Yank. 'All good news, I hope.'

'On my way to Amsterdam and Rome,' Brady said. He was fifty years old, but had a good thatch of silvery-grey hair and wore a dark suit and striped tie. If it were not for the scars on his face, he would have looked just like a regular businessman. He was handsome, but his skin was like chopped leather and his grey eyes were dead. 'I was asked to drop in here en route and report to you guys. Things are going well over there, but we thought you'd appreciate confirmation.'

'Damned right,' Hegarty said.

The ensuing conversation took a couple of hours and covered a lot of illegal business. Brady was a member of an Irish-American criminal fraternity stretched across the United States and now in charge of the illegal export of alcohol, tobacco, and drugs on behalf of the six local gangs, known as the Belfast Six. The organization, with backing from the Belfast Six, was also circulating approximately twenty-five million counterfeit dollars throughout the United States, as well as smuggling weapons into Ireland, usually through ports in Cork and Dublin. Some of these were for the growing arsenal of the Belfast gangs; others were sold to criminal elements and terrorist organizations in Europe, which explained why Brady was going there. In Belfast to conduct business, Brady had brought statements to show that revenue from the Belfast Six's cut in the counterfeit-dollar scam had been deposited in a secret bank account in New Jersey in the name of a well-known building construction company located there. In return for this, he received from the Belfast Six finance officer, Shaun Keenan, similar statements proving that the revenue due to the US side of the operation for their illegal exports had been deposited under various names in secret bank accounts held in the Channel Islands, the Cayman Islands, Geneva and the Isle of Man.

When the statements had been perused and approved on both sides, the meeting became more informal and Neil Byrne, now on brandy and smoking a cigar, his dark eyes squinting through the smoke, asked, 'So what about the immigrants?'

He was referring to the smuggling of illegal immigrants

through Canada and the US, which had proven to be highly lucrative for the US organization.

'No shortage and few problems,' Brady said. 'It's still being run by small groups of men who won't talk if they're caught by the border patrols. Most of the immigrants are brought in by boat. They're kept locked up in the hold until they reach shore and are sent on their way. If we get wind that the Coast Guard are on our tail, we leave a timed bomb on board and flee in a small boat. The immigrants go down with the boat before the Coast Guard can reach them. It's a pretty safe operation. A lot safer, we're beginning to think, than your drugs business here.'

'What d'ya mean by that?' Hegarty asked, waving Byrne's cigar smoke from his face and feeling annoyed.

'We're getting worried by the increasing amount of attention being given to your so-called drugs problem by the Irish and British media. That's too much attention for our liking. We think the authorities might be moving in on you and that has us unsettled.'

'Sure ya must scare fuckin' easily,' Hegarty said. 'It doesn't both us any.'

'It bothers *me*,' Byrne said.

Brady nodded in his direction. 'Right,' he said. 'For good reason. We don't scare easily, but we tend to be careful and we don't like what we're hearing about this place. Your media are in a frenzy over what's going on here. From what we gather, the drugs are being sold and used mostly by kids in the streets. This, we gather from the media, is creating another kind of problem entirely: a growing army of young drug addicts who turn to uncontrolled crime to feed their habit.'

'I didn't know ya were so concerned about the welfare of the young,' Hegarty said with deliberate sarcasm.

'We don't like *uncontrolled* crime. We don't like media attention. You might have to tone the operation down and let the dust settle. Pick it up again when silence reigns and then control it more tightly. Get those kids off the streets.'

'I agree,' Byrne said.

'Me, too,' Shaun Keenan said. 'Both Scotland Yard and the Gardai Special Branch are looking into the problem, which means the RUC will be brought in. That's the kind of attention I don't relish, so I agree we should tone it down.'

Hegarty was incensed by the high tone of Keenan's speech,

never mind what the jumped-up bookkeeper said about toning things down. Keenan had been to Trinity College and spoke like an Englishman and that was enough to get on Hegarty's nerves. He was convinced that Keenan, with his fancy education and good family, looked down his nose at him, viewing him as common muck from the bad end of Belfast. Hegarty thought that at best Keenan condescended to him and that was enough to make his hackles rise. Some day he'd show that bastard who was boss and that day might come soon.

'Yer all talkin' shite,' he said. 'Sure yer just runnin' scared. Fuck the Gardai, fuck Scotland Yard and, most of all, fuck the RUC. They couldn't touch us durin' the Troubles and they can't touch us now. We're cleanin' up here, takin' control of the whole damned city, and we've even got the criminal lice of Dublin eatin' out of our hands – and now you say we should tone it down. I say we do the very opposite: keep goin' while the goin's good, wrap this situation up and contain it while we've still got the chance. By the time those worthless bastards get themselves into gear, we'll have this city wrapped up so tight they won't be able to flush anything out of it. If we keep goin', we'll soon *own* this fuckin' city – and maybe Dublin as well. So I say let's keep goin'.'

'Al Capone owned Chicago,' Brady said, staying cool, 'but in the end, they got him for tax evasion. He had everyone in his pocket – the cops, the politicians, the businessmen, the goddamned works – so since they couldn't get him for what he was actually doing, they went through the IRS. What I'm saying, my friend, is don't get *too* big – 'cause if you do, they'll find a way to drag you down, no matter how smart you think you are.'

'I agree,' Byrne said.

'So do I,' Keenan added.

'More shite,' Hegarty said. 'Another time, another place. Sure Al Capone was just a plain gangster in a wide-open city. This isn't America, Brady, and it isn't 1930. It's Northern Ireland in 1998 an' it's a delicate subject. We're all former paramilit'ries – we're seen as freedom fighters – an' if the Brits move against us, if they turn the RUC loose, it'll be viewed as a political move, as overt provocation at a delicate time. So they're not goin' to do it too soon – and even then, they'll be careful. Sure we have all the time in the world an' I say we make use of it.'

'I say you're wrong, Hegarty.' Brady's dead gaze was steady. 'My friends across the Atlantic are worried and they want you to cool it.'

'I run my turf the way I want to,' Hegarty said, 'an' I'll continue to do so.'

'There are six turfs in Belfast,' Brady said, 'and you only run one of them. I want to know how the others think.'

Hegarty glanced at Byrne. 'I agree with Brady,' Byrne said, staring steadily at him. 'I believe we should cool it down. At least on the drugs. The rest we can run with.'

'And you?' Hegarty asked Keenan, staring him down until he lowered his gaze.

'I agree with Luke and Neil,' Keenan said, his gaze fixed on the floor. 'We won't lose too much financially if we cool it; we can make it up with the other things. We still have the fruit machines, the video trade, the social clubs. We're making a fortune from that counterfeit money and from our arms trade in Europe. Even the whores are bringing in good revenue, so all in all we won't feel the pinch.'

Hegarty could have killed him. 'Sure it's not just the money. I'm talkin' about takin' complete control while we've still got the chance.'

'We're in control of enough for now,' Byrne said. 'The rest can wait until later. So I say we cool it.'

'And the other three turfs?' Brady asked.

'I think they'll back us,' Byrne said.

Brady looked directly at Hegarty. 'So what do you say, pal? Why upset your good friends across the water when you're out on your own on this? Limit the drugs trade to overseas transactions. At least for a year. That's all we're demanding.'

Hegarty sighed. 'Ackay,' he said. 'Why not? Sure I don't want to cause a fuss.'

'Good,' Brady said.

But Hegarty was mad. He knew that when he left the meeting. He was so fucking angry, he walked down the stairs to cool off. Passing the bar, he glanced in, hoping to see Teresa Kiely. When he saw that she wasn't there, he remembered that she only worked the evenings and that made him angrier. Luckily, this being punishment day, he could take it out on someone. The very thought soothed his troubled soul.

Sitting in the back of the taxi that returned him to the Falls

Road, now crowded with carefree shoppers and busily being
modernized with fancy shops and the like, he decided that
Neil Byrne and his cronies were frightened of their Yank
counterparts and that he would soon have to go his own way
and, if necessary, turn against them and take control of them.
The drugs business with the kids was the best thing he had
going for him at the moment and no way was he going to stop
it when it was doing so well. If that meant a fucking range war,
well, so be it – a range war it would be. The fuckers wouldn't
scare him off.

Still, he was angry and he carried that anger with him into
the disused garage up a back alley in the upper Falls, located
not too far from where he lived. There, a long tabletop had
been placed on a couple of wooden pallets, raising it off the
ground. Hegarty's most trusted lieutenants (for so he called
his hard men) were already seated on four of the five chairs
behind the table, two on each side of Hegarty's, which was
in the middle. Hegarty's dickers – the young men who kept
their eyes out for RUC patrols, spied on their neighbours
and carried out punishment beatings and other forms of
intimidation – were grouped around the other unfortunate
men, mostly youths, brought in to be tried and sentenced for
real or imagined infractions. Taking his chair in the middle of
the table, Hegarty gazed balefully upon his minions and the
accused. Then the trial commenced.

The crimes, whether real, imagined or dreamt up by someone simply seeking revenge for some private grievance, were
rarely too serious, though Hegarty deemed them all to be
serious enough to warrant punishment. He did, after all,
take the *hands-on* approach and inflicting the punishment
was something that gave him deep satisfaction.

In fact, his punishments were the same as those he had
handed out during the Troubles: a variety of kneecappings,
each graded to match the severity of the so-called crime. The
kneecappings were designed to enable the locals to tell at a
glance that the wounded individual had somehow offended
the Belfast Six. The nature of the particular kneecapping also
enabled the locals to tell at a glance whether the 'crime' had
been minor or major. Last but not least, all of the kneecappings
were inflicted as gruesomely visible reminders to the locals
that something similar would happen to them if they stepped
out of line. For this reason there were plenty who still hadn't

comprehended that the Troubles had actually ended. The old ways still survived.

'Right,' Hegarty said loud and clear, judge and jury in one. 'Let's start the proceedin's.'

The first case dealt with at this particular 'trial' involved a fifteen-year-old lad, Tom Reid, who had gotten high on crack and, in that condition, had tried to break into a house on Hegarty's turf. Now shivering and sobbing, closely surrounded by Hegarty's hard-faced, smirking dickers, Tom insisted that he'd broken into the house only because he'd been desperate to obtain money for the purchase of more crack. He'd become addicted to it, he explained tearfully, from the minute he'd first taken it, having bought it off one of Hegarty's drug dealers in a local nightclub.

Refusing to accept the addiction as an excuse, but mindful of the fact that the burglary hadn't actually succeeded, Hegarty deemed the offence to be minor and meted out the least painful of the kneecappings. After stuffing a rag in the sobbing boy's mouth to prevent him from screaming, four of Hegarty's dickers pinned him to the ground, his arms and legs outspread, while Hegarty shot him at close range in the fleshy bit of the ankle with a dainty little .22 pistol. This hurt like hell and did a bit of bloody damage, but it didn't actually shatter the ankle-bone. You would not have guessed this, however, from the way that young Tom, when shot, spasmed and jerked practically off the ground as if electrocuted. When the punishment had been meted out, the boy, now groaning with pain as well as sobbing, was given a pair of crutches and sent on his own, painful way to the Great Victoria Hospital where, Hegarty knew, he would not say who had injured him, for fear of an even more painful punishment.

'Sure he took it like a man,' Hegarty said when the boy had hobbled out on his crutches, sobbing and dribbling. 'I hope the rest of ya do the same.'

The rest of the offenders, four in all, were standing in a single line across the garage, surrounded by Hegarty's smirking dickers. Compelled to watch the first punishment, they knew what to expect – what was the *least* they could expect – when it came to themselves. Inevitably, this led to tears, entreaties and fearful confessions, all of which Hegarty enjoyed hearing before passing sentence.

To put them out of their misery, viewing himself as magnanimous, he always dealt with the youngest offenders first.
Therefore, the next person he tried was another adolescent,
Jimmy Duggan, who had been charging twenty per cent more
for his crack than the street price set by Hegarty and then
salting that 'invisible' income away for himself. Outraged
to learn this, though taking note of Jimmy's tender years,
Hegarty decided not to inflict the major punishment: the
dreaded 'six-pack'. Instead, he had Jimmy held face down
on the ground – rag stuffed in the mouth as always – while
he, Hegarty, personally shot him in the back of the knee with
a high-velocity rifle, thus ensuring that the artery was severed
and the kneecap blown right off.

Shuddering and groaning, the wounded Jimmy was dragged
out of the garage by two of the dickers. These two hard-faced
young men would, Hegarty knew, drive to the gates of the
Royal Victoria Hospital, slow down, dump Jimmy out onto
the pavement, then drive away at high speed, leaving him
to be found by the first person to pass by. Hopefully, Jimmy
would then receive the treatment he now so badly needed.

'Sure let that be a lesson to ya all,' Hegarty said with a big,
vicious grin. 'Crime doesn't pay, like.'

The next two cases, tried quickly, involved the relatively
minor infractions of boys barely into their teens. Hegarty,
feeling magnanimous, sentenced each to the least painful
and damaging of all the punishments. a shot in the fleshy
part of the thigh with the .22 pistol. Each of the two boys
took his punishment like a man and was then permitted to
hobble out of the garage as best he could, either to go home to
his mammy, to his local doctor, or to the hard-pressed Royal
Victoria Hospital.

The fourth case, however, was that of a twenty-five-year-old
man, Danny Lenihan, one of Hegarty's lieutenants, who had
conducted the armed robbery of a local post office and failed to
tell Hegarty that he had done so, hoping to keep the money for
himself. For this offence there was no plea and no argument
about the nature of the punishment. Therefore, the unfortunate Danny Lenihan was given Hegarty's favourite: the good
old 'six-pack', which meant a bullet in each elbow, knee and
ankle. This guaranteed that he would suffer excruciating pain
and be on crutches for a very long time.

As his mouth was stuffed with the same rag that the others

had been forced to use – now soaked from their nervous vomiting – Lenihan could not scream, though the dreadful convulsing of his body as each bullet went in, shattering bone, severing arteries and drenching him in blood, was dreadful evidence of the pain he was suffering. When it was finished, when the last joint had been demolished, he was dragged out of the garage, thrown into the back of one of Hegarty's cars and driven by a dicker to a taxi rank controlled by Hegarty's gang. There, shuddering and groaning and almost senseless with pain, Lenihan was handed over to a taxi driver who was told to take him to the Royal Victoria Hospital and say that he had found him in the street. Naturally, seeing the state of his new passenger, the taxi driver agreed.

Pleased with his afternoon's work, filled with clammy excitement, Hegarty told his dickers to put the weapons back in the safe, mop up the blood and bone splinters, and lock the garage before they left. As they were dutifully getting to work, drinking beer and smoking fags as if nothing had happened, he hurried out into the alley, walked along to the first street, and from there made his way to the busy Falls Road where the lights were already coming on as evening's darkness descended. Taking a taxi back to the Europa Hotel, he hurried in and made his way to the upstairs bar. There he hoped to meet some friends, have a few drinks and, even better, catch sight of that freelance whore, Teresa Kiely.

This was Hegarty's lucky night.

CHAPTER EIGHT

As he was packing his travelling bag in the bedroom of his house in Redhill, Hereford, Burton realized that he felt clean inside, temporarily purged of his pain, his skin limned with a magical, lambent heat. This, he knew, was due to the fact that he had just made love to Deborah, pouring his hurt and longing into her as she clung desperately to him. They were good in bed together, always had been, still were, but this morning it had been even better than usual, perhaps because he was leaving. Burton had made love tenderly, almost frightened to touch her, as if her physical fragility, her quiet beauty, could be destroyed by his strength. He had kissed her all over, licked her smooth skin with his tongue, stroked her and squeezed her very gently until he could enter her. They had moved together as one, each melting into the other, until he had viewed the world through her eyes and glimpsed a much better place. Eventually, when they had finished and he had rolled off her slim body, the real world had rushed back in, though thankfully it still seemed slightly softened. He accepted that this feeling could not last, but to have it even briefly was a joy that made him feel almost whole.

He finished his packing, picked up the travelling bag and carried it down to the living room. Sharon and Grant were there, twelve and ten years old respectively, both still in their pyjamas and on their knees on the carpet, the former doodling on a large sketch pad, the latter playing with his toy cars and buses. The sun was shining outside, beaming in through the windows, making Deborah's blonde hair shine where she sat at the table in the open-plan kitchen, her green gaze turning towards him. She smiled, but he knew that she was troubled and that made him feel bad again.

'All packed,' he said, placing the travelling bag on the settee
and walking in to join her.

'Are you sure you don't want me to drive you?' she asked as
he leaned over her.

He kissed the top of her head and straightened up again,
then took the chair facing her. 'No,' he said. 'You'd have to
get the kids dressed and take them with us, so I've called for
a taxi. It should arrive any minute now.'

Deborah sighed and nodded. 'I guess that's best,' she said.
'No point moping at the station with the kids, which is what
I'd probably do. I still don't like it, Mike.'

'I've been away a lot before,' Burton said. 'It's no different
this time.'

'Yes, it is, Mike. It's another secret assignment. I've never
liked it when you went away – I always worried about what
could happen – but at least I always knew where you were,
which was something at least. Now you're not allowed to tell
me where you're going nor how long you'll be gone. That's not
very easy to accept and I'm worried already. Tell the truth: is
it dangerous?'

'No,' Burton lied. 'Believe me, it's not dangerous. It's classified because it concerns new problems and new weapons, but
it's still just a training exercise, so you've no need to worry.'

He hated lying to her, but he didn't have much choice. Each
time he lied to her, which he'd had to do often, he saw it as a
betrayal of her trust and suffered accordingly. Nevertheless,
as had happened in the past, he couldn't tell her the truth.
This aspect of his work, the need for secrecy, was the worst
part of it for him. Invariably, as it was doing this very second,
it filled him with guilt.

'You're lying,' Deborah said. 'I can see it in your face. You've
never been good at that, Mike, and I've always known when
you did it. I don't mind, believe me. I know you have to do
it. I'm just more concerned now than before because you say
you might be gone for a couple of months, but you don't know
when you're actually coming back, which means it could be
even longer. I think it's dangerous. I think that's why you don't
know when you're coming back. I'm worried sick about that.'

He should not have been surprised that she had seen through
him all these years – she knew him better than anyone – but he
was surprised and also a little embarrassed, which made him
look away from her. The sun was shining over the leafy street

outside and on the lawns of the red-bricked houses opposite. He was glad his kids were growing up here; this was a healthy, safe area.

'Stop worrying,' he said, turning back to face Deborah and reaching across the table to squeeze her hand. 'Believe me, it's just a lengthy training programme. It's really not dangerous.'

He squeezed her hand and then released it, but when he tried to withdraw it, she took it and held on, as if not wanting to let him go. 'We've been married for thirteen years,' she said, 'and I still love you, Mike.'

'I love you too,' he said and he meant every word of it.

'Have you ever had an affair?'

'No,' he said and it was true. He had been tempted now and then, particularly when overseas, but his love for her, his deep and abiding respect, had always made him pull back. Now, seeing the love in her face, he was glad that he had. 'Why do you ask?' he said. 'Did you ever suspect me?'

'No. I just wondered, that's all. A woman thinks about these things. Love and fear go hand-in-hand. Did you ever wonder about me?'

'No, Deborah, not ever.'

'That's nice,' she said, looking down at the hand she was squeezing, then shaking her head from side to side and pursing her full lips. 'Thirteen years married,' she said. 'That's an unlucky number. Maybe that's why I'm anxious.'

'You've always been superstitious,' he said. 'You won't walk under ladders, dread the sight of a black cat and won't light a cigarette from a candle for fear that a sailor will drown at sea. I've always been amused by that but I don't subscribe to it. It's been a good thirteen years, very good, and it'll only get better. Nothing bad is going to happen this year just because it's the thirteenth. I'll be all right, believe me.'

Deborah smiled, squeezed his hand again, then released him and glanced at the window. 'There's the taxi,' she said.

They both left the kitchen and went into the living room where Burton picked the children up in turn, cuddling them, tickling them to make them giggle, then kissing them on the cheek and letting them go. Finally, reluctantly, he picked up his travelling bag, slung it over his shoulder and let Deborah walk him to the door. He opened the door, then turned back to embrace her and kiss her and stroke her blonde hair.

'You take care,' he said.

'I will, Mike, don't worry. You take care as well.'

'I will. See you soon.'

'Yes,' she said. 'On your way now.'

He turned around and walked away from her tears and climbed into the taxi. The journey to the station took only ten minutes, but he was still feeling shaky when he got there. The train came five minutes later, on time for once, and he managed to find a seat in second class, sitting by the window. He spent most of the journey to London either glancing out at the passing countryside, still green and lovely for most of the way, or reading a paperback history of the SAS. Burton's interest in the Regiment was as deep and abiding as his love for Deborah. He was, in fact, interested in military history in general and in the peculiar psychology of professional soldiers. Though a civilized man, he felt happiest when fighting a war and had never worked out why this was so. He was not a violent man by nature, but he certainly thrived on risk and took pride in doing his duty well. As his duty included the sanctioned killing of other men, it was not one he was inclined to take lightly, though he did not suffer guilt. At least, he hadn't suffered guilt until the death of that child in Belfast; and that, he knew, was going to haunt him for the rest of his days. When he thought of his own children, he felt worse; and he thought often about them, as he did, with love and remorse, throughout the journey to London. Thus, when the train pulled into Paddington Station, he disembarked as if escaping from prison and immediately made his way to the Underground.

He took the Tube to Victoria, then walked from there to the Victoria Bus Station. Entering a pub facing the station's side entrance, he found SAS corporals Robert 'Rob' McAllister and Tony 'Slim' Dalton waiting for him, one relatively short, broad-shouldered and plug-ugly, the other tall, slim and handsome, both wearing casual civvie clothing and drinking pints of bitter. When Burton approached their table and placed his travelling bag on the third chair, he received a dark-eyed glance and crooked, Rotweiler grin from Rob, a familiar, sombre gaze from the blond-haired Slim.

'Can I get you another?' Burton asked, indicating their near-empty pint mugs.

'You're on your feet,' Rob replied.

Nodding, Burton went to the bar, ordered up three pints, paid for them and carried them back to the table, balancing them precariously between his hands. After placing the drinks on the table, he lowered his travelling bag to the floor and sat on the empty chair.

'Cheers,' he said, raising his mug.

'Cheers,' the other two said simultaneously, picking up their near-empty glasses to polish them off.

Burton glanced around the pub. It was filled with people either passing time until their bus came in – they had suit-cases or bags at their feet – or waiting for friends or relatives to arrive. It was a pub with a distinctly transient atmosphere, pleasant enough but rather impersonal. He turned back to his friends.

'Did you two have a good leave?' he asked.

'Not bad,' Slim said. 'I went to Spain with my girlfriend. Torremolinos. It's all gone to seed but at least the sun was shining and the wine was a lot cheaper than here. We had a pretty good time.'

'Not me,' Rob said. 'I went back to my missus and found her fucking an old mate, so I beat the shit out of him and then went on a bender that lasted the whole two bleedin' weeks. I'm *glad* to be going to Belfast. It can't be worse than my home life.'

Rob had a violent temper and, though plug-ugly, was a womanizer of little discretion, picking up his slags anywhere, sometimes in his local pub, and often being seen by his own children and caught out by his wife. He was also a good soldier who had trained in Hereford directly under Burton and proved himself in Northern Ireland and Iraq. Burton trusted him totally.

'You screw around as well,' Burton said, 'and you've always let your wife know it. That's why she turns elsewhere.'

'I'm a man and she's a woman,' Rob replied, looking indig-nant. 'The same rules don't apply.'

'Not in your view,' Slim said. 'Some women might dis-agree.'

'Like your girlfriend?'

'Right.'

'You must spoil her rotten.'

'She was born and bred in Oxford,' Slim explained, 'and was educated at Oxford University. She has these modern ideas.'

'I'd squash 'em right quick,' Rob said, 'before she gets out of hand.'

'I can handle her,' Slim said.

With his blond hair, blue eyes and rather wan, delicate
features, Slim seemed an unlikely candidate for the SAS, but
he was one of the best. Though generally quiet and certainly
never aggressive unless provoked, he was mysteriously gifted
with the instincts of a killer and absolutely ruthless in action.
Like Rob, he had trained in Hereford directly under Burton
and gone on to prove himself in Northern Ireland and Iraq.
He, too, was totally dependable.

'Anyway,' Burton said, being impatient to get going, 'I trust
you're both feeling well rested and are raring to go.'

Both men nodded: 'Yes.'

'Okay,' Burton said, checking his wristwatch, 'here's the
drill.' He had another sip of his beer and then put his glass
down. 'We travel at two-weekly intervals, carrying our false
passports, which hopefully we won't have to show anyway.
We won't be carrying arms. I leave first. In fact, I'm going
this afternoon, via Cork, travelling by bus and boat. From
Cork, I'm taking the train to Dublin, then taking another
bus from there to Belfast. Once in Belfast, I'll assume my
new identity, as Stanley Drummond, and rent a house in
an isolated location somewhere outside the city, probably
Antrim. Once established there, I'll purchase a second-hand
car, Belfast registration, paying by cash, and use that as my
transport.'

He had another sip of his beer, lit a cigarette, then turned
to Rob. 'You come two weeks later, flying directly to Belfast
by the Shuttle. You'll find a letter waiting for you in the poste
restante of the main Post Office in Castle Place. That letter
will contain my new address and details of when we can meet,
which will be in a pub located in Antrim City. By the time we
meet, I'll have found another house for you to rent, located
reasonably close – though not *too* close – to my own place.
Once you've rented your house, we won't meet again until Slim
arrives. While you're waiting, you'll purchase a second-hand
Transit van, paying by cash, and use it for general purposes
until we actually need it.'

After inhaling and exhaling a cloud of smoke, he turned
to Slim. 'You arrive two weeks to the day after Rob, flying
into Dublin, then taking the train from there to Belfast. Like
Rob, you'll find a letter waiting for you at the poste restante,
containing details of where you're to meet me that same day.
At that meeting, I'll tell you where Rob and I are located

and give you details of a third house you can rent, located somewhere in Antrim. Once established in the house, you'll also purchase a second-hand car, paying by cash. The three houses will have phones and you'll wait for my call. No later than five days after your arrival, I'll call you and fix up a meeting between the three of us. We proceed from there.'

'What about weapons?' Slim asked, staring steadily, his blue eyes unblinking in his matinée-idol face.

'By the time we three meet up, I'll have arranged for the purchase of weapons and explosives from an old UDA friend who still doesn't trust the IRA and owes me a favour. At the meeting between the three of us, I'll give Rob the details of the pick-up point. Rob will collect the groceries in his Transit van and stash them in his place. Within the next week, at prearranged times, on two separate occasions, you and I will visit Rob at his place and take our share of the goods. From that point on, we'll be ready to proceed properly.'

Rob and Slim nodded, both looking thoughtful. After drinking some more beer, Slim wiped his lips with the back of his hand and said, 'What's the game plan?'

'Right now, there isn't one,' Burton replied. 'However, once I'm in my place and have a car to travel around in, I'll start making daily trips to Belfast and survey the scene. By the time you arrive, I should know where the six targets live and what their daily routine is. Whatever we decide will be based on that intelligence and probably we'll have to play it by ear, on a day-by-day basis. We'll be living outside the city and fairly anonymous. We'll all be driving vehicles with Belfast registrations, so we won't stand out there. No one's expecting us. We can move pretty freely. As Northern Ireland's now filling up with tourists, even our accents won't stand out.'

'Well, that's a bleedin' relief,' Rob said. Though his parents were Scottish, he had been born and raised in Whitechapel, London, and sounded like an East Ender. 'I never *could* master that bleedin' Ulster accent. You'd enter a pub and ask for a pint of Guinness and they'd have you tabbed in two fuckin' syllables. A lot of good men have died tryin' that one.'

'Right,' Slim said. 'A lot of greens' – he was referring to British Army soldiers – 'learned that to their cost when they tried to go undercover during the Troubles, masquerading as locals. Just one word out of place and they were done for. We learnt from their mistakes.'

'Exactly,' Burton said. 'So when we talk to the locals, we say we've lived in England for years and have returned because the Troubles are over – coming back to our roots, so to speak. No Irish blarney. No accents. We talk just as we talk.' He checked his wristwatch and looked up again. 'Any questions before I leave?'

Rob and Slim glanced at each other, shook their heads, then turned back to Burton.

'Nope,' Rob said, offering his Rotweiler grin.

'It's sure nice to go travelling,' Slim said. 'I can't wait to get there.'

Reminded by that remark that Slim, though quiet and solemn, was a killing machine who loved taking risks, Burton pushed his chair back and picked up his travelling bag.

'I'll see you when I see you,' he said.

'You can bet on it,' Rob said.

Feeling confident that he had picked the right two men, Burton nodded, left the pub and crossed the road to find the bus to Belfast.

CHAPTER NINE

This time, when she entered the Gallery Bar of the Europa Hotel, Teresa was wearing a figure-hugging orange cashmere-blend jacket with black devorét scarf, a very short black shift skirt, black opaque tights and black suede high-heeled shoes. Taking a stool on the long bar, she crossed her perfect legs, putting them on display, then lit a cigarette and asked Jim Quaid to fetch her a large Bushmill's with ginger ale. While the drink was being mixed, she studied the tables behind her and saw that they were filling up rapidly with the customary mixture of tourists and locals, many of whom were already casting covetous glances at her.

'A good crowd this evenin',' she said to Jim when he came back with her drink.

'Ackay. Friday night. That usually brings in more than usual, so ya should be okay. How was the Yank?'

Teresa grinned and sipped some Bushmill's. 'Easy pickin's,' she said. 'All he wanted to do was watch me take m'clothes off, *very* slowly, and put 'em back on again. A sort of striptease, like. I had to do it a dozen times. Sure he worked himself up while I was doin' it and came all over the floor. He paid a lot for a little.'

'Ya should put 'im on yer payroll,' Jim said. 'It'd make your life a lot easier.'

'Sure he took the plane home the next mornin', leavin' a big stain on the carpet. He paid up, though – and plenty.'

'Bless the tourists,' Jim said.

Studying the large bar, she noted some familiar faces gathered around a table nearby: three men deep in conversation, all flushed with drink and none of them dressed well, favouring suits with baggy trousers and old-fashioned turn-ups, shoes in need of a polish. She couldn't quite place them, but she sensed that she knew them, possibly from a long time ago when she was just a wee girl. Two were fairly anonymous, but one was a big brute, tree-trunk legs and big belly, with thick, lascivious lips, a flat, broken nose and a hard, scarred, frightening face. They weren't tourists, that was for sure. They had the look of common muck. During the Troubles they wouldn't have gotten their foot through the door, but with the peace they'd probably moved on from kneecapping and killing to so-called legitimate business with a bit on the side. These days the slime floated on the surface and gave off a smell. As for that lot, she could smell them from here and she hoped to avoid them.

'Cyd Charisse legs!' someone exclaimed beside her. 'Sure I could make a meal of them!'

Turning her head, she saw Frank Cooney, the journalist, grinning at her as he leaned his elbow on the bar, fingers curled around a large glass of whisky.

'Sure it's a meal you couldn't afford,' Teresa told him. 'But feast on the thought.'

'Always quick with the comeback, Teresa. A woman of spirit. Sure this bar is enhanced with your presence and I have no complaints. How's the world treating you?'

'Not bad,' she said.

Cooney nodded, still grinning. 'I suspect it's going to treat you okay tonight. You've got a full house here.'

'It's full, all right, but mostly with riff-raff. Sure they let anyone through the doors these days.'

'Even you,' Cooney said.

'I wear expensive clothes and tip well and that makes me respectable. I come in, drink an' leave with male friends an' I never cause trouble. They've no reason to keep me out.'

'They've no reason to keep *this* lot out,' Cooney said, indicating the tables behind her with a nod of his head. 'They may look common to you, but they flash fivers like they're going out of style and that makes *them* respectable. These men are the backbone of the city and don't you forget it. Beggars can't be choosers, like.'

'I'm no beggar. I choose who I want an' I have my own standards.'

'What are those?' Cooney asked her.

'I like flush American tourists and local men of good

standin'. I don't like slime that floated to the top when the
Troubles were over – men like that lot over there. Who are
they, anyway?'

Cooney glanced at the table she had indicated with a nod
of her head. 'Not good news, Teresa. They're three former IRA
hard men, ASU leaders, now running respectable businesses
as fronts for a lot of more murky stuff. We can't pin them
down, we have no hard proof, but we're pretty sure that
they're behind a lot of the rackets that have turned this
town upside down.'

'What kinda rackets?'

'Drugs, fruit machines, pirated videos, organized prostitution, bank robbery, the theft and sale of illegal arms,
and various forms of extortion. The circumstantial evidence
certainly points in their direction, but we can't pin 'em down
because those that aren't already in their pockets are too
frightened to talk. They're a dangerous lot.'

Teresa studied the men in the mirror. 'And that's only three
of 'em?'

'Right. There are others, none better than they are.'

'You know 'em?'

'Don't tell me you're interested!'

'Jesus, no! Not as clients, for Christ's sake! I'd just like to
know, like.'

'You might get them as clients,' Cooney said, 'whether or
not you like it.'

'I'd turn 'em down, that's for sure, Cooney. Now who the
fuck are they?'

'Jack Hegarty, Michael Gallagher and Liam O'Shea. Used
to fight for the cause but now they're all gang lords for sure.
Hegarty's the big brute. He's the one to watch. He's buried old
friends and enemies alike and he kneecaps for fun. Mad and
bad, so I'm told. He has half the Falls terrified. I say he's the
one to watch 'cause he's been watching you since you came in
and that isn't a good sign.'

'A lot of 'em eye up me,' Teresa said. 'That's why I come
in here. I thought you knew that.'

Cooney ignored the sarcasm. 'Sure I'm not joking, Teresa.
That Hegarty's involved in organized prostitution and he's
got his eye on you. He might want you in bed – and that
would be bad enough – but he's more likely to want a slice
off you, and if he does, you're in trouble.'

'Sure he's a Catholic and this is Prod Land. Even if he has his own bit of turf, it won't include here. That bastard runs his trade along the Falls. That's his own little dung heap.'

'That won't stop Hegarty,' Cooney said. 'He's as mad as a fucking hatter. He's been inching all the way down the Falls and now his shadow's on Sandy Row. I'm told that some Prods tried to stop him and ended up in brown boxes. He won't stop till he drops.'

'Sure he won't get his fuckin' hands on me; I'm way out of his league.' She glanced over her shoulder and saw Hegarty staring at her. His was truly a frightening face and that made her defiant. 'I wouldn't work for that bastard if I was dyin' and I'm far from that yet. I can deal with him, Cooney.'

'I hope so,' Cooney said. 'Now I'm getting the fuck out of here before he comes over. I don't need the involvement.'

'Thanks a million,' Teresa said.

Cooney finished off his drink, winked at her, then hurried out of the bar. Jim Quaid, the flirtatious red-haired barman, gave her a grin.

'Cooney likes you,' Quaid said. 'He talks a bit rough and he's a cynic, but he has a soft spot for you.'

'He wants to get into my knickers,' Teresa said, 'just like all of the others. He just wants it for free.'

'That's not true at all,' Quaid said. 'Sure he told me so himself. He said ya shouldn't be in this business, that yer worth somethin' better.'

'He said that?'

'Ackay. Those were his very words. He said he'd never have picked you for a whore except for your foul mouth. Said you seemed like a real lady, well mannered an' high class.'

'That's my act,' Teresa said. 'I never swear when I'm talkin' to clients and *they* think I'm high class.'

'Sure yer classier than you think,' Quaid insisted. 'Ya just don't know it yet. Oh, oh, here comes Hegarty.'

Hegarty loomed up beside her, casting his shadow over her, and growled for another round of drinks, his grey eyes like stones. Jim turned away to mix the drinks. Hegarty stood there, breathing heavily. Teresa heard his breathing and thought of an animal in its dark lair, waiting to pounce. Even the breathing unnerved her. She tried to avoid those stony eyes, but Hegarty turned in towards her and seemed to press down upon her. She felt suffocated.

'How ya doin?' he said.

'Fine,' Teresa said. She exhaled a cloud of cigarette smoke and stared down at her glass.

'Name's Hegarty,' he said. Teresa didn't respond. 'Jack Hegarty. Sure you mighta heard of me.'

'No,' Teresa said, 'I don't think so.'

'What's *your* name?'

'Teresa.'

'Teresa *what*?' he asked. His voice was so harsh it seemed abrasive and made her skin crawl.

'Teresa Kiely,' she said.

'You don't talk much, do ya?'

'That depends,' Teresa said.

'Depends on what?' Hegarty asked her.

Teresa just shrugged. She couldn't help it: she felt frightened. Feeling that way, she tried to be defiant, but her voice didn't sound right. 'It just depends on whether or not I feel like it an' right now I don't.'

'You're too good for me, like?'

'Sure I don't want trouble, mister.'

'Would you be comin' from around here?' he asked. 'You seem to know a few people.'

'I come from Newtownards,' she replied, 'but I've lived here some years now.'

'Sure that's a real Belfast accent, darlin', so don't try to shite me.'

'I lived here as a kid. M'parents moved out to Newtownards an' I came back a few years ago.'

'You seem to know a few people.'

'You've already said that, mister. Sure the barman's just come back with your drinks. Why not return to your friends?'

'You want one?'

'What?'

'A drink.'

'No, I don't.'

'Yer thinkin' I'm not good enough for you?'

'I'm just not in the mood, thanks.'

'Yer drinks, Mister Hegarty,' Quaid said, gallantly trying to get Hegarty off her back.

'Aye, m'drinks,' Hegarty said. He breathed in and out like his lungs were great bellows, then he turned to stare stonily at Quaid, his scarred cheeks red with rage. 'So are ya standin' there wankin' or what?' he said to Quaid. 'Pick 'em up and take 'em over to the table before I smash yer gub shut.'

'Right, Mister Hegarty,' Quaid responded quickly. 'Anything you say, sir.'

Quaid placed the drinks on a tray, picked them up and walked off. Hegarty turned back towards Teresa, breathing into her right ear.

'You're a fuckin' whore,' he said.

'I'm a woman mindin' my own business.'

'You're a fuckin' whore workin' this bar an' a few other places. I know that much. I've asked around.'

'I mind my own business.'

'A whore's business *is* my business. You don't fuckin' work on my turf without payin' yer dues.'

Teresa took a deep breath, held it in, let it out. Though still frightened, she managed to turn her head and look into his stony eyes. 'I mind my own business,' she said, 'so you go an' mind yours. I work where and when I want – for myself – and I choose my own clients. So you go back to your slags in the Falls an' don't bother me, mister.'

She saw his fist clench on the counter. The fist looked like a mallet. She heard the breathing of an animal in its dark lair as his great chest heaved in and out. His face was flushed with rage, his stony eyes had turned to glass. He glanced around the bar, as if deciding what to do, then he opened and closed his fist a few times and finally seemed to relax. When he grinned, exposing a row of rotting teeth, she felt even more frightened.

'A tough wee bitch, aren't ya?'

'I can hold my own, mister.'

'Sure you probably think ya shit fuckin' gold bricks, but they stink just like mine.'

'Please go away,' Teresa said.

'Not until ya come with me.'

'If you don't go away, I'll ask the barman to call for the cops.'

'That wee bastard wouldn't dare.'

'Sure ya might be surprised. He works for the hotel an' I'm a customer and that means he'd have to.'

Quaid had come back to the bar. He was standing well back, listening. Teresa saw the pleading look in his eyes and that made her feel bad. 'An' if he didn't do it,' she added carefully, 'then the manager would. He can't have women molested.'

Hegarty glared at her. He was getting mad again. She heard his breathing and a chill went down her spine as she turned away from him. Another man was sitting beside her, oblivious to the conversation, so she leaned forward and tapped him on the shoulder to make him look at her. When he saw her face, the glory of her smile, he was instantly dazzled.

'Excuse me,' Teresa said, using her poshest voice and withdrawing a cigarette from her leather handbag. 'Could you give me a light, please?'

'Sure,' the man said, speaking with an American accent, reaching into his pocket, withdrawing a lighter and lighting her cigarette. 'Can I buy you a drink, ma'am?'

'Well, I really shouldn't . . .' Teresa pretended to hesitate.

'Please,' the man said. 'My pleasure. No offence meant, ma'am It's just nice to have someone to talk to when you're travelling alone.'

'Well, all right, then,' Teresa said.

She felt movement behind her and twitched with fearful expectation. When nothing happened, she glanced over her shoulder and saw that Hegarty had disappeared. Then she saw that he had returned to his table, but was still glaring at her. Turning back to the American, trying to keep her voice steady, she said, 'I'm Teresa . . . Teresa Kiely.'

'Bill Shaw,' the American said, stretching out his hand.

Teresa shook his hand, trying to hide the fear she felt. 'I'll tell you what, Bill.' She was still using her posh voice. 'I really shouldn't drink on an empty stomach and since both of us are on our own this evening . . .'

She let the sentence trail off, but Bill Shaw, no slowcoach, picked up on it. 'You mean dinner?'

'Only if you feel like it.'

'Gee, yeah, that sounds great.'

'Not the hotel. I don't like hotel food. I know this nice little restaurant.'

'Lead me to it,' Bill said.

Teresa let him take her hand as they hurried from the bar. When she saw that Hegarty had not moved from his chair, she heaved a sigh of relief. Nevertheless, when she and Bill had

left the hotel, she made him flag down a taxi. The trembling
of her limbs did not cease until the taxi had moved off.

This could be trouble, she thought.

CHAPTER TEN

A s he had done every morning for the past five weeks, Burton rolled out of bed at 0800 hours and, stark naked, did thirty minutes of rigorous exercises: push-ups, touching toes and physically exacting martial arts moves. When he was sweating from exertion, he showered, shaved and put on his working-class civvy clothes (open-necked shirt, faded denims and hush puppies), then had a high-calorie fry-up for breakfast. Finally, when the meal was finished, he pulled himself up into the attic above the second floor of this small house, located in a secluded green glen about three miles from Antrim City, and collected what he thought he might need for this particular day's work.

From the 'groceries', which included weapons and highly advanced surveillance equipment collected from Rob McAllister two days ago, he selected only the Browning 9mm High Power handgun and a 35mm Nikon F-801 camera with long-distance lens. After securing the '9-Milly' in the cross-draw position – hidden from view around the left side of the waist – he lowered himself out of the attic and tugged the trap door closed as he dropped back to the landing. Returning to the downstairs living room, he put on a well-used windcheater jacket, zipped it up halfway to ensure that his handgun was hidden, then left the house, carefully closing and locking the door behind him.

It was now 0900 hours and the morning was cold and grey, with tendrils of mist drifting over the low green hills surrounding the white-painted converted farmhouse that Burton had been renting since his arrival here. Glancing around him, he recalled the days when this beautiful bucolic landscape had been known as 'bandit country', its hills dotted with British Army OPs, its skies filled with the roaring of AH-7 Lynx

helicopters inserting replacements and taking off the soldiers
whose shifts had ended. A lot of men from both sides had died
in these peaceful hills; others, the victims of assassination,
were still buried in secret graves in the area. It was hard to
believe it now.

Slipping into the driver's seat of a second-hand, turquoise-
coloured 1995 Ford Escort, Burton placed the Nikon camera
on the seat beside him and covered it with a street map of
Belfast and its environs. He then turned on the ignition and
drove away from the house, turned onto a busy main road,
drove through Antrim town and then took the M2 motorway
to Belfast.

The journey was short and soon he was in the outskirts
of the city, passing the signs to Belfast International Airport where Rob McAllister had arrived by Shuttle two weeks
ago. Rob was now safely ensconced in a holiday cottage just
outside Ballyclare, about twenty minutes' drive from Slim's
house in Templepatrick, rented by him when he arrived by
train from Dublin less than a week ago. Burton's house, an
easy drive from the other two, was situated halfway between
Randalstown and the banks of Lough Neagh. All three houses
were located not much farther than ten miles from the centre
of Belfast.

As he came off the motorway and drove into the city, cutting
through the back streets and passing familiar landmarks, old
memories of the Troubles flooded in, bringing with them that
familiar discomfort. As always, he found it hard to accept that
there were no armed soldiers on the roads nor RUC check
points blocking off the streets, though the partisan graffiti on
the walls of ruined buildings reminded him that old hatreds
still flourished. Passing through the centre of the city, along
Royal Avenue and around the imposing City Hall, he was
impressed once more by the new shopping arcades and office
developments, by the sight of the many unconcerned shoppers
and lively buskers, where previously there had been bombed-
out dereliction, checkpoints in barbed-wire enclosures, armed
troops and a palpable atmosphere of unease. Now the atmosphere was bustling, energetic, optimistic, as if the coming of
peace had bought the populace a new lease of life.

The old feeling of unease did, however, return when he
left the centre of the city and drove along the Falls Road,
with its rabbit warren of side streets and alleyways. The

Falls itself was as busy as Royal Avenue, if considerably less sophisticated. Its shops, pubs, cafés, chippies, bookies, Xtra-Vision video shops and second-hand furniture shops, the furniture spread on the pavements, retained their often shabby, old-fashioned appearance, though certainly they were doing good business. Nevertheless, the gable ends of houses were still covered with Republican grafitti – *Free POWs!* and *Disband RUC!* – and many buildings were still enclosed in high mesh-wire fencing and steel shutters, indicating that they were IRA strongholds, often used for interrogation and torture. They were not a welcoming sight.

Burton knew this area like the back of his hand, having practically lived here for almost a year during the Troubles, engaging in a series of highly dangerous covert operations. Now, as he patrolled the area in his car, driving up and down the Falls Road itself, then exploring the side streets and their working-class terraced houses, keeping track of Jack Hegarty, Neil Byrne, Liam O'Shea and Shaun Keenan, all of whom lived in this area, he was constantly reminded of people and places he had known when last here. Very few of these recollections brought back good memories. Indeed, after nearly five weeks of this kind of daily reconnaissance, Burton knew that it hadn't really changed all that much: the teenage 'dickers' were still evident on the streets (grunge clothes and big boots, heads shaven, loud-mouthed and intimidating) and the men for whom they worked were still kneecapping and killing in the rubbish-strewn alleyways or fortified buildings, though for criminal profits instead of political freedom. In fact, this area was just as dangerous now as it had been during the Troubles.

Burton had spent the past five weeks following the movements of the Belfast Six, including Michael Gallagher and Patrick McCauley, who lived in Turf Lodge and Andersonstown respectively, both depressed Catholic ghettoes located east of the Falls. He had known all six men by name from his previous period in Belfast and been brought up to date with secret RUC reports on each individual. His personal intelligence-gathering involved driving into Belfast practically every day, parking near the home of the individual he had targeted, and then following him, either by car or on foot, wherever he went, taking long-distance photos with the Nikon camera and carefully jotting into his 'Bingo book'

relevant details about their daily activities. This included
home addresses, details of wives and children, descriptions of
their cars with registration numbers, the routes they generally
took to and from the city, the individuals they most frequently
met and where those meetings took place, their habits with
regard to eating, drinking and general socializing. And, most
important, the form of protection they had and who was
protecting them.

From this steady accumulation of intelligence, he was soon
able to ascertain that though the men he was after were still
living in their modest two-up, two-down terraced houses in
working-class streets, those houses were watched constantly,
unobtrusively by hard men, all of whom would almost certainly be armed. More crucial was the fact that gangs of
teenage dickers crowded the pavements on opposite sides of
the road at both ends of those streets, as if just lounging
casually, passing their unemployed hours with a bit of 'crack'
– conversation – when in fact they were there to ensure that
no stranger could walk or even drive in without being checked
and, if necessary, stopped. The six gang leaders, then, were
well protected when in their own homes.

They would have to be hit, Burton realized, when they
were somewhere else: either in the street, when travelling
in their cars, or when entering or leaving one of their many
meeting places. For this reason, accumulating intelligence on
their daily movements became ever more vital. Finally, after
nearly five weeks of observation, Burton's surveillance was
almost complete.

As usual, Burton did not have lunch, having filled up earlier
with his large breakfast. Instead, this particular day, he spent
the time in his parked car, smoking and watching the pub
across the road which Jack Hegarty had entered an hour
ago, presumably to have lunch or a pint with some of his
cronies. Burton was familiar with the Belfast Six from his
previous operations in Belfast, when they had all been highly
placed in the IRA and responsible for a great deal of mayhem.
However, having observed them in great detail over the past
five weeks, he had come to the conclusion that, though all of
them were still hard men, the monstrous Jack Hegarty was
the one most active personally in the daily business of running
his turf. Hegarty was far from being the most intelligent –
Neil Byrne and his best friend, Shaun Keenan, were that –

but clearly he was the one with the most enthusiasm when it came to the daily chore of visiting pubs, off-licences, video shops, betting shops and social clubs to collect his regular cut from their profits. He also stopped a lot en route to talk to adolescents and older men who were, Burton soon realized, selling drugs on the streets. Hegarty, therefore, was the most visible of all the gang leaders. Unfortunately, he was also the one best protected by hard men and gangs of youthful dickers who trailed his every move, their slitted eyes watchful. He would not be easy to get at.

Though Burton had not personally witnessed any incidents, he had learnt from one of his touts, or informers, that Hegarty was possibly mad, had a violent temper, and held weekly 'trials' in a back-alley garage, where he 'sentenced' those guilty of real or imagined crimes against him, then administered harsh punishments, mostly of the kneecapping variety. For this reason, he was the most feared of the six gang bosses – and also the one with the most enemies. This could come in handy.

When Hegarty eventually emerged from the pub across the road with Michael Gallagher beside him, Burton quickly took some long-distance photos with the Nikon camera, then drove off before he himself could be observed. The photos, like the many others he had taken over the past five weeks, would be developed in the dark room he had created in the rented farmhouse in Antrim. Copies of the photos would then be distributed to Rob and Slim for inclusion in their personal intelligence files, and also to some of Burton's most trusted friends in the community. Those friends were often able to identify the men photographed in the presence of the gang leaders and unknown to Burton.

He was about to meet one of those friends now. From the pub in the Falls, he drove back across the centre of the city and on to the university area. Parking his car on a meter near Queen's University, he entered the Botanic Gardens Park and walked to the Palm House, a curvilinear glasshouse and cast-iron conservatory surrounded by green lawns and colourful flower beds. Glancing around him, he saw Roy Moloney resting on a black-painted wooden bench near the Belfast Museum and Art Gallery. When Moloney saw him, he stood up and entered the museum. Burton followed him in and wandered casually to his side, where he was standing in the Local History Gallery

just off the lobby. He was studying the fire-box door of a boiler
made in Belfast in 1895 as part of a single-cylinder horizontal
engine. Other visitors were circulating through the gallery,
but they were well out of earshot.

'You come here often?' Burton asked.

'Only when meeting tourists like you,' Moloney responded
sardonically. 'Sure I like to think it'll help you understand the
Irish and be more sympathetic, like.'

Moloney was a former member of the IRA, tall, barrel-
chested, blue-eyed and red-haired, forced to retire prema-
turely when he lost his left arm in a bomb explosion during
a British Army ambush in 1985. Though viewing himself as
a soldier wounded in honourable combat and proud of his role
in the fight for Ireland's freedom, he had little love for the
present IRA which was, he believed, merely using the ceasefire
to buy the time needed to corrupt the organization's original
intentions and create instead a criminal empire. Disgusted by
this, Moloney was doing his best to prevent it by keeping his
nose to the ground and helping out erstwhile enemies like
Burton with information or weapons. They met here, Burton
knew, because there were too many sets of eyes and ears in
the centre of town.

'I believe the groceries were collected,' he said to Burton,
referred to the weapons and surveillance equipment picked
up by Rob McAllister a few days ago.

'Yes,' Burton said. 'Can you confirm that they're fresh?'

'Absolutely,' Moloney told him. 'They came straight from the
warehouse.'

By this he meant that the weapons and surveillance equipment had come from a secret RUC stash and had been passed
on with no questions asked. The goods would not have been
listed in any official RUC inventories and so, if destroyed
after use – as they would be – officially they would never
have existed. They were 'invisible' goods.

'Excellent,' Burton said.

'You require anything else?' Moloney asked.

'Only information,' Burton replied. He glanced left and
right, saw some people nearby and said, 'Let's walk around
the gallery. We're here to be educated, after all, so let's not
waste our precious time.'

Moloney grinned and nodded. 'Ackay.' They started walking
around the gallery, stopping at each exhibit, moving on when

other visitors came too close, talking on the move. 'So you've settled in nicely out in Antrim?' Moloney asked.

'Yes,' Burton said.

'What's your reason for settlin' in there?' Moloney asked. 'What's your tale for the locals?'

'Antiques,' Burton said. 'I'm here for six months to pick up antiques cheaply and take them back for sale in England. That explains why I drive around a lot. It works well in the pubs.'

'Good places for information,' Moloney said. 'So how can I help you?'

'You know why I'm here,' Burton said. 'You know the names of my six major customers.'

'Ackay, I do that, all right. You picked the right six.'

'Do they get on together or do they squabble? Knowing that would be helpful.'

'What I've got is all gossip and hearsay. I can't get that close to them.'

'How sound is the gossip?'

'Gossip's invariably based on somethin' solid. Though exaggerated, there's usually somethin' behind it, so it's well worth considering.'

'And what does the gossip say? Do they get on well together or are they fractious?'

'I'd say it's the latter. There's friction causin' heat. The divisions between them are growing wider and the main cause is JH.'

He was talking about Jack Hegarty. 'He's the one I'd have picked,' Burton said. 'I'd say that man's a loose cannon.'

'Loose and runnin' wild,' Moloney said. 'The grapevine has it that he wants to run the whole show and the rest of 'em know it. He's also refusin' to accept limitations imposed from outside.'

'The US?'

'Correct. A little matter to do with the importation and distribution of pharmaceuticals. For reasons which you may gather, the US has requested restrictions in this area and JH, though sayin' he'd accept them, is still goin' his own way. Because of this, the US is puttin' pressure on the other five and that's what's creatin' the friction between them. Their solidarity is weakening. They grow mutually suspicious. So if something happened to any of the other five, JH might be blamed. That would be the start of a range war that you could exploit.'

'I initiate the process, then step in when they're moving against each other.'

'You could do a lot worse,' Moloney said. 'That way you stay in the background.'

'I get the drift,' Burton said. They were standing together by a glassed-in collection of old Irish medals and when Burton saw a group of students approaching, he led Moloney back to the lobby. 'I have to be getting back,' he said. 'I'll leave you at the entrance.'

'Sure that's grand,' Moloney said. 'I want to go up to the Art Gallery and wander around. That should take me some time.'

'Good,' Burton said. They stopped near the revolving doors of the entrance, pleased that no one was there. 'Anything else you can tell me?'

'No,' Moloney said. 'I can't get that close to 'em.'

'I need someone who can,' Burton said. 'Do you have any suggestions?'

Moloney thought about it. He glanced repeatedly left and right, checking that no one was approaching, then removed his notebook from a pocket, scribbled a name, tore the page out and passed it to Burton. The latter placed it into his own pocket without actually reading it.

'Don't be surprised,' Moloney said. 'He's an old friend of yours. He's a Prod but he knows a lot more than he's likely to let on.'

'If he's a Prod, he's not likely to get very close.'

'He won't be close himself,' Moloney said, 'but he's likely to know someone who is and he'll be on your side.'

'Right,' Burton said. 'Thanks. I'll be on my way now.' He pointed back into the museum. 'The stairs are over there.'

'Aye, they are right enough,' Moloney said. 'Sure I'll go an' have a quick gander at the paintings before I head home. You keep in touch now.'

'I will,' Burton said. He waited until Moloney had disappeared up the stairs, then he turned around and made his way outside, into the afternoon's grey chill. Leaving the park, he returned to his car, sat behind the steering wheel, then checked the name on the slip of paper given to him by Moloney. Surprised by the name he found there, suddenly recalling that old friend, he didn't move for some time, his brow furrowed in thought. But eventually he took out his Zippo lighter and set fire to the paper. When it had burnt down to almost nothing, he opened the car's window and let the remaining charred pieces blow away on the fierce, biting wind.

He lit a cigarette with the Zippo, put the lighter back in his pocket, then started the car and drove back to the centre of town, circling around until he found a parking space near the entrance to the Europa Hotel. He sat there for a long time. He knew his old friend's habits. Eventually, ten minutes later than Burton had anticipated, a taxi pulled up in front of the hotel and Frank Cooney climbed out.

Burton watched Cooney as he entered the building. His old friend hadn't changed. He still wore a dark grey overcoat, a weathered pinstripe suit, a bright tie and black patent-leather shoes. He was still a big man with a shock of silvery hair and a floridly handsome, deeply cynical face.

Burton waited until Cooney had disappeared inside the hotel, then he smiled to himself and drove off, heading back to his isolated farmhouse in the green glens of Antrim.

CHAPTER ELEVEN

Joe Lynch was out to lunch when Hegarty had Mary Dogherty on Joe's desk in the back room of his offices in the Falls after weeks of sexual innuendo followed by overt demands and, finally, a threat to turf Mary out into the street with all the other unemployed or, if that didn't work, to break the legs and arms of her husband with a baseball bat. Terrified by the thought of unemployment, let alone the threat to her young husband, Mary allowed herself to be thrown roughly back onto Joe's desk and obediently spread her legs, sweeping letters and documents to the floor while Hegarty, already unbuttoned and erect, crushed her with his great bulk and proceeded to have his way with her.

Unable to stare into the void of madness that was Hegarty's eyes, mere inches above her, Mary closed her own eyes and tried to console herself by imagining that he did at least desperately want her. In fact, as Hegarty knew, he was really fucking that stuck-up whore, Teresa Kiely, whose image had come to haunt him and who would, in due course, whether she wanted to or not, end up on *her* knees, on *her* belly, on *her* back, doing exactly what he demanded of her. Even as he fucked Mary, sucking her nipples, biting her shoulders, thrusting into her with a vengeance, Hegarty was thinking of how that whore Teresa had insulted him in the Europa Hotel. She obviously thought he was scum, far beneath her, unworthy, and sooner or later he would make her pay for it by turning her into his slave.

Hegarty fucked the whore-bitch by sticking it in Mary and being none too gentle about it, expecting and eventually receiving the requisite cries of pleasure which, though clearly false, excited him enough to make him grunt and groan even more as

Mary hung half off the desk, the legs of which were squeaking in protest at the relentless pounding. More papers fell off the desk, littering the floor around it, as Hegarty worked himself up into a lather based on the rage, humiliation and lust caused him by Teresa Kiely. He cried out when he came, a strangled animal bellow, followed by fearsome breathing, and Mary made gargled sounds of pleasure because her torment was over, though Hegarty mistook this for gratification. Gasping and groaning, his sweat dripping onto her face, he rolled off her and sat up on the edge of the desk, then tucked his flaccid member back in and buttoned his trousers.

'That wasn't so bad, was it?' he asked. 'Seemed to me ya enjoyed it.'

'Sure it was grand, Mister Hegarty,' Mary said, also sitting up to turn her back to him and remove the remains of the panties he had virtually torn off her. 'Was it . . . ? Were you . . . ?'

'Yeah, yeah,' he said, impatient already now that it was over, wanting to get on with other things. 'Sure it was grand for me, too.' He glanced at the floor and saw the papers scattered all over it. 'Jesus,' he said, 'Joe's gonna go spare. Put all that shit back where it came from an' then get back to your desk, lass.'

'Yes, Mister Hegarty.'

Mary rolled her badly torn knickers up into a ball and tucked them down the top of her dress, between her heaving breasts, like a handkerchief. Trying to regain her dignity, she tugged the rumpled dress straight, then knelt low and proceeded to work her way around the desk, picking up the scattered papers and placing them back where she thought they might belong. When she had cleared Hegarty's side of the desk, Hegarty took his chair there and studied the phone messages that Mary had left for him.

The first was from Neil Byrne, reminding him that they were to meet that afternoon in Donovan's pub; the rest were routine calls from various business associates or locals trying to get in touch with him, probably to discuss money matters or to beg for favours. As none of the messages required urgent attention, he decided to deal with them at a later date and instead do his usual rounds as he made his way down the Falls to Donovan's. He was just placing the messages back in a wire basket when Joe Lynch walked in, blinking owlishly behind his spectacles, his Adam's apple bobbing in his throat, his cheeks flushed from his lunchtime pints.

'Have ya come?' he said rhetorically to Hegarty, using that oddity of greeting peculiar to the Ulster Irish as he removed his grey overcoat and hung it on the coat rack by the office door.

'Aye,' Hegarty replied, glancing at Mary as she placed the last of the scattered papers on Joe's desk and hurried out of the office, automatically tugging at the hem of her dress as if it was still too high on her thighs. 'Had a good lunch, did ya?'

'The usual,' Joe replied, adjusting his old school tie, straightening the jacket of his pinstripe suit and taking his chair at the other side of the desk. Reaching out for some papers, his hand wavered and then he studied his desk. 'What the hell's been goin' on here?' he said. 'Sure m'papers are all over the bloody place. Were we hit by a cyclone, like?'

'A little bit of an accident,' Hegarty replied. 'Ask no questions an' I'll tell you no lies.'

Joe glanced at the outer office, at Mary, then turned his gaze back on Hegarty. 'I won't ask,' he said.

'We've got a meeting this afternoon,' Hegarty told him. 'Will you be comin' along?'

Joe shook his head. 'No. It's nothin' to do with financial matters, so my presence isn't required, like. Some kinda war council, I'd imagine, so I'm well out of it, thanks. See no evil, hear no evil, speak no evil – that's my motto, like. I'll stay here an' tot up m'books an' let you get on with it.'

'A war council?' Hegarty said. 'What the fuck do they want to talk about now?'

'No idea,' Joe said.

'It's all blather-blather with that lot an' it never goes any-where. Sure I'm fuckin' fed up with it.' Hegarty sighed. 'Ah, well, I'd better git movin'. Hold the fort while I'm gone. I might see you before you leave an' I might not. Depends on what they've got cookin'.'

'Right,' Joe said.

Hegarty pushed his chair back and stood up to put on his overcoat. 'See ya.' Entering the outer office, he saw Mary at the computer keyboard, typing with fierce concentration. He passed her without the usual banter and hurried outside, into the Falls Road. He turned right and headed down the road, buttoning his coat against the cold wind, pushing against the tide of people, offering a smile to some, waving at others, nodding grimly to the gangs of dickers crowding the pavements at the corners of side streets. The dickers nodded respectfully, tipped their hats, gave him the thumbs-up, and they always parted like the Red Sea for Moses, letting him through. The Falls was busy as always, the shops doing good business, with video rentals up, all the bookies packed, and men entering and leaving the pubs like there was no tomorrow. Hegarty kept his eyes peeled, watching the kids on the pavements, seeing whispered conversations and furtive transactions as his youthful minions sold crack cocaine and other drugs to a growing army of addicts.

The word 'crack' intrigued Hegarty. It was another indication of change. Like all Irishmen, he had always thought of 'crack' as being good conversation and now it was also the name of the drug that made the most money for the Belfast Six. A man had to mind his conversation these days or he could put his foot in it. 'I'm off for a bit of crack,' he might say in all innocence and the cops would swarm all over him like flies and drag him in on a drugs charge. Not that Hegarty himself could ever be deemed that innocent, sitting on top of a whole heap of this new type of crack and reaping the benefits. He liked to change with the times, like.

En route to Donovan's, he made his customary stops at a variety of video shops, bookies, pubs and social clubs to check their takings and, where appropriate, pick up his cut in the profits. As usual, he was received with the usual mixture of suppressed contempt and respect based on fear, but most of the binlids paid up. Occasionally, those a bit more bold than average would voice tentative complaints about the size of his cut or their own shortage of cash, but few of them made an issue out of it when he fixed them with his mad, glimmering gaze. In one instance, a video retailer had doctored his books for no more than a few quid, but that was enough to make Hegarty put the man's hand in the cash register and slam the drawer shut on his fingers, breaking a few bones. In another instance, a publican lied about his take, so Hegarty picked up a chair and slammed it down on the nearest table, which was conveniently packed with innocent customers. The chair was smashed to pieces, the table collapsed, and the shocked customers were showered with flying glass and wood splinters and soaked in their own booze. Hegarty then threw another

chair across the counter, smashing the mirror above the bar
and the many bottles of spirits lined along it, at which point
the publican hastily begged him to stop and promised to make
up the deficit. When he did so, Hegarty shoved the money
into his pocket and marched out, feeling satisfied, confident
that neither the publican nor his customers would report the
incident to the cops. He was well protected around here.

He was, however, presented with a major problem when he
entered a broken-down social club located up a side street and
met the new owner for the first time. The previous owner,
Mick Slattery, had struggled in vain for months to meet
Hegarty's escalating demands for 'community support funds',
finally deciding that he was on a losing ticket and had best
get out while he was still relatively solvent. Which he did by
selling the club to Ralph Meeks, a former light-heavyweight
boxer with his own track record for violence. Though the club
was closed when Hegarty arrived, the front door was unlocked
and Hegarty was able to waltz right in, passing the chairs piled
on the tables and the silent fruit machines until he reached
the bar at the rear, where Meeks, a big man with a broken
nose, was cleaning some glasses. When Hegarty demanded his
cut from the previous week's takings, Meeks stared fearlessly
at him.

'We're under new management,' he said, 'and the rules have
been changed. We don't contribute to community support
funds or any other so-called fuckin' charity run by you and
yer cronies. Now get out of here, you fat, ugly bastard, before
I break every bone in yer fuckin' body and personally throw
you out.'

Instantly enraged, Hegarty stepped forward, raising his
clenched fists. But he stopped and then stepped back when
Meeks pulled a baseball bat out from behind the bar and
raised it on high.

'Sure I could beat you to a fuckin' pulp with my own fists,'
Meeks said, 'but not wantin' to smell yer foul breath, I'll use
this instead. If you're not outta here in sixty seconds you'll be
spread like jam on that fuckin' floor.'

'No one fuckin' talks to me like that,' Hegarty responded,
practically shaking with rage, his ham fists still clenched. 'I
don't . . .' But when Meeks started coming around the side of
the bar, raising the baseball bat to strike, Hegarty backed off
towards the door, saying, 'This isn't the end of this, you dumb

shite. I'll be back. Mark my words!' Meeks grinned savagely
and swung at him with the baseball bat as Hegarty made his
escape.

Humiliated and blind with fury, he continued on down the
Falls, venting his spleen by deliberately bumping into those
in his way and then violently pushing them aside. When one
man, not knowing him, turned back to complain, Hegarty
punched him in the mouth, kneed him in the balls, kicked him
in the ribs when he was down and then marched on, screaming
incoherent threats at anyone within range. He had managed
to contain himself by the time he reached O'Donovan's, but he
was still in a terrible rage and felt like murdering someone.
Though already late for the meeting upstairs, he stopped
in the downstairs bar and drank a double whisky in one
gulp. Taking a deep breath to slow down his racing heart,
he marched upstairs and into the back room being used for
the meeting. The other five gang leaders were already seated
at the table and the air was blue with cigarette smoke. They
all looked up when he walked in.

'Late again,' Neil Byrne said sarcastically. 'Always wantin'
to make the grand entrance like a tart at a ball.'

'Shut yer fuckin' gub,' Hegarty retorted as he pulled up a
chair and poured himself another glass of whisky from the
bottle of Bushmill's on the table. 'I've had enough aggravation
for one day. I don't need shite from you. So what's the reason
fer this fuckin' meetin'?'

'You're the reason,' Byrne said, always the spokesman for
the others.

'Sure it's nice to know I'm in your thoughts,' Hegarty said.
'What is it yer after?'

The other cowardly shits glanced at each other, but Byrne's
gaze was steady. 'We're getting bad wind from the streets,' he
said, 'about your activities.'

'I work my own turf,' Hegarty said, 'and what I do there's
my business.'

'Correction,' Byrne said. 'We're all in this together, so
what you do out there is *our* business and we don't want
it threatened.'

'So how the fuck's it being threatened? We've never made
more gelt in our lives an' the pile's growin' bigger every day.
You've no cause fer complaint.'

'Yes, we have, Hegarty. We're concerned about the way you

conduct your business; about the fact that we're receiving more and more complaints about your so-called punishments. The word's out that a lot of the punishments aren't justified or are too severe even when they are. There's talk of kangaroo courts an' beatin's in public an' what amounts, in general, to a reign of terror that's startin' to turn people against you.'

'I don't give a shit who's against me,' Hegarty told him. 'I can hold my own out there.'

'That's not the point,' Shaun Keenan said. 'If they turn against you, they'll turn against us and that's not in our interests. We need a certain amount of community support and you could lose us that.'

'If you frighten the bastards enough,' Hegarty said, 'you'll get their support. If you don't, you just bury 'em.'

'If we bury too many,' Patrick McCauley said, 'they might run to the fuckin' RUC. To be the law on your own turf is one thing; to practise indiscriminate terror is another an' it always backfires. The people on our turfs' – he nodded to indicate the other four – 'respect us enough to avert their eyes and keep their mouths shut. But if they start thinkin' that we're out of control, they'll run to the real law.'

'What's that got to do with me?' Hegarty asked him while including the others in his angry, accusing stare. 'Are you fuckers sayin' I'm out of control?'

'Getting that way,' Byrne said. 'To punish individuals out of sight and earshot is somethin' the locals will wear – they're not personally involved and they see it as us gettin' back at our own. But when someone like you starts wrecking pubs and the like with the customers still in 'em – or kneecaps sixteen-year-olds for pinchin' pennies or makin' a simple mistake – when someone does that, the people in the street start gettin' worried because they're personally threatened. They're worried enough already about us sellin' crack to their kids; but if they think they're in personal danger every time they go to a pub or club, they'll start lookin' to the law to protect 'em and we'll have a harder time.'

'So I'm the big bogey man, am I?' Hegarty said.

'At the moment,' Neil Byrne said. 'Our feelin' is that yer out there on yer own – a fuckin' cowboy – an' doin' things that are drawin' attention to the rest of us. We want you to stop it.'

'Fuck you,' Hegarty said. 'The day you run your turf as well as I run mine is the day I might consider what you say. In the meantime, I'll run my turf my own way an' you'll all reap the benefit, whether or not you like how I go about it.'

'That pits you against us,' Liam O'Shea said, 'and that's one against five.'

'Are you threatenin' me, Liam?'

'No,' O'Shea said quickly. 'I'm merely suggestin' that if we don't all row together – if even one of us is in disagreement – then the whole caboodle could come tumblin' down and we'd all lose out, like.'

Hegarty was boiling mad. They were all turning against him. He was better than the rest of them put together and they knew it and secretly resented it. Fuckin' amateurs, the lot of them, frightened to move into the big time, just wanting to sit on their arses and get it the easy way. Well, it wasn't for him. He had bigger fish to fry. He was going to go all out, the whole route, and no one would stop him. If needs be, he would go it on his own and let these bastards drown. That day might be coming real soon, and when it did, he'd be ready.

'Anything else?' he asked, trying to stifle his anger.

'Yes,' Shaun Keenan said. 'We promised the Yank a reduction in street trade – the crack and other drugs – and so far we haven't seen a reduction on your turf. Our friends across the water are getting worried and when they're worried, we are.'

'The Atlantic Ocean's between them an' us,' Hegarty said, 'so why the fuck do you even bother listenin' to 'em? Those bastards couldn't touch us if they tried, so we can safely ignore 'em.'

'They can reach us if they want to,' Byrne told him. 'They can reach us through their Mediterranean brothers – the Italians and Sicilians – and they'll do it if they think that what we're doin' is against their own interests. We're not alone in this, Hegarty. We import and export. We can't turn against our friends across the water and hope to survive. We need them in order to grow and that's what you want as well: steady growth through international trade. We can't do that alone.'

'So you want me to clip m'own wings and stay low to the ground.'

'Correct,' Neil Byrne said.

'An' if I don't?'

'Then we'll have to take remedial action. And that could be unpleasant.'

'That's a threat,' Hegarty said.

'Read it as you will, Jack.'

'Sure I can read perfectly well,' Hegarty said, 'and I say that's a threat.'

'We can't have cowboys in this organization,' Byrne said, 'and you've become our Lone Ranger.'

'Fuck you,' Hegarty said, pushing his chair back and standing upright. 'I won't have my fuckin' wings clipped by a bunch of wankers like you. I'll do what I want on my own turf and you can take that as read. Think about it an' get back to me when you see sense. Now I've got to make tracks.'

'Don't walk out on us, Hegarty,' Shaun Keenan said. 'If you do, you may not get back in.'

'Fuck off,' Hegarty said.

He stormed out of the room, made his way down to the bar and asked for another double whisky to set him up for the evening. Furious, he finished it in one gulp, then left and marched back up the Falls, now surrendering to darkness, the lights in the shops blinking on to beam over the pavements. Hegarty went on a pub crawl, working his way through his old haunts, getting free drinks wherever he went and growing angrier with every glass he polished off. By nightfall, when the shops were closing and people were pouring into the pubs and social clubs, he was well beyond his usual capacity, considerable at the best of times, and talking a lot to himself in his head.

Fuckin' timid cunts, he was saying to himself. *Gutless bastards filled with treachery and deceit, jealous of my success, my fuckin' authority in my own fuckin' turf, the fear I instil in all the binlids who try to do me down and have to be shown what law and order means with a bit of disciplinary punishment. They'll turn on me as sure as I have legs an' I'll have to retaliate. Move on them before they move on me. Fuck the bastards in every fuckin' orifice and make 'em bleed like stuck pigs. Wipe 'em off the map and take over. Let them know who the boss is.*

The more he drank, the more he was convinced that his old friends, the traitorous bastards, were planning to put him out of business and take over his turf. He was angry beyond words, feeling betrayed and humiliated, set upon from every direction as his enemies closed in. Why, even that whore, Teresa Kiely, had put him down in public – and then that locally famous light-heavyweight boxer, Ralph Meeks, had refused to pay his dues and even chased him, Hegarty, the gang boss, out of his sleazy social club with a baseball bat. Well, Hegarty knew about baseball bats – he was an expert with *that* fuckin' number – and he was going to sort out that bastard Meeks and to hell with the others. If they didn't like what he was going to do, they could go fuck themselves – he wouldn't take shit from anyone. And after Meeks, make no fuckin' mistake, he'd pay a visit to that stuck-up whore, Teresa Kiely, and show her what *real* humiliation was. Damned right, he would.

Drunk and blind with rage, Hegarty reeled out of another pub and approached a gang of his own youthful, hard-faced dickers. He told them to go back to his garage, grab a baseball bat each, bring one along for him, then meet him outside Meek's social club. Always grateful for a little personal attention from their fearsome boss, the dickers rushed away to do as they were told while Hegarty, in a fever of homicidal rage, made his way to the club and took up a position in a shadowed doorway just across the road from the entrance.

It was eight in the evening, dinner time was over, and men and women were pouring into the club to get pissed, work the fruit machines, play darts or billiards, and dance to a scummy local band. Hegarty observed them going in, arm in arm, laughing, some already drunk, and thought, *You won't be so happy in a short while. You'll all be shittin' your pants and lace knickers. After what's goin' to happen there tonight, you won't go back in a long while. That should fix fuckin' Meeks.* The dickers turned up soon after, all carrying baseball bats, and when Dick Connors gave one of them to Hegarty, he led the charge across the road. They just swarmed through the doorway, swinging the bats as they ran, and the bouncers at the door were the first to go down, arms flailing and blood pouring from their heads as they crashed to the floor. Hegarty stayed in the lead, always keen on the grand entrance, and swung his baseball bat left and right on the move, cracking the skulls of men and women alike as the dickers spread out to cover the whole room. Women screamed and men bawled, either scattering or collapsing, as tables were smashed, chairs went flying, broken glass flew in all directions and blood splashed on the floor.

Hegarty was fucking mad, smashing his way through the mêlée, but he really had eyes only for Meeks who was presently rising up behind the bar, holding his own baseball bat in his hands. Hegarty struck first, cracking Meek's skull open, sending him hurtling backwards against the mirror behind the bar, which broke noisily and showered him in falling glass. Hegarty ran around the bar and went in to get Meeks, raining more blows on his bloody head, pounding him to the floor, then smashing his arms and legs until he couldn't even crawl, which allowed Hegarty to put the boot in, kicking Meeks repeatedly, watching his body bounce, then bringing the baseball bat down on his head for a final blow before racing away.

'All out!' he bawled. 'Let's go!'

He led the dickers out of the club, back into the dark street, away from the weeping women and groaning, dazed men, from the broken bones and blood and ruin and gradually accumulating shock, all the way back to his garage, where they chortled and cheered and slapped each other on the back and then wiped the blood off the baseball bats and stashed them away. When that was done, Hegarty magnanimously opened the refrigerator in the garage and told the lads to help themselves to beer. He joined them in the booze-up, wanting to bless them with his presence, and eventually became maudlin and told them how much he respected them for what they had done. When they applauded him, he wiped tears from his eyes and knew what real pride was.

And now for that whore Teresa Kiely, he thought just before he fell asleep across the table where normally he sat to pass judgement upon those who offended him. *No fuckin' tart from Newtownards can humiliate me and get away with it. Your time has come, bitch.*

Then Hegarty, having put in a full day, fell asleep in his freezing garage and slept like a baby.

CHAPTER TWELVE

'So what do we have here?' Burton asked rhetorically as he flamed a cigarette with his Zippo lighter. He was seated at the big pine table in his rented farmhouse in Antrim with Rob McAllister and Slim Dalton facing him. A manila folder was opened in front of each man and photos of the Belfast Six were spread out between them. The folders were filled with the intelligence picked up by each man since his arrival in the province. Burton's was the thickest of the three folders because he had been here the longest, conducting his daily surveillance for almost six weeks as the others arrived at fortnightly intervals. 'We have six former IRA hard men,' he continued, exhaling a cloud of cigarette smoke, 'who've carved Belfast up between them and now run it as their criminal empire. Each has his own turf and they're all well protected by gangs of other hard men and the more youthful dickers. Their main source of revenue in the city comes from drugs, prostitution, video piracy, fruit machines, illegally imported alcohol and cigarettes sold in pubs and social clubs, and the rake-off from protection money and so-called contributions to various charities. The drugs are sold in the streets and in night clubs, mostly by, and to, young people. The addicts often become sellers in order to feed their growing habit. This in turn sucks them into the criminal underworld, keeps them trapped there, and effectively makes them a further threat to us.'

'Because they'd be aware of strangers in the community,' Rob said. Burton nodded, confirming. 'And the rest?' Rob asked.

'The prostitutes operate in the streets.' Burton said, 'and in pubs and hotels, though they're not allowed into the social clubs. Though they might not love the men they're working for

– by which I mean the Belfast Six – they're certainly going to be frightened of them and that makes them another potential threat to us.'

'Because those whores, like the drug addicts,' Slim said, his angelic blue gaze steady, 'will know everyone in the streets and could pick out strangers like us from a mile away.'

'You've got it,' Burton said. 'If they thought they could buy a favour by reporting our presence there, they'd certainly do so.'

'You're so fuckin' optimistic,' Rob said sardonically, 'I feel like dancin' on the ceilin' like Fred Astaire.'

'These are the facts,' Burton said, 'and we have to accept them.'

'So what *else* do we have here?' Rob asked. 'Make us shit more bricks, Sarge.'

In most regular British Army units, Rob's remarks would have been treated as insolence, but Burton was merely amused. Gazing at the corporal's battered, pugnacious features, which accurately reflected his rough background in the East End of London before reconstruction rendered that area anonymous, he recalled how this essentially uneducated man – often jokingly referred to as the shortest man ever to play rugby let alone get into the SAS; a bad husband, a womanizer and a drunken brawler – had fought beside him in Iraq, sharing the Pink Panther as it barrelled across Scud Alley during the appalling heat of the day, sleeping beside him in the freezing cold of the desert night, and fearlessly firing his 7.62mm GPMG in mobile attacks that would have tested the courage of any man to its limit. Rob had done all that and more. He had also deliberately revealed himself to vengeful Iraqi troops, acting as a decoy, inviting possible death solely in order to let Burton make his way across the Syrian border and take back invaluable intelligence to the Coalition Forces. Though captured and badly tortured by the Iraqis before being released at the end of that short war, Rob had repeatedly down-played his own part in the matter and insisted that it had all been a lark. Burton knew that it had not been, that it had been hell on earth, but he also knew that Rob would never admit that and he respected him for it.

'The criminal revenue is collected by the hard men,' Burton continued, 'and intimidation against those who refuse to pay is generally carried out by gangs of dickers. Sometimes, as with

Jack Hegarty, the revenue's collected personally, but mostly it's collected by the gangs, which means that the streets are always filled with them – the shock troops, as it were, of the Belfast Six. In short, we're talking about six gang bosses, each with his own turf, all with many hard men on the streets, so all well protected at most times of the night and the day. Our problem, therefore, is getting to those six men and somehow neutralizing them, preferably without being caught or killed ourselves. It won't be an easy task.'

Even as he spoke, he was quietly shocked by what he was proposing. Right now, back in Redhill, Hereford, Deborah was preparing the kids for bed in an environment so tranquil that violence would seem unimaginable to her. When Burton thought of Deborah's faith in him, her love for their children, her abiding belief in the essential goodness of life, he realized that the gap between her view of reality and his was as wide as the cosmos. He loved her and believed that she loved him, but they still lived in different worlds.

'What's the pecking order?' Slim asked.

'Pardon?' Burton responded, still distracted by his thoughts.

'The pecking order amongst the Belfast Six. Who's top and who's bottom?'

'Ah . . . yes.' Burton nodded, coming back to earth or, more accurately, being dragged back against his will by Slim's icily handsome blue gaze. 'Of the six men, Neil Byrne is undoubtedly the most intelligent and looked upon by the others as their unelected leader. Jack Hegarty resents the deference paid to Byrne, thinks of himself as the top dog, and may even be planning to take over the whole show – if necessary by force. The second most intelligent is Shaun Keenan, the organization's financial officer and also Byrne's closest friend. The other three – Liam O'Shea, Michael Gallagher and Patrick McCauley – aren't as bright as Byrne and Keenan, but at least they're not as mad as Jack Hegarty and all were efficient PIRA leaders during the Troubles. That means they're smart and hard enough to run their individual turfs with a great deal of competence. There are no soft targets here and the problem remains . . .'

In the manner of all Chinese parliaments, he wanted to let the others voice their own opinions and deliberately trailed off to encourage them. Slim came up with the anticipated response: 'How do we get at them?'

'The million-dollar question,' Burton said, which was a neat way of not answering the question and forcing Slim and/or Rob to do so.

'Well,' Rob said, running his fingers through his thinning brown hair and shifting restlessly on his hard wooden seat, 'as we've all observed during our reconnaissance, they co-ordinate their activities during weekly meetings that take place in a variety of pubs. That could be a possibility for hitting all six of them at once.'

'Not really,' Burton responded. 'We can't tell in advance where a particular meeting will take place, let alone which day they've chosen, so I can't see us targeting them together.'

'So if we don't know when they're going to be together,' Slim said, 'we'll have to take them out individually.'

'Exactly,' Burton said.

'Any particular order?' Slim asked.

Burton had known Slim so long that under normal circumstances, or in a world more normal than that inhabited by the SAS, he would have considered him to be a kind of brother. As it was, he still hadn't adjusted to the fact that his friend, blond-haired and blue-eyed, features refined, manners impeccable, was a clinically detached killing machine who had calmly fought his way through some of the worst bloodbaths on recent record. Though twenty-eight years old, Slim's delicate, indeed sensitive features made him seem younger than he was and Burton often found himself wondering, with a certain amount of guilt, if this was due to the fact that Slim was not, and never had been, married. This was not to question his sexual orientation – he was a renowned womanizer. Rather, it was a question of how Slim, being otherwise so ordinary, born in Richmond, Surrey to decent, middle-class parents and brought up there, had managed to become a civilized, thoughtful man who yet could kill without qualms. Burton had fought beside Slim in Northern Ireland and Iraq, but he had never found out what made him tick. Nevertheless, he trusted him.

'The most difficult to get at will be Hegarty,' Burton said, exhaling a cloud of cigarette smoke and tapping his Zippo lighter on the table. 'He's mad, bad, ruthless and absolutely fearless, but he's even better protected than the others.'

'He can't be that fearless if he has all that protection,' Slim said, thoughtfully studying the photos that Burton had

shot with his Nikon camera and processed in the darkened
bathroom of this house.

'The protection's nothing to do with the state of his nerves,'
Burton insisted. 'Hegarty's fearless as only the mad can be,
but he knows he has a lot of enemies and that sooner or later
someone's going to go for him. Also, he enjoys being the king
of his domain, being surrounded by flunkies or, in his case,
worshipful dickers and hard men, so he has a lot of them
about him at all times. Gangs of them guard his house –
they're always standing on the corners at both ends of the
street and others are in the street itself, pretending they're
just hanging around when in fact they're keeping their eyes
peeled. They also follow him at a discreet distance when he
goes on his walks along the Falls.'

'Which doesn't necessarily mean that we couldn't get at him,'
Slim said, placing the photos back on the table and running
his fingers through his hair. 'We could drive past in a stolen
car, fire at him from the window, then race away before the
dickers even knew what was happening.'

'At the risk of hitting innocent passers-by,' Rob said, 'and
that's a risk we can't wear.' He raised his glass of Guinness,
studied it admiringly with his dark, dangerous eyes, had a
sip and wiped his crooked lips with his hand. 'Anyway, as
Hegarty's going to be the hardest to get at, I assume he's the
one we're going to target last.'

'Yes,' Burton said. 'And not only because he's the most
difficult.'

Slim raised his eyebrows. 'What does that mean?'

'I recently had a talk with a friend,' Burton said, 'and he
suggests that the other five gang leaders are becoming wary
of Hegarty. The wild man is too ambitious for their liking.
He's also giving them problems with their US counterparts.
He refuses to take orders and he's even starting to trespass
on the other turfs.'

'That could be useful,' Slim said.

'Exactly,' Burton said. 'This friend suggested that if we
blow away one of the other five without being identified, the
remaining four are liable to blame Hegarty and that could
start a range war.'

'Which would work to our advantage,' Rob said.

'Right. At the very least, those bastards, blaming Hegarty,
won't even think that someone's come in from outside. They'll

be looking for their own kind in the Lower Falls – Hegarty's men – and are less likely to dwell on the possibility of clandestine British intervention. That takes the spotlight off us and gives us a lot of shadow to roam in. We move against the rest in that darkness.'

'That's one advantage,' Rob said. 'The other's that the other four bastards, suspecting Hegarty, will start looking suspiciously at each other. You know? If Hegarty can betray us, who's next in our formerly happy little group? And so, losing their mutual trust, they'll also lose what solidarity and cohesion they presently have. They might turn against each other. They might even start blowing each other away and save us the trouble.'

Burton smiled slightly. 'Wishful thinking with regard to the latter,' he said. 'But certainly they'd lose their solidarity, become less cohesive and, if not actually turning against each other, worry more about each other than about the possibility of outside intervention. Right now, no one even suspects that we're here. The first hit could keep it that way until we take out at least a couple more. After that, they're bound to suss that it's something bigger and look for outsiders. So let's take out that first target immediately and then move on pretty quickly to the others while we still have the advantage.'

'Who's the one to go first?' Slim asked pragmatically.

'Who do you think should be the first?' Burton responded, expecting to hear the right answer.

'Michael Gallagher or Patrick McCauley,' Slim replied.

'Why those two?'

'They live in Turf Lodge and Andersonstown respectively,' Rob said. 'They don't live in the Falls itself. That means they're the least protected. We can get at 'em a lot easier, probably when they're on the move, somewhere between their homes and the Lower Falls.'

'Correct,' Burton said, pleased that his two friends were on the ball. 'We start with one of those two. My personal recommendation is Patrick McCauley.'

'Why?' Slim asked.

'He lives in Turf Lodge and drives every day from there to his office, located near Divis Street. We can't attack as he leaves home because his street is protected and even if we got in, we'd never get out. For the same reason, we can't attack as he enters his office in the Lower Falls. Whatever we do, we have to do it without endangering the lives of innocents, which means we can't do it while he's driving in a built-up area.'

'Which leaves us absolutely nowhere,' Rob said.

'Incorrect,' Burton said. 'McCauley's not followed everywhere like that lunatic, Hegarty. In fact, living outside the Falls, where most of the criminal activity takes place, he seems to think he's relatively safe, so he only uses his hard men in the street where he lives and, of course, in the Lower Falls.'

'In other words?' Slim asked.

'In other words, he's relatively unprotected from the moment he drives out of his own street to when he parks at his office near Divis Street. We can't hit him there for reasons already discussed, so we hit him where he has to slow down at the Monagh Bypass to turn into Glen Road. We attack before he picks up speed again and we do it without endangering the other drivers.'

'Do you think we can manage that?' Rob asked him.

'Who dares wins,' Burton said.

CHAPTER THIRTEEN

Cooney was already leaning against the bar when Teresa entered White's Tavern in Winecellar Entry, not far from the offices of the *Belfast Telegraph*. It was Saturday lunchtime and the pub was busy, with most of the tables taken and shopping bags at the feet of many customers. Wearing his customary pinstripe suit and tie, drinking whisky and exhaling smoke from a cigar, the silver-haired Cooney looked raffishly distinguished and still attractive for his age, which Teresa judged to be just over fifty. He turned around when she tapped him on the shoulder, looked her up and down, and grinned.

'You're obviously not working today,' he said, referring to the fact that instead of her usual figure-hugging clothes she was wearing a windcheater jacket, loose roll-necked pullover, faded denims and flat, scuffed shoes.

'Not until tonight,' she replied. 'Sure I try to stay normal by shoppin' on Saturday like everyone else. When I get back, I'll give my flat its weekly cleanin' just like all the other decent wimmen.'

'Where's the flat?'

'Along the Malone Road.'

'I'm impressed,' Cooney said. 'Posh Catholic, that is.'

'Sure mine isn't as posh as it sounds,' Teresa told him. 'It's just a conversion in one of those big old houses, though it's done pretty nice.'

'You wouldn't get that working in Woolworth's.'

'Sure that's true enough.' She glanced at Cooney's drink. 'What's that you're havin'?'

'Bushmills.'

'That'll do fine.'

'Right.' Cooney called the barmaid over, gave the woman his order, then dragged a vacant stool into view. 'No tables left, Teresa, so plant your backside on that.'

'Thanks.' She sat on the stool, crossed her legs, lit a cigarette, glancing about as she inhaled and exhaled. 'Nice place, Frank.'

'A journalist's haunt during the working week,' Cooney said. 'Saturday shoppers today. You haven't been here before?'

'No. They wouldn't know me from Adam.'

'Good,' Cooney said.

Teresa noted the remark and wondered again why Cooney had phoned, asking to see her. 'Why good?'

'Well . . .'

'You don't want to be seen with me, is that it?'

'No,' Cooney replied. 'I'm seen with a lot of people and I've often been seen with you personally in the bar of the Europa Hotel, so it isn't social embarrassment.'

'It's one thing to be seen with me in the Europa Hotel an' another to invite me here for a drink. Sure what would yer nice wee wife be thinkin' if she saw us right now?'

'She'd almost certainly get the wrong idea, but she's not going to see us.'

'Some of her friends might.'

'We live out in Newtownbreda,' Cooney said, 'and her friends don't drink here. Besides, if they saw me talking to you, they'd probably just think this was an interview for the *Telegraph*. You can get away with murder being a reporter. You can even talk to whores with impunity, so I've nothing to worry about.'

'Lucky you,' Teresa said. She grinned and exhaled a cloud of smoke, turning slightly away from him so as not to blow it in his face. 'So what do ya want to talk about?' she asked, turning towards him again. 'You've never called me at home before, let alone ask me out for a drink. You've already said you're not the kind to pay for sex, so why am I here?'

'I haven't seen you in the Europa for the past couple of weeks,' Cooney said, deflecting her question with a statement of fact.

'You haven't seen me for the past couple of weeks because I haven't been there.'

'What's kept you away?'

Teresa knew exactly what had kept her away and the

very thought of it – of *him* – still chilled her bones. She had been very badly shaken by her encounter with Jack Hegarty and decided to stay away from that bar for at least a couple of months. Hegarty, she had deduced, was possibly mad, certainly violent, and clearly determined to make her work as one of his common tarts. Even worse, he obviously wanted her for himself and that thought made her shiver with revulsion. She had thought a lot about Hegarty since that initial encounter and doing so always filled her with dread. 'Just thought I'd change m'turf,' she lied to Cooney. 'Try some other hotels.'

'Why?'

Teresa shrugged. 'Just bored, I suppose.'

'You were a familiar sight in that bar. You did good business there.'

'I could do good business anywhere,' she said, 'so I thought I'd spread myself around, like, an' see what transpired.'

'And?'

'Good business as always,' Teresa told him.

'Glad to hear it.' Cooney turned back to the counter when the barmaid placed the drinks down. He paid the girl, then handed one of the drinks to Teresa and raised his glass in the air. 'Cheers,' he said. They drank and he placed his glass back on the counter and inhaled on his cigar.

'Sure that fuckin' smoke stinks,' Teresa said. 'You should smoke ordinary ciggies like the rest of us.'

'I merely stink while you get cancer,' Cooney replied. 'You don't inhale with cigars.'

'Then why smoke 'em?'

'For the aroma and taste.' He looked her up and down again with admiration. 'Even in those clothes, Teresa, you look like a million fucking dollars.'

'Sure I come cheaper than that, but I know you didn't call me as a client, so what's this all about?'

Cooney stared thoughtfully at her, as if undecided about what to say to her. He could be sharp with his tongue, but his florid, handsome face had the look of ruined innocence, of basic decency outraged once too often. Teresa had seen that look before, on the faces of some of her better clients: the shamed puritans and disillusioned idealists. She sensed that Cooney was a man who had seen too much for his own good and now found the knowledge hard to live with.

His cynicism was his one line of defence in a messy, corrupt world.

'The last time I saw you,' he said, 'you were about to be approached by that mad, bad bastard, Jack Hegarty.'

'Ackay,' Teresa said. 'An' you didn't want to be involved, so you got the hell out.'

Cooney grinned. 'Sure that's true enough. What happened after I left?'

'Nothin' much,' she lied, again recalling that particular evening with dread. 'He wanted me to leave with him an' I refused an' he made a few nasty threats an' then I left with someone else. I haven't seen him since then.'

'He's seen you,' Cooney said.

'What?'

'I think he's been following you,' Cooney said as Teresa fought the fear that slithered through her. 'I walk these streets night and day and I've seen you four times in the past two months, entering or leaving various hotels, though not the Europa. In every instance, I saw Hegarty as well – usually in a parked car and obviously watching you. Checking your movements, like.'

'Oh, Jesus!' Teresa murmured involuntarily, her skin prickling with the return of chilling fear, her heart starting to race.

'The last time,' Cooney said, 'which was only two days ago, he was waiting in his car when you came out of the Regency Hotel with one of your tricks. You hailed a taxi and got into it with that man and Hegarty followed your taxi. I was so worried, I followed Hegarty in another taxi and saw him parking where he could watch you as you led your trick into what I assume was your place. That was in the Malone Road.'

'It was my place,' Teresa confirmed, realizing that her throat was dry with fear and that her heart was still racing.

'I didn't know you took tricks home,' Cooney said.

'I didn't before, but after my confrontation with that bastard, I started doin' it when I picked the trick up in a bar in another hotel an' then learnt that he was actually stayin' in the Europa. I mean, I couldn't ask him to book a room in another hotel when he were already in the Europa, so I'd take him home rather than take a chance on runnin' into Hegarty. I was scared to run into Hegarty again; it was as simple as that. An' now you tell me he's followed me home, that he knows where I live. Jesus Christ, this is scary.'

'I didn't want to frighten you,' Cooney said, 'but I was convinced, when you stopped going to the Europa, that Hegarty had scared you off, so I thought you should know.'

Picking up her glass to have a sip of whisky, Teresa wasn't at all surprised to see that her hand was shaking. She sipped quickly, not wanting Cooney to see the shaking, then put the glass down again.

'Just how bad is he, Frank?'

'Very bad,' Cooney replied. 'The worst of the fuckin' bunch. If he's been threatening you, take note of his threats because that man doesn't make jokes. What he threatens, he'll do.'

'Oh, God!' Teresa exclaimed involuntarily.

'So what *did* he threaten?'

'He said that I was workin' his turf and that I couldn't do that without payin' my dues.'

'In other words, paying him.'

'Right.'

'And then?'

'When I told him to piss off, he insisted that I leave the bar with him. When I refused, he got mad. I thought he was gonna hit me, so I picked up this trick right beside me – a Yank tourist – and deliberately left the bar with him, leavin' Hegarty standin' there. He was real livid, though.'

'He would have viewed that as a form of humiliation.'

'Aye, he did. Sure I could tell that at a glance. He'd already accused me of believin' he wasn't good enough for me, of thinkin' I shit gold bricks, an' when I told him that I chose my own clients – implying that he wouldn't be one of them, like – well, he looked fit to burst. When I then left the bar with that Yank, I could tell he was hoppin' mad.'

'He wants you working for him, Teresa.'

'Sure that's why I never went back there.'

'But now the bastard knows where you live.'

'Christ,' Teresa said. 'Yes.'

'Please be careful, Teresa. This man can't be laughed away.'

'I won't laugh him away, but I won't give in to him. I won't let a pig like that into my life, no matter how much he wants in. I won't bend to that bastard.'

'So be careful, Teresa.'

Looking into Cooney's handsome, ageing face, florid from heavy drinking and jaded beyond its years, Teresa recalled Jim Quaid telling her that Cooney liked her and thought she was

worth something better than what she had gotten. Already
touched by this recollection, she was even more touched by
Cooney's obvious concern for her and seeming need to protect
her. She had judged him a cynical bastard – a 'shite-face', as
she had put it – but now she was seeing him in a different
light and she wondered why this was so.

'You like me, don't you?' she said.

Cooney wasn't embarrassed. 'Yes.'

'That's why you're worried about me, isn't it?'

'Yes,' Cooney said.

'Do you fancy me?'

'Yes.'

'But you won't buy me.'

'No.'

'I owe you one. Come back with me now.'

'No,' Cooney said.

'I won't charge.'

'I still don't want to know. You're attractive to me, but I can't
do that with you. It's something else I see in you.'

'What the fuck's that?' she asked. 'You fancy me and you're
trying to protect me, but you won't come to my bed, even
though it's for free. That's weird, Frank. Why is that?'

'You're the same age as my daughter,' Cooney said, 'give
or take a few months. You're roughly the same age and you
look like her and that probably explains it. You remind me
of her.'

'She's left home?'

'She's dead,' Cooney said. His voice was steady and controlled. 'A brain tumour at twenty-one years of age, dead and
buried a year ago. You could be her double.'

'Oh, Jesus!' Teresa said.

'Don't pray to *him*,' Cooney said sardonically, 'because he
doesn't spare anyone. But you look after yourself. You watch
out for that Hegarty.'

'I will . . . And thanks, Frank.'

'No sweat.' Cooney finished off his drink, put the glass on
the counter and said, 'Now I have to get back to my wee wife.
I'll see you around.' He turned away and walked out.

Shaking, Teresa finished her own drink and hurried out of
the bar. She spent the next two hours shopping, though her
heart wasn't in it, her thoughts scattered and diffused, limned
with the radiance of fear, by the recollection of Hegarty's

mad gaze and his heavy, relentless, animal breathing. She bought more than she needed, scouring the shopping arcades, protected by the crowds, helpfully dazzled by the bright lights, consoling herself by remembering what Belfast used to be like – the barricades across the streets, the contemptuous armed soldiers, the humiliating body searches, the constant tension – and comparing those recollections with this new, optimistic vitality that had only been dimmed recently by reports of a growing crime wave. Yes, she tried consoling herself this way but it simply didn't work, being darkened by the knowledge that that mad bastard Hegarty hadn't forgotten her and, even worse, was following her, determined to put her under his wing and turn her into his slave. Jesus Christ, what a thought!

Teresa completed her shopping in the full awareness that she constantly compared the old Belfast to the new because she could never forget where she had come from, what she really was, and Hegarty, that fucking lunatic, that frustrated moral puritan and perverted freedom fighter – another vicious shit who couldn't bear the thought of peace – had come into her life like the black plague, a nightmare's grim reaper, reminding her of all the bastards in her childhood that she wished to forget.

Don't let him get to you, she thought as if talking in her mind to someone else. *Don't let him bring back the past. He can't touch you through anything but fear and you don't have to bend to that. He's just another mindless thug, a gob of phlegm, and you've risen above that kind. You're above and beyond the likes of Hegarty. Believe that and you'll beat him.*

She ended up with a lot of shopping, much more than she needed, and had to take a taxi back home, having too many bags. The taxi driver was nice, helping her carry the bags into the house and up two flights of stairs, so she gave him a generous tip and sent him off happy. She felt better after that, being reminded of human decency, and drank a glass of whisky while unpacking the bags, putting the goods away in the refrigerator and cupboards, and gradually taking command of her own world.

A decent world, she thought. *My world. All my own. I may be a whore, no longer welcome in the church, but I'm a lot more than I was when I first left and I won't give it up. Not for him. Not for anyone. I have my pride and I'll keep it.*

Relaxed by the alcohol and feeling less threatened, she

kicked her shoes off, poured another glass of whisky, sat back in an armchair and looked around her, admiring the apartment that she had sacrificed so much to obtain. It was spacious and well furnished: white carpets, dark blue curtains, the cushions and duvets a golden yellow that made the place seem slightly more exotic than was normal in Belfast. She had made it all herself, knitting this, crocheting that, personally choosing the many paintings, all originals by unknown artists, and she had done so to create her own environment and keep out the world she had left behind when she had first left this city. She had no man in her life – only men who paid their way – and though she had often yearned for a real lover, a true companion, she knew that her fear of what men could do would keep her imprisoned. At least here, in this self-created world, her isolation was comfortable. She would rather be a whore, independent, than any kind of kept woman. She would live by her own terms.

The lock of her front door was blown to pieces and the door was flung open.

Teresa dropped her glass of whisky and jerked upright with shock as Hegarty came storming into the apartment, holding a silenced pistol in his right hand and using the other to slam the door shut behind him. In that terrifying split second, Teresa saw that two men were standing guard in the hallway directly outside her apartment, obviously there to protect Hegarty while he was inside.

The slamming of the door was like an explosion inside Teresa, making her jump to her feet and attempt to scream for help. She didn't manage to do so. The big brute was too quick for her. Before she could make a sound, he jammed the pistol into a holster strapped against his spine and then slapped her brutally across the face, sending her spinning backwards onto the armchair, knocking it over. Hitting the carpet belly down, feeling blood on her lips, she was grabbed by the shoulder and roughly flipped onto her back to find herself staring up at Hegarty. He had spread his tree-trunk legs to straddle her and was glaring down at her. His breathing was harsh and heavy, reminding her again of an animal in its dark lair, and she knew that if she attempted to scream he would most likely kill her.

'Ya fuckin' whore,' he said. 'Ya fuckin' jumped-up tart. Who the fuck did ya think ya were talkin' to in that pub a few weeks back? Did ya think I'd take that, bitch? Think I'd let you get away with it? Did ya think ya could treat me like shite an' then get on with yer business?'

He stooped low and grabbed her throat, squeezed until she couldn't breathe, waited until her lips had parted, then stuffed a handkerchief into her mouth to ensure that she couldn't cry out. Straightening up, he stomped on her right shin with the heel of his shoe.

The pain was horrendous, making her body convulse, and when he did the same to her other shin, she almost blacked out.

'Open yer eyes,' he snarled. 'If ya don't, I'll slice yer fuckin' eyelids off with a razor and you'll never be able to close 'em again. Now look at me, you whore.'

Teresa opened her weeping eyes and stared up at his mad gaze. He had taken a switchblade out of his pocket and it gleamed in the light.

'A whore's business is my business,' he said, 'and from now on you work for me. Let this be your reminder.'

He flipped her onto her stomach and she felt a sharp, savage pain that shot from between her shoulder blades to the base of her spine as he swiftly cut down her back. She tried to scream, but she was choking on the rag, so she could only make gargled groaning sounds as her body convulsed again.

'It feels worse than it is,' he said. She could hear his heavy, dreadful breathing. 'The scar will heal eventually. Sure I appreciate the value of undamaged merchandise, but I'll damage you much worse, for all time, if you don't do what yer told. Think about it, you dumb cunt.'

He flipped her onto her back, tramped again on each shin in turn, waited until her body's writhing had ceased, then stooped low again. For an instant, she thought he was going to stab her with the knife, but instead he slashed down the front of her pullover, cutting through her brassiere, then he roughly tore both garments apart, exposing her bare breasts. Grabbing her by the hair, he jerked her upright until she was on her knees in front of him, staring directly at the bulge of his groin.

'Look at me, whore,' he ordered. Teresa did as she was told. Staring up through the veil of her tears, she saw his flaring, triumphant gaze. 'Thought ya were above me, did ya? Thought yerself too classy for me. Well, now yer where ya belong, bitch,

on yer knees, and you'll do just what yer told. First ya satisfy
me. Do that an' you have a head-start. If I like what ya do
– and you'll have to do a lot – then I'll let you go back to
yer business in yer fancy hotels. When you do that, though,
you'll do it for me an' pay what I demand. If you don't, or if
you cheat me or try defyin' me, I'll cut yer fuckin' nose off.'

Reaching down, he jerked the handkerchief out of her mouth,
finally letting her gasp for breath.

'Now take it out,' he said, indicating his swollen groin, 'and
get to work with those luscious lips of yours. Show me what
you can do, you whore.'

Numbed by fear and shock, seeking protection in disbelief,
Teresa commenced to prove her worth in the basements of hell.

CHAPTER FOURTEEN

Patrick McCauley began the shortest day of his life by having his customary large fry-up, done by his wife Martha and consisting of two fried eggs, a couple of rashers of bacon, one sausage, baked beans and two slices of fried bread, all washed down with a mug of hot sugared tea. He wasn't worried about his heart because he didn't eat all that much and the breakfast was his main meal of the day. He would have a cheese sandwich for lunch, followed by a pint of Guinness, and a salad later in the evening, before his evening out in the pub. He certainly looked and felt healthy.

McCauley was a family man who took pride in having a happy wife and children, all of whom were having breakfast with him around the small pine table in the kitchen. The kitchen was not much bigger than the table because McCauley, though quietly rich from his many criminal activities, was mindful of his working-class origins and determined not to let success change him. He had therefore stayed on in his housing-executive home, modestly proportioned like all the others in Turf Lodge, terraced and totally anonymous in these parallel grim streets, though not so grim when the June sun was shining, as it was right this moment.

'A quare nice day,' Martha said, dabbing her lips delicately with a paper napkin and smiling contentedly. Like many women her age, born and bred in this area, she had never considered dieting and showed it in the weight she was carrying, though her face, which was as round as the moon, retained its childlike appeal. She was a decent if uninspiring woman and McCauley treated her well. He could have betrayed her, of course, with the whores he now had working his turf, but he had never done so. McCauley thought the men who

used his whores were filth and he didn't want to be one
of them.

'Ackay,' he said. 'Sure it's nice t'see the sun back again.
Makes ya feel like a new man.' He sat back in his chair, lit
a cigarette and exhaled a thin stream of smoke, smiling at his
two kids.

'Smokin's bad for you, Dad,' Janet said, brushing auburn
hair from brown eyes and grinning at him. She was thirteen
years old and rather pretty, even though, like her mother, too
heavy. 'Ya shouldn't do it at your age.'

'An' you shouldn't eat so many spuds,' he replied. 'That's why
yer puttin' on weight again.' It was the wrong thing to say,
he saw immediately, when a blush brightened her normally
pale cheeks. 'Though ya look really good with it, I'll admit,' he
added quickly. 'Sure yer the prettiest wee thing in this street
an' that's a damned fact.'

Janet smiled and seemed consoled. She wasn't all that
pretty, really. Like her mother, she had a certain sweetness
that made her attractive. McCauley loved her and felt very
protective towards her, regretting that she lived in these mean
streets and was forced to mix with kids too rough for her. In
fact, the few times he had thought of moving away from here,
he had been moved thus by his concern for her welfare. On
the other hand, this was his personal turf and he couldn't
bring himself to give it up. Like the rest of the Belfast Six,
he enjoyed his power too much to relinquish it and return to
a normal life. This personal need sometimes made him feel
selfish, but he just couldn't help himself.

'Yer blowin' that smoke right in my face,' his son, Liam, said
as McCauley exhaled again, 'and that could give *me* cancer,
Dad. You should think about that.'

Liam was grinning and McCauley grinned right back. Liam
was his pride and joy, his one and only son, to be cherished
and nurtured. A fourteen-year-old tyke, his face riddled with
acne, his head shaved near to the bone, he was constantly in
trouble at school, always beating up other boys, but always, in
his Dad's eyes, in the right and so always defended. He thought
his Dad was a hero and McCauley encouraged him to think so,
often telling him stories about the Troubles, which he could
scarcely remember. He'd only been a kid then, running wild in
the streets, but he'd thrown a few stones at the Brits when they
drove through in their armoured pigs. The Brits had come here

more than once, smashing the house up, bawling obscenities, and Liam, still only four foot tall, had gone at them with clenched fists. He was his Dad's son, after all, hating the Brits, fighting the Prods, and even now, with no Brits to throw stones at, he was always looking for action. He found it frequently at school, where he fought with his teachers, and in the streets where he ran with the teenage gangs, always the leader because he was McCauley's son and the other kids were in awe of him. McCauley liked that thought. His son was following in his footsteps. He just wished that Liam had something better to fight for, but those days were over, at least for the time being. Now the only cause was organized crime, but Liam didn't know that yet. He only knew that his Dad was still feared and he was proud of that fact.

'Yer sayin' you'll get cancer just by breathin' this smoke?' he asked mockingly.

'Aye, I am,' Liam replied. 'Ya can get cancer just by *breathin'* ciggie smoke an' that means yer endangerin' my health. It's a crime what yer doin'.'

'You read too many magazines, kid, an' they're all full of shite. You breathe worse from the exhausts of them fuckin' cars when yer walkin' to school. Which reminds me that it's time fer you to leave, so get out, the pair of ya.'

Liam rolled his eyes and Janet turned up her nose, but both of them picked up their schoolbags and reluctantly left the house. McCauley watched them go, passing by the front window, and he felt grateful that they no longer had to make their way past sneering, heavily armed British soldiers or brutal RUC officers, though they were back in the central streets of the city. The peace initiative had at least brought that benefit, but McCauley regretted the passing of the old ways, when he had felt like the hero his son seemed to think he still was. Now, though he couldn't resist the opportunities presented, couldn't give up the prestige and power that his criminal activities brought to him, he could not shake off a sense of unease at what he was doing.

Like Byrne, like Keegan – not like that bastard Hegarty – he still believed in the fight for Ireland's freedom and was still working towards it. True, he was now part of a growing criminal empire, but that was, to his mind, merely a way of staying engaged while waiting for the true fight to commence again. He had a lot of lads to look after – boys trained during

the Troubles and now grown men with no calling – and he
was doing it by keeping them busy with other activities that
would, in the long run, ensure that they were well prepared,
both financially and militarily, when the call came to return
to the real fight. The money and weapons being stockpiled
through his criminal activities would eventually be put to good
use. He soothed his troubled conscience with that thought and
felt better for it.

'So,' he said, inhaling on the last of his cigarette and stub-
bing it out in the ashtray beside his plate, 'I guess I'd better
be off, then.'

'Ackay, you do that, love,' Martha replied. 'No use wastin'
good time here. Yer always happiest when yer in the office
workin' an' that makes me feel easy.'

'Right,' McCauley said, pushing his chair back and walking
to the front door to get his jacket off the coat rack. 'An' I'm busy
enough now, I can tell you. We've never had it so good, love.'

'That's grand,' Martha said, standing up to clear the table
and start on the dishes. 'We do all right between us.'

They were, McCauley realized as he put on his jacket,
talking about two different things. McCauley ran a thriving plumbing business from premises near Divis Street and
Martha assumed that their good times came from this. True,
the business was thriving with no shortage of work in sight,
but what Martha didn't know was that the work came not
only from projects financed by the EEC – the restoration of
buildings destroyed during the Troubles – but, even more so,
from the various illegal rackets of the Belfast Six. Martha
knew that McCauley was a hard-line Republican who had
been a formidable IRA fighter, commanding his own active
service unit and serving his time in Long Kesh – she knew
and was proud. What she did *not* know was that her husband
was still training more ASUs in secret while simultaneously
helping to build up a criminal empire with his former IRA
friends. If she had known that many of the increasing number
of prostitutes in the city were under his personal control or
that the growing crime wave in the streets was partly his
doing, she would have been deeply shocked by the knowledge.
A religious woman, stout Republican and generally decent
soul, she believed in honesty, supported the fight for Ireland's
freedom, and often expressed her fears for the moral welfare of
her children in this increasingly violent city. That much of the

violence stemmed from McCauley's activities was something
she could not know.

'Right, love,' McCauley said, 'I'm off.' He kissed Martha on
the cheek, then left the small house, stepping out into the
warming sunlight of this fine June morning. Standing on the
pavement, he glanced left and right along the street, along
the rows of terraced houses, to check that his youthful dickers
were still on the watch. They were. Gathered in groups at
each end of the street, they looked like just another gang of
unemployed youths, bored and trying to pass the time with
idle banter and the endless smoking of cigarettes. They were,
however, McCauley's personal bodyguard, there to ensure that
no strangers entered the street without being seen and that no
one approached McCauley's house uninvited. Some of them
were former members of the IRA or its youth wing; others
were presently being trained in their spare time to become
members of future ASUs. The fight for freedom, as far as
McCauley was concerned, was still being engaged and would,
he hoped, explode back into the open in the near future.

Slipping into the blue Ford Escort parked outside his door,
he turned on the ignition and started off along the street,
watching the terraced houses slipping past on either side, the
housewives chatting on their doorsteps, a milkman doing his
rounds, and thought of how normal the area was compared to
what it had been. The normality, however, was purely on the
surface and during the daylight hours. When darkness came,
the pubs and social clubs would open to sell illegal booze and
cigarettes, fruit machines would rake in more money, drug
dealers would mix with prostitutes on dark street corners, and
'punishment' attacks against old enemies or those resistant
to the Belfast Six would break the silence with the sounds
of broken glass, women screaming, men bawling. McCauley
didn't like that part of it – his children lived here, after all
– but he kidded himself that it was necessary for the general
good of the community: that it was buying valuable time and
bringing in the cash needed to stockpile the weapons required
for the inevitable return to war with the Brits.

Alas, not all of them thought as he did. Turning out of
his own street, he passed the old hand-painted signs on the
gabled walls, proclaiming 'UP THE IRA!' and 'REMEMBER
1916', then headed for the Monagh Bypass. As he drove, his
good mood was dispelled by the recollection that yesterday

Ralph Meeks, a former light-heavyweight boxer and local hero, had been beaten to death with a baseball bat during a revenge attack on his club. According to the TV and newspaper reports, a gang of youths had burst into Meeks's club in the early hours of the evening, smashing up the premises, seriously hurting a lot of the customers, and leaving Meeks dead on the floor behind his bar. As usual, the shocked and terrified customers had refused to identify their assailants, but McCauley had no doubts about who was responsible. In fact, after learning of the incident from the TV, he had been on the phone all evening, either making calls to, or receiving calls from, the other members of the Belfast Six, all of whom agreed that the raid must have been led by that lunatic Jack Hegarty who was known to have a personal hatred for Meeks, who specialized in so-called 'punishment' beatings with baseball bats, and who was certainly violent enough to have clubbed the former boxer to death. It was no accident, therefore, that Hegarty was the only member of the Belfast Six not contactable that evening. For this reason, Neil Byrne had called for an urgent meeting of the Belfast Six, to take place in the upstairs room of O'Donovan's pub this afternoon. Now, thinking about what had happened, McCauley simmered with rage.

As he neared the roundabout that led on to the Monagh Bypass, he found himself tormented, as he often was these days, by the contradiction between what he was now doing and how he had started. Like the youngsters he was presently training to form new active service units, he had started as a fervent believer in the cause – his whole family was staunchly Republican – and joined the youth wing of the IRA like most of his mates. He had done everything asked of him – acting as a dicker, collecting revenue with threats, the odd bombing and assassination – and soon ended up commanding his own ASU. He had been caught, of course, and took his beatings from the RUC, did his stretch in Long Kesh, but he did it all believing that it was right, that he was fighting for a just cause. Then peace had been negotiated – a peace he didn't believe in – and, like many others who had lived their lives for the cause, he found himself at a loose end, feeling betrayed by Gerry Adams and not knowing what to do with the deadly skills he had learnt in the IRA.

Luckily, he was not alone. The city was filled with other frustrated hard men who wanted to keep hold of their weapons and put them to any use – men such as Jack Hegarty. It was also filled with men like Neil Byrne and Shaun Keenan, who believed that the peace was a sell-out and refused to give up the cause. Those men had gradually come together to form the six gangs that had gradually carved the city up between them. Eventually known as the Belfast Six, the gang leaders had continued to do what they had been doing during the Troubles but this time for very different reasons, some honourable, others sordid.

There had always been extortion and protection rackets and killing, but now it was done for personal gain, though some would say otherwise. McCauley liked to think he was different. He sided with Byrne and Keenan. They all believed that their drift towards organized crime could not be avoided; that they had to become more powerful through any means at their disposal in order to be prepared for the day when they could go back to war. When that day came, which it surely would, even if they had to force it, they would have the whole of Ireland stitched up and no one – not the Brits and not the Prods – would be able to touch them. This justified all the rest of it.

Unfortunately, there were those who were in it for their own gain and might have to be stopped. Those like Jack Hegarty, that heavy-breathing, insane bastard who clearly had no interest in the fight for Ireland's freedom, was merely using the umbrella of the Belfast Six as a cover for his own increasingly grandiose plans, and was now even threatening to turn against the other five gangs, if necessary with violence. Hegarty had always been trouble, a constant threat and embarrassment, and now, with the killing of Ralph Meeks, he had gone over the edge and would, if not stopped pretty quickly, go even farther.

McCauley had his principles and believed in some kind of order, but Hegarty lived by the rule of chaos and would listen to no one. A mad dog, he would have to be put down and relegated to history.

As he approached the roundabout, McCauley determined to impress this fact upon the others at the meeting planned for later that afternoon. He would do so whether or not Hegarty admitted to the killing of Ralph Meeks. That bastard had to be stopped.

In fact, it was McCauley who was stopped first. He had

entered the roundabout and was turning into Glen Road
when a battered white Transit van cut across on the inside
to reach the road first and forced him to pull out of the way,
back into the roundabout. In doing this, he crashed lightly
into the side of a red Honda Accord that was racing along
on his right. He felt the shuddering of his own vehicle, heard
the screeching of metal, and took the next available exit, into
the dual carriageway, heading towards the looming slopes of
the Black Mountain. He slowed down as the Honda bounced
off and swung around to brake a few metres ahead of him.

Cursing the Transit van as it continued along the Glen Road,
McCauley put his handbrake on and swung his legs out of the
car. As he was straightening up, he saw two men get out of the
front of the Honda and turn swiftly towards him. He realized
his mistake when he saw that both men had socks stretched
over their heads and faces, with slits cut out as eyeholes. He
was just taking this in, thinking *Hegarty! The bastard!*, when
the men spread their legs and raised their hands in the classic
firing stance, both aiming directly at him with hand guns.

'*No!*' McCauley bawled.

The shots ricocheted in his head as a hail of bullets hit him
and he was punched violently backwards, his body turning
numb. Then he fell spinning screaming into a bottomless well
of darkness, a black hole beyond time and space, where the
past and the present collided and from which there was no
return.

He was dead in an instant.

CHAPTER FIFTEEN

The meeting that afternoon was particularly tense because, contrary to everyone's expectations, Jack Hegarty turned up and Patrick McCauley, normally reliable, failed to materialize. A last-minute phone call made to McCauley's home by Shaun Keenan, using the phone in the upstairs room of O'Donovan's pub, elicited the information from McCauley's worried wife that he had left that morning as usual to go to his office. A second call made by Keegan to McCauley's offices near Divis Street revealed that McCauley had not turned up for work that day and no one knew where he was. Returning to the men gathered around the table, exhaling cigarette smoke and drinking Guinness or whisky, Keegan passed on the news and was met with a barrage of puzzled glances before the men all stared at one another, each man trying not to linger too long on Jack Hegarty's grim face. Only one man, the calm and fearless Neil Byrne, had the temerity to meet his gaze.

'You know anything about this?' he asked.

'Why the fuck should I know?' Hegarty responded. 'Sure I don't work for Pat.'

'Where the hell could he be?' Liam O'Shea asked.

'Probably pissed in some bar or in the bed of some whore,' Hegarty said. 'Probably just forgot, like.'

'McCauley's never missed a meeting in his life,' Neil Byrne reminded him. 'He left home and he never got to his office and I'd like to know why.'

'If even his missus doesn't know, sure you lot aren't goin' to know until he turns up again. Let's get on with the meetin'. I haven't got all fuckin' day and I can't wait for McCauley. Now what's this all about?'

Byrne stared steadily at Hegarty for what seemed like an

eternity, then said, 'Ralph Meeks was beaten to death with a
baseball bat last night in his own club. A whole gang broke
into the club and smashed it up with baseball bats, then one
of them went to work on Meeks, breaking practically every
bone in his body and beating his brains out.'

'I know that already,' Hegarty said. 'Sure I read the newspapers and watch the telly. You don't have to tell me.'

'Did you do it?' Byrne asked him.

'No,' Hegarty replied. 'Just because he happens to be on my
turf doesn't mean that I did it.'

'Then who did?'

'How the fuck would I know?'

'He *was* on your turf, Jack.'

'I've just acknowledged that,' Hegarty said. 'But that doesn't
mean I did it and it doesn't mean I know who did. Probably just
a bunch of fuckin' tearaways. I'll find out, don't you worry.'

'I'm surprised,' Shaun Keenan said in his quietly spoken
English way, 'that a man who keeps such tight control of his
turf would let such a thing happen in the first place.'

'Don't shite me, Keenan.' Hegarty's cheeks were turning red.
'This city's full of tearaways who get high on crack or Ecstasy
and do these things before we can stop 'em. Things like that
go down on your turf as well an' ya know it damned well.'

'What goes down on my turf,' Keenan replied levelly, 'is
that some kids get high or crack or Ecstasy and break into
someone's house for some gelt – they don't charge en masse
into a social club and beat someone to death with a baseball
bat. What happened last night was clearly organized – and if
you don't already know who did it, that means something's
amiss.'

'There's nothin' amiss,' Hegarty insisted. 'I didn't do it, but
I'll find out who did and I'll make sure they pay for it.'

'When you find out who did it,' Byrne said, his gaze steady,
'we'll want to know who it was and exactly *why* he did it.'

'That bastard Meeks had lots of enemies,' Hegarty told him,
'and most had good reason to want him dead.'

'We'll want to know the reason in this particular instance.
We'll want that information straight from the horse's mouth
and certainly before you administer punishment.'

'It's my turf,' Hegarty said.

'What does that mean?' Michael Gallagher asked.

'It means I deal with my problems my own way and I don't

have to report to you bastards. When the culprit's been found he'll be punished and I'll inform you accordingly.'

'You mean, you won't tell us who the culprit is?'

'That's right, Byrne. Sure you heard me right.'

'So why won't you tell us?'

'It's not your concern.'

'It *is* our concern, Hegarty. The killing of Meeks will cause disturbance in the community and bring the law in. The killing will put us in the spotlight and that *makes* it our concern.'

'Fuck the community and fuck the law. The community are shit-scared of us and they're gonna remain that way. The law won't find out a damned thing, so you've no need to worry there.'

'I'd still like to know why you intend keeping the culprit's identity secret. What's the harm in informing us?'

'It's a matter of principle,' Hegarty said. 'I won't answer to anyone. I run my turf my own way and I won't take fuckin' orders from you or anyone else around this table. What goes on on my turf is my business and I'll make sure it stays that way.'

'What goes on on your turf is *our* business,' Byrne said, clearly trying to contain his anger, 'and if you don't want to tell us who killed Meeks, you must have a good reason.'

'What reason?'

'Because you're the one who killed him,' Byrne said.

The silence was almost palpable as Hegarty turned beetroot red and quivered where he sat, his hands opening and closing on the table on each side of his whisky glass. He glared at each of the men in turn, trying to drill them into submission with the intensity of his look, and only Byrne managed to hold his gaze, not flinching at all.

'So what if I did?' Hegarty said finally. 'The bastard had it comin' to him. When I went to collect my dues, the fucker went at *me* with a baseball bat, so he had to be punished.'

'Punishment's one thing,' Byrne said. 'Killing's another. So's smashing up a local social club with everyone in it. There must have been a hundred people in that club and all of them witnesses. From what I hear, you bastards didn't even bother to cover your faces. Is that what you call sense?'

'They'll all keep their mouths shut,' Hegarty said. 'Sure they know what's good for 'em.'

'They don't talk when we kill our own,' Byrne said icily, 'but

now you're threatenin' *their* lives. If they think they can't go
out at night in safety, they'll talk soon enough – they'll choose
the law over us. We told you that before, you dumb bastard,
but you completely ignored us.'

Hegarty nearly jumped out of his chair, but he managed to
control himself by clenching his ham fists and glaring at each
of them in turn. Then he turned back to Byrne. 'Just watch
yer fuckin' mouth, Byrne. No one talks to *me* that way.'

'I'm talkin' as I feel,' Byrne responded, 'and what I feel is
contempt. Isn't it true that the reason Meeks wouldn't pay is
that you were demanding a bigger cut than usual?'

'I demand what I please,' Hegarty told him, 'and they either
pay up or pay the price.'

'The six of us agreed that we'd all demand the same percentages and co-operate in every other way. You broke that
agreement with regards to your demands for payment and
you're breaking it in other ways. You're punishing people
just for fun. You're asking for money they can't afford. You've
already screwed some people for so much that they've gone out
of business. You've increased the sale of drugs in your streets,
instead of decreasing it as promised, and now we're having
problems with the Yanks. Finally, you're now running a reign
of terror in your turf and turning your own people against you.
In doing that, you're also turning them against us and drawing
the attention of the RUC to what's going on up here. In short,
you're endangering us all and you've got to be stopped.'

'Who's goin' to stop me?'

'We are,' Byrne said.

'An' how the fuck will you do that?'

'Is that a sign that you won't do as you're told unless we
force the issue?'

'I don't take orders from weak bastards like you and I run
my own show as I want. You yella bellies won't stop me.'

'That's grounds for divorce.'

'We were never married, Byrne.'

'Then we're formally disassociating ourselves from you as
from this moment on.'

'Good,' Hegarty said. 'I'm fuckin' glad. I've been strainin'
at the bit for too long and now at last I can do what I
fuckin' want.'

'He wants it all,' Michael Gallagher said, addressing the
other three. 'We've already had to reprimand him more than

once for doin' things on our turfs an' from what I've been told
he's still doin' it. He's also made it clear that he doesn't give
a shit about the Yanks or our friends in the EEC an' that
he thinks he can do better without 'em. So fuck 'im, I say.
He's already actin' against us all an' that means he wants
all of it.'

'Look at *me* when you say that, you wee shite,' Hegarty
snarled. 'Sure I'm sittin' right here in front of ya. I'm not a
dog on a leash.'

Gallagher surprised him by turning his pink baby face
towards him and staring directly at him, his big blue mur-
derer's eyes unblinking. 'Go fuck yerself,' he said loud and
clear. 'Yer off my list, Hegarty.'

'I'll fuck your mother instead,' Hegarty retorted, pushing
his chair back and standing upright. 'I'm told she can't get
enough of it.'

Gallagher rose out of his chair as if propelled by a spring, his
hands already outstretched to grab Hegarty and throttle him,
but Liam O'Shea grabbed him by the shoulder and pulled him
back down. Gallagher quivered, his baby face red, his big eyes
bright with rage, his fists clenched on the table, but he managed to keep control of himself and remained where he was.

'You foul-mouthed cunt,' he said.

'That's enough,' Byrne told him. He looked up at Hegarty
and said, 'That's the end of it, Jack. You're on your own now.
We've already reason to believe that you've been moving
against us in various small ways, but if you try anything
bigger, anything serious, we'll take remedial action. Now get
out and don't come back.'

'If I come back, it'll be with good reason,' Hegarty said, then
he turned and stomped out.

The other four men said nothing for quite some time. They
were listening to Hegarty's footsteps thundering down the
stairs and considering just what his departure might mean
to them. The silence was only broken when his footsteps
faded away.

'Well, that's that,' Byrne said.

'Fuckin' good riddance,' Liam O'Shea said. 'Sure that big
bastard's mad.'

'An' gettin' worse every day,' Michael Gallagher added. 'He's
causin' fuckin' mayhem in the streets and not all of those
streets are his own. Sure he's all over the place.'

'Right,' O'Shea said. 'More an' more of my boyos are bein'
beaten up when they're out on their daily business – beaten
up by other kids their own age but not, so they report, from
where they live. That means they come from someone else's
turf and it's not one of ours.'

'Hegarty's,' Gallagher said.

'Right.' O'Shea nodded.

'And he's certainly getting worse,' Shaun Keenan said.
'From what I gather, he recently fucked his secretary, Mary
Dogherty, let her unfortunate husband know he'd done it and
was going to do it again, and threatened to break his legs if he
complained. According to my source, he's still fucking Mary
on his desk on a regular basis and she's not exactly complying
because she wants to. That bastard is now right off the wall
and that means we're going to have serious trouble.'

'You think he'll go directly against us?' Byrne asked.

'Yes,' Keenan replied. 'I agree with Mike on this. Liam's
lads aren't the only ones to be beaten up by other gangs
and those gangs certainly aren't any of ours – they've got
to be Hegarty's. As for our healthy relationship with our
Irish-American friends across the water, not to mention the
Europeans, he's already disrupting that and has made it clear
that he won't be cowed by them and will, if necessary, turn
directly against them. My assessment, therefore, is that he's
now going to turn against us and, as Mike here has suggested,
try to take over the whole organization.'

Byrne sat back in his chair and rocked lightly to and fro
whilst drumming his fingers rhythmically on the table. He
was still doing this, obviously deep in thought, when they
all heard footsteps coming up the stairs. Expecting to see
the missing Patrick McCauley, they glanced at the door,
but instead of McCauley another man, Keenan's trusted lieutenant Gerry Lenihan, rushed in. Mustachioed and long-
haired, he was dressed in blue denims, a black leather jacket
and red tee-shirt. Though slim and obviously fit, he was out
of breath and his pock-marked, angular face was flushed
with excitement. He stopped in front of Keenan, took a deep
breath, let it out in a sigh, then said, 'Hi, boss. Sure I know
I'm not supposed to be here, but I didn't think this could
wait, like.'

'What is it?' Keenan asked.

'I've just had a call from our tout in the Woodbourne RUC

Station, telling me that Patrick McCauley was shot and killed this morning on his way to work.'

'*What?*' Shocked, Keenan glanced at the impassive Byrne, then turned back to Lenihan. 'McCauley's dead?'

'Yes, boss.'

'Who shot him?' Byrne asked. 'The RUC?'

'No,' Lenihan said. 'The body was whisked away by the RUC and they're keeping tight on the details. But according to eye-witnesses, it seemed like a professional, paramilitary assassination – like one of our own.'

'What does that mean?' Keenan asked.

'McCauley was involved in what seemed like a routine accident as he was taking the Monagh Bypass roundabout – except it wasn't an accident. Apparently a white Transit van cut across the front of him and forced him to swerve back into the roundabout and crash into a passing Honda Accord. A broadside collision, just a scrape, like, not serious at all. Anyway, McCauley and the driver of the Honda both braked to a halt in the dual carriageway – obviously McCauley intended exchanging details with the other driver – but then two men got out of the Honda, both with socks stretched over their heads, just like paramilitaries, and shot him at close range with handguns. The two men then got back into the Honda and raced away from the scene.'

The ensuing shocked silence was only broken when Byrne, speaking quietly and authoritatively, asked, 'Have the RUC found anything out yet?'

'Yeah,' Lenihan replied. 'They found the white Transit van and the red Honda abandoned at two separate locations in deserted roads just outside the city. Both vehicles had already been reported as stolen and the owners, one Catholic, one Prod, were at work at the time of the incident.'

'The police are sure they'd nothing to do with it?' Byrne asked.

'They're pretty certain,' Lenihan said.

The men around the table just stared at one another until Keenan asked: 'Anything else?'

'No, boss,' Lenihan said.

'Okay, you can go now. Thanks – and keep in touch with our friend at Woodbourne.'

'I will, boss. I'll be seein' ya.'

Just as they had done with Hegarty, the men around the

table did not speak until Lenihan's footsteps had faded out below. Again, the first man to speak was the thoughtful Neil Byrne. 'It had to be Hegarty,' he said. 'He's already made his first move.'

'I agree,' Keenan said.

'So what do we do now?'

'Getting him personally won't be easy,' Liam O'Shea said. 'That bastard's too well protected.'

'We *have* to get him,' Keenan said. 'We have to do that before he picks off more of us – and that's what he'll try doing. The problem will be getting our lads near him without them being recognized. Here in the Falls we live on top of each other and that makes it difficult.'

Byrne pursed his lips thoughtfully, then raised his steady gaze to Michael Gallagher. 'What about you, Mike? You're out in Andersonstown. Your boyos aren't well known here in the Falls and that gives you the upper hand. We won't force you – it's purely voluntary – but I think you're our best hope. If your boyos can put that mad dog down, we'd all benefit from it.'

'My pleasure,' Callaghan said. 'You can start carvin' his tombstone.'

'We will,' Byrne replied.

CHAPTER SIXTEEN

It was a lie. Frank Cooney's daughter had not died of a brain tumour as he had told Teresa Kiely; in fact, she had been shot by accident in an aborted IRA bank robbery in Belfast just before the peace initiative had commenced. Cooney was thinking of this, with deep and abiding pain, as he walked away from his car in the afternoon sunshine and began the circular walk to the Giants' Causeway in North Antrim, heading for a meeting that he had not anticipated and was still surprised at.

As he made his way along the cliff path, high above the eerie lunar landscape of the Giants' Causeway with its bizarre rock formations and amphitheatres of stone columns, looking out at the calm but always ominous dark sea, he wondered why he had told Teresa Kiely that lie and realized that it was because she was a Catholic and he, a Protestant victim of Catholic violence, hadn't wanted to make her feel bad.

As a journalist for a Unionist newspaper, Cooney had been forced to tread a fine line between his detestation of Irish violence, both Catholic and Protestant, and his sympathies for the Irish cause. Though Protestant, he had been brought up by liberal parents in Donegall Avenue, where Protestants and Catholics had then lived side by side. His mother in particular, a volatile, principled woman, had been adamant that he must not hate the Catholics in general and had forced him to learn about Irish history, which was not taught in Protestant schools, where British history prevailed. Because of this, Cooney had learned to weigh both sides of the coin and, while still detesting the sectarian violence he grew up with, had accepted that the Catholics had a just cause that must sooner or later be recognized and properly dealt with.

This, however, was not an easy belief to live with, particularly for a Protestant working for a Unionist newspaper. Indeed, it became even more difficult to live with as the years went by and Cooney, reporting constantly on the Troubles, saw how both sides were conducting themselves in the bloody intercine struggle. Judging by what Cooney had witnessed, honourable men had initiated the war against the British. But the rules and aims had changed gradually and too many men on both sides had started using their mutual hatreds as a cover for all kinds of self-interested crime, including the terrorizing of their own communities for the profits to be had from protection rackets and other forms of extortion. Cooney's cynicism about the Troubles had grown accordingly over the years and had only been increased when his daughter, his beloved Suzanne, only twenty-one years old but standing in the wrong place at the wrong time, was riddled with bullets as some IRA thugs panicked and shot their way out of the bank they had failed to rob. That incident had occurred mere months before the peace initiative commenced and Cooney, racked by grief and abiding hatred for the hard men, had to force himself not to hate all Catholics for what had occurred. Nevertheless, when eventually he had managed to come to terms with his grief, his cynicism about the hard men on both sides was greater than ever.

Making his way along the winding, windblown cliff path, glancing down at the stepping stones formed by a mass of basalt columns packed tightly together and lined with bizarre rock formations known as the Honeycomb, the Wishing Well and the Giant's Granny, he realized also that he was worried about Teresa Kiely because he hadn't seen her for some time, whether in the Europa Hotel or in any other. Recalling that Jack Hegarty had been watching her, he was worried even more and bemused by the depth of his concern. About that, however, he had told Teresa the truth: she was the same age as Suzanne would have been this year and, with her long black hair, green eyes and delicate features, looked the spitting image of Suzanne. Cooney's interest, therefore, was not sexual but purely paternal, and it grieved him that the lovely Teresa Kiely made her living in bed. More so because, he believed, she was not a commonplace whore but one who seemed troubled by some secret grief and was morally above what she was doing. Cooney, therefore, apart from feeling paternal towards her, was intrigued by her mysterious nature and wanted to know more about her. Now he silently prayed that she was all right and not in Jack Hegarty's brutish hands.

He kept following the narrow, grassy path, breathing heavily, realizing that he was out of shape, and staring beyond the Grand Causeway to the tall, bizarrely shaped rock formations known as the Chimney Tops soaring high at the far side of the Amphitheatre. As he turned another bend in the path, heading for the first viewing point, Weir's Snout, he saw his old friend, SAS Sergeant Mike Burton, wearing a windcheater jacket and faded blue denims, standing as still as a rock and gazing out to sea. As Cooney approached him, Burton turned his head towards him, his senses still finely attuned to unexpected movement. Cooney saw that his face was still lean and oddly handsome, almost austere, and that his grey gaze, though as disconcertingly steady as always, was veiled to hide the suffering of his troubled soul. That look reminded Cooney of Teresa Kiely, whose nature was also troubled, but in Burton's case he knew exactly what had caused it: the accidental shooting of that child in Belfast many years ago.

Cooney stopped in front of Burton and said, 'Long time, no see, old friend.'

Burton grinned in his slight, pained manner as the two men shook hands. 'Good to see you,' he said.

'I'm *surprised* to see you,' Cooney replied. 'I was surprised when you called me. I didn't know you'd come back.'

'I'm not supposed to be here,' Burton said. 'That's why we're meeting here.'

Cooney nodded, glanced out at the murmuring, heaving sea, then turned back to Burton. 'Are you still with the Regiment?' he asked.

'Yes,' Burton said.

'Then what the hell are you doing back here? The Troubles are over.'

'The peace has brought a new kind of problem and I think you know what it is.'

'Let me guess. Organized crime being run by the former paramilitaries.'

'That's it,' Burton said. He glanced left and right, along the cliff face, then said, 'You fancy going for a walk?'

'I normally hate fresh air,' Cooney replied, shivering from

the chill wind blowing in from the choppy grey sea. Then he shrugged. 'But why not?'

They walked together along the edge of the cliff, the sea on one side of them, sheep grazing in the fields to their right, the grass smooth and bright green. Glancing at Burton's angular, ascetic profile and windblown brown hair, Cooney thought of all the things the SAS man had done and wondered how he had managed them. Burton was a decent man, a man of strong principles, but like everyone involved directly in the Troubles, he'd had to stoop to some dirty tricks. Killed men as well. A great many, by all accounts. Cooney knew that he didn't take his work lightly and respected him for it.

'How's your family?' Cooney asked.

'They're fine,' Burton replied without elaboration. He had always been a man of few words and Cooney was used to it.

'I'm glad,' Cooney said. 'Sure if a man has a good home to return to, he can take all the rest of it.'

'Right,' Burton said. 'And you? I heard about . . .'

'Yes,' Cooney interjected, not wanting to discuss his dead daughter, 'I'm sure you did. But it's all right. I'm okay. It's all well in the past now.'

Burton nodded and was silent for some time, as if deep in thought. 'I don't suppose you thought you'd see me again,' he said finally.

'I certainly didn't,' Cooney replied. 'Sure I thought you'd be dismissed from the Regiment after that . . .'

Now it was his turn to tail off, reluctant as he was to mention Burton's accidental killing of that child all those years ago.

'No,' Burton said, letting him off the hook. 'They kept me on in the end. I had psychiatric treatment, as you'd expect, but here I am, still serving.'

'Hard to believe it, Mike. Sure it all seems so long ago, doesn't it? It was all very different then.'

'Not much different now, Frank. You still live here and those bastards are still around. If they discovered that you'd helped me out then, they'd still want a piece of you.'

'I don't doubt it,' Cooney said, recalling how, back in 1987, he had been introduced to Burton by an officer with the British Army's 14th Intelligence Company – an intelligence unit that had replaced the discredited Military Reconnaissance Force (MRF). From his first meeting with Burton, he had been impressed by his decency, integrity and lack of prejudice towards the Irish, but later, working with him, he had been even more impressed by his ability to do what he had to do in an impartial, though deadly efficient manner. Even now, walking beside him along the windblown path, high above the murmuring sea, he felt the inner strength of the man and remained impressed. 'Anyway, what are you doing back here? And why this meeting with me?'

'You remember what we were doing back in 1987?'

'Ackay,' Cooney replied. 'I doubt that I'll ever forget it. Some things you just don't forget.'

'I need something the same from you now.'

'I should have known,' Cooney said.

In 1987, the UDA, composed of hard-line Loyalist para-militaries and responsible for the assassination of many Catholic civilians, had already become heavily involved in protection rackets and other forms of gangsterism; and the 14th Intelligence Company, using covert SAS operatives, was trying to put them out of business. In order to do this, they planned to let one of the SAS's best men, Burton, loose in the community, working undercover, to wreak what havoc he could, but they also needed a civilian with strong contacts in the streets and inside knowledge of what the UDA was planning at any given time. Cooney was then reporting the Troubles in detail, albeit from a Unionist point of view, and had the required contacts in the form of 'friendly' Prods and touts, or Catholic turncoat informers. Like many a Protestant, though he had no truck with the IRA, he certainly did not approve of the gangsterism of the UDA and was therefore willing to help. So it was that, for the next eighteen months, he was Burton's covert source of information for what was going on in the streets controlled by the Loyalist hard men. Throughout that whole eighteen-month period, he had lived with the knowledge that if found out he would be tortured for information and then killed, but his admiration and respect for Burton kept him at it and they soon became firm friends. Cooney was therefore saddened when he heard of Burton's accidental killing of the Catholic child and his subsequent transfer back to Hereford. They had not communicated since – at least not until the recent phone call – but Cooney's high opinion of Burton had never changed and he still thought him a friend.

'I should have known,' Cooney repeated, 'but I thought it might be something else.'

'Why?'

'Because the political peace is ongoing and most of the Brits are out of the province. I suppose that's why, though surprised by your call, I thought it might be just a social call. It never entered my head that the British government would send in the SAS to sort out what's essentially a civil problem. I find that hard to believe.'

'I repeat,' Burton said, 'I'm not supposed to be here. I'm here under an alias, with false identification. Officially, I don't even exist.'

Cooney smiled. 'The British government can't be seen to be involved.'

'That's right,' Burton said.

'And the SAS?'

'The same,' Burton said. 'As far as the Regiment is concerned, I no longer exist. That goes for my two friends.'

Cooney glanced at him. 'Sure that's some shit to eat.'

'We don't always get the menu we want. I need your help. Will you help me?'

Cooney didn't answer immediately. He was thinking of how, the last time he'd helped Burton, he had done so in the knowledge that he was risking not only his own life but the lives of his beloved wife and daughter. Throughout that whole time, as he now recalled vividly, he had suffered tremendous guilt and constantly wondered if he was doing right or wrong. How ironic it had been, therefore – how dreadfully ironic – that his daughter was not killed because of his activities but because of a random accident of time and place. He had thought about this many times and questioned what it might mean. He had not found an answer.

'You better tell me what it is,' he said to Burton. 'I'm not too sure of this. I don't know that I want to be involved or even if I can help. So what is it, Mike?'

'Let's turn back,' Burton said.

They started walking back the way they had come, towards the outthrusting Weir's Snout. The waves were breaking over the rocks far below and exploding into great clouds of spray that made the light bend and shimmer. Though the sun was blazing over the cliff top, the strong wind was chilling.

'You've heard of the Belfast Six?' Burton asked.

'My God, yes,' Cooney replied. 'Heaven help us, don't tell
me it's *them!*'

'Yes,' Burton said. 'You know what they've been up to.
They've turned Belfast into Al Capone's Chicago and that's
only the start of it.'

'That's right, Mike – I know. Sure they also control organized
crime in Dublin and Cork and they seem to be getting stronger
every day. They're a serious threat – no doubt about it – but I
still can't believe that the British government—'

'It goes farther than that,' Burton interjected. 'According
to MI5 and the CIA, they're using Irish-American gangs to
run rackets in the United States. They're also believed to be
working with the Mafia in Italy and Sicily. Last but not least,
they're liaising with criminal gangs all over Europe. So this
is no longer politics and certainly it's no longer localized. It's
the view of the British government, supported by Scotland
Yard and Interpol, that the IRA is on its way to becoming the
biggest criminal organization in the world. That's why it has
to be stopped – and the neutralization of the Belfast Six is the
first step towards that.'

Shocked, Cooney froze where he stood and then turned to
stare directly at Burton. 'Holy Jesus!' he exclaimed. 'One of
those bastards, Patrick McCauley, has already been assassinated – yesterday morning. Did you . . . ?'

Burton had also stopped walking and now he smiled slightly
– the only way Cooney had ever seen him smile – and said, 'I
can't confirm or deny that, Frank. What have *you* heard?' He
started walking again.

Following him, catching up with him and again walking
beside him, Cooney said, 'A paramilitary-style killing. Two
men wearing socks over their heads and using handguns.
They used stolen cars, so they can't be traced. Apart from
that, the RUC aren't talking.'

'Not surprising,' Burton said. 'Any word from the streets?'

'About what?'

'About the reaction of the rest of the Belfast Six?'

'Jesus, Burton, it *was* you and your pals, wasn't it?'

'Of course not,' Burton said. 'So was there any reaction?'

Still shocked, hardly believing what he was thinking, Cooney
said, 'Yes. The word's out that of the remaining five gang
leaders, four of them think it was Jack Hegarty. There's talk
of a range war.'

'They think Hegarty's turned against them?'

'Yes.'

'Excellent,' Burton said. 'When gangsters take to fighting amongst themselves, their defences start cracking.'

'Jesus, Burton, it *was* you!'

'I didn't say that, Frank. It's best that you never hear me saying that. The question remains: will you help me?'

They had reached Aird Snout and could hear the sea smashing over the rocks along the Giants' Causeway. Burton kept walking and Cooney fell in beside him, thinking of how what he was contemplating could endanger his wife. It wasn't only himself involved. Those bastards didn't think that way. If they found him out and they couldn't get at him, they would go for her instead. Then he thought of Suzanne, of the bastards who had killed her, and of the whore, Teresa Kiely, who looked so much like Suzanne and was possibly in danger from Jack Hegarty, the worst of a rotten bunch. He weighed the good against the bad, right from wrong, and came to his decision.

'What do you need?' he asked.

They were heading back to Weir's Snout, once more overlooking the Giants' Causeway. Far below, looking like ants, a lot of tourists were milling about on the stepping stones and bizarre lava-rock formations, reading guide books and taking photographs. The wind was rising and the sea was turning rough, with waves breaking in increasingly large clouds of silvery spray that fell back over the stones of the Causeway and drenched some of the tourists.

'I need someone inside,' Burton said. 'Someone close to at least one of the remaining five. That number will soon be reduced again, but after that I'll need someone.'

'Reduced by how many?' Cooney asked. 'And how soon will that be?'

'A matter of days,' Burton replied. 'There'll be four left after that. After that, I'll need a set of eyes and ears. Do you think you can be that?'

'Not me,' Cooney said. 'Sure I can't get near that crew. During the Troubles I'd get in as a reporter, but that lot wouldn't welcome me. It would have to be someone else – someone close – and I can't think of anyone.'

'Will you keep thinking about it?' Burton asked.

'Yes,' Cooney said. 'But I don't hold out much hope.'

'It's important,' Burton said. '*Very* important. So please try every avenue.'

'I will,' Cooney said.

When they reached the fenced-in viewing bay of Weir's Snout, Burton stopped walking and turned away to look out to sea. When Cooney stopped beside him, Burton handed him a piece of paper with a name and telephone number scribbled on it. The telephone number had an Antrim prefix and the name wasn't Burton's.

'We'd better say goodbye here,' he said. 'If you come up with anyone in the next five days – and please do – contact me at this number. My name, as you can see, is Stanley Drummond and that's the name you should use. Memorize the name and telephone number and then destroy the note. Thanks, Frank. I'll be seeing you.'

'How are you getting back?' Cooney asked him.

'Never mind,' Burton said.

Cooney nodded and walked away, heading back to his car. Just before the grassy path curved out of sight, he turned around and glanced back. Burton was still standing there, at the far edge of Weir's Snout, not moving, just looking out to sea, his tawny hair windblown, the bizarre rock formations of the Chimney Tops soaring far beyond him. He looked very lonely out there but he didn't seem lonesome. He was one of the rocks.

That thought made Cooney smile.

CHAPTER SEVENTEEN

'McCauley's death did the trick,' Burton told Rob and Slim in the kitchen of the farmhouse in Antrim a few days after his meeting with Cooney. 'The other four think Hegarty was responsible for the killing and there's talk in the streets about a range war.'

'Who told you that?' Slim asked. He had tilted his wooden chair back and stretched out in a languid pose, as cool and as handsome as a matinée idol about to be photographed. The morning sunlight, beaming in through the window, had turned his thick blond hair golden.

'A friend,' Burton replied.

'Right,' Slim said with a grin, knowing to ask no more questions. 'So assuming that it's true – that there might be a range war – those bastards will be concentrating on each other instead of suspecting outsiders. That's a definite advantage to us, but it might not be enough.'

'There speaks the eternal optimist,' Rob said. 'Always looks on the bright side.'

'He's realistic,' Burton said. 'The death of McCauley has divided the group – it's now four against one – but they might still need another push.'

'We take out someone else and do it quickly,' Rob said, anticipating his boss, 'to make them think that Hegarty's really gone on a rampage.'

'Exactly. You've got it.' Burton nodded in Rob's direction. 'We've got to make another hit and we've got to do it now, before they tighten up their security and make things more difficult. And since four of them are firmly ensconced in the Falls, which is already like an armed fortress, I suggest that we go for the isolated man.'

'Michael Gallagher,' Slim said.

'Yes. He lives slightly out – in Andersonstown. That makes him the first choice. Not necessarily easy, but still the easiest.'

'Maybe easier than you think,' Slim replied.

'I'm glad you think so,' Burton said. 'Since you're the one who's had him under surveillance, I assume you say that with confidence.'

Slim grinned. 'Yeah.' Looking enthusiastic, he let his chair drop forward, propped his elbows up on the table and spread his hands in the air as if delivering a sermon. 'I could never get into the street where he lives because both ends are guarded by gangs of dickers, all trying to look like your typical Belfast unemployed youth, just passing the time of day. But those kids had eyes and ears. They were watching all the time. So all I could do was follow Gallagher back from his office in the Falls – he has his own betting shop – and then watch him turning into his street. Because of the dickers, I then had to keep driving and so I couldn't even check out Gallagher's house. He's not listed in the phone book – only his bookie shop is – so I don't even know the number of his house and can't say which one it is. That leaves the street out of it.'

'A fabulous start to the day,' Rob retorted, grinning crookedly, wickedly. 'Keep the good news flowing, pal.'

Slim just grinned again and then turned back to Burton. 'Gallagher's shuffled to and from work – in fact, everywhere – in a car driven by one of his dickers, with another dicker sitting in the back. Obviously, they're both armed. They stand guard outside his betting shop, checking everyone who goes in and out, and I assume that when he's driven back into his street, they also stand guard outside his house.'

'So hitting him in his car could lead to a fire fight,' Burton said.

'That's right,' Slim replied. 'And we could be the losers.'

'Just tell us what you're planning,' Rob said. 'I can't stand the suspense.'

'We can't hit him in his car and we can't hit him in the Falls,' Slim said calmly. 'Twice a week, however, always in the evening and always on the same days, he gets driven to a fancy house on the Newtownbreda Road and remains there all evening, usually until the early hours of the morning. As usual, the dickers always stand guard outside, but the house is backed by the Belvoir Golf Course and those dumb bastards haven't given that fact a thought. So, one night last week, I crossed the golf course under cover of darkness, clambered over the fence, and got into the rear garden of the house with no trouble at all. I found a low outbuilding, annexed to the house, with its roof sloping up to just below the windows of the upstairs rooms. I clambered up onto the roof and found myself kneeling just below the window of what was obviously a bedroom. I heard low moans and groans. Peering in, I saw Gallagher, stark naked, a right tub of lard, stretched out on the spine of another man and going hard at it.'

'Jesus Christ!' Rob exclaimed softly, screwing his face up in disgust. 'My stomach churns at the thought of it.'

'According to our intelligence,' Burton said, more calmly, 'Gallagher is not, and never has been, married. This would explain why.'

'Correct,' Slim said. 'Anyway, I couldn't place a bug on the window with them on that bed, so I just slipped away. What I know for a fact, though, is that Gallagher is going to that house twice a week to play with his boyfriend and there's no one guarding the back of the house.'

'You think you can hit him from there?' Burton asked.

Feeling vaguely troubled, he realized that in the back of his mind he was still thinking of his own assassination of Patrick McCauley. The dead Irishman, though a villain, had been married with two children and Burton, with two children of his own, could well imagine the grief he had caused. Such thoughts came to him often these days, disturbing him greatly, and he constantly feared that if they came at the wrong time, they could damage not only himself but those working with him. He had never had such thoughts before the killing of that child and now that he was back in Belfast they were troubling him even more. Every day he was in the city, he passed the street where that child had lived and he never did so without a tremor passing through him. As a man who took his pride from being cool under pressure, from being the Compleat Soldier, he found those tremors to be almost unbearable and far too distracting. For this reason in particular, he wanted to finish this job as soon as possible and get the hell out of here. Yet he also wanted to do the job thoroughly to make amends for his sins. In cleansing Belfast of its filth, he might set himself free.

'Are you listening?' Slim asked him.

'What?' Burton responded.

'I just said, yes, I think I can hit him from there – and you didn't respond.'

'Sorry. Go on.'

Slim nodded. 'He visits the house the same two evenings every week, so I know when he'll be there. I simply clamber back up onto the roof, wait until Gallagher and his boyfriend are sweatily engaged, then smash the window and pop him with a silenced handgun.'

'What about the dickers out front?'

'They always stand by the car, out on the pavement, well away from the house, so there's a good chance that they won't even hear the sound of the breaking window. As I said, I'll use a silencer for the actual shooting. Gallagher will be dead before he even knows what's hit him. Even if the dickers hear the sound of breaking glass, I can be off that roof and heading back across the golf course before they get around to the back of the house to take a shot at me.'

'Do you know who Gallagher's boyfriend is?'

'No.'

'What if there's someone else in the house?'

'Gallagher always goes in alone and I doubt that he'd fuck his boyfriend with someone else present. If his boyfriend doesn't live alone, he's almost certain to make sure he's alone when Gallagher calls. I don't think it's a problem.'

At least Gallagher's not married, Burton thought. *No wife or kids to worry about. And if they fuck in that bed, then the boyfriend probably has no family either. That's something, at least.* Yet he was shocked to find himself thinking this, knowing that he shouldn't even be considering it. That child who died all those years ago must be turning him soft. *I better get a grip on myself*, he thought. *This won't help me at all.*

'When does Gallagher make his next visit?' he asked.

'Tomorrow night,' Slim said.

'Then do it tomorrow night.'

Slim leaned back in his chair again, grinning from ear to ear, pleased with Burton's decision. 'Good,' he said. 'Perfect.'

'Don't use the Browning High Power,' Burton said. 'It's been associated with the SAS for too long. Use a SIG-Sauer P228 instead. It's still not widely associated with us, though it's known to be in use by the IRA. Reportedly, they smuggle them in from Switzerland, so let's use what they use.'

'So the RUC blames the IRA while the remaining three members of the Belfast Six blame Hegarty again.'

'Fuckin' beautiful,' Rob said.

'What about the getaway?' Burton asked, trying to pull himself together and concentrate on the hit.

'I'll park the car a long way down the Newtownbreda Road and make my way back there by foot.'

'No,' Burton said. 'That's not good enough. You might not make it back to the car on time and, if they happen to find the car, they can trace it to you.'

Slim sighed. 'Okay. I'll use a stolen car and park it as near to the golf course as possible. I'll abandon it completely. When I make the hit, I'll make my escape back across the golf course under cover of darkness, until I reach the River Lagan. I'll dump the handgun in the river, then make my way to the old towpath leading to Annadale Avenue. I can easily make my way back from there to the university area, where I can pick up a taxi.'

'No taxis,' Burton said. 'You'll be anonymous on the pavements and that's your protection. My suggestion is that you use your own car to get from Antrim to the university area. Park it there, then steal and hot-wire another car. Use that car for the drive to Newtownbreda, then abandon it exactly as you've planned. Make the hit, take the escape route you've described, but then, when you're back in the university area, instead of picking up a taxi, use your own car to drive home in. That way you're just another face in the crowd and there's no taxi driver to see you up close and maybe recall you.'

'Right,' Slim said. 'I've got it.'

'We can't help you,' Burton said. 'You'll have to drive there and back by yourself. If you go down, that's your problem.'

'Understood,' Slim said.

'Don't let yourself be captured.'

'I won't,' Slim said.

'If you get wounded and you see the dickers coming at you, you know what you have to do.'

No one wanted to mention the Exit Club – suicide – but Slim knew that this might be his only option and he nodded. 'I know.'

Rob coughed into his fist, lit a cigarette, then blew smoke

rings and studied them thoughtfully. 'So where do we go from here?' he asked eventually, breaking the silence.

'You keep your eye on Hegarty,' Burton said, 'while I track the other three.'

He said this knowing that Rob, who had the face of a gnarled spud and the general appearance of a navvy, had been successful at trawling the streets of the Falls Road area, keeping his eye on Hegarty from a distance. Though strangers had once been unwelcome in the Falls, and therefore noticed immediately, tourists were now being bussed into the area, Protestants were shopping there, and strangers were no longer viewed with automatic suspicion. It was, however, one thing to watch Hegarty from a distance and quite another to get up close, since the dickers were always in his vicinity, keeping a watchful eye on him. The same could be said for surveillance of the other four gang leaders, which was Burton's responsibility; nevertheless, he and Rob between them had managed to keeps tabs on the separate movements of the four men and now knew their general routines and most of the places they frequented daily. The problem was how to get through their security, make the kills and get out again. It was not a small problem.

'I can keep my eye on 'im,' Rob said, 'but I still can't get at 'im. Those dickers have eyes in the back of their bleedin' heads and there's an awful lot of 'em. They're armed and they're experienced and they're vicious. So what about your four?'

'Three,' Slim corrected him, clearly confident that Gallagher would be no problem after tomorrow night.

'Right,' Rob said, 'three. Me mum always said I couldn't count. So what about your three, Sarge?'

'The same,' Burton said. 'I can track them, but I can't get up close – and that problem will become more acute when Gallagher's taken out.'

'Why?'

'The remaining three are bound to tighten security around themselves while deciding how to neutralize Hegarty. The latter might work to our advantage, but the main problem remains.'

'So how do we solve it?' Rob asked.

Burton glanced beyond Rob's head, which was framed by the window. He saw the rolling green hills of Antrim, bright and cheerful in sunlight. He also saw dark clouds on the horizon, drifting south, bringing rain.

'We need someone in there,' he said. 'Someone right in the thick of it. Someone who can tell us what's happening each time they make a move. We need to know what they're doing before they do it and I'm working on that.'

'You have someone in mind?' Slim asked.

'I have someone looking for me,' Burton said, 'but he can guarantee nothing.'

'And if he comes up with nothing?' Slim asked.

'I don't want to think about it. It doesn't bear thinking about. If we can't get someone in there, someone close, then our problem is major.'

'I still think we can get them,' Slim said stubbornly.

'I don't think we can hit the others in the Falls,' Burton replied, 'so we have to know when they plan to go somewhere else and where they're actually going. I'm thinking of an ambush. An assault on premises outside the city. Maybe bombs instead of bullets. Some way to hit them when they're on the move or when they're somewhere more open and less protected. Those men are trading across the border. That means they must travel. They must have meetings all over the place – in Cork and Dublin, for instance. We have to know when such a meeting has been arranged and take it from there. So we need someone inside. We *have* to have someone.'

'And while we're waiting for your friend to come up trumps?' Slim asked with a grin.

'We kill Gallagher,' Burton said.

CHAPTER EIGHTEEN

Stepping out of his terraced house that evening, Gallagher was annoyed because it was raining again. It was summer in Ireland, but it was raining as usual and he longed to be where the sun shone and he wouldn't get windblown. As he usually did when preparing to visit his paramour, James Reid, he had showered and drenched himself in aftershave and put on his best clothes. He felt like a million dollars and knew that he looked it, but the wind and the rain combined could make a bloody mess of him. He hated the Belfast weather, the cold wind and frequent rain, and yearned to be where he could wear more colourful clothes and keep his hair tidy.

Cursing softly to himself, he locked the front door behind him and turned around to face the street as one of his dickers, young Jim Hewitt, hurried to hold an umbrella up over him.

'Evenin', Mister Gallagher,' Hewitt said, grinning nervously out of a gaunt, pimply face. 'Sure wouldn't this be a pisser?'

'Ackay, it's bloody awful,' Gallagher replied. 'So let's get to the car right quick.'

The car, a metallic-grey Volvo 340 GL, was parked by the pavement directly in front of him, but he found himself glancing automatically along the street in both directions, mindful that Hegarty had killed McCauley and might be gunning for all of them. As expected, some of his dickers were lounging about in separate gangs on opposite corners at both ends of the street and others were leaning casually against the walls of houses within the street itself, smoking fags, chatting to each other and eyeing up any young girl who passed by. Gallagher was well protected, but he still had good reason to be nervous about what Hegarty might do. That bastard was mad and would stop at nothing to get at the other four if he wasn't stopped first. Gallagher, tasked with doing just that, was still working out how to do it.

'Right,' he said, 'let's go.'

It was only a few feet to the car, but young Hewitt held the umbrella up over him as he made his way to it and slipped in through the already opened front passenger seat door. Gallagher liked to be driven, but he also liked to sit up front and see what was going on in his streets – even more so now that Hegarty could no longer be trusted and his hooligans were all over the Falls. As Gallagher settled into his seat, Hewitt collapsed the umbrella and ran around to take the driver's seat. A second dicker, Phillip Quinn, was already sitting in the rear seat and both dickers were armed. Hewitt handed the umbrella to Quinn and then started the car and drove off.

'Mr Reid's house as usual?'

'Aye, that's right, Jim.'

'Okay,' Hewitt said. He knew enough not to ask questions about James Reid or anyone else that Gallagher met. If he needed to know, he'd be told and so he kept his trap shut. He probably assumed that Reid was in the organization and that these visits were some kind of business meeting. It was best that he think that.

'Any sign of unusual activity on the street?' Gallagher asked, thinking of Hegarty.

'Naw,' Hewitt replied, 'not a thing. It's as quiet as a morgue out there.'

'No sign of anyone from the Falls?'

'Not a trace, boss.'

'Good,' Gallagher said.

Glancing left and right at the terraced houses on both sides where his dickers, not wearing overcoats, were now drenched and shivering in the rain, he felt a deep depression and wondered if he could ever get out of here. He had joined the IRA years ago, when he was barely into his teens, but he hadn't done so because of his love for Ireland. In fact, he had always hated this place, its grim streets, its religious fervour, its sexual puritanism, and had spent most of his troubled adolescence dreaming of faraway, exotic places drenched in sunlight and populated with his own kind. It was a dream of escape.

Why had he wanted that? Because he had always been different: too fat and with an oddly unformed face that seemed never to age. His friends from boyhood and adolescence had called him 'Baby Face' from as far back as he could remember and even now, when he was in his late thirties, though no one would have dared call him that any more, he knew that his face was still unnaturally youthful, his skin too pink and smooth, his cheeks too round, his lips too dainty, and that his body, though big, was all blubber, making him seem like an overgrown child. He had been tormented by this all his life, mocked because of it in childhood, and it had filled him with secret shame, hatred and the need for revenge. He had joined the IRA, then, not only to prove his manhood, but to give his inner violence full expression and exact his revenge. He had killed, first for revenge and then for pleasure, and taken his strength from his sense of power. Ireland's freedom? To hell with it.

'What a shite-hole this place is,' he said. 'Sure it's as grim as a prison yard.'

'It's not bad,' Hewitt said.

'Sure it's all you know, boyo. That's why you think it's normal. If you'd done a bit of travellin' in yer time, you'd think a lot different.'

'I once thought of Australia,' Hewitt replied, 'but the shites wouldn't have me. Said they only wanted people with professional skills and I didn't have any. Left school too young an' all.'

'That's the problem with all you boyos,' Gallagher said. 'You only know one thing and it's not what they're lookin' for out there.'

'Damned right,' Hewitt said.

As the car took him out of Andersonstown, heading for Stockman's Lane, Gallagher thought yearningly of James, his soft buttocks and loving lips, his compliance and sexual greed, and realized that he could not halt this affair, no matter its dangers. It had always been dangerous, of course – his secret homosexual life – and he had lived for too many years with the fear of being found out. Knowing that, he also knew that he had taken up with the IRA to prove that he was a man – a *real* man, just like the others – and to hide his more feminine, secret side. As an adolescent, then as a young man, his homosexuality had terrified him, more so because he knew that it was not acceptable in a world of hard men. So he had fought to become a hard man, even harder than the others, and his violence, which was nurtured by his fear, had finally gained him respect. Now he was the one who terrorized, ruling his turf with an iron fist, but everything he had gained from this – his authority and wealth – would be lost if his friends found out about him. This was something he dreaded.

Sooner or later, I'll have to leave here, he thought, *and make a new life for myself elsewhere – some place where the sun shines and I can wear pretty clothes and reveal my secret self without shame and show off my lovers. Anywhere but this grim, colourless city with its sexual hypocrisy. I can't wait for that day to come.*

That day would not come soon, he realized with some bitterness as the car headed along Balmoral Avenue, between the green fields of Finaghy and Malone, where the Protestants flourished. James Reid was a Protestant, but Gallagher didn't give a damn, wanting only what it was that James could give him as no one else could: emotional release and sexual satisfaction without guilt or shame. James was lovely that way. He was Gallagher's passive victim. Much finer than the whores that Gallagher used in the streets, he had been educated in England, spoke with a posh accent, and behaved like a perfect gentleman, except when in bed. Gallagher liked that, appreciated that touch of class, felt raised above the squalor of his existence by James's good breeding and exquisite manners, which he liked to degrade. James was upper-class Belfast, the only son of wealthy parents, but he had made his own small fortune out of property speculation and normally mixed with the kind who played golf and had grand dinner parties. Gallagher had always fancied that, a bit of posh to elevate him, and not being able to attain it, feeling uncomfortable with it, he settled for degrading James in bed and bringing him down to his level. James often wept when he did that. He pleaded for mercy when Gallagher hurt him. Gallagher had met him in a club where those with guilty secrets gathered and had known at a glance that James liked rough trade and would thrive on submission. He had submitted to Gallagher, sexually aroused by his fear of him, and now Gallagher was addicted to the thrill of their unequal relationship. In hurting and humiliating James, in making him weep and moan, he temporarily conquered all his fears about his own masculinity.

Before James, he had only managed to do that when he tortured or killed and he had done that a lot. A man did what he had to do.

'Excuse me, boss,' Hewitt said as they travelled along a short stretch of the Malone Road, where birch trees were outlined by the stars on this finer summer's evening, 'but what's this business about lookin' out for gangs comin' up from the Falls? Is it serious, like?'

'If I tell ya to do it, it's serious. Sure ya should know that, boyo. Why the fuck are ya askin'?'

Hewitt flushed bright red. He knew enough to be scared of Gallagher. 'Sorry, boss. I'm not bein' a cheeky git. I just wondered, that's all.'

'You and yer mates have been talkin', like.'

'Just talkin', boss, honest. Like, we're told to look out for our own kind from the Falls and we're wondering if there's somethin' going on that we don't know about. We're worried that we might do the wrong thing because of what we don't know, like. Swear to God, that's all, boss.'

'Just keep yer traps shut and do as yer told and you'll be told if ya do anything wrong. Pass that on to yer mates.'

'Sure, boss. No problem. No offence meant.'

'An' none taken, boyo.'

He glanced past Hewitt's head, at the heavy traffic of the Outer Ring Road, and saw the Belvour estate beyond the houses, slipping past as a series of dimly lit slopes that melted into the lowering sky. You didn't see stars here too often. You had to travel for that. Though Gallagher had mentioned travel to Hewitt, he hadn't done it himself yet. He blamed that on the Troubles, which had sucked him in and trapped him, and now that he was one of the Belfast Six he was trapped even more. Once in, you couldn't get out. There was too much blood to wash off. You were a marked man wherever you went and needed constant protection. Not only from the RUC or the long arm of British law: you also had to think of bastards like Hegarty, a mad dog on the loose. He was foaming at the mouth, sniffing blood, in constant heat, and his killing of McCauley was a sign that he had started the range war. That bastard had to be put down – the others were right about that – and Gallagher was going to have to get his best men together and work out a game plan.

Not that he needed one. The way to get Hegarty was suddenly
clear cut in Gallagher's mind. You couldn't get him on the sly,
not with an ambush, not long distance, so the best thing was to
get him at home and God help his missus. Gallagher knew now
what he would do and there was little to think about. The only
way to get Hegarty was to organize a riot – get a hundred-odd
good men – and charge en masse into Hegarty's street, firing
on the move. Take out his fucking dickers, shoot all the shits to
shreds, and then throw a CS grenade through Hegarty's front
window and wait until he came stumbling out. Shoot him down
like the mad dog he was and then run like the blazes. Gallagher
planned to do that very thing the day after tomorrow. The very
thought made him feel good.

'Here we are, boss.'

Hewitt pulled the car into the kerb outside James Reid's
house in leafy Newtownbreda Road, near the Knockbreda Parish
Church and its old graveyard, a few houses down from the
entrace to the Belvour Golf Club. He braked to a halt and
then turned the ignition off. Gallagher glanced along the street,
which ended in a cul-de-sac. It was lamplit and quiet, the rain no
longer falling, but Gallagher waited until Quinn had clambered
out of the rear before he released his own safety belt. Hewitt got
out as well and ran around to open Gallagher's door as Quinn
took up his position by the front gate, his eyes flitting left and
right. When Hewitt opened Gallagher's door, the latter stepped
out, glanced left and right automatically, feeling haunted by
Hegarty, then hurried around the car and walked up the garden
path to James Reid's fine house. Glancing back, he saw Hewitt
and Quinn taking up their watch positions, the former leaning
back against the car to light a fag, the latter remaining by the
garden gate and already smoking. Satisfied, Gallagher turned
away and rang the door bell.

The door was opened by James, who lived here alone, not
having married, as many Belfast homos did, to disguise what
he was. He was a beautiful young man, wanly handsome,
sophisticated, as slim as a reed in a snow-white roll-neck pullover and immaculate grey slacks. Seeing Gallagher, he smiled
in nervous anticipation and stepped aside to let him in.

'Evenin',' Gallagher said.

He stepped inside the house and James closed the door
behind him. Gallagher slipped his overcoat off and James took
it and hung it on the rack in the hallway then followed him in.

'I'm so glad you could come,' he said softly. 'I've been *dying* to see you.'

Knowing his silences frightened James, Gallagher didn't reply. Instead, he walked into the lounge and went to the drinks cabinet. The house was really posh – paintings and antiques everywhere – and the drinks cabinet was better stocked than any pub that Gallagher had ever been in. He pointed to the brandy bottle and James poured him a large one. Gallagher finished it in one gulp. James poured him another and then Gallagher led them both up the stairs and into the rear bedroom, overlooking the dark slopes of the golf course. Once there, he sat on the edge of the bed with the drink in his hand, gently shaking the glass.

'Miss me?' he asked.

'Yes,' James replied.

'What did you miss the most, boyo?'

'I missed everything, Michael.'

'What would you do without me?'

'I'd kill myself. You know that.'

'I know that you're a fuckin' wee liar an' an arsehole for everyone.'

'That's not true. It's unfair. You're just trying to hurt me, Michael. You're strong and I'm weak and you know that and try to exploit it. You know how to wound, Michael.'

'That's what you want, boyo. A bit of rough trade. You were born with a silver spoon in yer mouth an' you want to eat shit. You think I'm shit for your gullet.'

'God, you're crude,' James said. 'I can't believe that tongue of yours. You're like something just released from the cave and wondering what you can slaughter. You wouldn't know normal speech if you heard it and you're sniffing for blood. You're so crude, I can't stand it.'

Gallagher finished off his brandy and stood up to put the glass down. He set it down carefully on the bedside cabinet and then flexed his fingers. Turning back, he saw James staring at him with that slight, nervous smile. James had brown eyes that were big and filled with fear, though he was also excited.

Gallagher stepped up and slapped him on the face. James's eyes filled with tears.

'You liked that?' Gallagher asked.

'Of course not,' James replied.

Gallagher slapped him even harder, once, twice, a third time. His head jerked from side to side and he quivered as tears rolled down his cheeks.

'What about that, boyo?' Gallagher asked. 'Was that even better?'

'No,' James said. 'Please stop.'

Gallagher punched him in the stomach. James grunted and collapsed. He was kneeling in front of Gallagher, his head bowed, and his whole body was shaking.

'You weak turd,' Gallagher said. 'You filthy Protestant shit. You're on yer knees because ya want to be converted an' find the true faith. Say ya want that. Just say it.'

'Yes,' James whispered. 'Oh, yes!'

Gallagher grabbed him by the hair and jerked his head up. His brown eyes were swimming in tears, bright with fear and excitement.

'Yer worthless meat,' Gallagher said. 'An arsehole that needs pluggin'. Ya want to be punished for yer sins and ya want me to do it. Isn't that right? Just tell me.'

'Yes,' James whispered, 'that's right.'

Gallagher jerked James's head back and slapped his face a few more times. Then he threw him on the floor and kicked his ribs until he cried out for mercy.

'That's what I like to hear,' Gallagher said, feeling strong and in control, consumed in a rising sexual heat that made his head spin. 'The sound of a Prod sufferin' for his heretical sins. Now take yer fuckin' clothes off.'

James stood up and took his clothes off, doing it slowly, like a stripper. He didn't turn around to face Gallagher until he was naked. He looked fragile and fearful, as white as snow, making Gallagher's blood boil.

'Now *you* can undress *me*,' Gallagher said, speaking hoarsely and feeling choked up, hard and hot where it mattered, 'and just make sure yer careful about it.'

'Yes,' James said. 'Of course.'

He undressed Gallagher, fondling him as he did so, kissing up and down his body, devouring him, massaging him, and soon they were both stretched out on the bed, one on top of the other. They were in the throes of punishment, one giving and one receiving, when the glass in the bedroom window was smashed and all hell was let loose.

James Reid screamed hysterically.

CHAPTER NINETEEN

Dressed completely in black – windcheater, roll-neck sweatshirt, trousers and soft-soled shoes – and with a loaded SIG-Sauer P288 handgun holstered in the cross-draw position under the windcheater, Slim drove from his house in Templepatrick, Antrim, to the university area of Belfast. There, in a quiet sidestreet, lined with birch trees, lamplit, he parked the car with confidence at a meter in the evening's free period. After securing the car, he explored the area until he found another quiet sidestreet with many cars parked in it. Stopping at a white Peugeot 106 cluttered with pop music magazines, a blanket, car maintenance tools and oily rags – obviously a student's car – he picked the lock, slipped inside, hot-wired the engine – the steering wheel had not been locked – and drove off unnoticed, heading along Stranmillis Road.

Nice and busy out there, he thought, taking in the street lights and the brightly lit shop windows and the many people out walking, taking advantage of the warm summer weather. *I can lose myself easily enough out there when I'm making my way back. No problem at all.*

Once across King's Bridge, which spanned the River Lagan, it did not take him long to reach the house in the Newtownbreda Road. Entering the road by Purdis Lane, he saw Gallagher's Volvo parked outside, with two dickers keeping watch, one leaning against the bonnet of the car, the other by the front gate. They were smoking cigarettes and having a chat and didn't seem too concerned.

That's a big mistake on your part, Slim thought as he turned right and drove away from them. *At least one of you should be out the back. Who trained you dumb bastards?*

He parked his stolen car a few hundred metres farther

along the road, closed the door but left it unlocked with
the key still in the ignition, then entered the driveway of a
big detached house where no lights were showing. Padding
along the side of the house, he emerged onto its rear patio,
overlooking the darkened golf course. Checking that no one
was in sight, he clambered over the low fence, dropped down
onto the golf course and made his way along to the rear of
James Reid's house. The ground here was lower, the steel
fence a lot higher, so Slim lifted his roll-neck and unravelled
the length of abseiling cord-with-hook that he had wrapped
around his muscled torso under the sweatshirt. Expertly
trained in this, he threw the hook up over the fence and
tugged on the abseiling cord until the hook had caught on
the top. He tested it by tugging at it, then clambered up over
the fence, pressing his feet against the meshwire and hauling
himself up by the cord, until he was balanced precariously on
the top. He left the hook attached to the fence, letting the cord
dangle down to the ground, in readiness for when he made
his escape. After checking again that no one was in sight, he
dropped down the other side, landing with scarcely a sound
on the smooth, damp lawn.

So far, so good, he thought.

From where he stood, he could see that the upstairs bedroom
light was on. Almost certainly this signified that Gallagher
was in there with his boyfriend.

Pausing only to check that no one was walking around on
the dark golf course behind him or out in the gardens of
the other detached houses, Slim ascertained that all was
clear and made his way across the lawn, glancing along
the side of the house to the street at the front. He saw the
hood of the parked Volvo, the dicker leaning against it, and
the back of the other dicker, still leaning against the front
gate. Satisfied that they presented no immediate threat to
him, he turned away from them and moved stealthily, at
the crouch, across the back of the house to the outbuilding
with a tiled roof that sloped up to that brightly lit window.

They're not shy with each other, Slim thought, *if they do it
with the lights on. But that's a bad mistake for Gallagher to
make. Love must have rendered him brainless.*

The outbuilding was unlit, but Slim glanced through the
window and saw, in the shadow darkness, that it was a kitchen

extension and laundry room. From what he could see beyond it, the rest of downstairs was in darkness, except for a thin blade of light falling obliquely from the entrance hall into the front lounge.

Satisfied that there was no one downstairs, he carefully clambered up onto the roof as he had done on his earlier reconnaissance mission. He stood on the rubbish bin placed foolishly beside the wall, placed one foot on the metal grip of a waste pipe, then grabbed the pipe and pulled himself up until he was high enough to place the other foot on the lower edge of the roof, just above the guttering. Thus secured, he was able to clamber up over the guttering, making practically no noise in his rubber-soled shoes, and then pad lightly, carefully, up the sloping roof until he was kneeling just below the window of the brightly lit bedroom. There he rested, getting his breath back and preparing himself for the hit.

'God, stop it!' he heard a man cry out from inside the bedroom. 'Please, Michael, you're hurting me!'

'Oh, fuck!' Michael Gallagher responded, sounding hoarse and gasping for breath. 'Fuckin' Jesus, ya soft cunt!'

Not wanting to see what was going on in that room until he had to, mindful that he was here for one purpose only, Slim reached across his waist with his right hand and withdrew the P228 from its holster. It was a double-action handgun with a fifteen-round magazine; he screwed a modified silencer onto the barrel and looked around him again.

The golf course was dark and silent. The neighbouring gardens were empty. Slim took a deep breath, let it out slowly, then released the safety catch on the handgun and straightened up. He smashed the window with the barrel of the gun and immediately opened fire.

He saw two milky-white bodies, one on top of the other, and recognized the one on top by his bulk. Gallagher jerked his head around, his attention drawn by the smashing glass, and Slim aimed for the visible part of his chest as he raised himself off the other man, frantically trying to roll away. Slim fired as the broken glass was still raining onto the floor: four shots in quick succession into Gallagher's chest, then another two into his head when it was well clear of the other man. Gallagher's head seemed to explode and blood splashed from his naked body as the man under him, prone but peering back up over his shoulder, his eyes wide with shock until they too were drenched in the blood, screamed hysterically and grabbed the sides of the mattress, holding on as if in a crashing car. Gallagher collapsed on top of him, his body still shuddering, drenching him in more blood and pinning him still harder to the bed. The trapped man, by now also thoroughly blood-drenched, continued to scream hysterically as Slim slithered back down the sloping roof, still holding the handgun. He dropped off the roof and bent his knees as he hit the ground, then rolled over as if landing by parachute and jumped back to his feet.

He heard the bawling of the dickers out front as they rushed up the garden path.

Wasting no time, his concentration razor-sharp, he raced back across the garden, holstering the handgun on the move, and used the abseiling cord still hanging down from its hook to haul himself up the side of the fence. He pulled the cord up after him and was balanced on the top, his ears ringing from the constant, hysterical screaming of the other man, when the first dicker raced into the rear garden and let out a hoarse shout.

Slim jumped off the fence when the first shot rang out. He heard the bullet whining above his head as he fell to the ground. He bent his knees to take the impact, rolled over a few times, then jumped to his feet and raced away across the golf course, unholstering his handgun again as he ran and glancing repeatedly back over his shoulder to see if the dicker was pursuing him. So far he was not.

Slim kept running, crouching low and zigzagging, crossing a two-tone jigsaw of darkness and shadow, heading for the river. He heard the other man still screaming, the two dickers bawling, then the noisy smashing of another window lower down. He assumed from this noise that at least one of the dickers was attempting to break into the house to find out what had happened.

He'd better have a strong stomach, Slim thought. *It won't be a pretty sight.*

Hearing more shouting, this time a lot closer, he glanced back over his shoulder and saw that one of the dickers had now emerged through a side entrance in the garden fence and was chasing him across the dark golf course. The dicker stopped, fired a shot, then started running again. The first shot had been a wild one, going wide of the mark, but the second, fired when Slim was racing across open ground, whipped dangerously close by his head.

Realizing that the next shot was likely to hit him, he dropped onto his belly, wriggled around to face the way he had come and saw that the dicker was still pursuing him. The dicker was pretty dumb, running upright, not zigzagging, and further indicating his position by bawling repeatedly for his unseen partner to join him.

Slim stretched his arms out in front of him, elbows hard on the ground, holding his weapon two-handed as he took aim. When he had the dicker in his sights, aiming squarely at his body, he restrained his breathing, applied pressure equally between the thumb and fingers of the firing hand, then squeezed and maintained the pressure on the trigger until the round had been fired. He fired again on the instant, slightly moderating his aim, and the dicker jerked twice, first left and then right, flung his arms up, went into convulsions and fell back into darkness.

Slim jumped up and ran off again, still heading for the river.

The hysterical screaming stopped abruptly, as if the man had been gagged, and was replaced with the shouting of the neighbours as they emerged from their houses. A car roared and Slim assumed it was the other dicker racing away from the house.

Slim kept running, still crouching low and zigzagging, and didn't stop until he reached the old ruined wall of the estate, where he made his way down to the River Lagan. He dropped the pistol into the river, not caring if it was found – indeed, that would be a bonus – then, turning away, he splashed through a narrow tributary stream and scrambled up another slope, through hawthorn trees and cutting brambles, until he reached the towpath. Walking steadily, with no sign of urgency, he made his way along the winding towpath until he emerged to Annadale Avenue.

Stay cool, he thought. *Don't increase your pace. You're just out for a stroll. Let yourself melt into the scenery. It's just a matter of walking now.*

He walked along the Embankment, passing a block-like high school and rows of housing-executive flats, and saw people on the other side of the river, drinking at the lamplit tables outside the lively pub on Cutter's Wharf. Still walking casually, as if just out for a stroll, he crossed Governor's Bridge to the far side of the Lagan, made his way through the crowd of people outside the Lyric Theatre, then strolled at a leisurely pace alongside the Botanic Gardens until he was back in University Road, brightly lit and lined with trendy restaurants, all doing good business. He crossed the road, just one pedestrain out of many, and walked casually to where his own car was parked along a quiet lamplit sidestreet. He slipped into the car, turned on the ignition, pulled out and commenced the long drive back to Antrim, feeling as cool as a cucumber and well pleased with his evening's work.

Less than an hour later, he was back in his rented house in Templepatrick, having a glass of Guinness and watching the news on TV. During the course of the programme, he was informed by the newscaster that Michael Gallagher, a former IRA member and reported gang leader, had been shot to death in the home of the prominent local businessman James Reid. Precise details of the crime had not been released by the authorities and James Reid, unhurt but reportedly in a state of shock, was unavailable for comment.

Slim had just switched the TV off when the telephone rang. He picked it up and said, 'Yes?'

'I'm told the fishing was good,' Burton said, clearly having seen the TV broadcast also.

'It was great,' Slim replied. 'I caught a salmon the size of a fucking whale. Eat your heart out, boyo.'

'Congratulations,' Burton replied. 'I'll drop in tomorrow night, bring a bottle of Bushmill's, and fix a date for our next fishing trip together. I'll even bring Rob along. How does that sound?'

'It sounds perfect,' Slim said.

Burton put his phone down.

CHAPTER TWENTY

Burton, being the closest to it, was the first to arrive at their chosen meeting place, Cranfield Point on the banks of Lough Neagh, on a wooden jetty overlooking the vast expanse of darkly glittering still water. Living only a few miles away, he often came here when he wanted to be alone, closeted with his thoughts as the curlews and other wading birds searched for food on the mudflats. He had always liked water: the sea, rivers and lakes. Even after going into the Atlantic in the crashed Sea King Helicopter during the Falklands War, surrounded by drowned friends and almost frozen to death before being rescued – a nightmarish experience that still haunted him – he could still find solace by being close to water, particularly great lakes like this, where he could wander to his heart's content, looking for the sun stars and curled octopus that sometimes appeared near the shore. For the moment, however, waiting for his friends to come, he was content to sit under a hawthorn tree, smoking a cigarette and gazing out at the vast body of water and the fishing boats in the distance. It seemed a long way from Belfast.

Burton could still not think of Belfast without a tremor of guilt and fear passing through him. The guilt was what he suffered for having accidentally killed that child years ago; the fear was caused by his seeming inability to shake it out of his mind and heart. He had returned to Belfast in a state of confusion, thinking vaguely of finding redemption, even if only by paying his dues by eradicating the Belfast Six. But he'd had to drive too many times past the street where that poor child had died and his own peace of mind had been brutally shattered. He sometimes thought of going back there to talk to the mother, to beg her forgiveness for what he had done, but he had deprived her of a husband and child all at once and for that there could be no forgiveness that wasn't hypocrisy. So he had stayed away, even avoided the street where possible, and now spent too many nights in his lonely house not far from here, imagining the agony that he and Deborah would feel if one of their own children was killed. The thought was unbearable.

Hearing the sound of an approaching car, he glanced sideways and saw Rob's second-hand Nissan Sunny coming around the bend in the road and braking to a halt just behind him. Rob climbed out, slammed the door shut, then turned around and waved and walked towards him. He would have had a short drive as well, having come from his rented holiday cottage in Ballyclare. Slim would be coming from his house in Templepatrick, only twenty-odd minutes drive from Ballyclare. The three of them were in reasonably close proximity to each other, but far enough away to ensure that the locals did not link them to each other. They communicated by phone and visited each other for war councils, fondly known as 'Chinese parliaments', but they never socialized together in their respective towns; they always did that elsewhere, where none of them were known. So far this had worked and no enquiring eyes had been turned upon them, at least as far as they knew.

Looking scruffy in a faded black leather jacket and loose grey pants, Rob gave Burton his crooked, wicked grin. 'That's some bleedin' lake,' he said in genuine awe, staring out over the dark, sun-stippled water. 'About the biggest I've ever seen.'

'It's certainly the biggest in the British Isles,' Burton informed him. 'A hundred and fifty-three square miles.'

Rob gave a low whistle. 'Are those fishing boats out there on the horizon?'

'Yes,' Burton said. 'They're probably fishing for eels.'

'They eat 'em?' Rob asked, turning up his nose in distaste at the very thought of it.

'Yes. I'm surprised you haven't had some. I thought you Cockneys lived on jellied eels. They're an Ulster delicacy and the Irish also export tons of them every year.'

'I'd rather lick my own vomit,' Rob told him. 'Bloody strange lot, the Paddies.' He lit a cigarette and sat on the ground beside Burton to blow a series of smoke rings, which was one of his habits. '*Bloody* strange,' he emphasized.

'No stranger than the English,' Burton said. 'Just strange in their own way.'

'I wanna get out of here,' Rob said. 'I'm bored livin' all alone there. I wouldn't mind if I could mix with the locals and maybe get me some nooky, but you won't let us do that.'

'No,' Burton said.

'I'd be discreet, boss.'

'No, you wouldn't, Rob. You'd try, but you couldn't guarantee it because things would just slip out. You socialize in pubs where you live and they're bound to become curious and ask you a few personal questions that'll force you to lie. All lies are potential mistakes and we can't afford those. As for nooky, it's hard to keep secrets when in bed with a woman, so that's out as well. So no pubs where you live and no nooky. Drink at home or in Belfast where you're not known, but no women at all. Not until you go home. Any problems in Ballyclare?'

Rob shook his head. 'No problems, boss. The locals just say hello. I've spread it around that I'm just there temporarily, trying to pick up some cheap furniture to take back to England. They all assume I'm just a Limey on the make, buying cheap here and selling high back in England. They nod and smile and I do that right back and we're no closer than that, so you've no need to worry.'

'Good,' Burton said.

Rob blew another couple of smoke rings and watched them dissolving like ghosts against the white-clouded blue sky. 'Two down and four to go,' he said. 'Slim did okay last night.'

'He killed a dicker as well,' Burton said. 'I wish he hadn't done that.'

'He probably had to, boss. That dicker was found on the golf course behind the house, so he was probably chasing Slim when he was popped.'

'Yes, I know. I just wish it hadn't happened. He was just a young boy.'

'A young hooligan with a weapon and murd'rous intent. So fuck 'im, I say. He got what he deserved.'

Burton sighed. 'I suppose so.'

A coughing and rattling in the distance announced the arrival of Slim's second-hand, badly battered Renault 5 van. They both glanced sideways and watched it approaching and braking to a shuddering halt, belching clouds of black smoke.

'Diesel engine,' Rob said. 'I wouldn't have one of those as a bleedin' gift. I prefer good old petrol. But I suppose it suits a down-and-out antiques dealer of the kind he's supposed to be. Do you think he's convincing?'

'Too handsome,' Burton replied without the trace of a grin. 'Too much like a movie star. But he plays his role like an eccentric aristocrat and says it goes down a treat.'

'I'll bet,' Rob retorted.

Slim jumped down from the van and came towards them, his blond hair blowing in the breeze and turned to gold by the sunlight. He looked too slim to be a soldier and had the face of an angelic choir boy. But even in Iraq, where he had fought for the first time, he had, from the very start, killed the enemy without batting an eyelid. Burton remembered that. It had surprised him at the time. And later, in Northern Ireland, working covertly from Q cars, Slim had surprised him once again with his ability to stay cool under pressure and kill in close-quarter combat without hesitation. Burton had often thought about that, wondering where Slim got it from. He was a quietly good-humoured, thoughtful, decent young man from a respectable middle-class family in Richmond, but he lived for the excitement of danger and suffered no guilt when killing. A good soldier, Burton thought, was a mystery beyond reckoning, a man who had to be prepared to kill without becoming a beast. For that very reason, good soldiers were a rarity and Slim was certainly one of them.

Like me, Burton thought. *It's my pride, what I live and breathe for, yet it's the thing that most frightens me. At least, ever since the killing of that poor child, which pushed me close to the edge. Since then, I've been wondering just what kind of man I am – good or bad, civilized or violent – and knowing Slim hasn't helped me to find an answer. He's too much like the man I used to be before this guilt started eating at my innards. God, I wish I could run from this.*

'I don't see any fishing rods,' Slim said when he reached them and stood in front of them, looking down and grinning.

'What the fuck are you talking about?' Rob retorted. 'I've never fished in my life.'

'Never mind,' Slim said, still grinning as he kneeled on the grass beside them. 'Any Bushmill's, boss?'

'Yes,' Burton said. He had brought along a shoulder bag and now reached into it to pull out a bottle of Bushmill's Irish Whiskey and three plastic cups. He gave a cup to each of the other two and then poured the Bushmill's in. When he had filled his own cup, they all drank and then Slim sat on the grass in front of them.

'Congratulations,' Burton said.

'Thanks,' Slim replied.

'This morning's papers were full of it,' Rob said. 'All taking the line that it was an inside job, a case of dog eat dog, just like the death of McCauley, and suggesting that it's the start of a gang war. It worked a treat, Slim.'

'I read the papers,' Slim said.

'Were the cunts in bed together?' Rob asked, turning his nose up in disgust at the very thought of it.

'Yes,' Slim said. 'But I managed to do it without touching the other man. He screamed like an hysterical woman, but he didn't even get nicked.'

'Good shooting,' Rob said.

'The papers didn't mention them being together,' Slim said. 'No word about hanky-panky. Just said that Gallagher had been killed in Mister Reid's house. They didn't mention the bedroom.'

'And they won't,' Burton said. 'Mister Reid is a prominent businessman and respectable Protestant. They won't mention that he was found in bed with another man, let alone a Catholic and former member of the IRA. They'll keep the lid tight on that. What about the young dicker?'

'He was chasing me,' Slim said, 'with a handgun. You must have guessed that.'

'I had to ask,' Burton said. 'It smells bad when it's a kid. On the other hand, when they found him lying in that field, the authorities assumed that he'd died in a fire fight with another criminal gang. The neighbours – at least those within earshot – described hearing other guns firing from the golf course.'

'One gun,' Slim said. 'The one fired by the dicker. He fired a couple of times before I got him and they would have heard those shots. I was still using a silencer.'

'Frightened people exaggerate,' Burton said, 'and what they heard was a fire fight. Good. That's why the authorities now think it's a gang war – and the remaining members of the Belfast Six will think the same, which is just what we want. We should blow on the embers while they're hot and keep that fire burning.'

'Another hit while those bastards are confused.'

'Exactly. They'll now be under pressure from the RUC and the media, and they'll also be confused by what's happened, with the other three blaming Hegarty and vice versa. They won't be thinking too clearly right now but that could change soon, so let's strike while we can. Hegarty's out of the question until we get someone inside. Neil Byrne and Shaun Keenan are too close – we'll have to take them together. That leaves us with Liam O'Shea. So what have you got, Rob?'

'Plenty,' Rob replied. 'They talk a lot in the Falls Road pubs. They talk compulsively about the Belfast Six – or the Belfast Four, as they're now called. They won't talk to the Press or police and they won't talk to strangers, but they're Irish and they talk amongst themselves and they all have loud voices. They talk about the little they know and while that doesn't include secrets, nothing about the actual business, you still get to learn, by cocking an ear as you drink your Guinness, what they think of the gang lords.'

'And what do they think?'

'They think that Hegarty's mad and bad and needs to be put down; that Byrne and Keenan are the brains of the outfit, both still dedicated IRA men even though they're involved in crime; and that O'Shea's the least intelligent of them all, though he isn't much nicer. According to gossip, he licks the boots of the others, does what he's told because he can't think for himself, boasts far too much when he's drunk, which he is a lot, and won't survive as long as the others because he's so dumb.'

'Do you think that's correct?'

'I've followed him, boss. He's more careless than the others. He's so busy showing off in the pubs that he's not always watchful and he doesn't always invite his dickers in. That's a real possibility.'

'You hit him in a pub and you won't get out, so I think we'll leave that one.'

'He samples his own whores, boss. That's another possibility. He sometimes picks them off the street, just when they're trying to do business, and he takes them back to their own rooms and stays there for some time.'

'With the dickers standing outside?'

'Unfortunately, yes. Though he also attends one of his own brothels and I *could* get in there.'

'Rob just wants his nooky,' Slim said, grinning. 'He'll risk anything for that.'

'No, I'm serious,' Rob said, not seeing the joke at all. 'I *could* get into that fuckin' brothel. I mean, it's there for the street trade. You get Protestants and tourists in there as well as the Catholics. If I see him enter, I could follow him in, going in as a customer, and put the bastard down with a double tap just like Slim did with Gallagher. Put him down while he's on the job and distracted as any man would be. Then I make my escape by simply running outside and shooting my way past the dickers. That's a bit of a gamble, I know, but I'd be willin' to take it.'

'Where's the brothel?' Burton asked, feeling uncomfortable just asking, being reminded of just how sordid his undercover activities had become in the past few years. It had been bad enough in 1988, but this seemed even worse.

'In the lower Falls,' Rob said.

'Then even if you managed to put the dickers down, you'd be running out straight into trouble – so, no, I don't think so. Think of something else, Rob. Just what does this man do?'

Rob sighed with disappointment. 'He's a butcher by trade. He still runs his own shop. He runs his turf just like the others, raking in a lot of gelt, but he stills runs his butcher's shop during the day and pretends to be normal.'

'He can't run it all day,' Burton said, 'if he's running his turf.'

'I said he *runs* it, boss. That doesn't mean he's there all day. He does his rounds just like the others and attends the weekly meetings, but he runs the shop with the aid of two assistants and they're there when he's not around.'

'Is he ever there alone?'

'Yes, sometimes – in the evenings. Just before the shop closes. He sometimes keeps the shop open for half an hour or so after both of his assistants have left. He serves the last-minute customers, jokes with them, his PR bit. He also has friends in in the evenings, having drinks in the back room. I think he has a few private conversations, 'cause he often pulls the blinds down. He probably does a bit of trade on the side, out of sight of the other gang bosses and, if so, that would explain the blinds. All those bastards, they cheat on each other and O'Shea is as shifty as the rest. That would explain it.'

'What about the dickers? Where are they when he pulls the blinds down?'

'He leaves them outside – just like he does at the pubs. He tends to treat his dickers like shit and forgets what they're there for. He certainly never invites them in for a drink, if that's what you mean. He locks the door and pulls the blinds down and leaves the poor sods outside, just cooling their heels. Why? You think . . .'

'You've been hanging around there a lot,' Burton said. 'You're even known in the pubs. Have you ever been checked?'

'No. I've been given the eye now and then, the odd question's been asked, but I've never been actually challenged. See, I do a lot of talkin'. A bit of drunken crack with the boyos. I'm always boastin' about how I buy old furniture cheap in the Falls and flog it for twice the price back in Petticoat Lane. And I've made sure I was seen buying the stuff and taking it away in my van – a hired van, of course. So, you know, they all think I'm just another fuckin' Limey taking advantage of the peace to wander safely up and down the Falls Road, picking up their old tat. In short, yes, boss, I'm a recognized face and I've never been challenged – though that probably wouldn't hold if I tried to approach Liam O'Shea or any other gang boss.'

'But you could enter O'Shea's shop as a customer just before his shop closed?'

'Yes, boss, I could.'

'And if O'Shea locked the door and pulled the blinds down, with you still inside the shop, the dickers might assume that you'd been invited into the back room for one of those private talks.'

'Damn it, boss, that's a thought.' Rob's eyes were growing bright as he caught Burton's drift and Burton, knowing what they were discussing, felt a coldness swimming up from his centre to numb him to feeling. He needed that right now – he couldn't go through with this otherwise. He was a husband and father who respected human feelings and now he was descending to the depths because this was his calling. He had once been a soldier and was still proud to be so, but the nature of war had changed with the passing years, becoming covert and sordid. This was not an honourable war in the clean light of the desert, on the sea or in the air: it was spying and sanctioned murder and, if necessary, blackmail, and it took place in the midst of innocent people who could well become victims. It was unavoidable, but that didn't make it right and he could never forget that fact. This was not the way for him to find redemption or compensate for his past. It was a road without end.

'I just have to persuade him to lock the door and pull down the blinds,' Rob continued, glancing from Burton to Slim and becoming excited. 'Then I neutralize him—'

'Silently,' Burton interjected.

'—and then I simply walk out.'

'Correct,' Burton said. 'Do you think you can manage that?'

'Just watch me, boss.'

CHAPTER TWENTY-ONE

Teresa felt that her heart had died, though she was some-how still alive, barely conscious of herself as a human being, deprived of the will to live. She had felt this way for weeks, from that first awful night with Hegarty, and she felt it more acutely right now as he laboured on top of her. He was a brute of a man, a dreadful weight pressing upon her, and his love-making – though those words were misplaced here – was inept and unfeeling. *He* felt something, of course: self-satisfaction and triumph, exciting himself with her abject subjugation, humiliation and fear. He took his pleasure from domination, thriving on her degradation, and as he fucked her, using his cock as a weapon, he was hoping to cause her pain.

'Fuckin' whore!' he grunted as he thrust hard inside her, clearly wanting to split her asunder and reduce her to pulp. 'Ya filthy cunt! Ya snot-nosed, superior, bitch! How do ya like *this*, you fuckin' tart?'

The insults stimulated him, helping *him* to feel superior, and he often grinned, before the grimaces of orgasm, when he felt her recoiling. He gasped into her ears, his foul breath filled her nostrils, and she closed her eyes and thought of a ravenous beast in its dark, fetid lair. Like a beast, he often bit her, leaving marks on her fine skin, and he squeezed her breasts and thighs, not with affection, but in order to make her wince. She had tried not to do that, wanting to cheat him of satisfaction, but the pain was usually too much to bear and too often she winced and even cried out with tears in her eyes. He licked her tears up as he came, slobbering over her, grunting and groaning, and her sole moment of triumph was to feel his body shuddering for that all too brief moment when, in the helplessness of release, he lost his power over

her. Though only a short-lived moment of triumph, it was
what kept her sane.

'Ah, Jesus!' he gasped as he finally collapsed upon her,
soaking her in his sweat, his body, that great barrel of lard,
crushing her and squeezing the breath from her. 'Ah, Christ,
that was good!' Eventually, when he had gotten his own breath
back, he rolled off her and stared up at the ceiling, a smirk
on his scarred, frightening face, now breathing like that same
ravenous animal picking over some bones. After a moment,
before her silence could embalm him, he sat up and grinned
at her. 'Did ya like that?' he asked.

'Sure it was grand,' she replied, now knowing all too well
that if she expressed her true feelings, he would beat her
black and blue with his ham fists as he had done many times
now. Naturally, he knew that she was lying, but his huge ego
protected him.

'I hear the tone of yer voice,' he said, 'an' I know what it
means. Ya couldn't help enjoyin' it but ya don't want to give
me satisfaction by admittin' the truth. Ya hate me because yer
now in my power an' that's what really riles ya. If it wasn't for
that, you'd have to admit it was fuckin' good, which ya will
soon enough.'

'When will that be?' she dared to ask sarcastically.

'When ya get used to the fact that I own you; when you
take it as nat'ral. That'll come with time – it does with all the
whores – and when it comes to you, when ya finally accept it,
sure ya'll lie back an' enjoy it.'

Teresa sighed and rolled over, turning her back to him,
resting her cheek on the pillow and staring at the opposite wall
as he slid off the bed. She didn't want to watch him dressing,
didn't want to see him naked, and she tried to forget that he
was still there, though this wasn't easy. She kept recalling
the last few weeks, beginning with that first evening, the
living nightmare that commenced from the minute he burst
through the door to slap her around and cut her back with
his switchblade and force her onto her knees. That was just
the start of it; what came later was even worse. After the
fellatio, which aroused him but did not make him spend, he
had made her stretch out on the bed while he had his way
with her. Degradation was what stirred him, inflicting pain,
arousing fear, and when she had tried to resist, which she
had done when she knew no better, he had taken his fists to

her, carefully avoiding her face, explaining thoughtfully that he didn't want to cause damage where it showed because the punters, *his* punters, would be put off and that meant loss of business. But he beat her black and blue, concentrating on her body, and then took her any damned way he pleased, engaging in every perversion. When he finally left, in the early hours of that dreadful morning, she threw up and then sobbed uncontrollably, accepting defeat. He was mad and she knew that he would kill her if she tried to resist him.

Since then, he had not let her go back on the game, insisting that he wanted to get his fill of her first, teach her a thing or two, namely obedience and some new tricks, and in general let her know her place in life. He also wanted the many bruises on her body to fade away before she stripped again for a punter, which she would do eventually. When that day came, he informed her, she would be working for him and would pass over most of her earnings to him. If she tried to cheat him by withholding some of the money, he would chop her nose off. When he told her that, she believed him.

Hegarty liked her apartment, which was flashier than his own place, and apart from fucking her on the floor, on the kitchen table and in the bed, he started using it as his home away from home, appreciating the luxury. He made her cook for him. He liked to watch her clean the place. He told her that he liked a neat house and a woman who knew her place. She was his slave and he made sure that she knew it and often beat her to prove it though, now mindful of her value in the marketplace, he inflicted no more bad bruises. His beatings still hurt, but now they didn't leave any marks, except on her soul. When sleeping alone, she suffered nightmares for the first time since childhood.

Now, pressing her cheek to the pillow, she heard him dressing behind her, breathing like the animal he was and sometimes cursing softly. He was too big for the clothes he was wearing – a sign of his vanity. When he sat on the edge of the bed to put his shoes on, the bed creaked and the mattress sank.

'Ya all right?' he asked.

'Yes,' Teresa replied.

'Good,' he said as he tied his shoelaces. 'Sure I'm glad to hear that. I like my wimmen to feel all right when they're on the game. Makes the punters feel good, like.'

Surprised, Teresa rolled over to stare at his broad back, now covered in a dirty white shirt and tucked into his pants. 'What does that mean?'

'Yer goin' back on the game,' he said. 'Ya can start when ya want. Do all yer old haunts – the Europa in particular, which suits yer high-flown notions – but make sure I get to see every penny or I'll cut ya to shreds. Don't even think about hidin' the odd punter, 'cause you'll be watched every minute. I have eyes an' ears all over the place an' they know you're mine now. Do ya understand that?'

'Yes,' Teresa said, hardly believing what she was hearing, having thought she was trapped here forever, condemned to hell in her own home. She felt an odd exhilaration and at first it had her baffled; then she realized that it was not because she was going back to work – she would now be working for this bastard, after all – but simply because she was going to get out of this hell and taste a brief, welcome freedom. The very thought of speaking to someone other than Hegarty filled her with immeasurable joy. She would work for him, his degraded, helpless slave, but at least she would have some time to herself and mix with real human beings. She had friends out there, people she could talk to, and the degradations that Hegarty would inflict would be worth it for that alone. Like someone who'd spent too long in prison, she simply wanted her freedom.

'One more thing,' Hegarty said as he stood up, tightened his tie and put on his jacket. 'Ya can work yer old haunts an' pick up who ya like, but every now an' then I'll send someone to you – send 'em here – and when I do, ya'll do whatever they demand and ya'll do it for free, no questions asked. Is that understood, bitch?'

'There's some things I don't like to do,' she said, though she knew it was pointless.

'You'll give 'em *everything* they want, no matter what the fuck it is, and ya'll keep yer gob shut unless they want to shove their dicks into it. No questions. No arguments. If I hear otherwise, if I get one complaint, I'll make ya rue the day ya were born. Do ya get what I'm sayin'?'

'Yes,' Teresa replied, thinking with dread of the kind of perverts he might know and of the licence he'd give them. 'You won't get any complaints.'

'Good,' Hegarty said. Leaning over the bed, he grabbed her

viciously by the hair and jerked her head up. 'I like a woman that knows her place,' he said, 'and does what she's told. You'll do that, won't you, Teresa?'

'Yes,' she said.

'Yes, *Mister Hegarty*,' he emphasized.

'Yes, Mister Hegarty.'

He jerked her head from side to side a few times, almost tearing her hair out by the roots and bringing tears to her eyes. 'One last thing,' he said, still holding her hair like a vice. 'This is a nice wee place ya've got here. Real upmarket, like. It's a good place to entertain friends and conduct business, so I'll be inviting a few friends around now an' then and you'll make 'em feel good. You'll cook and pour the booze an' in certain cases show 'em what ya can do in this very bed. You'll be a good little hostess. How's that for starters?'

'I understand, Mister Hegarty.'

'Fuckin' right, ya do,' Hegarty said. He released her hair by throwing her back onto the pillows, then he turned away and walked to the front door. 'I'll see ya when I see ya,' he said. 'In the meantime, start workin'.' He opened the door, turned back briefly to leer at her, then stepped out and slammed the door behind him, leaving merciful silence.

'Jesus Christ!' Teresa said, then she gasped with relief, stretched out properly on the bed and stared at the ceiling for some time, torn between despair at her situation and exhilaration that she was free, albeit temporarily, for the first time in weeks. 'Get out,' she said. '*Right now!*'

Hardly able to bear another minute in the flat, which formerly she had loved, she slipped off the bed and went into the bathroom for a hot, cleansing bath. She scrubbed Hegarty off her, rid herself of his smell and touch, then put on her finest underwear, sheer stockings, the black shift skirt and cashmere jacket and stiletto-heeled shoes. Renewed, feeling human again, she picked up her leather shoulder bag and hurried out of the flat.

It was seven in the evening but the sun was still bright and the Malone Road was busy with commuters driving home from work. Teresa walked along the pavement, looking about her for a taxi, and the eyes of male pedestrians turned to follow her, which made her feel good as well. She felt the breeze against her face, the warmth of the sun, and grew giddy from the unusual sensation of being out in the open. The

noise of the traffic was music to her ears and it raised her
on high.

She caught a taxi soon enough and asked for the Europa
Hotel, then sank back in the seat and looked out the window,
seeing everything as if for the first time, just like a tourist.
Belfast was a small city and the journey was a short one,
taking her past the Botanic Gardens, along University Road,
then across Donegall Pass and on to the Europa. She was
thrilled to see the latter, as if coming home after too long an
absence, and when she paid the driver and entered the hotel
she felt ten years younger. She went straight to the upstairs
bar and took one of the stools. Seeing her, Jim Quaid stroked
his red hair and offered his fond, lopsided grin.

'Long time, no see,' he said. 'Where the hell have you been?'

'On vacation,' she replied.

'Sure ya didn't come back with a suntan.'

'I never left my hotel room.'

Jim grinned again, blinked his watery blue eyes and distractedly scratched his pink, freckled face. 'So what'll it be,
Teresa? The usual?'

'That's right,' she said.

As Jim was mixing the drink, Teresa glanced around the
bar and saw that it was busy with the usual mixture of locals
and tourists. She felt their eyes upon her and was pleased
with the attention, which had not been the case, she realized,
before Hegarty had entered the picture to devastate her life.
Now, even the thought of selling herself to a stranger was
preferable to being cooped up in her apartment with that mad
dog breathing heavily all over her. Being on the game, even
if for that bastard's benefit, was infinitely preferable to being
with him, so when one of the strangers in the bar smiled at
her, she was quick to smile back.

'You've just caught a trick already,' Jim said, having noticed
the silent exchange as he brought her the drink. 'It didn't take
ya long, did it?'

'Missed me, did you?' Teresa retorted.

'Life was dull,' Jim confessed. 'Sure I get my little pleasures
just standin' here watchin' ya operate.'

'And your little percentage,' Teresa reminded him.

'Ackay, that as well.'

'So who's the one who just gave me that smile? Have you
seen him before?'

'He's here for a convention. Telecommunications. Up from Dublin and enjoyin' himself. You'll come to no great harm there.'

'If he asks, you can say I'm available.'

'Sure I'll do that all right.'

Teresa's good feelings survived for most of the evening. The telecommunications salesman approached her as expected and was knowledgeable without being arrogant with it. He'd had a few words with Quaid and knew what she was up to and when eventually he stood beside her, by way of ordering another drink, he engaged her in good-humoured conversation before making his pitch. He was not the pitiful type – no stories about his unhappy marriage. He just bought her a drink, talked about this and that, then said outright that Quaid had put him in the picture and it was what he was after. Nothing fancy, just a woman for a few hours, to take care of his needs. Teresa liked him and went to his room with him and gave him a good time. In truth, she gave him better than he might normally have had because he had a sense of humour, he treated her with respect, and he was shy about taking off his clothes, which she found rather touching. More importantly, he wasn't that bastard Hegarty and the contrast was startling.

'I don't mean to be crude,' he said when they had finished and she was preparing to leave the room, 'but that was truly the best fuck I've ever had.'

'Sure it was grand for me, too,' she lied.

He stayed in his room, settling in for a good night's sleep, while Teresa went back down to the bar, hoping to find another trick before closing time. In doing this, she was aware that most of the income would go to Hegarty, but the thought of returning too soon to her prison – her own apartment with that bastard in it – was more painful than the thought of working for him, though that hurt as well. She just wanted to be free, to have a whole night on her own, but when she sat at the bar and sipped the drink that Quaid brought for her, another man, this one not at all friendly, came up to her and said, 'That was real quick. Ya didn't waste any time. Just remember that yer now bein' watched wherever you go. Ya try to do us down, ya try to hide a fuckin' penny, an' we'll pick ya up, right off the fuckin' pavement, an' take ya somewhere an' bury ya. Just remember this, whore.' Then, without another word, he walked out of the bar.

Teresa started shaking, spilling her drink when she tried to drink it, and felt her good feelings being swallowed by a dark well of fear. She was nervously lighting a cigarette, her hands still shaking badly, when Frank Cooney slipped onto the stool beside her and said, 'Well, well, where have *you* been?'

Teresa inhaled and exhaled cigarette smoke, trying to still her racing heart. 'I don't know what you mean.'

'You know damned well what I mean. You haven't been seen around for the past few weeks. Even Jim Quaid was wondering.'

'Well, he would, wouldn't he?' Teresa said sarcastically, taking courage from anger. 'He has his own interests, like.'

'He was worried about you,' Cooney said. 'And in truth, so was I.'

'What the fuck were you worried about? I don't live here, you know. I mean, I have other places – other bars, other hotels.'

'You weren't in any of the other bars or hotels. I know. I trawl them all. You haven't been seen by anyone for three weeks, so where were you, Teresa?'

'What's it to you?'

'I'm just asking as a friend.'

'As I told Quaid, I was havin' a vacation. Doesn't a poor wee workin' girl get time off?'

'Not your kind, Teresa.'

It seemed like an insult and she turned to glare at him, but she melted when she saw that his face showed only concern. She had once thought him a cynical bastard, but now she knew different: if he was cynical it was because he had covered the Troubles for years, seen all there was to see, and what *that* was, as she knew from personal experience, was more than the heart could bear.

'Just what does that mean, Frank?'

He smiled, but she saw the pain behind it. 'Let me answer your question with another question. Did Hegarty get to you?'

The question came as a shock – the fact that he'd already guessed it – and she felt her cheeks burning with the shame of what she had come to. She had never felt that as a common whore, but she felt it right now.

'What's it to you?' she said.

'That means yes,' he replied.

'You want a story, go and find it elsewhere. I don't talk to reporters.'

'I'm not asking as a reporter.'

'Don't fuckin' kid me, Frank.'

'You're frightened and I can see it in your face and that means he got to you. It doesn't help to insult me.'

'So what's gonna help?'

'Does that mean it's true?'

'What's true is that you're gettin' on my nerves and I wish you'd piss off.'

'He followed you home, didn't he? He put the screws on you. Whatever he did, it scared you enough to make you go into hiding. If he threatened you, Teresa, or if he insisted you work for him, you're either back here as one of his whores or you're risking your neck. Either way, I'm concerned.'

Teresa felt like crying and had to fight to control the urge. She had fought for years to be free, to make herself independent, to forget the past and build walls around herself that would not let the pain in. Now those walls were tumbling down, letting in what she had locked out, and all the terrors of her past were rising up to take her back to the old days. She wanted to tell Cooney about those, unburden herself, pass it on, but she knew that talking about it would resurrect it and she still could not deal with that. Let the past be dead and buried; let it lie in hallowed ground. She could not unlock the secrets of her sorrow and hope to survive.

What she could do was endure, as she had done in the past, though how long she could endure with Jack Hegarty was an issue of doubt. But she had to unlock something, at least her fear of that mad bastard, and knowing this, she sighed in defeat and said, 'Yes, Frank, he's got me. I'm all his, signed and sealed.'

'I can help you,' Cooney said.

CHAPTER TWENTY-TWO

L iam O'Shea spent his final afternoon in a pub in the lower Falls, playing snooker, downing a lot of lager and enjoying a bit of crack, the conversational sort, with anyone who happened to be standing near him. When drunk, O'Shea boasted a lot about his former experiences in the IRA and his present high status as a member of the Belfast Six, but he knew that he was on safe ground here because fear kept mouths shut.

With his wild blue eyes and twisted lower lip, O'Shea was not a pretty sight and he had suffered the slings and arrows of mockery from an early age. He had responded with violence, fighting his way through his schooldays, and then joined the youth wing of the IRA, determined to make himself respected regardless of his appearance. Irish history meant little to him and the political issues were beyond him, but his fierce desire to be respected by his peers made him fearless in action. With the physique of a professional wrestler and a strictly limited intelligence, he was ideal as cannon fodder, going where others feared to tread, taking on the most dangerous and thankless tasks with a sublime disregard for his own safety or the suffering of his unfortunate victims. He started by spying on his neighbours, moved on to administering punishments – beatings with fists or baseball bats; kneecappings of every kind – and then, when he had been promoted from the youth wing to the provisional IRA, doorstep assassinations and cold-blooded executions, often after torture, on quiet country roads and in green fields. For this reason, if for no other, he soon rose through the ranks and eventually was put in charge of an active service unit that specialized in the bombing of RUC police stations and the ambushing of British army convoys outside the city. He did the lot – and he did it very well – until the peace came.

Like many others of his ilk, O'Shea didn't want peace because it threatened to leave him out in the cold by returning him to his former anonymity, with no more than his butcher's shop to keep him going. Luckily, by this time he was the boss of his own turf and had the weapons and muscle to keep it going. It was therefore no accident that when Neil Byrne and Shaun Keenan, both dedicated IRA men, both feeling betrayed by Gerry Adams, decided to go their own way and tighten their hold on the city instead of turning away from violence – in preparation, as they insisted, for their return to the fight for freedom – they had included O'Shea as one of the Belfast Six. When they did so, they made him even more powerful than he had been during the Troubles.

O'Shea loved that power and the fearful respect it brought him, but he also wanted to be one of the boyos and loved for himself. He forgot his twisted lower lip when publicans gave him drinks for free, when women smiled instead of sneering, when the youthful dickers practically fought with each other to gain his attention. Having power, he would not be humiliated, as he had been in childhood, because he was considered ugly and dumb. Having power, he would be treated with respect no matter how he behaved. He had not had that until he joined the IRA and now he needed it desperately.

Though publicans gave him drinks for free, O'Shea also liked to treat the whole bar, enjoying the fact that he could afford it and not immune to the slavish thanks of those drinking from his purse. He had done that this afternoon, buying drinks for all present, and had held court at the bar, accepting thanks and being drunkenly magnanimous to all those around him. These included the short, powerfully-built Englishman, Trevor 'Trev' Manning, who thought he was being smart by taking advantage of the peace to trawl the poorer sections of the Falls for cheap furniture that he would renovate and sell for twice the money in London. O'Shea liked the Englishman because he felt superior to him, thinking him pretty dumb in imagining that the tat he was buying had any value at all. He also liked him, however, because he had a ready wit, was always quick with a good joke, and seemed intrigued by what O'Shea told him about his time in the IRA. Like many working-class Englishmen on the loose in Belfast, he enjoyed rubbing shoulders with the hard men and had a perverse fascination with their world of violence. Just another English wanker, according to O'Shea, but at least he was entertaining, amusingly pugnacious and, most important, he knew enough to treat O'Shea with respect. That made him okay in O'Shea's books and so he bought him free drinks as well.

'Sure I bet you never thought you'd see the day,' O'Shea said, putting his arm around Trev to give him a friendly hug, 'when an Englishman like yerself could have a drink in the Falls without getting a fuckin' bullet through his crust.'

'I was nervous when I first came here – I can tell you that, Liam – but I 'aven't 'ad an unkind word said to me in all the time I've been 'ere. You Irish are so bleedin' friendly, I just can't believe it.'

'Ackay, we are that right enough,' O'Shea replied. 'An' let bygones be bygones, like.'

'That's true enough, Liam. I feel safer 'ere than in London and that's sayin' something.'

'Not really,' O'Shea said. 'Sure that London is a piss-hole. Filled with niggers and other coons from the West Indies and them other banana republics. Just down out of the trees, those fuckers are, an' a right violent lot. The Big Smoke was always a dangerous place and it's because of them blackies. Get rid of them and ya'd be a lot better off. Sure ya can take that as read, Trev.'

'Absolutely,' Trev said. 'You're not workin' today, then?'

'Sure I just took the afternoon off to come down for a few pints.' O'Shea checked his wristwatch. 'I'll have to make tracks soon. I like to lock the place up myself and attend to the books.'

'I might come along later,' Trev said, 'and buy a nice slice of bacon.'

'What we've got is the best in town,' O'Shea said, 'so you wouldn't go wrong there.' He finished off his pint, placed the glass back on the counter, and wiped his wet lips with the palm of his hand. 'Ah, well,' he said, sighing, 'I'd better be off then. Can't have those fuckin' assistants of mine stickin' their hands in the till. I'll see you later, Trev.'

'It's a date, mate,' Trev said.

Feeling drunk and in a good mood, O'Shea reeled out of the smoky bar and turned right to make his way back up the Falls Road. It was busy at this time, with the shops still open and lots of people either walking home from work or packing the double-decker buses, the 'safe' taxis not being in such demand now that the Troubles had ended. Even now, before darkness, young men were loitering on street corners, furtively exchanging crack or Ecstasy for cash, and the whores, some of whom worked for O'Shea, were standing outside the pubs and betting shops as if waiting for boyfriends or husbands when in fact they were touting for custom. Occasionally the RUC would make a swoop on the area, hoping to pick up drug dealers and whores alike, but they only did it when pressured by some ambitious politician and for the most part they stayed well away, still viewing the Falls as a Catholic ghetto controlled by the IRA and, more recently, by its criminal elements, notably the Belfast Six. It was the same in Sandy Row, the Protestant heartland, nearby – the UDA was still highly active there, though their rackets too were now more blatantly criminal in their nature and intent.

Some day, O'Shea thought, *another war will break out between Sandy Row and the Falls, though this time it won't be over fuckin' politics – it'll be over territory and criminal profits. Sooner or later, one gang will rule this city and it has to be ours. If I stick with Neil Byrne and Shaun Keenan, I should be okay. Those two know what they're doing. Not like that mad bastard Hegarty, who could ruin the whole thing. He's already killed McCauley and Gallagher, so I'd better watch my own arse. You can't trust your own friends these days.*

His obscene thoughts were in no way reflected in his face as he made his way back up the Falls, greeting familiar faces and cracking jokes with the women and generally acting just like any other tradesman keeping in touch. He soon reached his butcher's shop, located just off the main road, and was pleased to see that his hard-faced young dickers were loitering about there. He nodded at them, looking severe, not wanting to be too friendly, thinking it healthy that they should fear him and not get too close; then he entered his butcher's shop where his assistants Dennis Riordan and Bill Fitzgerald, known as Laurel and Hardy because one was short and skinny, the other tall and fat, were still serving behind the counter, both wearing white coats and bloodstained aprons. They were nice lads and did a good job, so O'Shea greeted them affably.

'How's tricks, lads?' he asked. 'Any problems? Any phone calls?'

'We've done a nice bit of business,' Riordan replied, 'and there's been no phone calls.'

'No news is good news,' O'Shea replied, walking around the back of the counter to remove his white coat and apron from their hook on the wall and put them both on. 'Now why don't you lads knock off early and let me close shop?'

'Sure that's grand, boss,' Fitzgerald said, wiping his hands on a bloody rag. 'I could do with an early pint.'

'Your missus'll kill ya if ya have more than one,' O'Shea reminded him. 'An' don't stop at the bookies on yer way home. Ya know she hates that as well.'

'Not when I win,' Fitzgerald replied, taking off his apron. 'She's all over me then, boss.'

'They're all mercenary creatures at heart. Sure it's part of their charm.'

'You coulda fooled me,' Fitzgerald said as he and Riordan disappeared into the back room to wash themselves clean of blood and then put on their jackets. When they emerged, O'Shea was wearing his white apron and had started tidying up. He liked the lads to see him doing his bit. It was good politics, like.

'We'll be makin' tracks, boss,' Riordan said.

'See ya tomorrow morning,' Fitzgerald added.

'Aye, lads. Have a good night.'

It was fifteen minutes to closing time and O'Shea gave his attention to tidying up and serving his last-minute customers. He had always liked serving – it was a chance for some good crack – and he joked a lot with those who came in, sometimes slipping the less well-off a little bit extra and taking his pleasure from the profuse thanks he received.

Deciding to close up, he was just about to take off his apron when the Englishman, Trev Manning, walked in, saying, 'Christ, I thought I wasn't gonna make it. Have you still time to serve me?'

'Forgot, did ya? Hangin' over your pint?'

'You know what I'm like, Liam.'

'Sure I understand a man that likes his drinkin'. So what'll it be, lad?'

'A few rashers of bacon's all I want. But you're gonna be here all night if more customers come in.'

'Sure that's true enough, Trev. Hang on an' I'll close that blasted door and then we'll have peace, like.' O'Shea hurried

around the counter, closed and locked the front door, then
turned back to return to the counter and stopped dead in his
tracks. 'What the fuck—?' he began and then went silent: he'd
seen the SIG-Sauer pistol in the Englishman's hand.

The handgun was being held close to the waist and could
not be seen from outside.

'What the fuck's this?' O'Shea asked, feeling no fear at all,
only outrage. 'Don't tell me yer plannin' to rob the till. Sure
ya can't be that desp'rate, Trev.'

'Desperate enough to squeeze the trigger,' Trev replied. 'Now
go and pull down the blinds.'

'Don't be fuckin' stupid, lad. If you need help, just ask.
Robbin' me's just gonna bring ya grief. Think about what
yer doin'.'

'Go and pull down the blinds,' Trev repeated, his battered
workman's face as cold as ice, his dark eyes, normally so full of
mischief, now extremely intense. 'And don't trying signalling
to those dickers outside. If you do, you'll be dead.'

'I don't fuckin' believe this.'

'Just do as you're told. I've already taken the safety catch
off and I'll fire if I have to.'

'All right, fuck it, okay, I'll pull the blinds down.' O'Shea
went to the window to pull the blinds down, convinced that this
stupid bastard was going to rob him and then try to run for it.
He glanced into the street and saw the dickers standing about
there, smoking cigarettes and watching those who passed by,
though a few were looking straight at the shop to see him
framed by the window. He wanted to signal to them, let them
know what was happening, but he realized that he wouldn't be
able to do it without at least moving his head, which Manning
would see.

Was Manning bluffing? Would he actually shoot him? O'Shea
couldn't be sure. You could never be sure what an amateur
would do if you made him panic. Best to humour him, play
his game, keep him calm as long as possible. Let the dumb
bastard take the money and run and then, if he wasn't shot
down by the dickers, go after him later. Sighing, shaking his
head in disbelief, O'Shea pulled the blinds down.

'What now?' he asked.

'Turn around,' Manning said.

O'Shea turned around and saw the handgun still pointing
at him. 'Have you done this before, Trev?'

'Yes,' Manning replied.

'I thought you were just here to buy furniture for Petticoat Lane.'

'You thought wrong,' Manning said. 'Now why don't you walk into the back room without starting trouble?'

'Just take the money and go, boyo.'

'Don't fuckin' boyo me. Put your hands on your fuckin' head and turn around and walk into the back room. I'll be right behind you with this handgun in your ribs, so don't try anything smart.'

O'Shea was livid. This little bastard had betrayed him. He'd befriended him and bought him lots of drinks and now the wee shite was robbing him. He wanted to kill Trevor Manning, wanted to strangle him with his bare hands, but instead he did what he was told and put his hands on his head.

'You're gonna lock me up in there?'

'That's right,' Manning said.

'Have a heart, lad. It's fuckin' cold back there. Just take the money and run.'

'You'll be hollering for your dickers if I do that, so the back room it has to be. Now turn around and start walking.'

O'Shea did as he was told. He didn't really have a choice. 'How did ya know they were my dickers?' he asked as he walked towards the back room with his hands on his head. 'That's not the kind of information ya pick up when yer out buyin' furniture. Have you bin watching me, lad?'

'Every day for weeks,' Manning replied. 'I always do my homework.'

'Not for furniture.'

'No, not for that. Now walk into that room.'

O'Shea walked into the room. It was freezing cold in there. He stopped in the middle of the room and flicked his eyes left and right. It was the cold-storage room where slabs of meat hung from hooks and refrigerators were stacked against every wall. A meat cleaver was resting on a wooden bench streaked with dried blood. O'Shea contemplated diving for the cleaver, but decided against it. Manning might not really shoot him – on the other hand, he might – and if he did so, O'Shea would have died for the few quid in the till. He glanced left and right again, wondering what he should do, and realized that his only option was to let the wee shite lock him up. It wouldn't be that bad, after all. He wouldn't have to stay here long. There was a telephone on the wall behind one of the refrigerators and once Manning had left, he would use it to call a friend to let him out. He would be out of this place in half an hour at the latest, then he'd go and find Manning and splatter his scrambled brains across the pavement. Too fuckin' true, boyo.

'All right, lad,' he said, hoping to keep the Englishman calm. 'You can lock the door now.'

Those were the last words he uttered.

CHAPTER TWENTY-THREE

Burton was staring out to sea, trying to look beyond the grey haze on the horizon to where England lay. In fact, he was looking towards Scotland, but he tried not to think of that. He wanted to go home, see his children, make love to Deborah, but the job wasn't finished by a long shot and that day was a long way off.

'You're one of the rocks,' Cooney said from behind him. 'Sure you were standing in exactly the same place when I left you the last time. You were so still, you seemed not to be breathing and you looked like one of those rocks.'

Burton smiled slightly and turned to face him. 'Right now, I don't feel like a rock,' he said. 'More like a hollow shell. So how are you, Frank?'

'Grand,' Cooney said. 'Nothing much has changed in my life since I saw you two weeks ago. But I take it, from what I've been hearing, that you've been a busy wee boy.'

'What have you been hearing?'

'Michael Gallagher following Patrick McCauley into an early grave. And now Liam O'Shea. Found dead in his cold-storage room with a bullet in the back of his head. I don't suppose you'd know anything about that?'

'No,' Burton said, feeling uneasy at the thought of it, thinking of Rob, as 'Trevor Manning', marching O'Shea into that cold-storage room and shooting him in the back of the head at close range with a silenced SIG-Sauer P228 handgun. Burton had killed men himself, but usually in the heat of battle and though occasionally he'd had to do it at close range, it had never been like that – not a cold-blooded execution when a man's back was turned to him. It was necessary, of course – there had been no other way – but between Slim's shooting

of Gallagher, in bed with his male lover, and the execution of
O'Shea in that cold-storage room, Burton felt that they were
entering dark territory that could only degrade them. The
IRA had killed like that, and the UDA as well, but Burton
felt an awful sickness in his soul at the thought of doing the
same thing. The war in the province had always been dirty, a
degradation of decent soldiering, and these last two killings,
even more than the killing of McCauley, had the stench of the
charnel house. He wasn't sure that necessity justified it and
he felt deeply troubled.

'You don't know anything about it?'

'No,' Burton lied.

Cooney smiled. 'I bet. Neither does anyone else, it seems.
Sure no one even seems to know how it was pulled off. It's a
right wee mystery, like.'

'What do you mean, it's a mystery?'

'Who did it? And how? O'Shea's shop was well protected. His
dickers were outside, keeping their eye on the place, and yet
someone managed to get in there and shoot O'Shea and walk
out again without being touched. There's no way to get out
the back of Hegarty's shop, so his killer must have left by the
front door. How the hell did he do that?'

Burton shrugged. 'Why ask me, Frank?'

Cooney stared thoughtfully at him, smiling slightly, trying
to read his impassive face. 'Sure I'm just speculating.'

'Go ahead,' Burton said.

'The shop was closed when the shooting occurred. The door
was locked and the blinds were down. If anyone else, a stranger, had pulled the blinds down, the dickers would have seen
them, so it had to be O'Shea himself who did it.'

'At gunpoint,' Burton said.

'Right,' Cooney said. 'So someone entered the shop just as
O'Shea was about to close, made him close up at gunpoint,
and then took him into the back room and shot him – all of
that makes sense to me. What *doesn't* make sense is how they
could have walked out the front door after the killing without
being stopped by the dickers. At least, it doesn't make sense
unless the dickers recognized the man as someone who knew
O'Shea well and might have been invited in by him for a drink
in the back room.'

'That seems likely,' Burton said. 'If it wasn't one of the
dickers themselves, then it had to be someone they recognized

as one of O'Shea's friends – maybe another member of the
Belfast Six. Maybe someone like Hegarty.'

'I thought you'd get to him,' Cooney said. 'But if Hegarty had
turned against the others, as we believe, then he wouldn't have
been allowed near that shop.'

'I'm suggesting that Hegarty may have been responsible.
That doesn't necessarily mean he was the one who actually
went to the butcher's shop. He could have sent someone else
– someone believed at the time to be a friend of O'Shea's. In
that case, neither O'Shea nor his dickers would have been
suspicious.'

'It could have been you or one of your friends.'

'I deny that,' Burton said. 'It's certainly possible that I or one
of my friends could have walked into that shop as a customer;
but if O'Shea had pulled the blinds down with a stranger in
there, the dickers would have enquired. No, Frank, not us.'

It was another lie, of course, and Burton felt bad about
it. As Trevor Manning, English trader in cheap furniture,
Rob had spent the past few weeks making himself known
the length and breadth of the Falls. He had also befriended
O'Shea, drinking with him in his pub, and had therefore been
able to walk into his shop without raising the suspicions of
the dickers. Burton hadn't heard from Rob yet, but he knew
that he had killed O'Shea and then probably just walked
out of the shop, carrying a package in his hands as if he'd
bought something after the door was closed. The dickers,
knowing he was a friend of O'Shea's, would have thought
nothing of it.

'I'm taking anything you say with a pinch of salt,' Cooney
said. 'My bet is that you'd something to do with it, but I won't
press the point.'

'Good,' Burton said. 'So what's the word on the killing from
the Falls?'

'I feel like an ijit standing here,' Cooney said, 'and I can't
be away too long. Do you mind if we walk back to our cars?'

'Why not? Let's go.'

They turned away from the sea, which was windblown and
stormy, and started along the clifftop, heading back to the
start of the cliff walk. They had been having an unusually
hot July this year, but today the sky was low and steely grey,
with a cold wind blowing.

'The word on the streets is that a range war's in progress

between Hegarty and the others and that the former might've
been responsible for the death of O'Shea.'

'What about McCauley and Gallagher?'

'Hegarty's under suspicion for those as well.'

'Does the RUC think the same?'

'So far, yes.'

'What about Neil Byrne and Shaun Keenan?'

'They haven't responded so far, so I don't know what they
think. I'd assume that they'd blame Hegarty and certainly the
word's out that they're planning to get him. That's why there's
talk of a range war. Of course, they also think it might be the
Prods – the Sandy Row gangsters.'

'That's interesting,' Burton said.

'Right. The RUC has always feared that the Prod and Catholic gangs will eventually grow ambitious and turn against
each other in an attempt to take over the whole city. For
that reason, they think it's possible that the three killings
were done by the Prods as the beginning of a systematic
elimination of all the Belfast Six. The Prods have their own
gang lords, as you know, but they don't have a fancy name.
It's just one big gang, based in Sandy Row, but it covers all
the major Protestant areas. So the killings, no doubt about it,
have caused a great deal of confusion and mutual suspicion. If
you're responsible, then you've done a good job so far – though
I know you're not gonna confess to that. I know you don't go
to confession, being a wee English Protestant.'

Burton smiled slightly, but otherwise revealed nothing.
'I'm not concerned with the Prods,' he said. 'They're just as
vicious as the Belfast Six, but they're not nearly as organized – nor as big – and if the gangs in the Falls can be
defeated, then the Sandy Row boys will fall as well. For
that reason, I have to concentrate on the three remaining
members of the Belfast Six. I have to know what they're
planning and what their movements are. And for that, I
need someone inside. Have you come up with a name for
me?'

'A possibility,' Cooney said.

Burton stopped walking and glanced down at the sea. He
was looking at the tourists on the stepping stones of the
Giants' Causeway, but Cooney knew that he wasn't really
seeing them – that he was looking inside himself. The wind
was blowing just as fiercely here, but it didn't bother Burton.

He was used to operating in all kinds of weather and his concentration was fierce.

'She's a whore,' Cooney said. 'Her name's Teresa Kiely. She's only twenty-two, but I suspect she's had a rough life and she's exceptionally mature for her age. She's also a looker and was running a high-class trade, mainly working the bars of good hotels and being pretty selective.'

'*Was*,' Burton responded immediately. 'You used the past tense. Is she off the game now?'

Cooney sighed and shook his head. 'No, she hasn't given it up. She's just lost her independence. She was pursued by Jack Hegarty, who wanted his fat cut, and when she tried to turn him down he smashed into her place and worked her over until she gave in. Now she's back on the game, but as his hooker, and she deeply resents that. She's frightened of him, but she hates him enough to maybe help you get rid of him.'

They turned away from the sea and started walking again, leaving Weir's Snout well behind them and heading for the Visitors' Centre, with its neat white-walled buildings. Burton glanced left and right, at the green fields and then the sea, feeling that he might as well be on the dark side of the moon, beyond all hope of returning. He felt divorced from himself, denuded of moral values, and wondered if he had made a big mistake in returning to Belfast. This operation was turning into a quagmire that was sucking him down. The light was dimming around him.

'Have you talked to her?' he asked.

'Not much,' Cooney replied. 'I only said that I might be able to help her. I said I'd talk to someone. She didn't ask any questions.'

'Do you think she can get in there?'

'She's already in there with Hegarty. That bastard has practically moved into her apartment and he keeps her enslaved.'

'What does that mean?'

'At first he just used her sexually, but now he's starting to hold his meetings at her place and she's always present. He likes her to be seen. He sometimes makes her service the guests. From what I gather, some of those guests are quite important and they talk serious business. If you can persuade her to pass on what she hears, you could come up with gold dust.'

'Do you think I can do that?'

'Persuade her?'

'Yes.'

'I think she hates Hegarty enough to risk a lot in getting rid of him, but what you want could endanger her life and I don't know if she'll go that far. She's smart and tough and resourceful, but she's also pretty damned scared. She knows that Hegarty wouldn't hesitate to kill her – and that's the danger you'll place her in. In short, I don't know how she'll respond, but she's the best bet you've got.'

They were now approaching the Visitors' Centre, where the cars were parked on smooth green lawns, and Burton, still feeling remote from himself, was wondering how he could do this. He was going to ask a woman already degraded to degrade herself even more. This was something he could not justify to himself, nor to Deborah, nor to the kids when they grew up. It was something so sordid, so alien to his nature, that it might scar him more than the killing of that child all those years ago. Yet he knew that there was no other way and that he had to proceed.

'Is she Catholic?'

'Yes.'

'That might put her on their side.'

'I don't know the reason, but I can certainly confirm that she despises the hard men of both sides and has no time for the politics of either.'

'Are you sure?'

'Yes. This is an unusual whore. She looks like a million dollars and dresses very high-class, but she talks as rough as any man you'd meet and there's something hidden about her. I think it's something in her past – something to do with the Troubles – and whatever it is, she still hasn't forgotten it, though she won't talk about it.'

'This could have some relevance,' Burton said. 'Have you any ideas?'

'She hates all the paramilitaries – even those on her own side – so I suspect some kind of punishment when she was younger, from some of that breed. Maybe a tar-and-feathering. That used to be pretty common. You know? A young girl gets involved with the wrong man, maybe a soldier, maybe a Prod, and so they drag her out onto the street, tie her to a lamp-post, shave her head and then tar-and-feather her, to make an example out of her. Maybe something like that. With her looks – and she really is a stunner – I'd say it's something like that. But there's no question – no doubt about it at all – that she despises the paramilitaries of both sides and, even more, the ones who've now turned into gangsters. As for that bastard Hegarty, she hates him with a passion, so whatever she decides in the end regarding you, religion won't even come into it, believe me. You're on pretty safe ground there.'

They were reaching the end of their walk and Burton, turning back to catch a final glimpse of the distant, eerie rocks known as the Chimney Tops, again thought of the dark side of the moon and its pitiless wastelands. He wanted to escape from here, to return to the real world, to wash himself clean in the arms of his wife and take succour from the innocence of his children. He wanted not to have to make a potentially lethal decision about this whore with the name of a saint. His stomach churned at the thought of it.

'I don't like to have to do this,' he confessed, 'but I don't have a choice.'

'Sure I know that,' Cooney replied. 'In your business, you have to do what you have to do even if you don't like it. I wouldn't help you if I didn't know that. It's not something I like myself.'

'That only makes me feel worse.'

'Don't let it. I didn't say it for that. I'm just saying that I know you wouldn't do it if you could think of another way.'

'I still feel bad – unclean. I can't help feeling that I'm going to be worse than a pimp because I'll not only be degrading the woman further; I'll be risking her life.'

'That's a risk you've got to take. If she agrees, if she decides to take that chance, look at it through her eyes. What's she got now? Nothing more than hell on earth. She's been tortured by that bastard, she's used as his sex slave, and now he's even turned her flat into a brothel for the worst of his bad friends. She's told me a bit about that and it isn't nice, believe me. He has friends who like to do things to women that you and I can't imagine. She has to do just what they tell her, no matter how bad it is. Some of 'em, she says, want to do things that are painful and dangerous. We're talking total abasement here. That woman's treated as raw meat. She has no life of her own any more and she's already in danger. Hegarty threatens her all the time. He slaps her around just for fun. She knows that he'd kill her without thinking twice and that

it wouldn't take much to make him do it. She's in the hands
of a madman and she knows it, so she's little to lose. For that
reason, I think she just might do it. Talk to her and see.'

'I will,' Burton said. 'Will you fix up the meeting?'

'Sure that's why I'm here. I'll ring you at the number in
Antrim when I've seen her again.'

'You won't be able to be there,' Burton said. 'I have to do
this alone.'

'I don't *want* to be there,' Cooney replied. 'The less *I* know
the better. Well, here we are.'

They were back in the car park near the Visitors' Centre. A
busload of tourists was milling about the shop and tea room,
but Burton, when he checked, saw no one who looked out of
place. He was always looking for someone.

Paranoia, he thought.

'So,' he said, 'I'll expect a call soon. Thanks for everything,
Frank.'

'Sure you've nothing to thank me for.'

Burton opened the car door, slipped into the driver's seat,
strapped himself in and turned on the ignition. He was about
to take off when Cooney indicated that he wanted to say
something else. Burton rolled the window down.

'Is there any way of protecting her?' Cooney asked.

'No,' Burton said.

He gunned the engine and drove off.

CHAPTER TWENTY-FOUR

'McCauley, Gallagher and O'Shea,' Byrne said tightly, facing Shaun Keenan across their usual table in the upstairs room of O'Donovan's pub. 'Now there are only two of us left – not counting that bastard Hegarty. We've got to put a stop to him.'

'It may not *be* Hegarty,' Shaun Keenan responded, gently swirling the whiskey in his glass and studying it like a fortune teller trying to divine the future from tea leaves.

'You mean the Prods?'

'Exactly. Those former UDA bastards in the Sandy Row gangs have been gradually creeping towards our turf, so a war between them and us is almost pre-ordained. They know that as well, so they could be the ones who jumped in first.'

Byrne always thought of the Sandy Row gangs with a mixture of contempt and wary respect because, as Keenan had just reminded him, they were mostly former UDA hard men and that meant they were bad. The criminal activities of the Provisional IRA had never sat easily with Byrne, but he consoled himself with the fact that the paramilitaries' drift towards crime had begun with those vicious bastards of the UDA. Formed in 1972 in the wake of Catholic outrage over internment and the Bloody Sunday massacre, the Ulster Defence Association was a Loyalist paramilitary group that soon became responsible for some of the most vicious activities of the period. With the RUC and the British Army helpfully turning a blind eye, the hooded and uniformed men of the UDA engaged in massive harassment, beating-up and intimidation of Catholics, forcing many of them out of their homes. Shortly after the emergence of the UDA, the Loyalists embarked on a campaign of random assassinations of and atrocities against

Catholics that shocked even the Protestants with their wanton savagery: a woman raped several times at gunpoint in front of her mentally retarded son before she and the child were shot, with only the unfortunate mother surviving; a Catholic UDR man tortured, branded with a red-hot iron, stabbed and eventually shot dead; a Catholic man hung up by the arms, stabbed about a hundred and fifty times all over the body, then eventually strangled; other men hacked to death with knives; and one so badly tortured with a blow-lamp that his hands and feet were almost burnt off. Most of these and similar outrages were widely viewed as the work of the UDA. By the end of that first year, the organization had been heavily infiltrated by gangsters and petty criminals and was involved in extortion, protection rackets and intimidation through violence, including beatings, shootings and bombings in Protestant areas. It was some of those same rogue Protestants, albeit now much older, who were presently running the criminal gangs of Sandy Row. Almost certainly, Byrne reasoned, they had cast covetous eyes at the territory of the Belfast Six; but he still doubted that they had made their move yet. He still thought it was Hegarty.

'It wasn't the Prods,' he said. 'I'm convinced of that, Shaun. Sure they'd like to take over, but we're still too strong for them an' I don't think they'd have risked the assassination of three of our top men. Besides, whoever killed O'Shea, in particular, got into his shop and waltzed out again through the front door, unmolested. I don't believe a Prod from Sandy Row could have managed that. It had to be one of our own kind.'

'Which gets us back to Hegarty,' Keenan said in his pragmatic English way.

'Right,' Byrne said. 'It had to be him. He turned against us and he knew we'd go for him, so he got in real quick, like. He's the bastard who did it.'

'I don't agree,' Keenan said. 'Given that we've told our dickers to watch out for that bastard – and O'Shea's dickers would have been told the same – I don't think that Hegarty could have waltzed in and out without being stopped.'

'It didn't have to be him personally,' Byrne insisted. 'It could have been one of his men. Not a dicker known to us – someone else. Someone local but not known as Hegarty's friend. That could explain it.'

'That's a possibility,' Keenan said, 'but how do we find out?'

'We pick that fucker up,' Byrne said, 'and ask him some questions.'

'That may not be easy, Neil.'

'We can do it,' Byrne said.

He and Keenan had been friends for years, maturing together through the Troubles and initiating the Belfast Six after peace was declared, but Byrne still thought of Keenan as the oddest candidate for the Provos that he'd ever known. Born of middle-class Irish landowners, educated at Trinity College and now married with three children, he divided his time between his big house on the Knockbreda Road, where his wife and kids resided, and his even grander family house with extensive gardens in Castleblaney, County Monaghan, just across the border from Antrim. His parents, both staunch Republicans, had died many years ago, but they had left a large inheritance and the country estate, when not being used by Keenan, was looked after by a married couple and a part-time gardener. Keenan, therefore, lived like a minor lord; and yet, though no socialist, was the member of the Belfast Six still most dedicated to the fight for Ireland's freedom.

Byrne thought of this with a certain amount of shame because he too had been dedicated to the fight for Ireland's freedom – or, at least, the fight against Protestant rule in Northern Ireland – and he had joined the Provos because they believed in direct action instead of slow political manoeuvring. However, somewhere along the line, the Provos, faced with the criminal activities of Loyalist groups like the UDA, had gone the same route and Byrne had been sucked into a mire of similar operations, including extortion and intimidation in his own community. By the time peace came, in 1995, he and others like him were so deeply involved in crime, so completely in charge of their own turfs in the Catholic ghettoes, that the formation of the Belfast Six seemed inevitable. Nevertheless, Byrne often felt himself yearning for the collapse of the political peace, if only to help him justify to himself what he was presently doing. He often wondered if Keenan felt the same way, but he had never dared ask him.

'We have to talk to him,' Keenan eventually replied in his thoughtful manner, 'if for no other reason than that our friends in the United States have been informed of the killings and have called to ask what the hell's going on.'

'Who called?'

'Mister Brady.'

'What did you tell him?'

'The truth: that we don't yet know who's responsible.'

'And how did our Irish-American friend respond?'

'He wasn't amused,' Keenan said. 'He and his friends – hopefully, our friends also – are worried that the Prod gangs will take the killings as a sign of internal strife in our organization and decide to attack us at our weakest moment, in order to take over the whole of Belfast.'

'Sure they might do just that,' Byrne agreed.

'Correct,' Keenan said. 'The only thing stopping them at the moment is their knowledge that we *do* have the backing of the Irish-American gangs, which is something that they, as Protestants, don't have.'

'Damned right,' Byrne said, grinning. 'The Orange State may be based on Protestant privilege, but that doesn't work in America. God bless the United States.'

'Nevertheless,' Keenan said, green gaze steady, smile slight, 'our Irish-American friends are concerned that the Prods might think we're fighting each other—'

'Which we are,' Byrne interjected.

'—and so they want us to find out who's responsible and put a stop to them.'

'Which gets us back to Hegarty again.'

'I guess so,' Keenan said.

Leaning back in his chair and lighting a cigarette, Byrne realized that he had been talking about the deaths of McCauley, Gallagher and O'Shea as pragmatically as Keenan usually talked about his long-term aims for the organization. He was quietly shocked by the realization that he had felt nothing at the deaths, other than rage at the thought that Hegarty might have been the perpetrator. There had been a time when Byrne felt real grief at the death of PIRA comrades, and yet these three recent murders hadn't touched him. Was this a sign that he simply hadn't cared for those men or that he was now completely hardened to the fate of his comrades, even of those closest to him? He then thought of Hegarty, who might have arranged the killings, and realized that he had always despised him not only because he was mad, but because he was as mindlessly violent as those Loyalists who had committed so many atrocities during the Troubles and were hardly less barbaric now.

Byrne had always felt distinctly uneasy about his own part in the various forms of intimidation required to keep first the PIRA, then the Belfast Six in command of the Catholic ghettoes; but he had been able to justify the 'punishments' as necessary. Hegarty, however, had not restricted himself to ritualistic kneecappings or straightforward, mercifully quick executions, but had, just like the Loyalists, resorted increasingly to lingering, often gruesome torture before putting the final bullet in the back of his tormented victim's head. Byrne secretly despised himself for letting Hegarty get away with it on the grounds that he was only doing it on his own turf. In fact, what Hegarty was doing was much worse than mere intimidation or punishment – and Byrne now understood, with a shock that chilled his soul, that he had ignored it because Hegarty's bestiality made his own actions seem less vile by comparison. He had used Hegarty to blind himself to his own sins and to help him live with himself. This knowledge now pierced his heart like an ice-pick and left a numbness within. He wondered how he could live with this.

'So let's get that bastard Hegarty,' he said, 'and make him squeal like a stuck pig. Let's put an end to it.'

'If we can,' Keenan replied.

Byrne was just about to make a retort when Keenan's trusted lieutenant, Gerry Lenihan, entered the room, flicking his long dark hair out of his eyes, scratching at his thick moustache, and looking as dishevelled as always in his black leather jacket, red tee-shirt and blue denims. Byrne was surprised to see that Gerry's hand was resting on the handle of the pistol holstered in the cross-draw position just behind his waist, as if he was preparing to use it. That made Byrne sit forward in his chair and do exactly the same.

'What is it?' Keenan asked.

'We've got Hegarty downstairs,' Lenihan replied.

'What?' Byrne asked, leaning forward even farther in his chair, hardly able to believe what he was hearing.

'Sure ya heard me right, Mister Byrne.' Lenihan returned his attention to Keenan. 'He came here of his own accord, boss. Says he wants to speak to youse both about somethin' urgent. We stopped him comin' up – drew our handguns an' frisked him – he wasn't carryin' any weapon – an' then he said to tell ya that if what he says doesn't satisfy ya, sure ya can put a fuckin' bullet in his brain and bring 'im down in a pine box.

Two of the boyos have 'im covered in the back room and want
to know what to do – bring 'im up or douse his fuckin' lights?
So what is it, boss?'

Catching Keenan's enquiring gaze, Byrne said, 'He's got a
fuckin' nerve comin' here, but at least now we've got him.'

'He wouldn't have come here if he didn't have good cause to
think he'd walk out in one piece. That means he has something
to tell us.' Keenan turned to Lenihan. 'You better bring him
up, Gerry.'

'Okay, boss, I'll do that.'

As Lenihan's footsteps retreated back down the stairs,
Keenan turned to Byrne and said, 'This should be interesting.'

'It better be,' Byrne retorted.

A few seconds later, they heard a door slamming downstairs,
then heavier footsteps coming up the stairs, followed by lighter
ones. Arriving at the top of the stairs, Hegarty entered the
room, breathing heavily, like an animal, followed by Lenihan
and another dicker, both of whom were covering him with
Czech-75 handguns. Stopping by the table, just beside Keenan,
looking across at Byrne, he said, 'Those two pricks have
already frisked me an' found I was clean. And sure I wouldn't
be here if I wanted to give youse a headache. I've got somethin'
to say and I've got the right to say it in private.'

Byrne glanced at Keenan, who turned to his men. 'Okay,
you can leave now.' When the two men had left the room, he
turned back to Hegarty. 'Okay, what is it?'

'McCauley, Gallagher and O'Shea,' Hegarty replied, shaking
his head from side to side in denial. 'I didn't do 'em. Not a single
one of 'em. If I'd done 'em, I wouldn't have come here on my
own. I'm as clean as a whistle.'

'If you didn't, who did?' Byrne asked bluntly.

Hegarty nodded at the bottle on the table. 'Is that whiskey
yer drinkin'?'

'Yes,' Keenan said.

'Sure can I sit down an' have one?'

Keenan nodded. 'Of course.'

Hegarty pulled up a chair and sat down and poured himself
a stiff drink. He had a good swallow, then placed the glass
back on the table and wiped his lips with the back of his big
hand. His breathing filled out the silence.

'I knew you two bastards would suspect me,' he said, 'so I

did a little bit of homework on m'own. Knowin' that O'Shea's hard men wouldn't threaten me with him bein' dead an' all, I drove down to his shop an' found his boyos still hangin' about like limp dicks at a weddin', doubtless wonderin' what they were gonna do with no one to take orders from. They all recognized me, of course, an' were very respec'ful, tippin' their hats and grovelin', hopin' to work for me, an' so I asked if anyone of 'em had been on guard the night of the shootin'. Naturally, they all grew cagey, so I said never mind, you boyos can work for me now, an' then I picked a couple as personal bodyguards and told them to hop in my car. The buckijits fell for it and I had one of 'em drive me back to my garage with the other boyo sittin' in the back, pleased as punch with himself.'

Hegarty picked up his glass of whiskey, had a drink, then put the glass down and wiped his lips with the palm of his hand.

'Once inside the garage,' he continued, 'with the doors closed and locked an' my own dickers standin' guard, I asked those boyos again if they'd been on guard outside O'Shea's durin' the evenin' of the shootin'. When they denied it, I had my boyos go to work on 'em and soon one of 'em was yelpin' that his mate had been one of those on duty that evenin' and his mate beside 'im, hearin' that, sobbed like a babe an' confessed that it was true. I let the first one go an' then asked the second if he'd seen anyone leave O'Shea's shop at the time of the shootin' an' though at first he denied it – he was obviously fearful he'd be punished for dereliction of duty – he soon changed his tune and started whistlin' about an Englishman, some kind of furniture salesman, who'd befriended O'Shea over the past few weeks and who'd entered the shop that evenin' just before closin' time. O'Shea locked the front door just after the Englishman entered, then pulled the blinds down, an' then a few minutes later, the Englishman came back out. The dicker thought that it had to be him – that the Englishman did it.'

Shocked by the implication of what he was hearing, wondering if it could be true, Byrne glanced at Keenan and saw a fleeting shadow cross his normally impassive face, though it was gone almost as soon as Byrne saw it. Troubled to see even this brief display of emotion in his friend, Byrne turned his gaze back on Hegarty and asked, 'Why didn't the dickers think it suspicious that the front door was closed

and the blinds were pulled down just after the Englishman
entered?'

'Sure it was well known that O'Shea often liked to entertain
his friends behind closed doors after closin' time – a few drinks
an' a wee bit of crack, like – and he'd always pull the blinds
down when he did it. He an' the Englishman were friends, so
the dickers didn't think it unusual when the Limey went in
there. Sure they assumed he'd just gone in to buy a bit of
meat and have maybe a quick drink in the back room. When
he came back out, he was carryin' a parcel in his hand an' they
assumed it was wrapped meat. In fact, someone had heard him
an hour or so earlier in Leary's pub tellin' O'Shea he'd drop in
for some slices of bacon. So it all seemed very nat'ral, like.
But that Englishman, he's the bastard yer after. It isn't me,
boyos.'

Feeling as if some dark shadow had moved in over him,
Byrne extinguished his cigarette, emptied his lungs of smoke
and stared steadily at Keenan. His friend's lean, pale face was
impassive and his green gaze remained opaque. Byrne turned
back to Hegarty. 'What else did the dicker tell you about this
Englishman?'

'Not much. Sure I didn't ask much. I've just finished
questionin' him an' I thought you might not believe me,
so I came straight around here to see you. He's still in my
garage, trussed up like a turkey, an' I'd like you to hear it
from his own lips, so you'll have t'come with me.'

Byrne stared thoughtfully at him, wondering if this was a
trap, but Hegarty, obviously reading his mind, grinned and
shook his head from side to side. 'Sure I know what yer
thinkin' an' it isn't that at all. I'm not after you two. If an
Englishman's involved in this, then it's bigger than all of us
an' we're gonna need each other to tackle it. If yer still worried,
bring yer dickers along. Ya'll walk out of there safe enough.'

'Let's go,' Keenan said.

He led the way downstairs, with Hegarty behind him and
Byrne bringing up the rear. Still not sure that Hegarty was
on the level, Byrne nodded at the two dickers in the pub
below, Gerry Lenihan and Tom Farrell, to fall in behind them.
Hegarty's garage was only a few blocks back up the Falls, but
during the short walk, Byrne could not take his eyes off the
unshuttered shop windows crammed with goods, the many
pedestrians walking freely on the pavements, and the many

men entering and leaving bookies and pubs. It reminded him all too vividly of how different it had been during the Troubles. At that time the streets had been blocked off with British Army checkpoints manned by grim-faced soldiers in DPM clothing, heavy fragmentation vests with protective groin panels, steel helmets with chin protectors and eyeshades, all of them armed with a wide variety of rifles, sub-machine guns, CS gas canisters, shields and truncheons. At the same time, the roads had been filled with other soldiers in Shoreland armoured cars fitted with Browning heavy machine-guns or with paddy wagons and 'cage' vans driven by flak-jacketed, heavily armed RUC officers. Byrne could still clearly recall August 1969, when an Orange march past the Unity Flats led to violent rioting that lasted for three days and led to the mobilization of the dreaded, exclusively Protestant B Specials. That riot was followed by the equally violent seige of the Catholic bogside in Derry when CS gas was used for the first time in Ireland. Though only a teenager, Byrne had been present when, ten days after the Unity Flats riots, people in his area were forced to raise makeshift barricades as angry mobs of Loyalists, including mobilized B Specials armed with rifles, revolvers and sub-machine guns, surged down the side streets towards the Falls, attacking and burning Catholic houses. Eventually, the mobs were driven back by armed IRA men, including Byrne's father, but not before the RUC had fired their machine-guns into the Divis Flats, killing a nine-year-old boy, and not before the Prods had burned out most of the Falls.

During those riots, five Catholics and one Protestant died, 150 Catholic homes were burnt out, internment was reintroduced and twenty-four men were arrested. However, even with the presence of British troops in the streets, the riots continued and by the end of September many more had died and nearly two thousand families, most of them Catholic, had been forced to flee from their homes. Though the riots were quelled, they erupted again repeatedly over the next two years and in July 1971, after 2,000 British troops were used in a series of dawn raids on Republican homes throughout the North, Byrne's father was one of those arrested and incarcerated in the Crumlin Road prison. Freed a few weeks later, he turned up at his home dreadfully pale, underweight, badly bruised, to recount harrowing tales of how he and his fellow prisoners had been routinely beaten up, forced to run barefoot across glass-strewn ground between rows of British army troops hammering at them with batons, and had even been blindfolded, dumped on the floor of a helicopter, and then threatened with being thrown out in mid-flight. Hearing such stories from his father, the teenage Byrne, already hating the British, came to hate them even more.

When it became apparent that the British Army was on the side of the Loyalists and that the IRA was still in favour of negotiation, thousands of angry young Catholics flocked to join the Provisional IRA. Byrne was one of them. Though aware of his father's experience during his incarceration in Crumlin Road jail, he still wasn't prepared for the shock of his own imprisonment in Long Kesh where he was held for seven days, in complete isolation and with a hood over his head. While there, and still hooded, he was repeatedly, severely beaten, given practically no food, prevented from sleeping, tormented by 'white' noise, and constantly interrogated while being forced to stand spreadeagled against a wall until he collapsed. He emerged from the experience a much hardened, more cynical man, with his hatred for the Protestants and the British 'invaders' made concrete. When he returned to his work for the PIRA, or the 'Provos', he did so with cold-blooded ferocity and never looked back.

Now, as he hurried along the busy Falls Road between Hegarty and Keenan, with the latter's two armed dickers keeping watch behind them, he realized that, though most of the British Army had gone home and the RUC was now keeping a low profile, this was still a city at war and he was one of its causes. Now, however, as he realized with deepening cynicism, it was not a war against the Prods or the Brits, but against his own kind. It was a war designed solely for profit and it was out of control. Byrne knew that there was no turning back, but this was no consolation.

'Here we are,' Hegarty growled.

They had arrived at Hegarty's notorious garage, located in a square-shaped, rubbish-strewn, walled-in space at the end of an alley behind a street of grim terraced houses. The garage was a good distance away from the back yards of the nearest houses – far enough away, Byrne judged, to ensure that nothing going on inside the garage could be heard when the steel doors were closed. Right now, a bunch of

dickers, mostly bovver-booted skinheads, were keeping watch
in the afternoon's fading light, with their customary sneers
of contempt changing instantly to grovelling obsequiousness
when the fiercely glaring Hegarty marched up to them.

'Everything quiet in there?' he asked.

'Ackay, Mister Hegarty,' the boldest dicker replied, scratching
his pimply face and exposing bad teeth in a wolfish grin.
'With that bit of rag stuffed in his gob, he can't make too
much noise.'

'Good,' Hegarty said. 'Now stay out here and keep yer fuckin'
eyes peeled.'

'Will do, Mister Hegarty.'

Hegarty pulled the steel doors far enough apart to let Byrne
and Keenan enter. When they had done so, he closed the doors
behind them, forcing them to adjust to the gloom inside.

Byrne, who had not been here before, saw that the garage
was still filled with repair equipment, though most of it was
stacked around the walls to make a cleared space on the
concrete floor. At the end of that cleared space, a long table
had been placed on a couple of wooden pallets, raising it off
the ground as if on a low stage. In the middle of the cleared
space, lying on his side on the concrete floor, was a teenage
dicker. He was lying on his side because his hands had been
tied together behind his back and trussed to his bovver-booted
feet, also tied together. A rag had been stuffed into his mouth,
to prevent him from screaming, and Byrne noted that it was
soaked with the blood that had spilled from his split lips.

'You've worked him over,' Byrne said.

'Damned right,' Hegarty replied.

'He told you about the Englishman before you worked him
over, so why did you have to do that to him?'

'Sure I wanted to see if he'd say the same thing under torture
– and he did. He stuck to it.'

'Jesus Christ!' Byrne exclaimed in disgust.

Before he could say or do anything rash, Keenan stepped
between him and Hegarty. 'All right, let's forget about that
for now. Just take the gag out of his mouth and untie him.
Let's hear what he has to say.'

'Right. I'm with you, Shaun.' Hegarty leaned down, raised
his index finger to his lips to indicate that the dicker should
make no sound, then removed the gag. The dicker gasped for
breath and then coughed a few times, but he didn't scream

and he didn't say a word. Hegarty then untied his hands and
feet, letting him roll over onto his back to stretch his cramped
arms and legs gratefully. A small, helpless moan escaped his
lips, but again he said nothing.

'Sit up,' Hegarty said. Wincing with pain, the boy did as he
was told. 'Now stand up,' Hegarty said. When the boy had
clambered painfully to his feet, Keenan nodded at Byrne.

Stepping out in front of Hegarty, until he was face to face
with the blood-smeared young dicker, Byrne stood very close
to him and stared steadily at him. Tears had streaked the boy's
gaunt face and dried blood had caked around his swollen, split
lips. He sniffed and breathed nervously.

'You know who I am?' Byrne asked him.

'Ackay, Mister Byrne.'

'Good. Now tell me exactly what you told Mister Hegarty
about the night of the shooting. Who went in and came out
again?'

Obviously still terrified, imagining that he was about to be
killed, the boy repeated his story. It matched Hegarty's report
in every detail. He confirmed that O'Shea had been seen in
Leary's pub with the Englishman that same afternoon and
that one of those present had heard the Englishman state
that he might drop around later to the shop for a couple of
slices of bacon.

'So when we saw him enter the shop that evenin',' the boy
said at the end of his recital, 'we weren't too surprised, like.'

'Do you know the Englishman's name?' Byrne asked him.

'No. We were never allowed into Leary's pub when Mister
O'Shea went in there – we always had to keep watch outside.
We only knew the Englishman by sight because he often came
out with Mister O'Shea and he gave us the wink, like, and
told us not to bother the Englishman – that he was kind of
a mate, like. So, you know, we were never bothered when
we saw the Englishman around. He was Mister O'Shea's
friend.'

'O'Shea never mentioned his name?'

'No. He just made jokes about him. Like, he'd call him that
dumb wee English shite or that funny wee bastard. An' he
told us the Englishman was okay and we weren't to worry
about him.'

'Would anyone in Leary's pub know the Englishman's name?'

'Ackay, Mister Byrne. Sure they're bound to, aren't they?

The Englishman boozed there a lot – with and without Mister O'Shea – so they'd all know his name, like.'

'Any idea what this Englishman was doing in the Falls?'

'I can't say for certain, Mister Byrne, but Mister O'Shea used to joke a lot about how the Englishman was dumb enough to believe that the worthless furniture he was buyin' in the Falls could be sold for a lot across the water . . . Sure he'll lose his socks on that furniture, Mister O'Shea would say. That shows how dumb the wee cunt is . . . But he thought the Englishman was good for a laugh, like, so he didn't mind that.'

'How long has this Englishman been hanging around the Falls?' Byrne asked.

'A couple of months, maybe less. No more than that, though.'

'Any idea where he lives?'

'No. But they might know that in Leary's pub as well – along with his name, like.'

'You know anything else about him, boyo?'

'No, Mister Byrne.'

'You're sure?'

'Swear to God, Mister Byrne, that's all I know. Sure I'd swear on the Bible.'

Byrne studied him for a moment and realized, from the pleading in his bright gaze, that he was telling the truth.

'What's your name?' he asked.

'Tommy McBride.'

'What are you planning to do, now that Mister O'Shea's dead?'

'Dunno, Mister Byrne.'

'You want t'come and work for me?'

The boy's eyes brightened with relief and excitement. 'Ackay, Mister Byrne! Sure that would be grand!'

'Report to me tomorrow morning at nine – not at my home – in my office at the taxi rank in the Falls.'

'Great, Mister Byrne. But what about . . . ?'

'I'll tell my other dickers to expect you.'

'That's grand, Mister Byrne.'

'Okay, get yer wee arse out of here.'

'Ackay, Mister Byrne!'

When the boy had rushed out, practically sobbing with relief, Byrne turned to face Keenan and Hegarty. 'If the English are involved in this,' he said, 'we're in really deep shit.'

'We have to find that fuckin' Englishman,' Hegarty said.

'He buys and sells furniture,' Keenan said, 'and does his drinking at Leary's.'

'Let's start there,' Byrne said.

United once more by this potential disaster, they left the garage together and went to look for the Englishman.

CHAPTER TWENTY-FIVE

Signing into the Europa Hotel, proffering his false passport, Burton felt that all eyes were upon him. He knew that this was only imagination, but the uncomfortable feeling persisted as he chatted to the desk clerk, letting him know that he was only here for one night and was looking for a good time. Deliberately avoiding an American accent, he made it clear that he was an English computer programmer resident in Los Angeles and here to sell new computer games to the Irish. Once signed in, he glanced around the busy lobby, saw that no one was studying him, then followed the bellhop across to the elevator. As they were carried up to the fifth floor, Burton joked with the bellhop, saying the city seemed livelier since he'd last been here and asking him where the action was these days. When the kid blushed and said that he didn't really know, that he couldn't afford it himself, Burton grinned and slapped him on the back. Once inside his room, he tipped the kid handsomely, told him to have a good day and walked him back to the door. When the door had finally closed behind the bellhop, Burton sighed with relief.

Going to the window, he looked down and saw an endless stream of buses and cars racing along Great Victoria Street, past the Crown Liquor Saloon on the other side. Burton knew that famous bar from past experience. When he had last been here, working undercover for the British Army's 14th Intelligence Unit, he had met his touts, informers and other friends there to trade information. Now, however, he had no wish to relive old memories and had to concentrate instead on making himself known to the staff of the hotel. To this end, he made a call to Room Service and asked them to send up a bottle of Bushmill's, a continental breakfast and the morning newspaper. When these were delivered, he handsomely tipped in cash after signing the bill.

Satisfied that the man from Room Service would, like the bellhop, talk about the Englishman from New York who was looking for a good time and ordered Bushmill's with his breakfast, he sat on the bed and withdrew a Browning 9mm High Power handgun from his overnight bag. He had no thought of using it, but he couldn't be too careful now that he was in this hotel where many former UDA and PIRA members met. This, in fact, was what had him intrigued about the prostitute, Teresa Kiely, even before he met her. When Frank Cooney had phoned him in Antrim to say that Teresa wanted to meet him in her usual haunt, the bar of the Europa Hotel, Burton had thought she must be going mad.

'No, she isn't,' Cooney had explained over the phone. 'She says she's now followed everywhere by Hegarty's men, so if she meets you at any of your normal meeting places, you'll both be picked up. Her suggestion, therefore, is that you approach her as a potential trick in the Europa Hotel and then arrange for her to come up to your room. You'll both be watched, of course, but if you play it right, Hegarty's men will assume you're a routine trick and Teresa will, of course, come back down those stairs with the money she earned, so you won't be suspected.'

Obliged to admire the whore's intelligence, Burton also had to give a nod to her courage, since what she was doing, no matter how clever, was still highly dangerous. Cooney had said that she was a tough, resourceful lady and that seemed to be true.

After loading and checking the 9-Milly, he holstered it and then positioned it practically behind his back where it was hidden by the loose shirt that he had deliberately left dangling over his pants. To encourage the hotel staff to think he was drinking his bottle of Bushmill's at eleven in the morning, he poured half the bottle down the sink, left the remaining half uncorked on his bedside cabinet, then spent the next hour finishing his continental breakfast and reading the newspaper. Shortly after noon, he put a corduroy jacket on over his loose shirt, checked that the shirt was pulled well down over the holstered handgun, then left the room and took the lift down to the first floor, where he entered the bar frequented by Teresa Kiely. He was not expecting to see her at this time of the day, but over a couple of whiskies he made himself known to the red-haired, freckle-faced barman, Jim Quaid, and emphasized that he was only here for one night and was out for a good time. When Jim asked him what kind of good time he was after, he replied with: 'A woman – something classy.' Quaid told him to come back about eight that evening and he'd have something for him. Knowing that Quaid would, in all innocence, introduce him as a potential trick to Teresa Kiely, Burton finished off his second drink and left the bar feeling satisfied.

He passed the afternoon by walking the city centre and noting, as he had done so often since returning here, how very different it was from the grim place it had been during the Troubles. Now, with its brightly-lit shopping malls, wide variety of fancy shops, packed pubs and restaurants and dense traffic, it could have been anywhere in western Europe.

Four hours later, when the shops were closing, he returned to the hotel, popped into the upstairs bar for another quick drink and chat with Jim Quaid, then returned to his room for a hot bath and change of clothing. Emerging dressed in a formal grey suit with shirt and tie and black patent-leather shoes, though with the Browning 9mm High Power handgun still hidden under his shirt, holstered slightly to the rear of his body, he made his way to the restaurant where he made a point of engaging in ostentatious conversation with all those who served him. As befitted someone from California, he drank only Perrier water and completed the meal with a cup of black coffee. After signing the bill, he left a handsome tip in cash and waved everyone goodbye on his way out.

Entering the upstairs bar at approximately 2000 hours, he glanced at the stools and saw no beautiful woman sitting there. Taking a seat at one of the tables, he snapped his fingers for Jim Quaid to come and serve him, which Quaid quickly did.

'I see no lady of interest here,' Burton said to Quaid when he had given his order.

'Sure ya won't mistake 'er when she walks in,' Quaid replied, 'and when she does, if you fancy 'er – and I'm sure you will – just give me the nod, like.'

'Right,' Burton replied.

He was still waiting for his drink when he saw Teresa Kiely entering the bar – and he did not doubt for one second that it was her. Frank Cooney had already given a physical description of her, so Burton was prepared for the gleaming long black hair hanging down to her waist, the exquisite legs in the high-heeled black shoes, and the deceptively simple black silk dress that appeared to ripple on every hollow and curve of her slim, full-breasted, perfect body. What he was not prepared for was the sublimely sensual grace of her movements as she walked in, surveyed the busy room, removed her leather bag from her shoulder, then removed her black coat, draped it over the back of her stool, crossed her long, silken legs and finally lit a cigarette. Nor was he prepared for the sheer beauty of her face which, even from this distance, struck a chord deep inside him with its milky white skin, high cheek bones, delicate, upturned nose, full, sensual lips and an expression that mixed carnality with cynicism and a thinly concealed air of defensiveness. She was very definitely *there* – an oddly mesmerizing presence – and she drew every male eye in the room by the simple act of being.

Trying to view her professionally, Burton found himself failing badly. Like every other man in the room, he could hardly keep his eyes off her and he therefore had to force himself to be more objective and remember what he was here for. This was a woman who could cut through to a man's core and that made her dangerous. He would have to be careful.

As the other men in the room gradually gathered their wits together and went back to their business, all the time trying desperately not to ogle, Burton erected an invisible wall between himself and the woman, then concentrated on the barman. Quaid was talking to her, joking with her, patting her wrist, and at one point Teresa Kiely glanced back over her shoulder, directly at Burton. He nodded at her, not smiling, and she turned away again, but eventually, as Quaid left her, going to serve another customer, he managed to give Burton the nod. Knowing that Quaid thought he was just another trick, an Englishman from Los Angeles chasing a good time, Burton nodded back, finished off his drink and then approached the bar. He positioned himself just beside the woman but did not immediately look at her.

'Another Bushmill's, thanks,' he said to Quaid.

'Right, sir,' Quaid said and went to pour straight Bushmill's on ice.

Burton looked sideways at Teresa Kiely. Her eyes, even behind a veil of cigarette smoke, were a striking, vivid, wild

Irish green that drew him to her mesmerizing, pale-skinned beauty like a moth to a flame. The cliché was apt, because he felt just like that: seduced by a magical light that had darkness behind it. There was a lost and lonely child in that darkness, crying out to be rescued. Burton sensed that, or possibly imagined it, and then he rescued himself.

'Hi,' he said, trying to sound like a traveller on the make, but sounding false to himself. 'Can I buy you a drink?'

'Why not?' she replied. 'Sure that'd be grand, mister. Jim there knows what I have.'

'Stanley Drummond,' Burton said, using the name on the false passport he had proffered to the desk clerk and holding out his hand to let her shake it. She shook it. He felt the delicacy of her fingers within his own, the soft warmth of a broken sparrow against his palm, a pulse that could not have been there and made him think he was dreaming. When he released her hand, he experienced a sense of loss that brought guilt in its wake and this, too, seemed unnatural. 'I'm just here until tomorrow, passing through on my way to Dublin. I live and work in Los Angeles—'

'In movies?' she interjected.

'Computers.'

'Ah,' she said, sounding disappointed. 'Teresa Kiely. Nice to meet ya.'

'Nice to meet *you*,' he said. It was an act and he felt foolish, but she was acting as well, and they both acted that way for half an hour, making small conversation for the benefit of those listening, until he finally came to the point. 'Do you mind if I ask . . . ?'

'You'd like me to leave with you?' she anticipated.

'Yes,' he said. 'Yes, I would.'

'I'm professional,' she said.

'I'd assumed so, Teresa.'

'You'd like me to come up to your room?'

'I'd like that very much.'

'Let's discuss terms,' she said.

It was an act for those listening, but Burton still felt sordid and as they negotiated terms, what he wanted and what she would charge, he realized that he couldn't help feeling that all of this was for real. He kept avoiding her green gaze, its thinly veiled cynicism, while thoughts of his wife and children tormented him, though he had no reason to feel guilty. *It's just a job*, he thought. *It's not a real transaction. Just go through it and get it over and done with and then you can go home . . .* But those eyes were unavoidable, that face was flame and heat, and like a moth, he *was* being drawn to his own destruction – or so his senses were telling him. He was confused by his own feelings, more frightened than he had ever been, and wondered why he was seeing in this lost child, this degraded woman, a future that made him tremble within because he could not define it. Badly shaken, he had to dip himself in psychic ice and emerged feeling numb.

He completed the charade, arranged to meet her in his room, then left the bar, returned to that room and waited for her to come to him. When, ten minutes later, he heard her knock on the door, he opened the door with his face carved in granite and his heart beating normally. He let her in, stepped aside to let her pass him and then closed the door again. She threw her leather bag on the bed and sat beside it, but she kept her overcoat on.

'You performed very well down there,' she said. 'You even had *me* believing you.'

'Let's just hope they all think I'm another trick. I'll send you back down with money.'

'Sure you'd better,' she said. 'One of Hegarty's men was sittin' at the bar, listenin' to every word. When I go back down, I'll have to pass the money on an' get my cut later. That's how those bastards operate.'

'I'm sorry,' Burton said.

'No, you're not. But sure ya don't have to be.' She sighed loudly and glanced around the room, then turned back to face him. 'So,' she said, 'you're Frank Cooney's friend. He said you could help me. How can you do that?'

'Can I offer you a drink?'

'No, you can't. Just tell me how you can help me.'

'This isn't going to be easy,' Burton said.

'It never is,' she replied. 'Now why don't you tell me?'

Burton told her. He took the chair that was facing the end of the bed, and with every word he uttered, he felt ever more sordid, more divorced from his decent self. When he saw her widening eyes, her spine's gradual stiffening, he understood that even she, with her undoubtedly broad experience of human corruptibility, was shocked by what she was hearing. Finally, when he had finished and the silence became unbearable, she said, 'Let me get this straight, mister. You're telling me that you want to bug my flat and listen in on every last little thing. Is that what yer sayin'?'

Burton sighed. 'Yes.'

'Do you know what goes on in there?' she asked him, sounding outraged. 'Has Frank Cooney filled you in? Do you know *exactly* what they make me do? Is that what *you* want to listen to?'

'Yes,' Burton said. There was nothing else to say. Already he was drowning in a sea of shame, but confessing that would not help her.

'Is that Bushmill's over there?' she asked, nodding grimly towards the bottle on the bedside cabinet.

'Yes. You want one?'

'Christ, yes.' She shook her head from side to side in disbelief. 'Pour the whole fuckin' bottle.'

Burton poured her a drink and handed the glass to her. When she looked at him, her green eyes were bright with rage and contempt. Her legs were crossed and he saw the pale line of her thighs and had to lower his gaze. This was a different kind of shame.

'You're gonna listen in,' she said. 'I'll have to do it knowin' that. Those bastards do things to me that you wouldn't do with an animal an' you're gonna be sittin' next door and jackin' off while I'm doin' it.'

'That's not—'

'Shut yer fuckin' mouth,' she said. 'All you men – yer all the same. You think wimmen are bits of meat that you can use for whatever purpose you fancy.'

'Please—'

'Shut yer gob. Don't try tellin' me yer different. You think you're just doin' yer job, tryin' to make right what's wrong, and because of that, you think I'm of no consequence and you can put me through this. Is that your way of helpin' me, mister? To put me through that for a purpose? You think because I'm a whore I can go through that shit while you bastards are listenin' in? How do you justify that, mister? Sorry, I should say *sergeant!* You're a soldier and yer fightin' for a cause an' I should show some respect. Well, fuck you, sergeant! What yer askin' is too much. I'll whore to survive and I'll whore to preserve my life, but I'm fucked if I'll do it with a microphone stuffed inside the mattress. There's a limit to degradation, Sergeant Burton, and I'm allowed to have mine. Oh, you bastard! You *cunt!*'

She slid off the edge of the bed and paced back and forth, then turned away to the side of the bed and lowered herself to the floor. Resting her back against the bed, she raised her knees and placed her forehead upon them. She placed both hands on the back of her neck, her right fist clenched around the whiskey glass. Her body shook as she sobbed.

'Don't you understand, you cunt? Those bastards *degrade* me! They make me do things you wouldn't believe and they laugh and share me around. I'm just a fuckin' animal there. I'm a side of beef to 'em. They take a bite here and there, have a bit of this an' that, an' I'm punished if I don't give satisfaction an' sometimes I can't breathe. They're *killing* me, those bastards! They're turning me inside out! They're doing all that an' you want to make it worse by listenin' in while it's happening. Is that what you call *help?* Oh, Jesus! You *shite-holes!*'

She burst into tears again and Burton felt that he might die. His heart was racing and he fought to contain it as he looked on, transfixed. She was still on the floor, forehead resting on her knees, beating her head repeatedly against her knees as if to block out her pain. He was looking at a lost soul, a child crying in the darkness, but her beauty – that perfect body in black silk – contradicted this image. Burton felt a great woe. He was throttled by lust and grief. Though ashamed, he could not stop himself from doing what had to be done. Taking a deep breath, retaining an iron control, he walked up to her and then knelt in front of her to stare steadily at her. He placed his hand on her shoulder.

'We'll get rid of them,' he said. 'That's why you have to do this. If you do it, we can clean this mess up and you'll be free again. It's not nice, but it's not worse than what you're suffering, so what can you lose? This is the one chance you've got.'

He shook her gently by the shoulder, trying to reassure her. Then, having failed and feeling like Judas, he removed his hand and stood up to stare down at her. She didn't move for a long time and he thought she might be sleeping, but eventually she sniffed back her tears and raised her head from her knees. She had a sip from the glass in her right hand, then looked up again. Her green eyes, though bloodshot from the weeping, were steady and bright.

'The one chance *I*'ve got?' she said. 'Sure that's a neat way of puttin' it.'

Burton shrugged. 'I'll admit, it's in my own interests, but you still stand to gain.'

'Ackay,' she said sarcastically. 'I'll try to bear that in mind when I'm sucking cocks and you're listenin' in.'

Burton turned away and went back to sit in the chair. He watched her as she climbed back to her feet and straightened out her tight dress. With her black hair flowing down her spine, she looked the picture of elegance.

'Why not?' she said eventually. 'Fuck it. When do we start?'

She walked around the bed to pour herself another drink. When she had done so, she sat on the edge of the mattress and stared steadily at him. 'I'm all yours now. So tell me.'

The remark was meant to humiliate him and it worked, but he didn't let her see that. He held the pain in. He swallowed it.

'I'm afraid it doesn't begin that easily,' he said. 'I have to know a few things first.'

'*What?*'

'I said—'

'You said you have to know a few things first. Sure there's nothin' you're *not* gonna know when you bug my damned flat, so you've no right to—'

'I'm sorry, but I have to ask you some questions. I have to know who I'm dealing with.'

'Jesus Christ!'

'He won't help us.'

She glared at him with a rage that burned like blue ice. Then, taking protection from contempt, she uncrossed and recrossed her legs, very slowly, deliberately, and offered a chilling smile.

'Sure I'm all ears,' she said.

Burton burned in his own heat, his shame and desire combined, and yet he still felt convinced that she felt lost beneath her cynical posturing. Though consumed with guilt that was building on many levels, he decided to press on.

'Frank didn't seem to know too much about you,' he said, 'and that makes me uncomfortable. I need to know what he doesn't know.'

'And what's that?' she asked.

'I know you were born and raised in Belfast, then went

with your family to Newtownards, then returned to Belfast and became a whore. I need to know how, or why, that happened.'

'That'd tickle yer fancy would it, Mister Soldier?'

'It's just something I need to know.'

'Why?'

'You're a troubled person. Even Frank picked that up. He seems to think it was something in your past – something to do with the Troubles. I have to know what that problem was, because it could have a bearing.'

'A bearing on what?'

'On exactly why you left Belfast and who was involved and whether or not that person, or those persons, could still be around to give us problems. I need to know where you came from.'

'I don't want to discuss it,' she said.

'Then it all stops right here.'

She looked steadily at him, swinging a long, exquisite leg, and finally, when she knew that he was uncomfortable, she offered a deadly smile.

'Can I smoke in this fancy room?' she asked.

'Yes,' he said, 'you can smoke.'

Teresa smoked a lot of cigarettes as she told Burton her story.

CHAPTER TWENTY-SIX

'You must know what it was like,' Teresa said. 'You bein' a soldier an' all – the SAS, no less – young an' healthy an' lookin' for some excitement an' comin' to Belfast during the Troubles to work undercover. Enjoyed it, did ya? Had a good time, did ya? Well, I didn't, Sergeant Burton. I wasn't there as a fuckin' visitor. I was twelve years old at the time an' all I knew about was RUC barricades and British Army checkpoints an' a lot of men armed to the teeth and treatin' me like a dog turd. You know what it was like to *live* there? I mean breathin' it in an' out. I was a kid but I couldn't walk the streets without tremblin' in my shoes, wonderin' who was gonna spit at me or call me a Catholic bitch. And not just your kind, neither. No, you weren't the worst. You Brits were bad enough, backin' up the fuckin' Prods, but my own kind were every bit as bad, though they thought they were better. A bunch of skinheads in fuckin' bovver boots callin' themselves freedom fighters. Fuckin' freedom! *Fuck* freedom!

'I was twelve years old,' Teresa went on. 'I couldn't walk to school in peace. It was so bad that the soldiers at the checkpoints even searched *me* for weapons. They use children, they told me. You fuckin' kids are little assassins. So they'd frisk me and get their little thrill from my ripening body. Of course, they were the real enemy. At least I could despise them. But my own kind, the brothers of the IRA, or the Provos, or whatever else those bastards decided to call themselves, were even worse 'cause they were right there on your doorstep an' they never stopped watchin'. Fuckin' freedom fighters, right! Our liberators, as they'd have it. They put up their own barricades an' hemmed us all in an' then financed their fuckin' glorious fight for freedom by bleedin' us dry. The protection rackets were the thing. We had to pay for our own protection. All the bars, all the bookies, all the shops, all the taxi drivers had to fork out a percentage of their meagre takin's to finance the cause. And the percentages kept gettin' bigger. The more they got, the more they wanted. My dad had friends who were runnin' small businesses and bein' sucked dry. So sometimes they said no. Can't afford it, they said. And then our own kind, the IRA or the Provos or whatever, would beat them black an' blue or set fire to their business premises or, if they still refused to pay, shoot the poor fuckers stone dead.

'They shot my father,' Teresa said. 'I was still twelve years old. He was just a taxi driver an' he kept to himself an' if you asked him what he thought about the Prods, he'd say live and let live. He agreed with the cause, mind you. He knew there were injustices. Sure he hated the Orangemen and knew about discrimination, but he didn't think that killin' them would help and so he stuck to his taxi. He refused to join the IRA. He thought the Provos were gangsters. He said the UDA are Protestant filth but I have Protestant friends. He said we can't win with violence, with the killin', and I won't subscribe to it. He was a kind, decent man and I loved him. God, I loved him. I did.

'Then they shot him,' Teresa said. 'Shot him dead on our fuckin' doorstep. I was only twelve years old when they knocked on the door and he opened it and two masked men were standin' there, aimin' their pistols. They fired and kept firing, though he was dead with the first shot. They kept firin' because they loved the sound of guns and liked to see people dyin'. I was standin' right behind him. He fell backwards on top of me. They kept firin' an' his blood splashed all over me as I wriggled beneath him. Fuck! Sweet Jesus! I'll never forget it, dear God. There was all that noise and those masked men and my Dad fallin' – no sound from 'im – and the fuckin' blood splashin' all over me and me screamin' and terrified. I was gibberin' and my Dad was twitchin' all over me and then those bastards walked off. I heard 'em laughin'. Just laughin'. Havin' a great fuckin' time. An' I almost went mad there and then an' that lasted a long time.

'Can you imagine it?' Teresa said. 'Can you think of a worse nightmare? My Dad's twitchin' and he's covered in blood and I'm soaked in that blood, I'm swimmin' in it, and then my mother starts screamin'. She's there above me, all eyes. I'll never forget those eyes. I'd never seen 'em so big or so large an' I'd never seen 'em so mad. She was out of her fuckin' head. Just demented, standin' there. She kept screamin' and wavin' her hands and then she reached down an' grabbed me. Pulled me out from under my twitchin' father an' then we both started howlin'. A fuckin' river of tears. Because of that, we were both done in.

'My mother became an alcoholic,' Teresa said, 'an' she never dried out. We buried my Dad and the shits who'd killed 'im paid their respects, actually turned up for the funeral, an' then it turned out that they'd killed 'im by mistake, goin' to the wrong door. It was as simple as that, like. They just knocked on the wrong door. The dumb fucks, the big heroes of the cause, simply shot the wrong man. They did that a lot those days.

'I was traumatized,' Teresa said. 'So was my Mum. They put us both under treatment, like we were a couple of nutters, and my Mum just kept drinkin' and falling to bits while I developed a pair of ripe breasts an' legs you could kill for. I became a tearaway. You name it an' I did it. At fourteen I was livin' like a woman who'd had twice the experience. Got pregnant an' aborted. Liked to show men what I looked like. I was lookin' for my Dad in all those men an' I never got near him. You know what I mean, Sergeant? No Dad and no real Mum. Just a tearaway on the loose in a place where the wrong move could kill you.

'They were always there,' Teresa said. 'The fuckin' dickers – always watchin'. Those bastards – the ones who'd killed my father – fightin' for their great cause. Had their eyes on me, didn't they? I was luscious an' made 'em ache. They'd make fancy remarks when I swished past because they knew I despised 'em. Then I fell in love. Sweet Jesus, did I ever! I wanted out of that fuckin' place, to go somewhere far away, an' when I met my off-duty British soldier, I was head-over-heels. He loved me too, I tell ya. We were cats on a hot tin roof. From the word go, we couldn't say stop an' we burned all our bridges. Of course, the Provos found out. Those fuckin' shite-holes were watchin' us. They always liked a good show – nothin' clean an' quick for them – so they caught us when we were comin' out of a pub and had their bit of fun with 'im. Put their bovver boots in. Smashed his nose with their shaven

skulls. Had him down on the ground and stomped all over
'im and then used their baseball bats. I could hear his bones
snappin'. He was screamin' somethin' awful. I was screamin'
as well but I was helpless 'cause two others were holding me.
They beat 'im to a bloody pulp, made 'im unrecognizable, then
they picked 'im up and stood 'im against the wall and said
how did you like that. He tried to reply. He tried to spit but
his lips were broken. When he tried that, they took out their
switchblades and took turns at cutting 'im. He was a fuckin'
pomegranate. I kept thinkin' that's what 'is face was. You split
a pomegranate down the middle and that's what he looked like.
Red and soaked in his own blood.

'They slit 'is throat,' Teresa said. 'They did it right there in
front of me. He didn't scream but I heard his gargling like it
was the fuckin' Niagara Falls and to this day I can still see the
blood that came out like a waterfall. I can't remember much
more about it. The shits marched me away from there. They
took me out to the nearest main road an' threw me on the
pavement an' said take yer British whore's arse back home an'
we'll come for you later. I got home, but I don't know how.

'They kept their promise,' Teresa said. 'They came for me
later. A couple of days, maybe a week later, they came to my
house. I was just sixteen then. I was lovely with long hair. My
Mum was stone drunk in the parlour when they knocked on my
door. How's the whore? someone said. I didn't get time to reply.
They hauled me out into the street – this was ten in the mornin'
– an' they roped me to a fuckin' lamp-post an' then started their
little game. Fuckin' freedom fighters, Sergeant. Defendin' the
cause. They strapped this sixteen-year-old girl to a lamp-post
an' then started in. Shaved my lovely long hair off. Left me bald
as an eggshell. Then took their switchblades out and cut away
my clothes and left me as naked as the day as I was born for all
the neighbours to see. A lot of the neighbours enjoyed it. God
knows, their lives were dismal. But some, God bless 'em, were
appalled, though they still couldn't help. There I was on that
lamp-post. Almost naked and bald. Then some fucker dipped
a brush in a bucket of hot black tar and proceeded to tar me
all over. It burned, I can tell you. It stuck to me like glue. Then
those bastards opened a bag of fuckin' feathers and threw 'em
all over me. An honourable war, right? It's how ya win yer
liberation. You take a sixteen-year-old girl and you shave her
hair off, then you tar-and-feather 'er and leave 'er dangling

there for the rest of the day as an object of sport. That's what they did to me, Sergeant.

'My mother cut me down at midnight,' Teresa said, 'when the spectators had gone. She stopped drinkin' after that. That's the good that came of it. Then she pulled herself together and said let's get the fuck out of here. So we left for Newtownards, found a small house, moved in, an' my mother went straight back to the drink and I knew we were finished. Fuck this for a joke, I thought. I don't need this anymore. Fuck the cause and fuck the fuckers who fight for it, I'm on my own now. So I left Newtownards. I left knowin' what men were. I left knowin' that I had what men wanted an' I decided to use it. I returned to Belfast. I let my hair grow back. I let it grow longer than it was before because that was my strength.

'I knew what those bastards had done,' Teresa said. 'They'd cut my hair out of vengeance. They'd seen me walking up and down, a lush plum ripe to be plucked, an' they hated me because they couldn't have me, so they cut my hair off. The fight for freedom? *Fuck* the fight for freedom! What they wanted was what they couldn't have – and I was that very thing. God, yes, I was that – I was lush at sixteen – and they'd killed my father and now they wanted to kill me by turning me into a whore. So I became a whore – but not for those bastards. I became a whore so high-class that those bastards couldn't possibly afford me. I picked my own clients. I said no to all the shits. I kept a million miles away from all the rubbish, all the arseholes, that I'd left behind and couldn't stand to think about – an' I did everything I could – sweet Jesus! – to make a life for myself. Then that bastard, that fuckin' lunatic, Jack Hegarty, burst through the front door of my flat an' my life ended overnight. That's my story. That's all of it.

'Now give me the money, Sergeant Burton,' Teresa finally said, 'for the fuck you didn't actually get. When I leave this room, I have to take down that dosh or I'll get my throat slit. Sure I hope you've enjoyed this.'

Burton gave her the money and she left the room without saying another word.

Burton was speechless.

CHAPTER TWENTY-SEVEN

'You can't go back to the Falls,' Burton said to Rob at the pine table in the small kitchen of the latter's rented house near Ballyclare, Antrim. 'You only got into O'Shea's butcher shop because the dickers knew you as a friend of his. They're going to remember that you were the last one to enter the shop just before he was neutralized and that means they'll be looking out for you.'

He was not unaware of the fact that he had used the word 'neutralized' instead of 'assassinated' or 'killed'. The terminology of modern warfare, particularly counter-terrorist warfare, had evolved as a means of making the unpalatable acceptable in a so-called civilized society. In truth, Rob had marched O'Shea into his cold-storage room and, albeit out of dire necessity, cold-bloodedly shot him in the back of the head. This was something that none of them liked to talk about and so far none of them had.

'I can't go back to the Falls?' Rob asked, looking outraged. 'You mean my work's finished here?'

'No, Rob, it's not finished. I'm just saying that they'll be trawling the Falls looking for you and if they find you, they'll pick you up and that'll be the end of you. So you can't go back there. There'll be plenty more work for you to do but, by necessity, it has to be outside Belfast.'

'But the people we're looking for are *in* Belfast,' Slim said, flipping locks of blond hair out of his blue eyes as he leaned back languidly in his wooden chair and smoked a filter cigarette. 'So what can Rob do outside?'

'Right,' Rob said, nodding emphatically and looking as fierce as a Rottweiler about to charge. 'I was just about to ask that.'

Burton smiled, briefly amused by Rob's concern. 'It's pretty
obvious,' he said, 'from what we've all seen in the Falls, that
we're going to find it extremely difficult to get at the remaining
members of the Belfast Six when they're on their own turf.
The deaths of the other three have made them tighten their
security and now, with this mysterious Englishman – namely
you, Rob – being related to O'Shea's death, they'll be looking
for outside interference. In other words, if we're going to get
near these people, it's going to have to be when they're not on
their own turf, which means outside the city.'

'So how do you plan to do that?' Slim asked. Though out-
wardly less agitated than Rob, Burton knew that Slim was
growing increasingly restless living alone in Templepatrick
and would be more so now that their surveillance of the Falls
had ended. Slim was a young and handsome man, in superb
physical condition, and apart from his boredom at not having
enough to do, he would not have found the enforced celibacy
of the past few weeks easy to deal with. Like Rob, he had been
living just outside his local town and only going into it for
groceries and the odd drink, when he could spread the word
that he was an English antique dealer just here for a few
months. His main temptation when he visited Templepatrick,
as he had recently confessed to Burton, was the need for the
company of a woman, if only for the odd night. So far he
had managed to resist such temptation, but now, like Rob,
he was finding the isolation more difficult to deal with and
either wanted the distraction of more work or a return to
his normal life back in Hereford. His present girlfriend, as
Burton knew, was extremely attractive and he was obviously
missing her – just as Burton was missing his wife and kids.
The quicker they completed this job and returned home, the
better for all of them.

'I've come up with someone,' Burton said. 'She's a professional prostitute, formerly independent, who's since been
taken over and seriously abused by Jack Hegarty. He now
uses her flat on the Malone Road as a meeting place and has
started meeting Byrne and Keenan there.'

'You mean they're talking to him again,' Slim said.

'Yes. Obviously they know that O'Shea was neutralized by
the Englishman who befriended him, not by Hegarty, and so
they've banded together again to track the culprit down.' He
smiled in Rob's direction, but received only a darkly intense

stare in return. 'So, though Byrne and Keenan still often meet in O'Donovan's pub in the Falls, when Hegarty calls a meeting he invariably holds it in this prostitute's flat. She hates Hegarty for what he's done and continues to do to her, so she's agreed to let us bug her flat in the hope that eventually we'll get rid of him.'

'Can we get in there?' Rob asked.

'I think so,' Burton replied. 'This woman is watched all the time – there are dickers outside her building – but I've told her how to cause a leak in the plumbing in her kitchen and she's going to do it when Hegarty next has a meeting. I'm hoping that Hegarty, when he sees the leak, won't think it unusual when she complains that she'll have to call the plumber.'

'He could insist on calling his own plumber,' Slim said.

'He could,' Burton acknowledged, 'but I'm assuming that he isn't that paranoid and will let her call the plumber used by the people who normally service the building.'

'And instead of the normal plumber,' Slim said, 'one of us will turn up in a plumber's van.'

'Correct. I've already checked out the plumbing company that services the building and I know what kind of van they use. I photographed the logo on the side of one of their vans, had it enlarged, and then bought a similar van and personally sprayed on the same logo, using an identical alphabetical template. It probably wouldn't stand up under close inspection, but it looks like the real job from a reasonable distance, so I doubt that the dickers will spot the difference.'

'I didn't know you were so artistic,' Slim said with a lazy grin.

'We learn a lot of different skills in the SAS,' Burton replied. 'That's one of its pleasures. Isn't that why you're here?'

Slim grinned, but Rob, more intense, just leaned forward and said, 'So you'll go in as the plumber and bug the place?'

'Yes. It's all miniature probes and I only need a few small tools – all of which will look perfectly normal in a standard plumber's kit. The probes will be strapped to my waist until I get inside.'

'You've fixed up next door?' Slim asked him.

'Yes. It's another red-brick Victorian mansion converted into apartments mainly used for short-term residents and located right next to her building. I've booked myself in for an unspecified period of time and I picked a room on the

appropriate side of the building, within a line-of-sight path
of the side window of the woman's living room. The STG
surveillance equipment will be moved in by a regular removals
company in normal packing crates, with the laser transmitter
packed in the box of a known-brand TV set.'

'Very neat,' Slim said. He stubbed his cigarette out in the
ashtray on the table, had a sip of his almost cold tea, then
leaned back in his chair again. 'What are we hoping to pick
up from this surveillance,' he asked, 'apart from the sounds
of this woman fucking her clients?'

Burton felt a hot flush in his cheeks and knew instantly that
it was shame, rather than anger. Though unjustified, Slim's
cynicism was perfectly understandable, but this knowledge
didn't help Burton.

'We'll certainly pick up the sounds of this woman fucking,'
he said, 'because Hegarty makes her service some of his
friends.'

'Jesus Christ!' Rob exclaimed in disgust. 'It's a bottomless
pit.'

'However,' Burton continued, ignoring him, 'since Hegarty
is now holding his important meetings there, I'm hoping we'll
pick up not only information about their movements regarding
us – they'll now be looking for that outside influence, starting
with Rob here – but also information regarding any moves they
plan to make outside Belfast. If we know in advance where
they're going to be, and when, we can set up an ambush.'

'Then I suggest we leave Hegarty to the last,' Slim said. 'If
we neutralize him first, those meetings in the whore's flat will
end and we'll lose our eyes and ears.'

'I agree,' Burton said. 'Even if we get the chance to hit
Hegarty, we'll have to ignore it until we can take out the
other two. Only when they're out of the picture can we move
against Hegarty.'

'That's gonna hurt,' Rob said. 'I mean, to get that big fat
bastard in my sights and not be able to do anything about it
– Christ, that's gonna be hard!'

'You'll just have to control yourself,' Burton said. 'Kill him
first and you'll kill the goose that lays the golden eggs, so make
sure you don't do it.'

Rob nodded. 'I think I've got the message. I'm just saying
that it's gonna be difficult. That's the bastard I want most.'

'Me too,' Slim said. 'So if I get him in my sights and feel the urge to squeeze the trigger, I'll just close my eyes and think of England, like all the nice ladies do.'

'That might work,' Rob said.

Glancing past Rob's head, Burton saw the window framing the green hills of Antrim and a hot, azure-blue, white-clouded summer's sky. It reminded him of Hereford, which was equally bucolic, but here the peace was all on the surface and that view was deceptive. Out there, in that pastoral landscape, many men on both sides had died violent deaths and were, indeed, lying in unmarked graves, their whereabouts still unknown. It was a chilling thought and Burton felt that cold inside him, making him want to get up and run and return to his wife and kids. He couldn't do that, of course, because he was here to do a job and, also, because he was here to make amends for his sins. When he thought of the woman, the prostitute, Teresa Kiely, he saw a glimmer of hope. It was just a glimmer, because although he wanted to help her, he would first have to place her life in danger. When he thought of that, he had to throttle the cry of rage that threatened to burst from him.

'This woman,' Slim said, as if reading Burton's mind. 'How far can we trust her?'

'I can't answer that,' Burton said. 'I can only speculate. Right now, I think she'd go a long way to get rid of Hegarty. He degrades her and she hates him with a passion, so she has strong motivation. I don't think it's a matter of trust; it's a matter of how long she can last. Once we bug her flat, she can't change her mind and tell Hegarty – he'd kill her if she confessed to that. By saying yes, she's committed herself outright and has to stick with it, either until we get rid of Hegarty or until she's found out. So, no, it's not a question of trust. It's just a question of whether or not we can neutralize Hegarty before he discovers that she's helping us. We only have to concern ourselves with that. The rest will play as the cards fall.'

'I don't envy that poor bitch,' Rob said.

'Neither do I,' Slim added.

Burton knew what they meant and it made him feel no better. He had placed the woman in a compromising situation and soon, the instant he bugged her flat, she would not be able to back out. No wonder he felt sordid – though that feeling was inextricably entwined with his obscure, faltering notion of somehow finding his own redemption by helping her escape from degradation. He was climbing a slippery rope and the fall could be hard.

'So when does all this start?' Slim asked after a lingering silence.

'Tomorrow,' Burton replied. 'I move into the adjoining building tomorrow morning and bug the woman's place the following day.'

'Best of luck,' Slim said.

CHAPTER TWENTY-EIGHT

Burton spent his first night in his modest, newly-rented studio apartment tossing and turning in a restless sleep. Once upon a time he had taken pride in his ability to sleep as and when necessary, under any conditions, but ever since his accidental killing of that ten-year-old child, he had suffered nightmares that either jerked him awake or made him slip in and out of consciousness to leave him finally exhausted. This was such a night.

He had spent the evening unpacking and setting up the STG laser surveillance equipment, aware every second that Teresa Kiely was just next door and that he was about to spend the next few days or weeks spying upon her. This made him feel bad enough, but even worse was the fact that he felt strongly attracted to her and was no longer sure if he could trust himself, either as a married man or as a soldier. She *was* physically attractive, certainly, and he had responded to that as most men would, but that wasn't the whole of it. He could have dealt with that alone, relegating it to base instinct, but what troubled him was the overwhelming feeling that she had already seduced him, irrespective of his feelings for his wife, Deborah. The seduction had been subtle, not based on flesh alone, and he felt as if he had been imbued with her presence and could not shake it loose. He was haunted by her face – its mesmeric combination of carnality, cynicism and, possibly, suppressed pain – but more than that, he had been stirred by the inexplicable feeling that here, in this beautiful, haunted child, he could find his means of atonement. It was a remarkable feeling, but not one that he could source, nor even accept as valid, and so, lying in his strange bed, aware every second that Teresa Kiely was

next door, he tossed and turned and had the old nightmares
and awakened exhausted.

Nevertheless, the next morning, he rolled out of bed, attended
to his ablutions, taped the 8mm high-grain microphone probes
with miniature lenses to his torso, then dressed in a threadbare shirt, jeans and tie, with a corduroy windcheater and
scuffed suede shoes. Finally, he packed a pair of deliberately
soiled overalls into a shopping bag and then he went out to
do what he had to do.

He had deliberately parked the resprayed plumber's van
far from where he was staying – from where Teresa Kiely
was staying – and the walk back to it took about half an
hour. When he reached it, he clambered into the back and
removed his corduroy jacket, then put the dark blue coveralls
on, over his threadbare pants and shirt and tie. Though he
doubted that the dickers watching Teresa Kiely's apartment
block would frisk anyone in the street, he had taken the
precaution of carrying no weapon, just in case they became
suspicious and broke their own rules. Then, after clambering
out the rear, closing the door, and going around to the front,
he placed the plumber's toolbox on the seat beside him and
drove off.

Ten minutes later, he was approaching the house where
Teresa Kiely lived and saw the two dickers sitting in a Ford
Cortina parked at the opposite side of the road. Aware that
they would have been informed about the imminent arrival
of a plumber, he confidently parked the van outside Teresa's
building and climbed out, carrying the toolkit. Deliberately,
he withdrew a piece of paper from his pocket and studied
it, then looked up at the house as if checking the address.
Looking satisfied, he shoved the paper back into his pocket
and walked up to the front door. There were six flats listed
on the sign by the intercom on the door and he pressed the
one for Teresa Kiely's flat. After a short delay, her voice came
on the intercom.

'Yes?'

'Miss Kiely?'

'Yes.'

'O'Grady Plumbing. You called about a leak in your kitchen.'

'Oh, right, come on up.'

When the intercom buzzed, Burton opened the door and
entered the hallway. Closing the door behind him, he realized

that he was nervous – not about the dickers, but about meeting Teresa Kiely again. Already obsessed with her for a variety of reasons, some clear, others obscure, he had been even more deeply affected when she had cleared up the mystery of her past with its manifold horrors. Now, as he walked up the stairs to the second floor, he realized that he felt threatened by her presence even as he was drawn to her. The feeling made him uncomfortable.

The door was open when he arrived at Teresa's flat and she was waiting there for him. Though unsmiling and dressed informally in a loose checkered shirt and washed-out denims, she still looked darkly beautiful. Her long black hair was hanging loose and the skin of her throat, framed by the open-necked shirt, was as fine and white as the surface of fresh snow. Her green eyes stared steadily at him, then she stepped aside and indicated that he should enter. When he did so, she sat on the settee and picked up a nearly finished glass of whiskey. It was not yet noon.

'So,' she said, 'you got in all right. Those two bastards outside didn't bother you.'

'No,' Burton said, placing his plumber's toolbox on the floor and glancing about him. The flat was spacious and well furnished, with white carpets, dark blue curtains and golden-coloured duvets. The walls were covered with paintings that looked very good and were mostly original, though Burton did not recognize any of them as being the works of famous artists. Clearly, Teresa Kiely had good taste, if leaning slightly towards the sunny and the exotic. The flat seemed to have been designed to counterbalance her dark personal world.

'Can I get ya a drink?' she asked, holding up her own empty glass and smiling sardonically.

'No, thanks,' he replied, lowering his gaze to where she sat on the settee, one long leg crossed over the other. 'It's too early for me.'

'Is that a reprimand, Sergeant Burton?'

'Don't call me that even as a joke. It might get to be a habit and you never know who's going to be listening. Just use my name.'

'What's that?'

'You know what it is.'

'I know your surname; I don't know yer Christian name.'

'Everybody calls me Burton. I don't know why, but they do.

It's what I've been called for years and it's what I respond to.'

'It's probably because you're so reserved,' she said, still smiling sardonically. 'You always seem somewhere else.'

'I didn't know that,' Burton said. Uncomfortable, he glanced down at the toolbox, then forced himself to look at her. She had regained her composure since that meeting in the hotel and there was little in her flawless beauty, or in her bold, challenging glance, to suggest that nightmare of the life she had recounted to him. Frank Cooney had got it right: she had suffered dreadfully in childhood, in the Troubles, and it was etched in her face. Hers was a dark, troubled beauty.

'So why are you like that?' she asked him.

'Pardon?'

'The way ya are. The way ya hold yerself in, showin' sweet fuck-all. Yer as distant as the dark side of the moon an' that means ya have secrets. What are they, Burton?'

'If I've secrets, they're going to stay that way. That's what secrets are.'

'I should've known not to ask.'

Burton smiled, though he wasn't amused. In fact, he felt hot and bothered. 'I was relieved to get your call,' he said. 'I wasn't sure if the trick would work. You had the leak when they came here?'

'Yes,' she said. 'They came yesterday as planned and had a good palaver and in the middle of it I let out a little shriek and Hegarty rushed in. I did just what you said – loosened those pipes under the sink – and the water was flowing out just enough not to make it seem like it needed emergency treatment, though it had to be done. Hegarty's a man's man – he thinks all wimmen are dumb shits – so he cursed like I was just a fuckin' nuisance, then got down on his fuckin' tree-trunk knees and wrapped some tape around the pipes until the water was just seepin' out. I'll get you a plumber, he says to me. One of my own boyos. So, knowin' he's a tight-fist, I said, it's not really that urgent. The people who run this place are responsible and they'll have to do it for free. I'll call them tomorrow. He had a good laugh at that. It tickled his fancy, like. He says, I like a woman that doesn't waste money and then he walks back out of the kitchen. The meeting continued, I didn't have to fuck anyone, and eventually they all went off an' left me alone. And now, here's the plumber right on time. I think the service is wonderful.'

Burton smiled, though he knew she was taunting him. 'Very good. Let's get to it. I'm going to have to take my shirt off. Do you mind?'

She stared at him in disbelief, then broke out in a soft, throaty chuckle. 'Sure that's a good one, isn't it? I'm a fuckin' whore an' I'm bein' asked if I'd be embarrassed if a man removed his shirt in my presence. You must lead a sheltered life.'

'Pretty normal,' Burton said, though he secretly felt embarrassed, almost naked, when he had to peel the overalls down to his waist and then take off his tie and shirt in order to remove the probes taped to his chest.

'You have a good body,' Teresa said. 'I don't know why you're embarrassed.'

'I'm not embarrassed,' Burton said, but he was relieved to remove the taped-on probes, then put the shirt and tie back on and pull up his coveralls.

Teresa just smiled. Burton knelt on the floor, opened the tool box, removed a small manual hand-drill from it and inserted an 8mm bit. 'There won't be much damage,' he said, 'and you won't see a thing.'

'That's nice to know.'

Standing on a chair with a newspaper spread across it, he drilled a hole through the top of the wooden window frame, then pushed a tiny fibre-optic probe into it until its miniature lens was flush with the wall. Opening the window, which was at the side of the house, facing the gable end of the house he was staying in – he could not, therefore, be seen by the dickers out on the street – he fixed the wired end of the probe to the outside of the window frame, attached a miniaturized transmitter to the frame, right next to the probe, and finally wired the probe to it. Though it would have been visible to a keen eye, it was unlikely that anyone not deliberately looking would see either the tiny probe or the small transmitter.

'That's a microphone?' Teresa asked when he had closed the window, stepped off the chair and turned back to face her.

'Yes.'

'How does it work?'

'It's a laser surveillance system that enables us to pick up sound through glass. Any conversation you have in here will create minute vibrations on the window-pane. Next door, my

laser transmitter will direct an invisible beam onto the window
and pick up those vibrations. The beam will then bounce back
to my optical receiver and convert the modulated beam into
audio signals. Those signals will then be filtered, amplified and
converted into clear conversations. I'll be able to monitor those
conversations through headphones and also record them. It's
pretty simple, really. So where's the bedroom?'

'You want to put a fuckin' probe in my *bedroom?*'

'Yes. Men often say revealing things when they're having
sex and we have to hear what they say. I'll fix the probe to
the bedroom window. I'm sorry. We need it.'

'Jesus Christ,' Teresa said.

But she nodded towards the bedroom. Burton went in,
carrying the hand drill, and she followed him in. As he
was bugging the bedroom, he was aware every second
that she was standing behind him. He was aware, also,
of the double bed beside him and what had transpired in
this room and would in the near future. The curtains had
been closed, leaving the room in semi-darkness. When he
had finished inserting the probe, he opened the curtains
again and turned back to face her. She was staring directly
at him, smiling slightly, obviously aware of his discomfort.
The light and shadow fell upon her face like the veins on a
windblown leaf. He saw her flame, felt her heat. He felt as if
he was touching her.

'That's it?' she asked eventually.

'Yes,' he said. 'Short and simple. Just try to forget that
they're there.'

'Are we being recorded right now?'

'No. I'll activate the equipment when I get next door. Once I
turn it on, it'll stay on for good, so please try to remember that.
If a conversation takes a turn that might be useful, please try
to encourage it.'

'It's exciting, being a spy.'

'It's also dangerous. Please don't ever forget that.'

He stepped towards her to get past her, but she didn't move
and he had to step around her, thus unavoidably brushing
against her body. He felt her failure to get out of his way had
been deliberate. She followed him back into the living room
and watched him pack up.

'You still don't want a drink?' she asked him.

'I'd better not.'

'A man who doesn't drink and drive,' she said. 'Sure that proves yer not Irish.'

'It's not that. I just can't stay here too long. Those dickers in that car outside will be checking their wristwatches. This is supposed to be a small, quick plumbing job, so I can't hang around.'

She went and poured herself another whiskey, then sat on the settee. He was aware of her long legs in the denims, one crossed over the other. He saw the rise and fall of her breasts, the smooth white of her perfect throat.

'Are you married?' she asked him.

'Yes.'

'Kids?'

'Yes. Two. A boy and a girl.'

'Is it a happy marriage?'

'Yes. Why do you ask?'

'Because you don't seem too happy.'

'That's in my nature. It isn't the marriage. It's just one of those things.'

'It's yer *secret* nature. It's what yer hidin', Burton. Come on, tell me! What is it?'

She had said it lightly, but he knew that she was curious and he wasn't about to discuss it. He felt a deep and powerful yearning for her, but that brought its own baggage of guilt. When he thought of Deborah and the kids back in Hereford, he was even more troubled. He hadn't laid one hand on Teresa Kiely, but he felt that he had.

'Stop playing your games,' he said, closing the toolbox and picking it off the floor, straightening up in front of her. 'I'm here to do a job and I've done it and now I have to leave. I'll have cause to meet you again where we won't be suspected by anyone watching, so I suggest that we do the same as the last time and meet in the Europa.'

'As one of my tricks.'

'Correct.'

Teresa smiled. It was a smile suffused with amusement and light mockery, but it was certainly genuine. He warmed to it and liked her even more for it; but he still felt uncomfortable.

'You're amused?' he asked.

'Yeah. It's like bein' in a movie. Here I've got this attractive man and he'll *pretend* to be a trick and we'll go up to his room but we don't fuck. You must like your wife a lot.'

'A lot,' Burton confirmed. He checked his wristwatch. 'Since those dickers watch you all the time, you won't even be able to call me from a public phone without Hegarty wanting to know who you called. Do you normally close the blinds in the evening?'

'Yes.'

'Okay. I'll check this house every evening – at least when I'm not elsewhere – and if you want me, leave the blinds open. The dickers will think you've just forgotten to close them, but I'll know you want me. I'll then go the following evening to the Europa Hotel and we'll meet in the bar and I'll invite you up to my room like the last time.'

'Sure isn't that clever?'

'Thanks. Do you need to know anything else?'

'No, I don't think so. Sure ya've been very thorough. My head's swimmin' with admiration already.'

'It's swimming with whiskey,' Burton said. He turned to open the front door, but her voice, thrillingly low but still mocking, pulled him back a little. 'Do I get a goodbye kiss?'

'No,' Burton said, but he felt his cheeks blushing as he opened the door.

'I wouldn't charge if you kissed me,' she said.

'You certainly like playing games.'

He left and closed the door behind him, feeling sweat on his brow.

CHAPTER TWENTY-NINE

Teresa walked around the living room of her own flat, pouring drinks for Jack Hegarty, Neil Byrne, Shaun Keenan and an American visitor, Luke Brady. They were discussing business in general, particularly the Irish-American side of it, and giving a feast of information to Burton through the miniature probe placed in the windowframe. Teresa had tried to make light of being bugged, but now she felt scared by it. Luckily, since she had never felt natural with Hegarty, any nervousness she displayed would be treated as natural. In fact, Hegarty took his pleasure from instilling fear and that could be her protection.

'We've read reports in the Press,' Brady was saying, 'about Gardai concern over increasing IRA involvement with Dublin's gangland. Reports like that give us troubled thoughts, so just what's happening there?'

'A lot,' Byrne replied, 'and most of it worth the risk. Initially, the biggest threat we had down there was one of the two competing gang bosses, Martin Craig, known as the Fox. He was taken out two weeks ago with a Magnum .357 when sitting in his car at the traffic junction in Ranelagh on the south side of the city. The other gang boss has since seen the light and is dealing with us right now.'

'Good,' Brady said. 'What's the source of the income?'

'Mainly various kinds of heists reaping big money,' Keenan said. 'Doubtless you've read about them. A 1.5 million pound jewellery job, a 1.4 million pound painting theft, a cash heist from the National Irish Bank, netting three hundred thousand-odd, and various ambushes of bank armoured security vans. Also, the sale of various drugs, including cannabis, crack and Ecstasy – most of which comes from your side, so you're doing well there. Finally, organized prostitution, the fencing of stolen paintings and antiques and, of course, the taxing of the major Dublin criminals. The growing concern of the Gardai is a risk, but it's one we think worth the taking.'

They're ruining this fucking country, Teresa thought, *and they're so full of themselves. They kneecap and murder and kill, and they all think they're grand men. They despise me for being a whore and this is what they get up to. Sure it beggars belief.*

'It's come to our attention,' Brady said, 'that since you were well armed by us—'

'Arms we paid well for,' Keenan interjected boldly.

'Now that you've been armed by us,' Brady continued doggedly, 'you've started a lucrative arms trade of your own. We don't mind that, but we have to know where the weapons come from. We don't want our lines crossed here.'

'They won't be,' Byrne said. 'We're not buying them from your European sources. Instead, we're concentrating on deactivated weapons which can be sold legally, since the buyers don't require a gun licence and no minimum age limit is imposed.'

'But the buyers can then reactivate them,' Brady said.

Byrne nodded. 'Another lucrative business for us. We have licensed armourers doing it all over the place and we get our cut off them as well. They use standard gun parts and components that are easy to come by and can be bought legally in Europe and America. Put simply, the weapon's stripped down to its basic components with a lathe, a small welder and a milling machine. The weapon will have been deactivated by having its barrel slotted through with a cutter, blocked with a pin and welded to prevent it from firing. The armourer merely makes up a new piece of tubing to the same specification as the original barrel and fixes it into place. Then he repairs the breech-block assembly and replaces the firing pin that was removed. Bob's yer uncle, it works again!'

'What are the weapons?' Brady asked. 'And where do they come from?'

'Heckler & Koch MP5s and other dismantled machine-guns are sold to us by former and still-serving British Army soldiers who send the kits to firearms dealers in our pocket. Other soldiers actually reassemble the weapons and sell them to us in one piece; we then mark the price up and sell 'em on, usually to criminal gangs located here, in England and in Europe. We've sold weapons that came in with a Home Office-approved deactivation certificate stating that they were harmless and couldn't be used, though most of them can be converted back to use in less than forty-five minutes. Occasionally, we pick up Czech Uzi sub-machine guns, others come from Germany, and we even get them from the former Yugoslavia, shipped back through dealers in Belgium and deactivated in London. So it works and it's growin'.'

'This all sounds hunky-dory,' Brady said, 'but what about your recent in-fighting? We're concerned by that, also.'

'Sure ya don't have to worry,' Hegarty said with a smarmy grin. 'The wee tiff between me and these two' – he nodded to indicate Byrne and Keenan – 'has been resolved an' now we're working together to find that English fucker who put out O'Shea's lights and did the same to the other two.'

'Him or *them*,' Byrne carefully corrected him. 'If there's outside influence, there's probably more than one man involved. We have to find all of 'em.'

'Agreed,' Hegarty said. 'I'm not arguin' with that. I'm just tryin' to convince Luke here that we're not havin' a gang war between us and spoilin' the whole show.'

'I accept that,' Luke Brady said. He glanced at Teresa and flashed a smile. He was a big man with a roughly handsome face that was not without humour. It was a cynical sense of humour, Teresa sensed, but at least it was there. He was probably a man used to getting his own way and therefore at ease with himself. Teresa knew the type. He was good-humoured when things were going his way, but look out when they weren't. He was smart, tough and dangerous.

'I'm just here to insist,' Brady continued, 'that you resolve this problem as soon as possible and make the streets safe for yourselves again. If you're in danger, we're in danger; and if, as you say, outside influence has come to bear, that suggests the involvement of the British government and that certainly doesn't sit well with us. We can deal with the Law, both here and in the US, but we can't become entangled with the British government, even if it's only by association. You have to find out what that outside influence is and then decide what to do. If you don't, we'll stop trading with you and go our own way.'

Having poured their drinks, Teresa sat back on the sofa

and sipped at her whiskey. She was wearing a skin-tight dress, which Hegarty had demanded, and when she crossed her legs, her perfect thighs were exposed and caught Brady's eye. Teresa suspected that she was here for him today and the thought made her tremble.

'You won't have to do that,' Keenan insisted. 'We'll find that English bastard. Don't you worry.'

'What have you got so far?' Brady asked, reluctantly removing his gaze from Teresa's exposed thighs.

'Well,' Byrne said, 'we know that he hasn't been seen in the Falls since he put O'Shea's lights out.'

'That figures,' Brady said.

'But we did find out,' Byrne continued, 'that he said he'd been living out in Antrim and it's possible that his van was hired from there.'

'The furniture van,' Brady said.

'Aye, that's right. So we're presently trawling all van rentals in Antrim, hoping to find one that was rented by an Englishman. We're also enquiring about any English bastard living out in that direction and tellin' the locals that he's there to find furniture. Between the van and local gossip, we should soon pick 'im up.'

'It better be soon,' Brady said, 'because there's only three of you guys left right now and if, as you say, there's more than one man involved, the others will have their sights on you. Keep that in mind if you start getting lazy: they have you in their sights.'

'Sure we know that all right,' Hegarty said. 'But we can live with that knowledge. I'll get that wee fucker if it kills me.'

'It might,' Brady said.

Listening to them talk, Teresa knew only too well that if Burton wasn't the one who'd killed O'Shea and the other two, then he was certainly responsible. He was here to get rid of all these bastards and she wished he would do it. She was risking her life because he might. It was a very big risk. In the meantime, she had to listen to these shite-holes talking their heads off. She was hoping they'd talk themselves into early graves. By God, she was. She wanted Burton to rescue her from all this, but she sensed it was more than that about him, something much deeper.

I'm going fucking mad, she thought. *He's just another man and he's using me and yet I'm feeling as if he's my knight errant. He's not doing it for me – he's doing it for himself – and there's something about him that makes me feel he could succeed, though that's not the whole of it. He's not like any of these bastards. He has something they don't. He fights by their filthy fucking rules but he's kept himself clean. I'm not sure what that means yet, but I feel it. I must be losing my marbles.*

'So what about this money?' Brady asked of the other three. 'You still owe us a lot. You owe us for the drugs and for the weapons we sent to you through Italy before you started trading in your own. You still haven't paid us.'

'We've had some setbacks,' Keenan said. He was studying the ledger in front of him. 'We lost out on a lot when you asked us to cut down on the street trade – the sale of crack and Ecstasy – and then, of course, we've had the deaths of McCauley and Gallagher and O'Shea, which caused a great deal of chaos. There was no one to run their separate turfs and we had to deal with that problem. You don't walk into someone else's turf and take it over that easily, but we had to gradually take control of those three turfs and get things going again.'

'And you were fighting amongst yourselves,' Brady reminded them. 'That wouldn't have helped.'

He's reprimanding the bastards, Teresa thought as she listened in from the sofa. *He should bring his Irish-American hooligans in and clean up the whole lot of them. That would solve a few problems.*

It was a vain hope, of course, and she knew what she was really thinking. She was thinking of Sergeant Burton, his reticence and odd dignity, the guilt she saw in his face when he looked at her and realized that he wanted her. She knew all about men, even the decent ones like Burton, so she knew that her senses would not have failed her when it came to his feelings. He had wanted her all right and it had caused him some confusion, and even now, when she recalled his embarrassment, she felt a warm glow. He was married and felt guilty. He hadn't touched her, but he had wanted to. He felt guilty even thinking about it and that somehow touched her. Unlike these animals – these bastards sitting in her place – he was mortified by the nature of his own desire and trying hard to resist it. Though he was doing that for his wife, he was also doing it for her, the whore, and it showed that he respected her as a human being, which was something no other man had ever done, except maybe Frank Cooney. No wonder Burton and Cooney were friends. They respected each other. She had come to respect Cooney as a friend, but this Burton intrigued her. She felt that she wanted him to touch her in a way she had never been touched before. She felt lost in her thoughts of him.

'We've stopped fighting amongst ourselves,' Keenan said to Brady, 'so let's drop the subject before it starts.'

'What?' Brady's eyes had turned to stones. 'I'm raising a concern from across the Atlantic and you're shutting me up?'

Keenan, always quietly spoken and calm, was clearly not fazed by Brady's gaze. 'I'm simply saying that our gang war never started, so it counts for little in the problems we're having. We've already told you that we'll track the Englishman down, so let's return to the money. We owe you because we lost in the streets, but we'll get it back soon.'

Brady continued to gaze steadily at Keenan, as if wondering just how insolent he was being behind his own calm demeanour. When Keenan did not flinch from his gaze, he simply asked, 'How soon?'

'How much time do we have?'

'I was sent here to demand the money,' Brady said, 'so that doesn't give you too much time.'

Teresa had listened to enough of these conversations to know that Brady represented the Irish-American gangs of New York and could, if annoyed, turn into a formidable enemy of the gangs in Belfast. She had always thought that Byrne was the natural leader of this pack, but now, as she watched Keenan's quiet performance, she saw him in a different light. He was the most sophisticated of them all, almost. Irish aristocracy, but clearly, if he could hold his own even with Brady, he was more formidable than she had imagined him to be. He looked like an academic, a professor, but the hardness had to be there.

'Can you give us a month?'

'No, Shaun, I can't. I came here to collect and I need a guarantee to take back. I need to know where it's coming from and I need to know when.'

'And if we can't supply an answer?'

'There'll be trouble. Let's all try to avoid that.'

Keenan glanced at Hegarty, then turned his gaze on Byrne.

The latter was leaning back in his chair, smoking a cigarette, but he sat forward when he caught Keenan's glance and then he turned to Brady.

'We'll fly back to London,' he said. 'Keenan and I have to fly over to deal with the laundry man. Why don't we fly back with you and do the paperwork there? Then you fly back to New York with the cheque and everyone's happy.'

'That sounds good,' Brady said.

'When are you leavin'?' Byne asked him.

'Wednesday,' Brady told him. 'I fly out at eight in the evening. Can you book the same plane?'

'It's a shuttle flight, so there should be no problem. We'll pick you up at the Europa at six-thirty and we'll all go together. We'll have an escort – a car front and rear – and we'll be met at the other side.'

'Great,' Brady said. He smiled at Teresa, then turned thoughtful and looked back at Byrne. 'You know what I'd really like?' he asked rhetorically, being a man who expected his requests to be treated as demands. 'I'd really like to visit the Republican Plot in Milltown Cemetery before I go back. I mean, they're all buried there, aren't they? The Gibraltar Three; the hunger strikers – all the others. I'd sure as hell like to pay my respects. Any way of arranging that?'

'No problem,' Byrne replied. 'We can drop in on the way to the airport, then take the back road over the Black Mountain. No problem at all.'

'Great,' Brady said again.

'Ack, sure everyone's happy,' Hegarty said. 'Sure that calls for another drink.' He turned to Teresa and snapped his fingers. 'We need some more drinks here.'

'Right,' she said and jumped to her feet to hurry into the kitchen. When she returned with a fresh bottle of Bushmill's, she poured drinks for the four of them. Hegarty leered at her, then he slapped her hard on the rump as he grinned at the others.

'Sure she's a nice piece,' he said.

'*Very* nice,' Brady said.

'An' a more agreeable wee woman you couldn't find,' Hegarty informed him. 'She's not the one to say no.'

'I'm glad to hear *that*,' said Brady.

Teresa caught his bold glance, its cold mockery, and it made her tremble again. She left the bottle on the table and sat down and sipped at her own drink.

He's good-humoured when it suits him, she thought, *but I'd better make sure I please him. Displease him and I'm likely to be on the floor with his boot on my face. So I'll please him. I'll do anything for his pleasure. That's all I've got left now.*

'So is there any more business?' Keenan asked.

'I don't think so,' Brady said.

'Then if you don't mind, I'll leave.'

'I don't mind.'

'Me, too,' Byrne said. 'I've got to be makin' tracks.'

Byrne, like Keenan, Teresa thought, seemed more civilized than he actually was. If it hadn't been for all the stories she'd heard about him, she would have deemed him a thoughtful man. He had that air about him – he seemed as thoughtful as Burton – but she'd even heard about him during the Troubles and she knew he was ruthless. Like the others, he'd begun as a freedom fighter and then drifted into crime. Though not mad like Hegarty, though looking civilized, he'd kneecapped and killed his fair share. Another swine in sheep's clothing.

Of course, Burton had killed as well, but certainly not the same way. You could see in his reflective gaze, hear in his quiet voice that he was a man of honourable intentions in a world where they weren't easy to preserve. She sensed that he was divided within himself and that was something she understood.

Christ, what am I thinking? she wondered. *You'd better watch yourself, girlie . . . Oh, fuck, Brady's staying.*

Byrne and Keenan had stood up to shake Brady's hand, but Hegarty remained at the table to have more drinks with Brady.

'See you on Wednesday,' Byrne said to Brady when he had opened the front door and was ready to leave.

'Me, too,' Keenan said.

'Adios,' Brady responded. The two men left and Brady closed the door behind them and then returned to the table. He sat down, stared steadily at Teresa, then drank some more whiskey. 'That's one fucking lovely piece,' he said to Hegarty, staring straight at Teresa.

'Ackay, she is that,' Hegarty replied. 'An' like I say, she's agreeable.'

They're talking about me like I'm blind and fucking dumb,

Teresa thought. *Like I don't have a feeling in my body – just meat for their pleasure. I don't think I can bear this.*

As if reading her mind, Brady turned to stare directly at her. 'Is that true?' he asked. '*Are* you agreeable?'

'Sure, why not?' Teresa said.

'Are you good?'

'Yeah, I'm good, Mister Brady.'

'You'd better be,' Brady said. He finished off his drink and stood up and looked down at Hegarty. 'You don't mind?'

'Of course not,' Hegarty replied. 'Sure that's what she's here for. You have a grand time, now.'

'Right,' Brady said. Looking every inch the civilized business-man, he turned back to Teresa, then nodded his head towards the bedroom. 'Get your ass in there, lady.' Teresa did as she was told. Brady followed her in. He closed the door behind him, plunging the room into semi-darkness as she turned down the covers on the bed and then turned back to face him. He was taking his jacket off, looking her up and down, and she felt the tightness of the dress on her body, which made her feel naked. He walked up to her and moved his hand behind her back and unzipped the dress. When it was loosened, he tugged it down along her body to expose her bare breasts. 'Those are something to see,' he said, now breathing heavily, like Hegarty. 'I've already got a hard-on just looking and you know how to start with it. So, lady, get started.'

Teresa started on her knees and ended up on the floor and finally found herself beneath him on the bed, being pounded hard by him. As he grunted and groaned on top of her, as she gasped and squealed with feigned pleasure – which, of course, she had to do in order to keep from being beaten – she kept thinking of Burton next door, listening in to their every sound. She felt herself filling up with pain and rage, with crucifying humiliation, and had to fight back the tears that kept threatening to burst forth and betray her. It was a fight and she fought it, losing herself in this squalid game, and in the end she managed to get through it without giving herself away. Nevertheless, she felt traumatized, racked by pain, rage and dread, and when Brady finished, rolling off her to get dressed again, she thought she was living a nightmare.

Brady didn't say thanks. He just grunted an obscenity. Then he left the room, leaving the door open, to let Hegarty see her shame.

Teresa didn't move from the bed. She wept quietly and at length. Brady and Hegarty were talking out in the living room and then she heard the front door slam. She stayed sprawled on the bed, feeling crushed, thinking of Burton listening in, and this time she was swept by a wave of hatred that was mixed with her need for him. Burton was using her – and he might just save her life – but she would never forget this.

She continued to lie there, still feeling traumatized, thinking that hell had no end. She was thinking this when Hegarty entered the bedroom to give her thoughts a hideous reality.

'Was that American shite as good as me?' Hegarty asked.

'Of course not,' Teresa said.

'Sure I'm just about to prove that,' Hegarty said, 'so don't get off the bed.'

Teresa wanted to cleave the darkness with her screaming but she kept her mouth shut. She thought of Burton and died there.

CHAPTER THIRTY

Slim and Rob arrived at Burton's house just after five that hot July evening to prepare for the ambush. All three men were wearing normal civilian clothing – denims, windcheater jackets and open-necked shirts – with their single nod to the military being laced-up rubber-soled canvas boots that would make movement in possibly wet fields easier. The weapons they had selected for the task were one GPMG (general purpose machine-gun), one M16 assault rifle with breech-loading 40mm M203 grenade-launcher, three Heckler & Koch MP5 9mm sub-machine guns, three L42A1 Lee-Enfield .303 bolt-action sniper rifles with Starlight 'scopes, four British L2A2 hand grenades each, and the ubiquitous Browning 9mm High Power handgun. All of these were concealed in the false bottoms and glove compartment of a Transit van stolen the day before from a street in Belfast and resprayed in Burton's garage in his rented house in Antrim.

Now, with the van packed and the summer sun still high in the sky, Slim and Rob clambered into the front of the van and Slim drove away from the house. Burton carefully locked the house and followed them in a rented red Ford Cortina. He soon overtook the van and raced ahead, then slowed down to enable Slim to follow him at a reasonable distance. Having already ascertained the best location for the ambush by taking the Black Mountain route the day before and scanning the landscape, he knew just where he was going and led the van away from Antrim, towards Belfast, but turned away well before he reached the city and headed for Aldergrove.

At this time of year, the sun took its time sinking and the evening was bright, with the rolling green hills streaked with ribbons of light and great, constantly shifting swathes of

shadow. It was a soft, pastoral landscape, with the quality of
a dream, and as he drove Burton thought of what they were
about to do and of how they had found the means to do it.

So far, the bugging of Teresa Kiely's flat had been successful
and the latest information to come out of it – details of the
travel arrangements of Neil Byrne, Shaun Keenan and the
Irish-American gangster Luke Brady – had been just what
they needed to enable them to mount an ambush that might
succeed in getting rid of the remaining members of the Belfast
Six. Though this information had thrilled Burton and, at the
least, vindicated what he was doing to get it, what he was
doing, or had been doing for the past few days, had still shamed
him immeasurably. Now, as he drove towards the selected
ambush site, he could not shake from his head the words
spoken between Teresa and the American and, of course,
Hegarty. Their treatment of her had shamed him – both as
a man and as an individual – but later, listening to what was
happening between them, first with Brady, then with Hegarty,
Burton had felt like a voyeur of the very worst kind.

Nevertheless, to his despair, those sounds had also aroused
him, setting fire to his imagination, and he had practically
seen Teresa in that bed and desperately wanted to have her.
He had been shocked by this desire – more so by what had
caused it – and ever since then, from that first awful night,
he had thought of her constantly. He still felt the need to
save her – she was his lost child needing help – but now
mixed up with that was a desire that he could not deny. He
was shocked by that desire, which in itself was a betrayal of
Deborah – but he was even more shocked by how it was being
aroused each time he spied upon her. He was listening in on
her most intimate moments and they were dreadful to hear.
Now, at least, something productive had sprung from it, but
this failed to ease the guilt he felt or clear up his confusion. All
the nightmares of the past were now trebled and he shuddered
to think of them.

Tormented by such thoughts, he was relieved to reach his
chosen parking spot, on a narrow, deserted road, almost a dirt
track, that wound around the back of the hill separating it
from the lonely road that wound up from Glen Road, across the
Black Mountain and on to the airport. Using a hand signal, he
indicated that Slim should park just off the track, in a natural
parking spot formed by the inward curving of the hedgerows,

then he drove on until he was around the bend and found a similar spot. After parking and locking the car, he walked back the way he had come, around the bend in the road, until he came to where Slim and Rob were standing outside the van, waiting for him, both smoking cigarettes. The evening was still bright, but the shadows were deepening all around them.

'So,' Slim said, his blond hair windblown, his blue eyes bright with anticipation, 'where to now, boss?'

Burton nodded towards the smooth green field that rose up to form a hill beside the car. It was not a steep hill. 'I've personally checked that field,' he said, 'and we can drive the van up and slightly over it, parking it just beyond the summit, which gives us a good view of the road on the other side. There isn't a house in sight for miles, so we should be okay. By that I mean that I don't think we'll be stopped or checked, so it's as safe as any area we're going to find. Put your fags out and let's go.'

'Happy fuckin' days,' Rob said, throwing his cigarette on the ground and stomping on it. 'I've waited a long time for this.'

'Damned right,' Slim said. He stomped on his own cigarette, then climbed into the driver's seat while Burton and Rob packed themselves into the other side of the cabin. It was a four-wheel drive vehicle and Slim managed the climb easily, soon stopping just over the brow on a long, level stretch where the van was almost certainly hidden from the road below while giving the SAS men a good view of it, as well as of the broad fields around it and the distant airport. The lights on the airport, Burton noticed, had not yet been turned on, which indicated that they still had some time left before darkness fell. This knowledge made him rest easier.

'Okay,' he said, 'all out.'

When they had clambered out of the van, Burton pointed down the gently sloping hill to the road below. The road ran roughly east to west, heading towards the airport. Between them and the road was a broad, smooth field, bordered with windblown hawthorn trees. Burton checked his wristwatch, then indicated the road with his index finger. 'According to what was said in Teresa Kiely's room, Byrne, Keenan and the American, Luke Brady, will be flying out of the airport at eight. Byrne and Keenan were going to pick the Yank up at the Europa Hotel at eighteen-thirty hours, visit the Milltown Cemetery in the Upper Falls, and then take the back route

across the mountain. Which means they should pass along
the road below about thirty minutes later. That gives us a
good half-hour to set up.'

'That isn't very long, boss,' Rob said.

'The less time we spend here, the less likely we are to be
seen,' Burton said. 'We can set up in that time.'

'So what's the set-up?' Slim asked.

Burton indicated the hedgerow to the west, on his right. 'We
can't move over that road to form a cross-fire,' he said, 'so we'll
be forced to attack just from this side. If we take up concealed
positions in that hedgerow, the setting sun will be behind us
and in the eyes of those down on the road. The GPMG's the
heaviest weapon to carry back to the van – it's also the one
with the most fire-power – so I suggest that we position it as
near to here as possible, say halfway down the field, hidden in
the hedgerow, with Rob manning it. You, Slim, will take up a
position lower down the field, about a third of the way down,
and initiate the attack from my hand signal by firing grenades
from the M203, first at the lead car, then at the other two. Rob
will then open up with the GPMG, spraying the whole convoy.
When the convoy stops, as it surely will, and when they spill
out of the damaged vehicles, you, Slim, and I will pick off as
many of them as we can with the Lee-Enfield sniper rifles
while Rob, leaving the GPMG behind, makes his way down
to join us. When he's there, we play the game as the cards fall,
advancing closer if necessary and finishing them off with the
MP5 sub-machine guns, hand grenades and, if necessary, our
Browning High Power handguns. Any questions?'

'No, boss,' Slim and Rob said simultaneously.

'Okay, let's unpack and get going.'

Opening the rear doors of the van, they removed the weapons, distributing them as required amongst themselves. After
glancing in all directions to ensure that no one was in sight –
the fields appeared to be empty for miles on all sides – each
man strapped a holstered Browning High Power to his waist
in the cross-draw position, then clipped four hand grenades
to his belt. When this was done, they made their way down
the hill in single-line formation, with Burton out front, as if
on point, Slim in the middle, and Rob bringing up the rear,
heavily burdened with the separate parts of the GPMG, as
well as a Lee-Enfield sniper rifle and Heckler & Koch MP5
sub-machine gun. Slim was carrying his M16 with the M203

grenade launcher and Burton had a Lee-Enfield sniper rifle and an MP5, which gave him the lightest burden of all. As they moved down the field, they dropped into their respective positions: Rob first, having the highest position on the slope, then Slim, about halfway down, and finally Burton, positioned dangerously close to the road. The three of them melted into the hedgerow and took up firing positions.

The sun had not yet sunk, but the shadows were deepening and shifting in great swathes across the darkening landscape. As this was a little-used country road, the traffic was sparse and Burton prayed that it would remain so until the ambush was over. Using his old, frequently sharpened switchblade knife, he hacked at the branches of the hedgerow until there was a body-sized recess into which he could squeeze himself. This accomplished, he carefully checked and loaded both the MP5 sub-machine gun and the Lee-Enfield sniper rifle and then sat back with the latter across his lap.

As he sat there, waiting for the approach of the car, he had to force himself to forget Teresa Kiely and the troubled thoughts she had given rise to; instead, he concentrated on the job ahead. He was hoping that with this one ambush they would be able to neutralize the remaining three of the Belfast Six and thus be able to return to Hereford immediately, but he couldn't be sure that this would happen. Nevertheless, he was silently praying that it would, because he desperately wanted to do something for Teresa Kiely and, at the same time, put a safe distance between himself and her by returning to his family. As long as he was here, dealing with the strange, tormented girl, he would not feel secure.

He checked his wristwatch repeatedly, but the time seemed to drag on interminably. Eventually, however, he saw the three cars in the distance, travelling close together, and he knew they could only be the target vehicles. A later conversation between Hegarty and the American, Luke Brady, picked up by Burton on his advanced STG laser surveillance system in the house next door, had produced a precise description of the cars to be used for the journey and now, as they drew closer, Burton was indeed able to identify them as being the target vehicles.

Instantly, he raised his left hand in the air and held it there for a moment. He was waiting for the first car to reach midway across the bottom of the grassy slope. When it did, he dropped his hand to his side, signalling that the attack should commence.

A short, sharp roaring indicated that Slim had fired the first missile from the M203 grenade-launcher attached to his M16 rifle. Even before the missile had exploded on the road, Rob's GPMG roared into life, pouring a hail of machine-gun fire into the moving convoy as Burton opened fire with his Lee-Enfield sniper rifle, carefully aiming at the front side window of the leading car. Slim's grenade exploded just in front of the same car and made it slew to the side of the road as a hail of bullets from Rob's GPMG and Burton's rifle slammed into it and smashed the rear side window. The second car, unable to brake quickly enough, smashed into the rear of the first as the third car veered sharply to the opposite side of the road and screeched to a halt, facing the bottom of the hill.

Men poured out of the first car just before the second grenade from Slim's M203 smashed through the rear side window and exploded inside, blowing glass and pieces of metal in all directions. Then the petrol tank exploded and the vehicle turned into a ball of fire ringed with black, boiling smoke.

Having raked the first two cars, which were jammed against one another, one blazing fiercely, Rob turned his GPMG on the third car as its occupants jumped out and took up positions behind it. Meanwhile, Burton carefully took aim at one of the three men kneeling at the bottom of the field in front of the burning car, firing blindly up the hill with their handguns. Burton squeezed the trigger, the rifle roared, and his target threw his arms up in the air, releasing his handgun, and fell back onto the road even before his weapon had reached the ground. Burton immediately fired at the second man, who also jerked backwards and collapsed as the third man threw himself face down on the grass in a desperate attempt to avoid being hit. Burton hit him anyway, pumping a couple of bullets into him, and the man twitched violently and then was still. As Burton turned his attention to the car in the middle, the one that had crashed into the blazing car, he saw its occupants taking refuge behind it and opening fire with handguns. Three of those men were the ones he wanted, but he couldn't get at them.

Another grenade from Slim's M203 exploded in the road beyond that car, but the position of the stalled cars, at this side of the road, had made the elevation too low for Slim or Rob to reach them. Hearing the abrupt silence of the GPMG, Burton glanced over his shoulder and saw Rob running down the hill, staying close to the hedgerow, carrying his Lee-Enfield sniper rifle and MP5 sub-machine gun, to join Slim halfway down. Both men then started firing their sniper rifles at the men exposed on the road between their undamaged car and the bottom of the hill. Burton also turned his sniper rifle on those men and soon all four were dead, leaving only the other four – the men he most wanted – bunched up behind the smashed middle car.

'Keep me covered!' Burton bawled as he lowered his sniper rifle to the ground and picked up the MP5 sub-machine gun. So far, the men below, with the sun in their eyes and their attackers hidden in the hedgerows, had not been able to see where the fire was coming from. Burton knew that he would be visible to them the instant he left the shelter of the hedgerow, so when Slim's M16 and Rob's Lee-Enfield started firing above him, he hacked his way deeper into the hedgerow, finally managed to crawl out the other side, and then ran down towards the road, hidden from view.

The fire fight was continuing on the other side of the field when he reached the hedgerow running parallel to the road. Again, he dropped to his knees and hacked his way through with his knife, then sheathed it and crawled through the hole until he could peer carefully out.

Looking along the road, he could see the front of the blazing lead car, now obscured in a pall of smoke, but that vehicle was blocking his view of the four men behind the second car. The men were still firing up the hill, trying to hit Slim and Rob, who were firing back with their rifles. Taking advantage of the fact that those men were being pinned down by the repeated firing of the sniper rifles, Burton crawled out of the hole and stood upright, holding his MP5 at the ready. Then he raced zigzagging along the middle of the road, hoping that the blazing car would prevent the IRA men from seeing him.

He was about twenty yards from the blazing car, smelling the smoke in his nostrils, when one of the Provos behind the second car glanced sideways and saw him. As the man straightened up, aiming his handgun, Burton wrenched a hand grenade from his belt, unclipped it and threw it, then hit the dirt and rolled over repeatedly, towards the side of the road. He heard the grenade bouncing off the first car and then exploding with a deafening roar.

With the explosion still echoing in his ears, he stood up and advanced on the run, firing his MP5 from the hip in a wide arc, hoping to at least keep the IRA men pinned down until he could see them more clearly. Just before plunging into the smoke from the first car, he glanced sideways and saw that Slim and Rob were zigzagging down to the bottom of the hill, now firing their MP5 sub-machine guns. The sound of gunfire and ricocheting bullets formed a hellish cacophony as Burton plunged into the smoke and advanced towards the flames of the burning car.

Turning around the side of the car, advancing at the crouch, his MP5 ready to fire, guided forward by the yellow flames and by shouting and gunfire, he saw a shadowy figure in the murk. Burton opened fire and heard a scream as the figure jerked, then he emerged from the smoke and saw a bulky stranger in a grey suit – it had to be the American, Luke Brady – straightening up again with his left arm all bloody, his right hand holding a pistol. Brady was gritting his teeth and raising his pistol to fire again, but Burton opened up first, putting a burst into his chest. This time Brady didn't scream – he just convulsed against the car and appeared to jackknife, then he straightened up and staggered awkwardly backwards and finally fell out of sight. Burton heard his pistol clattering on the ground as three more figures materialized in the murk, the nearest one turning towards him. Burton recognized Neil Byrne.

Keenan was right behind Neil Byrne. Hegarty, behind Keenan, was the one standing closest to the undamaged car. He made a run for it.

Byrne was staring straight at Burton and raising his hand-gun to fire when a bullet from one of the men on the hill sent him bowling sideways. He hit the ground and rolled over, coming to rest on his back, as Burton advanced out of the smoke, taking aim with his MP5.

'Help me!' Byrne bawled.

Burton was just about to open fire on Byrne when he saw Keenan turning around as if to help his wounded colleague. But Keenan didn't help him. He glanced down at him, then at Burton, then he stepped back, quite deliberately, and ran towards the undamaged car as Burton fired into Byrne.

Byrne screamed and jerked repeatedly. 'Oh, fuck!' he bawled. 'Fuck you!' Though still twitching and drenched in his own blood, he tried to raise his handgun. Burton fired another burst and Byrne's chest was smashed open. He seemed to lift off the ground, his back arched, his arms flailing, then blood burst from his mouth and he collapsed and did not move again.

Burton checked that Byrne and Brady were both dead, then he looked at the third car. Keenan was throwing himself through the open front door as the car, driven by Hegarty, reversed on screeching tyres and then lurched forward in the direction it had come from. The front side door slammed shut and then Keenan started firing out the window, keeping Slim and Rob pinned down. Burton raised his MP5, locked it into his shoulder and fired repeated bursts at the retreating car. The glass in the rear window exploded, but the car kept going and had soon raced out of range of the MP5. It disappeared around the bend in the road and then there was silence.

'Shit!' Burton exclaimed softly, lowering his MP5 to his side and then glancing sideways. Slim and Rob had advanced to the road and were walking up to him.

'They're dead?' Slim asked, nodding towards the bodies of Neil Byrne and Luke Brady.

'Yes,' Burton said.

'Those other two fuckers got away,' Rob said.

'Yes, I'm afraid so. Now let's get the hell out of here before another driver comes along. Let's disappear pronto.'

Leaving behind them the two smashed cars, the dead men, and the flame and smoke obscuring a darkening road strewn with bullet casings, they clambered back over the hedgerow and headed back up the hill, sticking close to the hedgerow. As they made their way to the summit, they collected the weapons left in the three separate assault positions, picking up the GPMG last. Heavily burdened again, they made their way across the brow to the van still parked there, heaped the weapons into the rear, then drove back down to the narrow road at the bottom. There they turned left and drove along to the parked Ford Cortina. The weapons and ammunition were stored under the false bottom of the Ford Cortina and then, while Burton and Rob kept watch, Slim poured gasoline over the van and set it alight. Confident that when found it would be burned beyond easy identification, the three men piled into the red Ford Cortina and Burton, at the steering wheel, headed back towards Antrim.

'Keenan deliberately let me kill Byrne,' he said when he had driven well away from the ambush site and was on the road home, heading into the deepening darkness. 'That really surprised me.'

'That means he's more than we imagine,' Slim said. 'He's not just some mild accountant.'

'It means he's more dangerous than Hegarty,' Rob added. 'And he's fooled the whole lot of 'em. Which means he's fooled us.'

'Well, I'll be damned,' Burton whispered.

CHAPTER THIRTY-ONE

U pstairs in O'Donovan's pub, the morning after the ambush, Keenan faced Hegarty across the familiar table in what seemed like an oddly empty haunted room. Gallagher, McCauley, and O'Shea were missing – and now, so too was Byrne. Keenan had been wondering for a long time how he could get rid of Byrne and that unknown ambush team had solved the problem for him. Now the problem was learning who those hit men had been and retaliating in kind.

'Sure I can't believe Byrne's dead,' Hegarty said between impressively long gulps of Guinness, still gathering his shocked senses together. 'That bastard shot him to pieces with an MP5 an' made a thorough job of it. I still can't believe it.'

'Neither can I,' Keenan lied. 'I tried to save him, but I saw it happening too late. He was dead before I could help him.'

'Ackay, I understan' how ya feel. You and he were good friends, like. Him and me, we had our differences as you know, but I always respected him.'

Keenan sighed. 'Yes, he was one of the best. Apart from our friendship, he was invaluable to the organization and his loss will be felt.'

'Damned right,' Hegarty said. 'This is a real blow to all of us, I tell ya. The organization's gonna be in disarray if we don't do something about it. You and me, we'll have to take over the whole show between us. I think that's the simplest way.'

'Right,' Keenan said, appalled at the very thought. 'In the meantime, we have to think about what happened and make sure it doesn't happen again. We have to know who those men were.'

'Sure it was a fuckin' professional job,' Hegarty said. 'Those

bastards were organized, they knew exactly what they were
doin', an' they had a fuckin' impressive arsenal with 'em. That
arsenal included Heckler & Koch MP5s, which most of us here
in Belfast use. I say it was those Prods from Sandy Row an' we
should go in an' wipe 'em out.'

'The Brits use MP5s as well,' Keenan said softly. 'Especially
the SAS. Those bastards gave us problems during the Troubles
and some might have been sent back.'

'The SAS?'

'Why not? If it's from outside, who'd be better? We both know
that the British government has expressed concern about our
activities, so if they decided to put a stop to us, who better to
send in? The SAS are masters of covert work – they also know
this city – so sending in a few of their top men, particularly
those with previous experience in Northern Ireland, would
certainly make sense.'

Hegarty stared at him, trying to think. It rarely came easily
to him. Keenan despised him and couldn't wait to get rid of
him and the time for that would come soon now. Keenan had
let Byrne die because Byrne was his last impediment to the
taking-over of all six turfs – except, of course, for Hegarty who
was as thick as two planks and could now be more easily dealt
with. Keenan and Byrne had once been friends and Byrne
had never stopped thinking they still were. But Keenan could
never forgive his old friend for losing his beliefs and, along with
lesser men than himself – the likes of Gallagher, McCauley,
O'Shea and this mad bastard, Hegarty – leading his former
IRA freedom fighters into organized crime. Keenan had seen
it coming and had tried to prevent it, but then he realized that
the only way he could stop it was to join them, gradually make
himself invaluable to them and then somehow subvert their
intentions. They had turned the honourable fight for Ireland's
freedom into a squalid wallow in the filth of organized crime
and he had loathed them for it.

'The SAS,' Hegarty said, his eyes gleaming with the light
of understanding. 'Sure yer right, come to think of it. They're
the boyos who worked these fuckin' streets like a bunch of
invisibles. They'd know Belfast, right enough. An' they know
some of us by sight. For sure they'd be a good fuckin' choice if
the Brits wanted some men in here who knew what they were
doin'. An' that bastard who killed O'Shea was an Englishman,
so he fits what yer sayin'. Jesus Christ, this is serious, like.'

God, this Hegarty was loathsome and typical of the breed: the very opposite of the men good and true who, over fifty years ago, had fought here and in Dublin and in Cork to get the Black and Tans out. Keenan's grandfather had been one of those men – a dedicated freedom fighter – not scum like this, who used the legitimate IRA as an umbrella for crime. Keenan's grandfather had been a landowner, aristocratic and wealthy, and he had not fought to make himself filthy lucre, which he didn't need, but because he was fiercely patriotic and defending his homeland. He had been killed by the Black and Tans, tortured and shot in a roadside ditch in the county of Monaghan, but his son, Keenan's father, had then taken up the cause and handed down to Keenan his love for Ireland, his urge to defend it, and his determination to wrench it back from the Brits. Keenan was brought up believing that and he had never forgotten it.

He had been born and bred in his family estate, in Castleblaney, County Monaghan, a far cry from the dismal hovels of the poor that then littered the countryside and filled the mean streets of Belfast. He had always been separate, therefore, from the common herd of the poor, and was separated even more by his expensive education at Trinity College; but he had been brought up to believe that all Irishmen, whether rich or poor, should have the right to be free and rule themselves in the land of their birth. Keenan's father was killed as well, accused of subversion and executed by the Brits, but then Keenan, like his father and his grandfather, had picked up the banner. He had not done so for profit, nor indeed out of vengeance, but because he believed that it was right and that a man did the honourable thing. Then these jackals, all the scum like this Hegarty, took over the streets and the cause became criminal. Keenan's shame was that he'd been forced to work with them and pretend to be one of them. Now he wanted to get rid of them all in a cleansing operation that would enable him to lead his erring flock back to the fold. He wanted to cleanse the ranks of the filth and return to the true fight. And ironically, the SAS – if such they were – had helped him to do that. Now he only had Hegarty to deal with and they might help him there as well.

'Yes,' Keenan said. 'Serious. If they've sent the SAS in, *they're* serious and we've got to move fast. We've got to find the Englishman and learn from him who and where his friends are. We've got to do it right now. To pull off that ambush, they had to know in advance we'd be travelling to the airport at that time. How the hell did they find that out?'

'Fucked if I know,' Hegarty said. 'The only ones who could have known about our movements are those who went with us – ten men plus us two – an' now all of 'em dead. Maybe one of 'em was a tout who didn't realize he'd be killed as well. You know? They tell 'im they'll make sure he's not harmed durin' the ambush, then they ice 'im to make sure he can't squeal on 'em. That used to happen a lot.'

'It surely did,' Keenan said. *That and a lot of other filth,* he thought, recalling how, when he had first moved to Belfast and joined the IRA, he had been filled with an idealism that was soon to be shattered. At that time the IRA had been based firmly on the historical organization and viewed itself, rightly in Keenan's view, as a legitimate army of freedom fighters trying to drive out an invading force. As in any such war, dirty tricks were played on both sides and some of the measures taken were harsh. Nevertheless, Keenan had felt them to be necessary and so engaged in his fair share of bombings, ambushes and executions, both of the enemy and of traitors on his own side. However, in 1969, when Loyalists rampaged through the Catholic ghettoes and the official IRA, with its gradualist policies, was unable to stop them, the hardliners of the movement broke away and formed a dissident group, the Provisional IRA, or PIRA. Frustrated by the gradualist attitude of the IRA, Keenan and Byrne were two of the many who joined the Provos on the promise of arms and military action. Soon, heavily armed and taking direct action against the Loyalist mobs, the RUC and the British Army, the Provos rapidly grew in strength. Unfortunately, they also showed a lack of moral restraint not seen in the 'Officials' and soon they were engaging in the same criminal activities initiated by the more fanatical Loyalists, financing their operations through intimidation, extortion and bank robberies. From there, the drift towards organized crime for non-political reasons was almost inevitable and finally, when the political peace came, many former freedom fighters, men such as Byrne, had become no more than gangsters who justified their unsavoury activities with a thin veneer of ongoing political commitment. At least Hegarty, with his increasing egomania and ambition, held to no such hypocrisy. Lacking Byrne's relatively sophisticated and convoluted self-justification, he was open about being in it for wealth and power. An increasing number of former paramilitaries, now members of the criminal gangs, were equally blatant about their motivation and so had turned Belfast into a gangland. Keenan loathed them, as he loathed this bastard Hegarty, and he would put an end to them. Once he had done that, he would build up a more dedicated, highly-motivated army and turn it against the Brits. He would give Ireland back to the Irish and take pride in so doing.

'What about your whore?' Keenan said. 'She was present at the meeting with Luke Brady, so she knew what we were planning and she knew the exact time. Do you think she'd have talked?'

'I thought about that,' Hegarty replied, 'and she certainly overheard everything, but sure she knows she'd get her fuckin' throat cut if she mentioned a word.'

'She still might have done it,' Keenan said. 'She might have decided to take that chance, assuming that none of us would survive. I think she might be their source.'

'I still say she'd be too fuckin' frightened. She's scared shitless of me.'

'If she's scared shitless of you, she might hate you enough to take that chance, so I still think she's their source.'

Hegarty was exasperated and soothed his angst with another slug of beer. He wiped his lips with the back of his hand, then said, 'Look, even if she wanted to pass on information, there's no way in the world she could have done it. I have dickers watching her house night and day, her phone has been bugged, an' even when she's on the game, pickin' up tricks in hotel bars, there's always a couple of my men sittin' within earshot to hear what she says. She can't even use a public telephone without our permission, so she's never used one since I took 'er over. She just couldn't have talked.'

Keenan recalled how British Intelligence, including the SAS covert teams, had operated during the Troubles. He thought he knew what the answer was. 'Her flat's been bugged,' he said. 'It's been bugged by an outside influence. Probably all the rooms and even the bedroom. If that's true, she wouldn't have to talk to anyone. We were the ones doing the talking and those bugs picked it up.'

Hegarty was silent for a moment, deep in thought again, then he shook his head and said, 'No, that's not possible. We watch her house night an' day an' sure no one could have entered without us seein' 'em. No way could that happen.'

'It's not her house, Jack. It's a house converted into flats. The residents come and go all day long.'

'We know all the residents,' Hegarty insisted.

'But one of them could have done it.'

'Shit!'

'Or one of their guests. You don't know their guests.'

'Shit!' Hegarty said again.

'But let's assume it wasn't them, has she had any visitors of her own? Anyone you don't know?'

'No, I wouldn't let 'er have visitors that I didn't know personally.'

'Any tradesmen who had to enter the house?'

'Shit!' Hegarty exclaimed for the third time, his pink cheeks giving away his embarrassment. 'Come to think of it, she had a leaking pipe one night when we were there and I let her call 'er own plumber. He came the next day in a plumber's van – it belonged to a company known locally – and he was in there for nearly an hour. Oh, shit, come to think of it . . .'

'He's our man,' Keenan said. 'He bugged the flat. I'm damned certain of that.'

'Jesus Christ! Christ, I'll kill 'er.'

'Where would she be now?'

'On the game as usual. I make her work all day.'

'Do you make her be back by a certain time?'

'Ackay. Never later than three in the mornin'.'

'And she's reliable?'

'Yeah, very reliable. Like I said, she's scared shitless.'

'Then make sure you're there when she gets back tonight. Then give me a call. We'll question her and then tear the place apart until we find where the bugs are.'

'An' if it's true?' Hegarty asked. 'If she confesses an' we find the bugs?'

'We take her out of the city and kill her and bury her deep. Then we find the people she's been working for and we terminate them as well.'

Hegarty looked a bit brighter, as if forgiven for his sins. 'I think we've already found the Englishman,' he said. 'The one who put O'Shea's lights out.'

'You *think* you've found him?'

'I haven't had time to get out there,' Hegarty said, sounding sarcastic. 'I was out gettin' shot at.'

Keenan ignored the sarcasm. 'So why do you think you've found him?'

'As I told you, he'd talked up and down the Falls and let slip that he was out in Antrim, so we trawled that whole area for weeks, askin' about an Englishman who'd recently arrived an' was spreadin' the word that he was here to buy second-hand furniture. Yesterday, just before we picked up Brady to go to the airport and get our balls shot off, I received a call from one of my boyos, sayin' that he'd been told of an Englishman supposedly looking for second-hand furniture an' living out in a rented cottage near Ballyclare. They say he was called Trevor Manning – the same name used by that bastard who befriended O'Shea in the pubs and went into his shop the evenin' he had his head blown off.'

'He's our man,' Keenan said.

'Right,' Hegarty said, looking satisfied with himself. 'So, havin' found this out, my boyo checked the local car-and-van rental companies and found that Mister Trevor Manning had rented a furniture van a couple of months earlier. My boyo jotted down the registration number and then drove out to have a look at the cottage near Ballyclare. He saw the van – same registration number – sittin' outside it. My boyo's still there, keeping watch, an' I'm goin' out there this afternoon.'

'You do that,' Keenan said. 'Try to take him alive. If you succeed, keep him there and do anything required to make him talk. Out there, no one will hear him scream.'

'A real blessin',' Hegarty said.

Keenan nodded, not smiling, knowing that Hegarty was a sadist, but accepting that in this case he had to let him do what he could do as no one else could. Clear this mess up and he could soon get rid of Hegarty and take over himself. Alone, with no one to contradict him, he could amalgamate the six turfs of West Belfast and build himself a real army. His day would come soon.

'When he's talked,' Keenan said, 'kill him and bury him where he'll never be found. Set fire to the house and the van. Then get back to Belfast and go straight to that whore's flat and wait for her. When you have her, call me.'

'Good as done,' Hegarty said.

He stood up, walked out and descended the stairs, leaving Keenan, the last true freedom fighter, alone with his thoughts.

The end will come soon, Keenan thought, *and then we'll have a new beginning. The political peace will be broken and the war for Ireland's freedom will be engaged again.*

This thought consoled him.

CHAPTER THIRTY-TWO

Teresa had already had three tricks in two different hotels by the time she arrived at the Europa that evening. One trick had been easy ('Face to face, lady, and no fancy stuff') but the other two had been more demanding and now she felt bruised and soiled. Nevertheless, she had showered and made herself up afresh in the room of the final trick and knew, as she entered the upstairs bar, that she looked as good as always.

Jim Quaid gave her a nod as always when she walked through the door and she saw Frank Cooney sitting on a stool near to where she usually sat. Her heart skipped a beat when she saw him, particularly when she also saw that two of Jack Hegarty's more mature hard men, both dressed in conservative suits with shirt and tie, were sitting on the stools beside Cooney, close enough to hear everything she said to him or anyone else. Nevertheless, she had to sit beside Cooney, silently praying that he would have sense enough not to offer anything other than light, bantering conversation. She was not disappointed.

'So how's the sexiest hooker in Belfast?' Frank asked. 'Still doing good business?'

'Doin' fine, Frank. No problems. Will ya buy me a drink then?'

'Sure what do I get in return, gorgeous?'

'My ravishing company.'

'I think that's worth a wee drop. The usual?'

'Ackay.'

Cooney ordered two more drinks, Jim Quaid gave her a wink, then Cooney said, 'Pick up anyone special? Any rich millionaires?'

'Nah,' Teresa replied. 'Just the usual windbags. Little men

with very big wallets, but no millionaires. The day I find a fuckin' millionaire I'll go back to the church.'

'You do that and I'll become a Catholic and we'll get blessed together.'

'Jesus, Frank, yer jokes are dreadful.'

'But I'm paying for the drinks.'

'Why not pay me for a night up in a room and give yer wife a night off?'

'I'm a happily married man.'

'I confess, yer my first. I haven't met one since the day I was born, so you've just made my day.'

Teresa glanced around the room. She was pretending to be working. She wanted the two goons beside Cooney to think this was a normal night. 'Anyone in here worth knowin'?' she said to Cooney, turning back to the bar. 'I've still a few hours to fill, like.'

Cooney shrugged and grinned. 'Just the usual, gorgeous. A few tourists, a few pot-bellied businessmen and some of the regulars. Nothing new or startling that I know of, but you'd better ask our wee barman.'

'I will. Here he comes.'

Jim Quaid brought the drinks and set them down on the counter, then grinned, looking Teresa up and down, and said, 'Sure ya look like a wet dream.'

'Don't come while yer workin',' Teresa said. 'That could be an embarrassment. Frank here tells me this room is like a morgue and the stiffs are all wiltin'. Do you know better or not?'

Quaid automatically glanced around the bar and then shrugged, turning back to her. 'These stiffs are all horizontal,' he said. 'I think yer in for a bad night.'

'Thanks a lot,' Teresa said.

'On the other hand . . .' Quaid glanced towards the door and Teresa turned and saw Burton. Her heart skipped a beat again. Burton was wearing an immaculate grey suit with shirt and tie and black patent-leather shoes. He looked handsome and rich.

'Looks like one of your regular tricks has arrived,' Cooney said, loud enough to ensure that the two goons beside him would hear. 'I think that one likes you. What's he like in the sack?'

'Not as good as he looks,' Teresa replied, 'but he's easy to handle. If he's here, my night's made.'

Burton stared directly at her – a bold, deliberate stare – then raised his hand and pointed from Jim Quaid to a table located close to the bar. When Quaid nodded in return, Burton walked to the table, sat down and lit a cigarette.

'He wants the usual,' Jim Quaid said. 'A large Bushmill's on the rocks. That means he's gonna drink until he can approach ya. Yer luck's in, Teresa.'

'Irish luck,' Teresa said.

As Quaid went to pour Burton's drink, Cooney deliberately looked back over his shoulder at Burton, studied him at length, then turned back to Teresa and said, 'Why is it that it's always the handsome bastards who're no good in the sack?'

'He's probably a closet gay,' Teresa replied, 'who's tryin' to convince himself that he's not by picking up whores.'

'That's what I like about you, gorgeous. I learn so much from you. I'm a happily married man with a wife and kids and you show me a different world.'

'You're a voyeur who gets yer rocks off by hearing about what others do. So what do you want to know?'

'You really think that one's gay?'

'I don't know, but he might be. Sure he's okay, but he has to work up to it an' he fumbles a lot. Like, he practically apologizes. Sorry, I can't get it in, he says. So I help 'im an' he whispers his thanks and sort of leaves me to do the rest. I think that's funny, don't you? I mean, he's really pretty handsome. You'd think he'd had so many women that he'd be pretty confident. But he isn't – he's kinda nervous. He's even shy of taking his clothes off. I think that shows he's not comfortable with it an' that could mean he's gay. So why are *you* interested? Do you recognize the breed? Are *you* like that as well, Frank? I've often wondered why you buy me all these drinks an' make sexist remarks, but never actually ask me for the business. Sure I have m' doubts there, Frank.'

Cooney grinned. He was acting as well. He finished off his drink and put his glass down, then pushed back his stool. 'On that note, I'll leave,' he said. 'I can't stand the heat in here. A man asks a simple question and gets rubbished by a whore with a heart of stone. I'm not gay – I just can't afford your rates like that closet gay over there. What's the cost, Jim?'

Quaid made out the bill and slid it across to Cooney. The latter paid and waited for his change and then turned back to Teresa. 'Your friend's waitin' to get his arse on this stool and make you an offer you can't refuse, so I'll bid you good evening.'

'Same to you, Frank.'

'Sweet dreams.'

Cooney left the bar and Teresa ordered another drink and tried not to look at the two goons sitting farther along. They were watching and listening, which was frightening enough but, talking to Cooney and now waiting for Burton, she felt even more frightened. This was a dangerous game that could end in death if the wrong word was spoken. When you acted, when you played this dangerous game, it was easy to say the wrong word. Teresa prayed that Burton would make no mistake as he walked up behind her. She felt him before she even saw him and she thought this was magical. When he slipped onto the stool vacated by Cooney, she felt a lot better. She had confidence in him.

'Hi,' he said. 'Good to see you again.'

'Well, well, look who's here,' Teresa replied. 'My old friend, Mister Drummond. What brings you back?'

'Business. I'm just here for the night. Can I buy you a drink?'

Teresa held her glass up. 'Got one,' she said.

'I don't really want another,' Burton said. 'I just wanted to say hello.'

'On yer own again?'

'I just came for a meeting. I wondered if . . .'

'Don't be shy, Mister Drummond. I enjoyed it the last time. Stayin' here again, are ya?'

'Yes. I always stay here. It's the best place in town. And I remembered you and saw you sitting here, and so I . . . Well, are you free?'

'Not free for you,' she replied, 'no matter how much I like you. How long do you want?'

'I have to fly back to London tomorrow, so I think I should sleep. What about until midnight?'

'I'm yer woman,' Teresa replied. 'You want to go up right now?'

'That's fine by me,' Burton said.

'All right,' Teresa said, 'you toddle on up and I'll be up in another five minutes.'

'Good. See you then.'

Burton left the bar and Teresa sat on, trying to slow the racing of her heart as she finished her drink.

'Sure it's a treat watchin' ya operate,' the goon nearest to her said. 'It's good to know ya've got regular customers – those who come back for more. I might try it some time.'

'Fuck off,' Teresa said. 'Just make sure yer sober enough to drive me home when I come back down from there.'

'Some day that mouth'll get ya into trouble.'

'Not with you,' Teresa said.

She picked her bag off the counter, slung it over her shoulder, smiled at Quaid and then walked out of the bar. Two minutes later she was knocking on Burton's door and holding her breath. When he opened it and gazed steadily at her, she let her breath out again.

'Come in,' Burton said.

'Jesus!' She stepped in quickly. He closed the door behind her and then turned to face her. He was still wearing the grey suit with shirt and tie. He hadn't taken the jacket off. 'My heart was hammerin' down there, I can tell ya,' she said. 'First I walk in an' find Frank Cooney sittin' there with two of Hegarty's goons sittin' right beside him. So we're both sittin' there actin', tradin' cynical wisecracks, an' all the time I'm waitin' for one of us to make a slip, say the wrong thing, an' I'm also sittin' there knowin' you were about to come in as well an' I'd have to go through the second act. I kept wonderin' what you'd say, how I'd reply, and I'm talkin' nineteen to the dozen and thinkin' every second of those two hoodlums listenin' in. I can't take too much more of this.'

'You won't have to,' Burton said. He hadn't moved from where he was standing. He was holding her gaze with his own and it made her feel better, but her heart was still racing.

'What do ya mean?' she asked.

'I'm going to have to pull you out. Neil Byrne was killed yesterday – and a whole lot of others – and the survivors are bound to know that the ambush team was aware of their movements. They'll want to know about that. How the information got out. And if they believe that it didn't come from inside – from one of their own – they'll realize that the only other person who knew of those movements was the lady listening in to their conversation. That lady was you.'

Teresa felt a hot blush of rage burning her cheeks, even as fear slid icily through her and tightened her stomach.

Drinking in Burton, she was overwhelmed with emotions
that left her confused: a kind of love – she wasn't sure if it
was that – combined with hatred for how he was using her.
She was drawn to him as she had never been drawn to a man
before – she felt her blood surging towards him, her nerves
trying to reach out and touch – but she was also frightened
by something buried inside him, something withdrawn and
deep and yet faintly recognizable – and she wanted to slap
his face and then embrace him and fade away in his arms.
She hated him for this as well – for confusing her emotionally
– but she hated him too, even in her growing love, for what he
was telling her.

'Ackay,' she said, 'they're bound to know it was me – and you
must have always known they would once you'd used what you
picked up. You knew that and still bugged my flat and placed
me on a hot rock. Oh, God, I can't believe it. You fuck-face!
You shite-hole! You came in there and did what you did and
then you left me exposed. Sure I should've known better. What
bastards you men are.'

He reached out to grab her shoulder and shake her gently,
insistently. 'It never entered my head,' he said. 'Believe me,
it didn't. I knew I was placing you in danger and I told you
so, but I didn't think of this part of it. It was my mistake. I'm
sorry. When I bugged your place, I couldn't predict what would
happen and now we have to deal with this. I'm pulling you out
of there right now.'

Though she liked the feel of his hand on her shoulder, she
shook it off angrily. 'Pull me out? What the fuck does that
mean? Are you tellin' me I can't go back home? Is that what
yer sayin'?'

'Yes,' Burton confirmed.

Christ, she hated him! The bastard! How could he have done
this to her? She was still uncertain about what he was saying,
but it didn't sound good. She felt fear in her soul.

'I'm not allowed to go back there? What else? Do I have to
leave Belfast? Are ya sayin' it's all over for me? That I have
to get out?'

'No,' Burton said. 'I'm not saying that. Calm down. I'm not
saying that.'

Boiling with rage, feeling betrayed, Teresa turned away
from him and stood at the foot of the bed, aware that she was
trembling. She wanted Burton on that bed, she realized, and

this need only made her hate him all the more. She wanted to break his reticence, to unravel what he was hiding, to discover what it was about him that she feared because it struck a deep chord in her. She knew that this could sometimes happen – an instinctive drawing together – two people recognizing something in each other that others could not see. He was haunted and hurt, as she was, and that told the whole story. She wanted him on that bed because she knew what she could do there to help unravel their mutual torment. Beds were made for unravelling.

'So what the fuck *are* you saying?'

Burton walked up behind her, took hold of her shoulders, turned her around and then pressed her gently down until she was sitting on the bed with her feet on the floor. Looking down, he seemed taller than he was, making her feel like a lost child.

'It's not permanent,' he said. 'It's only temporary. We've got rid of them all, except for Keenan and Hegarty, and when they're out of the picture you can return and live a free life. You don't have to leave Belfast. This will only take a few days. You're coming with me, to stay with me in Antrim, and when we clear up the rest of this mess, you can return home in safety.'

'I'm going with you, Burton?'

'Yes,' he said. 'Right now. My feeling's that if you go home tonight, you'll find Hegarty there. He'll be wanting to talk to you. You know he can make you talk. If you refuse, he'll go to work on you and eventually you *will* talk. When you talk, when you confess that the place is bugged, he'll almost certainly kill you.'

'Jesus, thanks a lot, Burton.'

'We have to leave right now,' he said. 'I'll drive you back to Antrim. Those two animals downstairs aren't expecting you till midnight, so we'll leave now and go down by the stairs and they won't even see us. I'll drive you out to Antrim, you'll stay there until this has ended and then, when Keenan and Hegarty are no more, you can return to a normal life.'

'What's that mean?' Teresa asked.

She wanted a cigarette, but she decided not to have one because she wanted to get him down on the bed and learn more about him. She wanted him for that, but for the other thing as well, and when she realized she wanted him for the other thing

– for himself, for love or some equally unimaginable return –
she was shocked and shaken to the roots of her soul. She had
not dared to want a man for love since her poor British soldier
and now the thought of it frightened her.

'Sure that all sounds very promising,' she said, 'but nothin's
guaranteed, is it?'

'No,' he replied.

'So why should I trust you again?'

'It's either me or Hegarty.'

Christ, he was sharp. Not half as soft as he looked. He
was sharp and hard when he had to be, yet he also had
that old-fashioned, almost stern morality and the pain that
only decent men can shoulder. He was the kind of man she
had dreamed about when still an adolescent, but he was also
the dark creature of her nightmares, bringing doubt and
confusion. It was either him or Hegarty, he had said. No
false promises there. Where did men like him come from?

'I'm fucked either way, aren't I?'

'I don't know what you mean,' he said.

'I go back to Hegarty and I get my throat cut. I go with you
an' I'm as helpless as a child, totally dependent upon you. Sure
that's no grand choice, Burton.'

'It's not a matter of choice,' he replied. 'It's a matter of life
or death. Stay here and you'll be buried and forgotten. Come
with me and you might live. There's no choice. We all want
to live.'

'Well, don't we just, mister?'

She couldn't help smiling, admiring his pragmatism, but she
knew that he wasn't as calm as he seemed, because her heart
told her so. She knew all about that as well – the beguiling
mysteries of the heart, the yearning heart, the broken heart
– and so she knew that Burton's heart had been broken and
he was trying to live with it. She had to know why. Knowing
that, she would know him. She had to know him because she
recognized something in him that struck a chord in her own
heart. Like her, he was living on the edge and trying not to
fall off. She had to know what it was about herself that she had
seen in his eyes and she decided to ask him. She'd asked before
and he'd managed not to tell her, but now she had something
on him. He had the need to protect her – that was clear – and
she would use that against him.

'We all want to live,' she said. 'Sure that's a grand truth, isn't it? You give me this choice between life an' death and say there's really no choice. But I have to choose, don't I? There's no choice about *that*, is there? But what about you, Burton, who says there's no choice and yet looks at me with yearnin' in yer eyes but does nothin' about it? Isn't that your choice, Burton? To have me or not? To think ya *might* want me an' want to know if ya do, but can't decide if ya should find out by tryin' me out or stickin' to yer sweet wife and kids in the green hills of Hereford. That's a choice that hurts, doesn't it? You accept or decline the pain. Most men would take the chance but you can't because there's somethin' that stops you. So what is it, Burton? That I'm a whore? I don't think so. Yer here to do a job an' I'm part of the job, but I mean somethin' more to ya than that and the pair of us know it. Ya really wanna help me, don't ya? Save m' soul or whatever. Ya *need* to do that – I've sussed that – it's a *need* – and now I have to know why ya feel that way and where the need came from. So you tell me, Burton. If you don't, I won't go with ya. You think I'm bluffin'? I've got little to lose and I'll risk it by sayin' no. Let Hegarty cut my throat. That could be a fuckin' blessin'. I won't go if you don't tell me what it is that makes you want to protect me. Redemption – is that it? Some slime of sin to be washed away? Quiet men – an' you're a *very* quiet man – always have somethin' to hide. So what are you hidin', Burton? What's the secret of yer solitude? You look at me with eyes filled with pain an' ya think I can help you. I can't. I can help an awful lot of men, but I have to know what they need. So tell me what you need, Burton. Tell me what it is yer hidin'. Tell me that an' I'll make ya feel better by lettin' ya protect me an' be my knight errant. That's yer choice, Burton. Talk or not. If ya don't, I walk out alone.'

She saw the look in his eyes and it was the kind of look that kills, but she had seen even worse in her lifetime and she didn't yield one inch. He didn't yield either – or at least, he didn't move – but he seemed to tremble (though this may have been an illusion) and then he turned away from her. He walked to the nearest wall and then stopped to stare at it. He stared at that wall a long time and then he finally told her.

'It's fairly simple,' he said. 'There's really not that much to tell. I killed a child in Belfast ten years ago and I've never forgotten it. It was an accident, of course. It happened in the upper Falls. I can't remember the name of the street, but I'll

never forget what it looked like. It was a cordon-and-search
sweep of the kind you may remember and we went in to pick up
some terrorists and put them in prison. The child's father was
one of those. Just your average-day terrorist. So we burst into
his house and his wife was there screaming and we went up
the stairs to look for him and I killed the little girl by accident.
She was only ten years old. Her father was Mick Hennessey.
He was hiding a PIRA friend, Dennis Flagherty, up in his loft.
There was a fire fight on the landing. We got Flagherty – we
killed him – then we concentrated on Hennessey by throwing
flash-bangs into the bedrooms to start clearing them out. A
little girl rushed out. She was screaming hysterically. She ran
down the stairs and then I entered the bedroom and someone
moved and I fired and fired again and then there was silence.
Two people were dead in there. One was Mick Hennessey. The
other was his other daughter, ten years old, and when I saw
her, I died as well. I had to pick her up. I wanted to give her
back to her mother. It was insane, but I felt I had to do it
and that's what I did. Her mother was already screaming.
She'd been doing that since the break-in. So I picked her dead
daughter up and carried her down the stairs and then – I was
weeping; I remember that – I held the dead child out to her
mother. That poor woman, she went mad. She fell apart before
my eyes. She reached out to her dead daughter, almost touched
her, but jerked back; then she turned away – she didn't attack
me – and just screamed at the walls. She was screaming and
sobbing. I'd never heard that sound before. It was screaming
and sobbing all at once and it sounded like hell. I placed her
dead child on the floor. I didn't know what else to do. I turned
away and I walked out of the house and I never looked back.
Shortly after – maybe minutes, maybe hours – I started falling
to pieces. I kept cracking and I stayed that way a long time,
though they finally cured me. But they didn't. I'm not cured.
I had nightmares for years and those nightmares are with me
still and until I find a way to make amends I will not have a
restful night. So that's it. It's really not very much, but it's
all that I've got. If you want anything more, anything deeper,
you'll have to look elsewhere. There's no great mystery to it.'

He didn't say another word. Teresa sat there, shocked
speechless. She was ashamed that she had asked, but she also
felt rage and grief, and then she saw the endless nightmare of
her life from a different perspective. There was pain on both

sides, but no pain could match your own; given that, there was little she could do except live for the moment. Standing up, feeling murderous and maternal, she walked over to Burton. She wanted to cut his throat, to drink his blood, and then to die in his arms. To die with him, both of them together. But knowing what derangement was, what pain bred, she could only console him.

'I never wanted to hear that story,' she said. 'It's not what I expected. Sure I should never have asked. Fuck me, I shouldn't. Let's get out of here, Burton.'

He turned away from her, avoiding her face, and walked to the door of the room like a vanishing shadow. He stopped there, as if forgetting what he was doing, and she caught that brief moment. It was that moment, coming once in a lifetime, that you grabbed at or lost. Teresa grabbed it and held on.

'Burton,' she said.

He turned around to face her. His handsome face was gaunt with grief. Teresa took a step forward, feeling almost ethereal, and stopped when she was practically touching him, her breasts grazing his chest. She had to look up at him, craning her neck, drinking in his tortured face, overwhelmed by her contradictory emotions and knowing where they would lead. For her, no good could come from such emotions, given what he had told her.

'You want me, don't you?' she said.

'Yes,' Burton confessed. Then he led her out of the room and down the stairs, into the dark, dangerous night.

CHAPTER THIRTY-THREE

When the front door burst open, smashed in with a sledgehammer, Rob was sitting at the kitchen table oiling his Browning 9mm High Power handgun, his beloved 9-Milly, in order to keep himself busy and avoid temptation. Yesterday's ambush had been the only action he had seen since his killing of O'Shea and it had reminded him of just how dull his life here in Ireland was otherwise. No longer able to trawl the Falls for information, which had afforded him much pleasure, he'd had little to do until the ambush and knew that he could now do nothing other than sit around and wait for Burton to decide on their next course of action. As Burton was a careful man, that might take a bit of time and Rob, though he accepted the wisdom of Burton's caution, felt increasingly restless. He was tired of living alone, of jacking off forlornly instead of having real sex, of not having any contact with his fellow human beings, so he was tempted to break Burton's rule that he wasn't to socialize more than necessary with the locals and certainly wasn't to involve himself with any woman. This was the hardest bit of all – so hard, in fact, he was even beginning to have sexual fantasies about his missus, with whom he hadn't had sex for years. They had a good relationship, though – she went her way and he went his – and now he was thinking fondly of his social life back in Hereford and in the East End of London, where he'd been born and bred. Of course, the East End wasn't quite what it used to be: it had been drastically altered over the years by the property speculators who had obliterated a lot of the charming old areas and replaced them with hideous modern complexes. Nevertheless, Rob lived with his missus and kids in one of the few remaining old streets and always had a good time when he was there, boozing it up in the pubs, playing darts and billiards, picking up his fancy women, and even playing rugby occasionally – although he had to go down to Richmond for that. Certainly it was a damned sight more interesting that sitting here in this lonely cottage in Ballyclare waiting for something to happen. Rob was thinking about all this and oiling his handgun when the front door burst open.

Looking up, he saw the door falling to the floor and a bunch of men charging across it, kicking furniture aside and swinging baseball bats. Instantly recognizing Hegarty, Rob grabbed a 13-round magazine for the Browning High Power and tried to load the weapon while throwing himself to the floor and rolling onto his belly. He was too late. Just as he was slotting the magazine into the handgun, the first man reached him and kicked the weapon from his hand. Before Rob could do anything else, the man kicked him in the ribs and sent him flying across the floor. The man kicked him again: Rob felt a sharp pain and heard the snapping of some ribs. Then he was kicked a few more times, filled with pain and rendered breathless, before being grabbed by the hair, hauled to his feet and slammed back into his chair.

'Fuckin' English cunt!' Hegarty bawled. He punched Rob in the stomach, then in the face, breaking his nose and making his head feel like it had exploded. 'Fuckin' murderous bastard!'

Though dazed and blinded by pain, his nose flattened and pouring blood, Rob felt his arms being tied behind his back so tightly that he thought they would break. Hegarty slapped him a few times, making his head jerk left and right, then his legs were also tied to the chair and his drooping head was hauled up. He looked straight into Hegarty's glassy-eyed mad gaze and was chilled by the sight. Hegarty held up Rob's handgun and waved it under his broken nose.

'Fuckin' Browning High Power!' Hegarty bawled. 'That's fuckin' SAS – right?'

'I don't know what you're talking about,' Rob said.

Hegarty punched him again, in the stomach and in the face, then he slapped him so hard that the chair fell sideways, taking him with it. When Rob hit the floor, pains shot through his legs and arms and he nearly passed out.

'Okay, you lot,' Hegarty said to the other men, 'I want ya to turn this place inside out, includin' the attic. Make sure ya miss nothin'.'

'Right, boss,' one of the men said. Then they scattered through the house, including the upstairs, smashing furniture and ripping down curtains and tearing the sofa to shreds with knives, while the one who had remained in the kitchen with Hegarty heaved the chair back up onto its legs with Rob still tied to it. The pain in his bleeding, broken nose was atrocious and he had to breathe through his mouth. He felt fear such as he had never known before and he had to fight to control it.

Hegarty threw Rob's handgun on the kitchen table and then turned back to face him. The other man took up a position behind him, holding onto his shoulders, as Hegarty leaned over him again and glared into his eyes.

'Trevor Manning, my arse,' he said. 'Yer no furniture salesman either. You're fuckin' SAS and ya killed O'Shea and took part in that ambush yesterday. Now isn't that right, boyo?'

Rob didn't reply.

'Refusin' to talk, are ya? Well, we'll see about that. You'll fuckin' talk, ya'll sing like a fuckin' bird, before I'm through with ya. Save yerself an awful lot of pain, boyo, an' tell me yer real name.'

'My name's Trevor Manning,' Rob replied, 'and I deal in second-hand furniture. My van's outside and—'

'Ackay, yer van's outside. That and yer fuckin' rented Sunny Nissan. Both rented a couple of months back when ya arrived here from England. You and yer fuckin' friends – those bastards who shot us up yesterday. Now isn't that the truth, boyo?'

'I don't know what you're talking about,' Rob said, finding it hard to breathe, let alone talk. 'My name's Trevor Manning and I'm here to buy second-hand furniture. You must be crazy to think that I'm—'

Rob's face seemed to explode again – another crazed blow from Hegarty's fist – then he took another vicious punch in the stomach and coughed up some vomitus. His head was reeling and he felt his heart pounding as Hegarty turned away from him.

'Fuck this for a joke,' Hegarty said, turning to the table and picking up a baseball bat left there by one of his men. 'I don't have the patience for this.'

He smashed the baseball bat against Rob's shins and Rob heard himself screaming. He heard the scream before he

realized it was because of the pain, but when that came it
was terrible.

'Now tell me who ya are, shite-face,' Hegarty said, 'or ya'll
get that again.'

Blinded by tears and dazed by the pain, Rob desperately
wished he could reach his cyanide tablets and put himself
out. The pain consumed him and filled him with a nausea
that almost made him throw up again. He choked it back,
swallowed it, tried to keep it down, but then the baseball bat
hit his shins again and it came out with his screaming. He
felt the vomitus splashing on his shirt as he fought to get his
breath back. He tried not to sob, but his eyes were weeping
and he felt ashamed of himself.

'What's yer real name?' Hegarty said. 'Spit it out before I
use this bat again an' leave ya crippled for life.'

'Trevor Manning,' Rob gasped.

This time the baseball bat smashed across his feet and the
pain made him pass out. He recovered to find Hegarty pouring
a saucepan of cold water over his head. When Hegarty placed
the saucepan back on the table, Rob tried to twitch his toes
and realized, from the extent of the pain, that the bones in
his feet and toes had been broken. He would not be walking
out of this house. He would not leave alive. He knew this in
the dim recesses of his mind where the fear also lurked. This
was the end of the line for him.

'Yer a tough wee bastard,' Hegarty said. 'I'll give ya that
much. But yer gonna talk before this day's through, so ya
might as well do it now. What's yer name, boyo?'

'Trevor Manning,' Rob gasped.

Hegarty was just about to swing the baseball bat again when
some of his men came down the stairs, carrying the weapons
Rob had hidden in the attic. They laid them down on the table
and stepped back to let Hegarty study them.

'He had a whole fuckin' arsenal up there,' one of the men
said. 'Not the tools ya'd use for renovatin' furniture. We've a
right one here, boss.'

Hegarty picked the weapons up one by one, shaking his head
from side to side in disbelief and glancing repeatedly at Rob.
'Fuckin' right,' he said. 'Look at this! An L7A2 GPMG – one
of the fuckers that fired on us yesterday. And this: an M16
assault rifle with an M203 grenade launcher – also used in
that fuckin' ambush yesterday. And lookahere! The good old

Heckler & Koch MP5 sub-machine gun – used by us as well as by those SAS bastards – and an L42A1 Lee-Enfield sniper rifle with a Starlight 'scope. Last but not least, a whole fuckin' bagful of British L2A2 hand grenades. Sure this second-hand furniture salesman from England has some unusual interests. Second-hand furniture my arse! This wee bastard is SAS.' He turned back to Rob. 'Yer not Trevor Manning and yer not a man who knows about fuckin' furniture.' He pulled a pair of pliers from his hip pocket and waved them under Rob's broken nose. 'Yer fuckin' SAS an' we know it, so why not admit it? Ya've just lost yer legs and yer feet an' the next is yer fingernails. Now let's start with yer real name.'

When Rob did not respond, Hegarty pulled out the nail of his left thumb with the pliers and Rob heard his own screaming reverberating in his head's pain-filled darkness. When he recovered, he saw the weapons on the table, his SAS weapons, and accepted that further denial was useless. They knew already, so he might as well tell them and get this over and done with.

'Corporal Rob McAllister, D Squadron, 22 SAS.'

Hegarty patted him soothingly on the head and said, 'Good boy. That's the spirit. Now what the fuck are ya doin' in Northern Ireland? Just spit it out, boyo.'

Consumed by pain and feeling sick to his soul, Rob whispered, 'I came to neutralize the Belfast Six. I was told to get all of you.'

'British government, was it?'

Rob nodded.

'So ya were sent in here to put our lights out – and so far ya've got four of us. Is that right, boyo?'

Rob nodded again.

'You an' who else?' Hegarty asked him.

As best he could think through his pain and shame, Rob thought about it. 'Just me,' he finally groaned.

'Just you,' Hegarty said.

'Yes,' Rob muttered. 'Just me. They didn't want to send in too many men. They thought one man would work better.'

Hegarty grinned. It was a sight to chill the soul. 'So who the fuck were those bastards who shot us up yesterday?' he asked. 'I counted three men. You an' who else?'

'Two Prods,' Rob gasped. 'I don't know their real names. They came to me through a second source and I was told

not to ask. They're just gangsters, mercenaries for hire, and I
hired them for that single job. The other killings I did alone.'

Hegarty laughed and then glanced at the other men gathered around him. They all laughed together. 'Sure the man's
a wit,' he said. 'He has the gift of the blarney.' He turned back
to Rob and punched him in the face. The pain was appalling.
Rob threw up and then sobbed. 'Don't shite me,' Hegarty said.
'Sure ya came here with some friends. Those two bastards
who were with you yesterday were professional soldiers. That
whole thing was an SAS-style ambush an' all of us know it. So
I want to know their names, who they are, where they are now,
an' I want to know how you knew about our movements and
could set up that ambush. First question: who are your fuckin'
mates? Just give me their names.' Holding the pliers up, right
in front of Rob's face, he opened and closed them as if pulling
out more fingernails. 'Start talkin' or else.'

Rob refused to talk. At least, he tried to refuse. When he
stayed silent, the real torture commenced and the pain was
too much to bear. They did things beyond imagining, induced
pain beyond belief, and he screamed and sobbed and begged
them to stop and still tried not to talk. They kept working at
him. When one grew tired, another started. Each man had his
own speciality and each one was a killer. But Hegarty was the
worst, a man who loved what he was doing, and when he'd had
his little break, letting the others have their fun, he returned
with even more enthusiasm and Rob could not fight him. Rob's
throat was raw from screaming, his shirt was soaked in sweat
and vomitus, his heart was pounding and his thoughts were
lost in the chaos created from boundless pain. He sobbed
and finally broke, giving them everything they needed – the
addresses of Burton and Slim, the whereabouts of Teresa Kiely
– and then he sobbed in his despair, like a child, and wanted
to die where he sat. He was shuddering violently and racked
with pain and shame when they threw him back on the floor.
They loosened his bonds and kicked him across the room until
he lay in the corner. His bruised and lacerated arms were
wrapped around his battered body, when Hegarty came to
him. Hegarty went down on his knees in front of Rob and
looked him right in the eye.

'You've been a good wee boy,' he said. 'Ya sang like a fuckin'
bird. I can't be sure if all ya told me was true, but now we're
gonna find out. We're gonna find yer friends, boyo. If they're

home, they're dead meat. If they're not, we'll just sit tight and
wait for 'em and put an end to 'em. You're stayin' alive for now,
under guard, till I get back, an' if I find out that ya told me
some fibs, I won't be in a good mood. Ya think what I did was
bad? Jesus, boyo, that was nothin'. If ya've lied, if ya've told
me a few wee fibs, yer gonna know what *real* pain is. So you
sit here, ya fuckin' wee squealer, an' think of what ya've just
told me. If ya've lied, ya'll rue the day ya were born, 'cause I'll
do to ya what ya've never imagined an' then I'll bury ya deep.
If ya've told the truth, ya've condemned yer friends to death
an' yer own death will be harder. So think about that when
I'm gone and then suffer accordingly. Sure there's nothin' any
lower than a squealer an' that's what ya are now. I'll see ya
later, boyo.'

Rob had told him the truth and that made it even worse. So
when Hegarty stood up and turned away to leave, Rob reached
quickly into his shirt pocket, withdrew his cyanide tablets and
popped them into his bloody mouth.

'What's he swallowing?' someone bawled.

For all his bulk, Hegarty spun on the balls of his feet like a
ballerina and rushed back to Rob, slapping hard at his face
and then kneeling down to try prising his jaws apart. Rob's
throat was raw from screaming, but he managed to swallow
the tablets and knew, through his shame and pain and grief,
that he had put an end to it. He felt Hegarty slapping him,
heard his bawled oaths, felt his kicking boot, but the tablets
had slipped down his gullet and that, at least, was a victory.

'Ya fuckin' shit!' Hegarty bawled. He kicked Rob across
the floor. 'The shite's poisoned his fuckin' self! The fuckin'
bastard's dead meat!'

Rob was turning numb all over, taking the kicks without
hurting. He shuddered as he felt his lungs constricting and
floated out of himself. He drifted high above his body, looking
down upon himself, feeling the ebb and flow of the pain and
then its final retreat. Someone grabbed him by the hair and
dragged him out of the house. They threw him back down on
the ground, left him lying there like a turd, and then hurriedly
set fire to the house and emerged from the streaming smoke.

Rob saw it all from afar. He assumed that he must be dead.
They poured gasoline over his rented van and car, set fire to
both vehicles, then hurriedly drove away in their own car.
They took Rob with them in the boot of their car. He was

there, in that cramped darkness, in that tomb, but he was also drifting high overhead, tied to himself by a thin cord.

The car turned off the road, bounced and rattled across a field, and when it stopped they dragged Rob out of the boot and threw him back on the ground. He was vomiting and choking, coughing blood and shuddering, as they hastily dug a deep hole in the earth, heaping the soil up on both sides. Rob drifted high above, no longer feeling any pain, looking down upon himself, his other half, as they finished digging that deep hole. They picked him up and swung him like a rag doll and threw him into the hole. When they shovelled the soil back over him, when the darkness rushed in, the thin cord tying Rob to his other self was released and he drifted free.

He drifted over his resting place, which had been covered by grass turves, and he kept watching as his tormentors climbed back into the car and drove away from his hidden grave. When they drove away, Rob saw nothing but green fields, the white clouds, the radiant blue sky beyond. Then he entered the vast realms of the cosmos . . . Beyond that, there was nothing.

'Now let's get those other two bastards and the whore,' Hegarty said as he was driven away from the flame and the smoke and another unmarked grave. 'Let's put an end to it.'

Rob didn't hear those words.

CHAPTER THIRTY-FOUR

Making love to Teresa, Burton felt victimized, racked with guilt and yet helpless, unable to resist her mesmeric beauty or his own heart's fierce pounding. He had wanted to resist her and stay loyal to his wife, but the minute Teresa entered his rented house, he knew he would fail. She had taken her coat off, looked around her with interest, then stretched her body, which even in a sweater and blue jeans was still an exquisite sight. Then she had turned to him, her smile like ice and fire, walked up to him, placed her hands on his shoulders and said, 'Well, Sergeant Burton, if you want me, I'm yours for the taking.' After that, there was no hope.

Now, as he made love to her, Burton knew what true desire was, his need for her transcending his whole life's history and melting guilt in its heat. He knew that the guilt was there, floating around him like a fog, but he could no more have stopped what he was doing than he could have held back the raging sea. When he kissed her lips, she sucked his tongue; when he licked her throat, she bit his neck; and when he kissed his way down her writhing body, she held his head with her thighs. Down there, in that silk-smooth vice, in the darkness of her centre, he used his mouth and tongue in ways he had never before imagined and would never again forget. She gave herself to him, pushing down, opening and closing, and he knew the deep despair of a man for whom passion is dangerous. When she released him, when she opened her legs and sighed, he raised his head and was dazzled. He saw the glory of her supine, arching body and was stunned by the sight of it.

'Come here,' she crooned. 'Come back where ya belong. Let me look at yer face. Sure I need ya on top. I want ya stretched

out above me. God, yer eyes. God, yer face. Kiss me, Burton.
Just kiss me. Take me out of this fuckin' world an' leave me
wasted. That's it. *Kiss me*, Burton!'

He lay his body upon her softness, felt her breasts, the
sweat-slicked belly, and sank into her as into a deep well
where the darkness was magical. There was warmth and
electricity, streams of light that stroked the skin, and in
the cavern of her mouth and in her cunt he felt the joining
of opposites. He kissed her to devour her, tugging her hair,
jerking her head back, slid his tongue between her lips and
touched her centre and then slid smoothly into her. Once there,
in that moist, pulsating warmth, he lost the last of his will.
He hardly knew what he was doing but his body did and her
body rose up to help him. He moved in and out, they moved
together, in tandem, and this made them as one. When she
sighed, when she murmured soothing words, it was a sound
deep inside him. She was within him and he was part of her
and the real world did not exist.

'Oh, Burton,' she whispered. 'What is this? What is it yer
doin'? Do it, Burton, just do it. Do it as ya would like it. Mary,
Mother of Jesus, sure that's grand. Oh, dear God, don't stop
movin'. Do it now and for always.'

There was need and there was greed and he felt that mindless hunger, overriding all other considerations and making
him lose his identity. He had wanted to resist her, to keep
her at a distance, but all that came to nothing in this bed
in the darkness and silence. It was not a real silence – that
distant roaring was his breathing – but it helped him rise out
of himself and look back down in wonder. She had her arms
and legs around him, trapping him in her web, and she moved
with the seductive rhythm of a spider hypnotizing its prey. He
felt victimized, yes, and yet he also felt in control: as if, in the
very act of being taken, he had somehow exploited her. He had
done that, of course, in various ways, but none had come close
to this. As he rose and fell upon her, thrusting hard and deep
inside her, he sensed that, in letting himself be seduced, he
had finally broken through to her. Though a mystery that had
yet to be unravelled, she was opening out to him.

'Don't say nothin',' she said. 'Let me do all the talkin'. Let
me hear m'own voice to make it real, but don't you make a
sound. I wanna hear yer breathin', Burton, hear yer sighs. I
want yer wind in m'sails. You be quiet now. Just do it. Ah,

that's grand, that's the business. Sure there's no gettin' away from this at all. Fuck me, Burton, just fuck me. All the rest is a nonsense.'

He plunged into her, trying to find himself in there, where blood and bone were the essence. Inside her, in her pulsating heat, was the self she would not reveal. He probed deeper, draining into his own centre, trying to find what it was she had seen in him but refused to acknowledge. She had sensed his pain and listened to his outpouring of grief and then taken him in. Her reasoning was beyond him, at once fearful and calculating, and he sensed that in cleaving to her body, he had somehow enslaved himself. He was swimming in her treacherous tides and she would not let him go.

'Try it this way,' she murmured.

She turned onto her hands and knees and he knelt behind her and fell upon her, curved over the white snowscape of her spine with its ribbons of black hair. He grabbed her hair with both hands, a pair of reins that he could cling to, and tugged her head this way and that as he entered her from the rear and rode like the wind through a stormy night. His belly slapped against her buttocks, his sweat dripped onto her white skin, and he reached down to cup her breasts in his hands and feel her taut, tingling nipples. He crushed her breasts and pulled her to him, pressing himself tighter to her, and she rolled her buttocks and seemed to spiral around his cock as he threatened to come.

'Not yet,' she said with uncanny intuition. 'It's too soon for that. Let me go and turn around again, then lie down on yer back. That's it. God, ya look good. That body! An' so big and so hard. I've gotta have a taste of it. Close yer eyes and don't move.'

But he couldn't help moving. What she did was too much for him. He felt her tongue and the back of her throat and couldn't get enough of her. His body arched as he thrust upwards, wanting more, giving more, and she sucked him up into her and swallowed him and made him shake like a windblown leaf. The shaking started in his legs and moved up through his body and then, when his arms started trembling, he grabbed her hair with both hands again, his set of reins, and tugged her down even lower. He ran his fingers through her hair and grasped her head and moved it up and down, gently, this way and that, to make her cover the whole of him.

She took him in as much as she could and then her soft lips
slid off him.

'Come inside me,' she said. 'I want to feel ya – what yer like
when ya come. Let me lie there. Turn over. That's it, Burton.
Ah, Jesus!'

She spread her legs as he slipped in and then she clamped
her legs around him and he felt her fingers pressing on his
spine and then her fingernails cut him. He was trapped in her
web, in the strands of her limbs, and he tried not to come and
then came as if exploding from inside. He was uncontrolled,
helpless, a victim of his own lust, and as he poured himself
into her, one spasm piling on the next, he felt the ecstasy of a
bird taking wing before being shot down. He had to have that
one moment, freedom's light before the storm, and so he came,
and came again, and came a third time, and then gasped and
collapsed.

He lay upon her body for a long time and she didn't complain.
Then eventually, not believing what he had done, he rolled off
her and lay there beside her, staring up at the ceiling. He didn't
know what to say.

'Are ya all right?' Teresa asked after a lingering, unreal
silence.

'Yes,' he said. 'I'm all right. I'm fine. I'm just . . .'

'Yeah,' she interjected. 'Right. Sure ya don't have to say
another word. There's not much to say, really.'

'What does that mean?' he asked.

Still naked, she slipped out of bed and went to her shoulder
bag. She lit a cigarette and picked up an ashtray and then
walked to the window. Looking out of the window, she smoked
the cigarette and occasionally tipped the ash into the ashtray
held in her left hand. Naked, she was even more remarkably
beautiful, the long black hair spilling down her spine to touch
white, perfect buttocks. Burton thought he was dreaming.

'What it means,' she said, 'is that ya did what you wanted
and now yer filled with guilt and shame. You've nothin' to say
because of that, but that's somethin' I'm used to. I know ya
want me, Burton. In yer own way, yer in love with me. But
ya also want to save me to make amends for what ya did to
that poor wee child all those years ago.'

'That's true,' Burton said.

'Damn right it's true, Burton. It's as true as my naked body.
Ya want to save me, but ya also want my body an' maybe me

for myself. I was touched by that, Burton. Not many men see me that way. They think I'm beautiful an' they want their hands on me but you wanted all of me – and that's somethin' to cherish, like. But though you want me, and maybe want me the right way, ya can't accept the truth of it. Yer thinkin' of yer wife and kids, of betrayin' them though me, an' right now yer regrettin' what ya just did and maybe blamin' me for it. I could hate ya for that, Burton, I really could, but that isn't the half of it.'

'What's the rest?' Burton asked her.

'The way ya used me, for a start. That wee carelessness of yours. You were honest enough to tell me it was dangerous, but then ya dropped me right into it. You were too busy thinkin' about you an' me to think *only* of me. So ya set up yer fuckin' ambush an' have yer wee victory an' only then do ya think about the consequences for Hegarty's whore. You wanted me from the minute ya saw me and yer guilt made ya careless. I could hate ya for that, too.'

'You don't hate me for that,' Burton said. 'You've known too many men for that. I'm not perfect and you wouldn't expect that of me, so that's not what it is. What is it, Teresa?'

'Life's shit, you know that? It's been shitty from Day One. I've lived a life you just couldn't believe an' I want to get out of it. Oh, I know I told ya about it. I mean, I told you certain things. But there are things I can't even begin to tell ya an' they're eatin' me up. It's because of you, Burton. Things you've said in yer innocence. They've made me hate ya and love ya at the same time an' I don't like the feelin'. What I heard, I won't forget. My heart's been withered like a raisin. I think I love ya, but that won't make a difference when this has all ended. So just tell me one thing, Burton, and make it straight an' true. I know ya love yer wife and kids an' I respect that, I admire it – I even envy yer wife – but I need to know if even lovin' yer wife as you do, you still love me in yer fashion. Maybe different, not the same way ya love her, but a kinda love just the same. If ya can say it – and I know it won't be easy – I'll believe it an' cherish it. I'll do that no matter what comes next, when all this shit has ended. Yes or no, Burton. Tell me.'

Naked, Burton slid off the bed and walked up behind her. He placed his arms around her naked body and kissed the back of her neck.

'I love you,' he said.

'Now yer mine,' she said. 'Always.'

She leaned against him, communicating with her body, and then she walked away from him. After placing the ashtray on the table, she lay back on the bed. She lay there, breathing deeply and evenly, with tears in her eyes.

'I love you,' she said. 'Don't ever forget it. No matter what happens in the future, always remember I said that. It's not somethin' I've said for a long, long time. Now please let me sleep, Burton.'

'I will,' Burton said.

Still naked, he left the bedroom and went down the stairs. In the kitchen, he poured himself a large whiskey and then lit up a cigarette. He felt confused and badly shaken, but he also felt redeemed, as if the love that had been given and received had healed the scars on his broken heart. She was a mystery and there were things she still hadn't told him, but he wouldn't worry about that, at least not right now. In admitting he loved her, he had set himself free and no longer felt guilty or ashamed – and that, in its very simplicity, had made it all worth while. Now he only had to ensure her future safety and the rest would work itself out. He had to finish the job.

The telephone rang.

CHAPTER THIRTY-FIVE

S hocked back to the real world by that intrusive ringing noise, Burton placed his whiskey glass on the table and picked up the telephone.

'Yes?' he said, almost whispering.

'Is that you, Burton?'

'Yes, Slim, this is me. What's going on?'

'You'd better get over here real quick. I'd suggest you come right now.'

'Why?'

'I can't discuss this on the phone. Just get over here, Burton.'

'I'm on my way,' Burton said.

Knowing that Slim's refusal to talk on the phone meant that the matter was serious, Burton put the phone down and hurried back up the stairs and into the bedroom. Teresa was still stretched out on the bed, her eyes closed, fast asleep. Burton didn't want to waken her, but he didn't have a choice: he didn't want her to wake up and find him gone, so he gently shook her awake. He was already slipping into his pants when she opened her eyes.

'What . . . ?'

'I have to go out,' Burton said. 'I'll try not to be too long. Now you go back to sleep.'

'Don't leave me, Burton.'

'I have to,' Burton said.

'Will I be all right here?'

'Yes,' Burton said. 'You've nothing to worry about. Nobody knows I live here and nobody calls. You'll be all right. Go back to sleep.'

She closed her eyes and slept instantly. Burton put his clothes on. He strapped his Browning High Power handgun over his shirt in the cross-draw position, then put on his jacket and shoes and walked back to the bed. Teresa was still asleep, looking as innocent as a child. Burton leaned down and kissed her on the forehead, then he left the bedroom. He went downstairs and out the back door and locked it carefully behind him. Then he climbed into his rented Ford Escort and hurriedly drove off.

He was at Slim's house in no time, having driven in a trance-like state, and when he reached it, he saw the lights blazing out into the night. Climbing out of the car, he was aware of his nervous tension and he was glad when Slim opened the door and he could step inside. He turned around as Slim was closing the door and said, 'So, what is it?'

'I couldn't risk telling you this on the phone,' Slim said. 'It's pretty bad news.'

'Just tell me,' Burton said.

Slim took a deep breath and let it out in a sigh. 'I've just been to Rob's place. It's been burnt down to the ground. His van and car have also been burnt and there was no sign of him. I checked the whole area, but there was no sign of his body. What I *did* find was a lot of footprints around the front of the house – or what's left of the house. But no sign of Rob. Nothing. I think he's been taken.'

'Shit!' Burton exclaimed softly. He was shocked and his heart was racing. 'They've either taken him or they've already killed him and buried the body. They wouldn't do that near the house. They'd do it somewhere else. They'd burn the house and cars and take him, leaving no trace behind.'

'If they took him alive, they'd have tortured him before they killed him. If they did and he talked, we're in trouble. What the fuck do we do now?'

'If he talked, he'll have told them where we are, so we'll have to move out.'

'I don't think Rob would talk.'

'If he was tortured, he'd talk. Maybe not at first, not for a long time, but in the end he would talk.'

'He might have joined the Exit Club – taken the cyanide tablets. He might have done that before he talked. I know he would if he could.'

'They burned the house down. They also burned the cars. They wouldn't have done that if he wasn't there, so they must have burst in. He might have had time to take the tablets, but

I doubt it and they probably tied him up. Maybe not, but we can't take that chance. We have to assume that they took him alive and made the poor bastard talk. And if he talked, that means they'll know where we are and we'll have to move on. We'll also have to finish this job quickly and get the hell out of here.'

'Fucking A,' Slim said. 'So where do we go from here? It's practically midnight, for Christ's sake. That's not a time to be moving.'

'We'll find somewhere,' Burton said. 'We'll drive around and find a farmhouse. I've seen quite a few empty ones around, so we'll break in and bunk up in one. You'd better pack up straight away. Make sure you take the weapons. In fact, make sure you don't forget a thing and then light out for my place. I'm going back for Teresa. I'll take her out of there immediately. You'll find my car parked about half a mile away, to the south, where the road forks. When you get there, you can stick on my tail and we'll go in search of a farmhouse. Somewhere a good distance away, well outside Antrim. Now I'd better get going.'

'See you soon,' Slim said.

Burton went back to his car and then drove at reckless speed through the dark night, back to his own house. This time the journey took forever – or so it seemed to him – and he kept his eyes peeled for other cars or a potential ambush. The journey was uneventful and his tension started easing, but when he reached his own house his stomach heaved when he saw all the lights on. He was about five hundred metres away from the house when he braked to a halt.

After turning the ignition off and dousing the lights, he slipped out of the car and quietly closed the door. There was no-one in sight, but he advanced at the half crouch, sticking close to the side of the road, in the shadow of the line of hedgerows, well away from the moonlight. When eventually he reached the open ground in front of the house, he knelt on one knee and carefully studied all the windows, seeing nothing but the lights blazing out and hearing no sound at all. Withdrawing his Browning High Power handgun from its holster, he removed the safety catch, then advanced again, zigzagging, at the half-crouch. The front door was open and he knew that was bad news, but he carefully moved up to the open door, then turned sideways against the wall beside it.

There was no sound of movement inside. There was no sound at all.

Raising his handgun, he held his wrist with his free hand, then glanced around the doorframe and quietly scanned the living room. A small table had been knocked over and a lamp lay on the floor. Burton strained to hear movement from upstairs, but he heard nothing at all.

Spinning quickly on the balls of his feet, he rushed into the living room, swinging the handgun from left to right and preparing to fire. Seeing no one, he checked the whole of the ground floor and found all of it empty. The place had been ransacked, however, and the floor was a mess.

Burton advanced towards the stairs, still moving his handgun left to right, and when he reached the stairs he stopped and looked up and again strained to hear. He heard no sound at all.

He advanced up the stairs.

The climb took an eternity, one step at a time, and he never stopped listening for a sound that would indicate movement. Again, he heard nothing.

The first bedroom was the guest room and Burton went in there first, moving quietly and swinging the handgun left and right, preparing to fire.

The bedroom was empty.

Burton went to the next bedroom. He advanced very slowly. He thought of Teresa lying there sleeping and he dreaded what he might find. He took a deep, even breath, making no sound, and then spun on the balls of his feet and rushed into the bedroom.

Teresa was missing.

CHAPTER THIRTY-SIX

When Cooney, windblown and out of breath, made his way to Weir's Snout high above the Giant's Causeway, he saw Burton in exactly the same spot, staring out at the stormy sea. Burton merged with the landscape, standing still as a rock, and he only turned his head at the last moment, just as Cooney approached him. He smiled, but he seemed far away. Then he held out his hand.

'Hi, Cooney,' he said.

They shook hands. Cooney glanced out to sea and said, 'Sure you're trying to see England again. You're yearning for Hereford. Home and hearth, wife and kids.'

'I guess so,' Burton said. 'How are things with you?'

'Nothing's changed much in my life since a couple of nights ago. I sweated blood pulling that act with Teresa, but I'm my old self again. I note she hasn't returned to the bar. Did you get her out safely?'

'I got her out and then I lost her,' Burton said. 'That's why I wanted to see you. I lost her and I'll never forgive myself and I have to find her and finish this. If nothing else, I've got to finish the job to buy her a safe life. I owe her that much.'

'Yes, you do,' Cooney said. He had seen the pain in Burton, but now he sensed something else: an inner calm that had not been there before and now was thinly obscured by the concern he was feeling for Teresa. Burton had somehow found release from the torments of his past, and sensing that, Cooney knew without doubt exactly where he had found it. 'You slept with her,' he said.

Burton sighed. 'Yes, I did. I broke my own rule. I told my men they mustn't involve themselves with any local women –

my concern was for security – and then I turned around and slept with Teresa. So much for my rectitude.'

'Leave rectitude to the priests,' Cooney said. 'So when did it start?'

'Last night,' Burton said. 'When I took her home. We only did it one time. That one time is going to last me a lifetime and I won't think bad of it.'

Cooney smiled. 'What a moral man you are. So when did you lose her?'

'That was last night as well.'

'A busy night,' Cooney said.

Burton didn't smile, but he stared out to sea again. The wind was blowing his hair around his face and it made him look wild. There was something ancient about him, something primal, and he seemed carved from stone. That's why he looked like one of the rocks. He was as timeless as they were.

'They got one of my men,' he said. 'They burned his house down and set fire to his van and car and they didn't leave a trace of him behind, so I think he's a dead man. Almost certainly they tortured him and I think he must have talked, because that same night, when I was seeing another friend, they came to my place. When I got back, Teresa was gone and now I've got to go find her.'

'You think Hegarty took her?'

'Almost certainly,' Burton said.

'Then she might be hidden somewhere in the Falls and that place is a labyrinth.'

'I don't think she's there,' Burton said. 'If they have her, they're going to kill her. For that, they'll take her somewhere outside and I need to know where.'

'I can't help you,' Cooney said, 'and I don't know who can. They could have taken her anywhere in the Province and your guess as to where is as good as mine.'

'Tell me about Shaun Keenan,' Burton said. 'What's he like? What makes him tick?'

'Why do you ask?'

'Because I think he's the leader of the pack and that he was all along. I also know that he let his good friend Byrne die, so I think he's more than he looks.'

'He let Byrne die?'

'Yes, he did. And it was absolutely deliberate. I never asked about him before because I thought he was just an accountant, but now I know he's a lot more than he seems – and he's certainly ruthless. So just what is he, Cooney?'

'What I have is a mixture of fact and speculation, but it carries some weight.'

'Just tell me, Frank.'

Cooney sighed and glanced about him at the rocks and tumbling hills far below. The wind was bending the trees on the grassy slopes and the grey sea was roaring. Ireland, even the North, was a wild country and its passions ran deep. Beneath the charm of this place were murderous feelings that blew in on the wind.

He turned to Burton and saw that steady, questioning gaze and thought of what he had done here, both now and during the Troubles. Burton had seen enough to last him a lifetime, enough to break many men, but he stood there unbroken. Cooney knew that when this job was over, he would never come back. At least, he would never come back if he survived and that issue was still in doubt.

'Keenan,' Cooney said. 'I always wondered about him. There are an awful lot of stories about him, but you can't always pin 'em down. You'll have his basic details, of course – his aristocratic background, Trinity College and all the rest. He's certainly not a lout picked off the streets and handed a baseball bat.'

'Yes,' Burton said, 'I know that much. Just how deep does he run?'

'Pretty deep with strong roots. He did his time in the streets. He was never thrown in jail like his father and grandfather, but he certainly took part in a lot of business of the unpleasant kind. But he was too bright for that, too educated, sophisticated, and he rose very quickly through the ranks and soon had his own ASU. He was good at that as well, though it wasn't really his kind of thing, and soon he was transferred to an operational planning wing, using his brains instead of brawn. He was brilliant at the planning because he had the long-term view and his proposals fitted in with the IRA's gradualist politics. Keenan originally believed that the problem could be solved that way, with negotiation, but then, during the Troubles of '78, he lost his patience and joined the Provisionals. Things became pretty murky after that and he sank into the background, though the word was out that in his shadowy way he'd become pretty powerful. By that time

he was running the business side of things and he knew how
to do it. He was flying in and out of the country, buying arms
and soliciting funds, and from what I hear, he shook an awful
lot of the hands of fellow travellers worldwide. He became a
power, I think, during that time. And then the peace came.'

Burton had turned sideways to look out to sea again, but
Cooney knew that he was hanging on every word. When
Cooney followed Burton's gaze, he saw a transport ship out
on the horizon, hazed in mist, looking ghostlike. The ship was
clearly heading for England and Burton was following it. He
was looking towards home now.

'From what I picked up,' Cooney said, 'when Keenan became
one of the Belfast Six, his situation was slightly different from
that of the others. The others had their own turfs, but Keenan
shared his with Byrne – combined, their two turfs made up
the largest of them all. And while Byrne concentrated on
the active side of things – the extortion and intimidation,
the bank robberies and hijacking, the street trade in drugs
and so forth – Keenan quietly ran their business affairs and
made them a mint. He was also flying in and out again,
making connections overseas, and there's no doubt that the
American-Irish connection was set up by him. Now, from
what I gather, he's into Europe in a very big way. So he's
shadowy, but he must be pretty powerful and I think he would
use that.'

'What for?' Burton asked.

'The new war,' Cooney replied. 'He's never believed in the
peace initiative. The political peace has never really worked
– it's crashed more than once – and I believe he's going to
encourage the next crash and then march in with an army.
Sure his men are still training ASUs and gathering arms on a
huge scale. Keenan's not the criminal type – he really believes
in the cause – and he's never lost the dream of a united Ireland,
with the Brits out for good.'

'But why, given that, would he let Byrne die?'

'Because Byrne lost the faith. They were best friends, but
Byrne turned to crime and degraded the cause. If Keenan
wants what I believe he wants – to build an army of dedicated
freedom fighters and return to the fight – then Byrne, having
turned to organized crime, would have been in his way. With
Byrne dead, Hegarty's next on the list. I'm pretty damned sure
of that.'

Cooney looked straight at Burton, trying to save him from himself, wanting to keep this good man alive and let him go home in one piece. 'Why waste your time, Burton? Why risk your life for nothing? Let Keenan put Hegarty out of the way for you, then go for Keenan alone. You might finish it that way.'

'I'm going for both of them,' Burton said, 'because time's running out. I don't think they'll have killed Teresa yet, so I'm going for her as well.'

'Why won't they have killed her?'

Burton looked distraught. 'They'll want as much information as they can get, so they'll put her to torture. That's why I have to move fast. If she's not in the Falls, if they took her outside the city, where do you think they might have taken her?'

'Keenan's house,' Cooney said. 'I've heard stories about that place. It's a big, rambling mansion in Castleblaney, Monaghan. South of Armagh, a good distance from Belfast, but not really that far. There's been talk about interrogations in its basement – an enormous basement that used to be a wine cellar, big and cold and soundproof. Those stories might be rumours – I can't say one way or the other – but certainly Keenan has used his house for years for upper-echelon meetings of the IRA and, later, the PIRA, so the idea that he might take prisoners there for interrogation isn't all that outlandish.'

'I think that's where he would have taken her,' Burton said.

'It's a possibility,' Cooney said. The wind howled and beat at him, making him shiver with cold even in this summer month, and he turned up the collar of his overcoat and stomped his feet on the ground. He knew that Burton would go out to Keenan's place and that nothing would stop him. 'Do you know where it is?' he asked.

'Yes,' Burton replied. 'It was in his intelligence dossier, clearly marked on the map. I don't think I'll get lost.'

Cooney smiled. 'So what happens if you find them both?' he asked. 'I mean Keenan and Hegarty.'

'They'll both disappear,' Burton said. 'There'll just be an empty house.'

'More unmarked graves on the green hills of Ireland. No wonder this country is haunted.'

Burton actually smiled. 'Yes, I guess that explains it.' He

ran his fingers through his windblown hair and squinted at
the horizon. The ghost ship that had been gliding through the
mist was nowhere in sight. 'Thanks,' Burton said. 'I'd better be
going now. As you've probably sussed, I won't ever be coming
back, so this is goodbye.'

He shook Cooney's hand and the latter turned to walk away.
He had only walked a few paces when he stopped and turned
back to his friend.

'Will I know if you've survived it?' he asked.

'No,' Burton said. 'We'll just vanish along with the dead men
and you won't see me again.'

'I'll find out if Teresa materializes,' Cooney replied.

'She won't talk,' Burton said.

Cooney smiled and waved his right hand, then turned away
and walked off. This time, though he felt a lump in his throat,
he did not look back. He knew that Burton would be standing
there like a rock, at one with the landscape. This thought gave
Cooney solace and hope as he walked out of Burton's life.

Cooney silently prayed for him.

CHAPTER THIRTY-SEVEN

Burton and Slim approached Keenan's house under cover of darkness after parking a good half-mile away and cutting obliquely across an intermittently moonlit field surrounded by whispering trees. They emerged onto a driveway that circled around the house and saw the lights gleaming over the gravel from its high, narrow windows. It was a very large house, though not quite a mansion, and two cars – a Mercedes and a Ford Cortina – were parked just out front. Beyond the house, beneath a sky filled with scudding black clouds, the hills curved like great waves.

'Only two cars,' Slim whispered. 'That's a pretty good sign. I know that Hegarty drives a Ford Cortina. The Mercedes must be Keenan's.'

'I don't think they'd come alone,' Burton replied. 'There'll be more cars around the back.'

Slim grinned. 'Right,' he said, 'the servant's quarters. Or maybe the stables. No horses these days – just dickers' cars. That makes sense to me, boss.'

'There'll be a guard out front,' Burton said. 'We're still too far away to see. At least one man out front at any time and a couple inside the front door. There'll be similar around the back of the house, so let's take it from front and rear.'

'Suits me,' Slim said.

They had considered bringing along some high-tech surveillance equipment that would enable them to eavesdrop on what was happening inside; but Burton, upon reflection, had decided against it because it would need setting up. There were two strikes against that: one, that it would need time; two, that the equipment could be traced if he and Slim copped it. So, instead, they had agreed to make it simple: they were each

armed with a Heckler & Koch MP5 sub-machine gun – which
the IRA also used – and the ubiquitous Browning 9mm High
Power handgun, now widely used everywhere. If they made
it but had to leave behind their weapons, they'd still have
anonymity. Though wearing civilian clothing – open-necked
shirts, windcheater jackets, denims and rubber-soled shoes
– both men had webbed belts around their waists, with a
couple of L2A2 hand grenades clipped to them. Last but not
least, they were both carrying a Sykes Fairburn commando
dagger, strapped to the waist. So, given this relative sparsity
of hardware, they could move quickly and quietly.

Which they did.

Slim went loping at the half-crouch along the driveway,
cutting around the side of the house, heading for the back, as
Burton advanced towards the front by circumnavigating the
moonless edge of the driveway, keeping close to the hedgerow.
He was holding his MP5 in the position known as the 'Belfast
Cradle' – crooked in the forearm – when he reached the side
of the big house. Still hidden by the hedgerow – the moon was
casting shadows – he glanced along the house and saw a single
guard standing outside the front door. Not an inexperienced
teenage dicker, he was obviously a hard man, middle-aged
and bulging out of his grey suit like a bouncer at a club in
West Belfast. He was smoking a cigarette and occasionally
scratched his short-cropped hair, and though he wasn't holding a weapon in his hand, he almost certainly had one.

Knowing that some more hard men would be in the hallway,
Burton took a deep breath and moved forward very slowly,
crouched so low that he thought his back would break. He
advanced along the front of the house, keeping close to the
front wall, and kept looking from the guard to the ground
beneath his own feet. He was looking for loose gravel, large
stones, other debris, for anything that could make the slightest
noise and give away his position. But nothing obstructed him:
his progress was smooth and soon he was five metres from the
guard, who kept smoking his cigarette. Burton froze where he
was and remained there for some time. He was checking that
the guard hadn't heard him and assumed eventually that he
had not. Satisfied, he lowered the MP5 to the ground, laid it
down gently, then withdrew the Fairburn Sykes commando
dagger from its old leather sheath. He would have to be
careful now.

He advanced across that final few metres like an invisible man.

The guard, looking stiff and uncomfortable in his tight suit, threw his cigarette butt on the ground, crushed it under his foot, then reached down to scratch his balls distractedly. Burton moved very fast now, like an uncoiling spring, and came up from the shadows of the front wall like some dark beast of prey. The guard heard Burton's movement, the rush of air past his body, but by then Burton's hand was across his mouth to prevent him from screaming. Burton slashed his throat with the dagger, from left to right in one movement, and as the guard went into a spasm, his heavy body shuddering, Burton jerked his head back, his hand still covering the mouth, and let the blood spurt out, away from him, and then hugged the dying man to keep him still. The guard made a macabre rattling sound, jerked his legs and then sagged. Burton lowered him gently to the porch floor and removed his hand from the open mouth. The blood was still spurting from the dead man's throat but he was no longer moving.

Satisfied that his silence had been maintained, Burton went back to pick up his MP5 and then returned to the front door. He pressed his ear to it. He heard a murmured conversation inside, so he listened some more. One voice. Then two. Was that three? No, only two. There were two guards inside: they'd be armed and Burton had to deal with that.

Unclipping an L2A2 hand grenade from his webbed belt, he released the firing pin, but kept his thumb upon it. He was using his left hand. With his right hand, he aimed the MP5 sub-machine gun at the lock in the door, steadied the weapon between his elbow and hip, then fired a short burst from the waist and blew the lock apart. He kicked the door open, threw the grenade in and then spun backwards and pressed himself to the wall, waiting for the explosion.

The noise, which was deafening, was followed by screams and bellows. Burton spun around and raced through the front door, crouched low, his MP5 at the ready, moving the barrel from left to right. He saw streaming smoke, a body lying on the floor, clothing tattered, soaked in blood, and then he crashed into a man who was staggering as he clawed at his blinded eyes. Burton fired a short burst into the man's body; it shuddered under the bullets' impact and spun away. Thinking of nothing except what he had to do, Burton ran, still crouched low and zigzagging, into the brightly-lit entrance hall. He heard sporadic gunfire from the back of the building, signifying that Slim was fighting his way in.

Good boy, Burton thought.

He continued to think of nothing else except what he was doing right here and now – moving forward into that large house full of spacious rooms. Burton wanted the basement, where he sensed that it would happen, but he had to check all of the rooms first while Slim fought his way in from the back, his MP5 making a jarring sound that reverberated through Burton's head. Burton checked the downstairs rooms, which were luxuriously appointed, with fine old paintings hanging on the walls between curtains of velvet. Someone came out of nowhere, another gorilla in a grey suit. Burton fired his MP5 from the hip and the man screamed and fell away. Stepping over him, through another doorway, Burton heard a soft squeaking from above. He glanced up and saw a man on the stairs, taking aim with a pistol. Burton caught him with a short burst and the man jerked epileptically, then dropped his pistol and fell over the balcony and thudded onto the hallway floor.

The house is full of them, Burton thought.

He wanted to clear the upper floor, but he didn't have the time. He was fearful that Keenan and Hegarty might escape through a door in the basement. So he ran to the basement door, located under the stairs, and was just about to enter and go down when Slim rushed into the hallway.

'Upstairs!' Burton bawled. 'Clear the whole area! If you can't, set the building on fire!'

'Fucking A,' Slim replied.

Slim ran up the stairs as Burton entered the basement, moving slowly, with infinite care, down into that dank gloom. He saw light down there, wavering tendrils of whiteness, motes of dust at play, and heard the kind of silence that has the resonance of bells in a ghostly dream. A tap was dripping down there. The stairs creaked beneath his feet. He was wearing rubber-soled shoes, yet he could hear them as they pressed on bare boards, the squeaking dreadfully amplified. The dripping tap was his metronome, drip, drip, an eerie sound, and he strained to hear the sound of something else, but heard only his own breathing. He was breathing like a man asphyxiated and his chest felt that tight.

Don't consider her, he thought. *Don't let concern distract you. It's a job and it has to be done and when it's done you'll be clear of this. Christ, it's dark in this bloody hole.*

The cellar floor was bare concrete and the walls curved around him, forming a series of arch-shaped tunnels where formerly the wine vats had once stood. The tunnels went back a long way, into a deepening gloom, but he saw striations of light at the far end and moved carefully towards them. Smaller side passages ran off the tunnels and he checked them as he advanced, aware that men could be hiding around the corners, preparing to fire at him.

He heard movement, the soft pad of a single step, and then a man stood half exposed at one corner, taking aim with a pistol.

Burton fired his MP5, raising the barrel high and dropping it low, firing in a vertical arc to hit as much of the man as he could see. The man let out a brief scream and his pistol fell to the floor. As he disappeared back into the passageway, obviously wounded and falling, Burton heard movement behind him and spun around and kept firing his MP5. Another man, emerging from the passage behind him, was chopped across the stomach, doubled up, then jackknifed and fell backwards to thud onto the floor. Burton checked that no one else was coming at him from that direction, then he turned to the front and advanced again towards the light at the far end.

He heard movement from down there – the brief scurry of running feet – and he checked the MP5 and saw that it was empty. Lowering it quietly to the floor, he unholstered his Browning High Power handgun and released the safety catch.

A pistol shot rang out above, followed by a sustained burst from Slim's roaring MP5, as Burton advanced carefully along the cellar, hugging the damp wall. Catching the faint whiff of smoke, he guessed that Slim had started setting the house on fire. When he reached the end of the tunnel, where the light was shining dimly, he dropped onto one knee, pressed himself to the wall, then steadied his right wrist with his left hand and took a deep breath. Very carefully, he stuck his head out and peered around the corner.

The passageway ran away about thirty feet, its stone walls

damp and dripping, to another wall with a door leading
outside, almost certainly into the side garden. In the gloom
at that far end, Teresa was tied to a wooden chair, her arms
and legs bound with rope, a gag in her mouth. Even from here,
Burton could see that she had been beaten black and blue.
Her shirt had been pulled off, leaving her breasts naked, and
her skin was badly blistered from cigarette burns. Her eyes,
though black and swollen, were also wide and alert.

Burton burned with a smouldering rage when he saw what
they had done to her.

Whether or not she had seen him, Burton couldn't tell,
but certainly she did not move a muscle when he advanced
carefully into the passageway and headed towards her, still
moving at the half-crouch and holding his Browning High
Power with both hands, preparing to fire.

He heard the pad of running feet, from his left and from his
right, indicating that men were in the other passageways – at
least two, maybe more. They were clearly running in opposite
directions to box Burton in.

He continued advancing towards Teresa, but gradually
turned his body sideways to enable him to glance left and
right, at both ends of the passageway. The running feet muted
into a silence broken only by sporadic firing from upstairs –
it was all handguns now – accompanied by the crackling and
snapping from what undoubtedly was the fire started by Slim.
Smoke was drifting down into the basement and the distant
tap kept on dripping.

Still advancing sideways, Burton eventually reached Teresa.
He was shocked by the burns on her naked body – the shirt was
hanging loose around her waist – and by the bruises around her
eyes and on her split, bloody lips. Kneeling lower, still glancing
left and right, still holding his handgun, he tugged the gag off
Teresa's mouth and whispered, 'Don't make a sound.'

'*Behind you!*' Teresa screamed.

Burton spun around to see Hegarty rushing at him, his great
bulk casting a shadow before him, his eyes gleaming with rage.
He was aiming a pistol and Burton heard the first shot as
he fired his own handgun. The single bullet from Hegarty's
pistol whistled past Burton's head and ricocheted off the wall
behind Teresa as Hegarty jolted to a halt, looking surprised,
and then took a step backwards. Burton kept firing, six more
shots in a sustained sequence. Hegarty, amazingly, despite

being punched backwards and staggering drunkenly from left to right, remained upright until the seventh shot made him fall and hit the floor with a solid thud. Even then, he didn't die immediately but kicked his legs and cursed and groaned. Then he shuddered, went into a violent spasm, coughed blood and died. More blood, spreading out in a pool around him, turned the concrete floor purple.

Turning away, Burton removed his commando dagger from its sheath and started cutting the ropes binding Teresa. Something punched him in the shoulder and sent him spinning and only then did he hear Keenan's shot. The sound of the firing pistol filled his head as he fell to the floor and heard his handgun rattling away across it. His head was spinning and filled with cascading stars. Then he blinked and looked up. Keenan was standing above him, staring down with a thin smile. He held a Czech 75 in his right hand and was preparing to fire it.

'You English bastard,' he said. 'Coming here to cause havoc. My family home is on fire and that fire can't be put out and that's what you fucks have done to my country for two hundred years. Did you think you'd win, mister? Did you believe the shite they told you? Well, you didn't win today and your English friends will never win while Irishmen live and breathe in this country and stand up to be counted. You're fucked, my nameless friend, just as your English friends are fucked, and what I'll do to you is what we'll do to all the rest who come over here to try stopping us. Say your prayers, you English bastard, say them quickly, because it all ends right now.'

A single shot rang out.

Keenan gasped and leaped forward, as if punched from behind. His pistol went clattering to the floor as he fell past Teresa and slammed into the wall just behind her. He slid down the wall, leaving a trail of blood above him, and had managed to turn painfully to the front as he came to rest on his haunches. He was breathing in short, agonizing spasms, but his eyes were still bright.

Slim walked along the passageway, holding his handgun with both hands, and he stepped around Burton and Teresa to stop directly in front of Keenan and aim the handgun at him.

'Fuck you,' Keenan gasped. 'Our day will come.'

'Not today,' Slim replied.

He fired two shots – a double tap – into Keenan's heaving chest and Keenan jerked convulsively, as if tugged by invisible strings, then fell slowly sideways and died.

'Fuck you, too,' Slim said.

He turned away, dropped to his knees beside Teresa, and untangled the ropes not already sliced apart by Burton. Teresa gasped like a newborn baby taking its first breath, then she silently rubbed her bloody, scarred wrists and took deep, even breaths. Slim grinned at her and then turned away to look down at Burton.

'Your shoulder's a right bloody mess,' he said, 'but otherwise you're okay.'

'Thanks,' Burton replied. 'What's happening upstairs?'

'I flushed out the last of those bastards and then set the house on fire. That fire's going to burn a long time and leave nothing standing. A good day to be leaving.'

'Damned right,' Burton said.

At that moment, a great roaring emanated from the far end of the basement and they saw the gloom of the cavernous ceiling illuminated by boiling yellow-blue flames. The fire had rushed down into the cellar and smoke billowed before it. The smoke spread out and thickened.

'We'd better get the hell out of here,' Slim said.

'Damned right,' Burton repeated.

Slim turned towards Teresa and Burton saw the girl's movement as she twisted sideways and slipped off the chair, pulling her shirt back on, quickly reaching down to the floor for Burton's handgun. She grabbed the weapon, straightened up again, turned around and fired twice. Punched backwards by the impact of the bullets, Slim slammed into the wall facing Burton and remained there, standing upright, bemused, staring down at his bloody chest.

'What the fuck . . . ?' He raised his eyes, stared at Teresa and then slipped to the floor. After rocking on his haunches for a few seconds, he fell sideways onto the floor, coughed blood and then died.

Burton didn't say a word. He knew what Teresa was doing. It was a fitting and proper end to this whole business and it would bring him relief. He sat there, propped up against the wall, shivering with cold, one shoulder still seeping blood, as Teresa, visibly trembling, walked up to him. She looked down

at him through tearful, blackened eyes as she took aim with
the handgun. Burton noticed that her hand was shaking badly
and his heart went out to her.

'Fuck ya, Burton,' she said. 'Damn ya to hell, Burton. I love
ya, but ya've brought me to this and now there's no gettin'
away from it. I've lived with ya for years, Burton. You couldn't
have known that, but I did. All that stuff I told ya, all that
shite about tarrin' an' featherin', sure it never happened at
all. Oh, it happened to some others. Other poor wee friends of
mine. Teenage girls who just wanted a little love and picked
the wrong man – a fuckin' Brit or a Prod. They tarred an'
feathered 'em, just like I told ya, but I was too young for that
then. Ya remember it, don't ya, Burton? That poor wee child ya
killed. Shot her Dad an' then shot her as well before ya knew
what was happenin'. Her fuckin' Dad, Burton! It was him an'
then her. Ya shot her Dad – that was my Dad as well – an' then
ya shot her. Ya remember me, don't ya, Burton? Sure you've
remembered me all this time. Ya still have nightmares about
the other one, that poor wee child who ran screamin' out of
there. Yeah, that was me, Burton. That was me at nine years
old. Ya shot my Dad an' my sister and that drove m'Mum mad
an' then you an' I shared our separate nightmares, though
we both had the same dreams. Sure I dreamt about ya and
remembered ya, for years after, night an' day, an' I knew that
I could never forget it till I wiped the slate clean. I didn't know
how I could do that – I just couldn't think how, like – an' then
you came back into my life an' at first I still didn't know. I
didn't recognize ya, Burton. I mean, I did an' I didn't. When
I first met ya, I thought I recognized ya, but I didn't know
where from. Then ya told me yer story, Burton. Poured yer
fuckin' heart out. An' by that time, I loved ya – yes, I did –
an' then I knew that God hated me. I mean, how could He do
that to me? Make me love the man I'd hated. When ya told me
yer story, not knowin' who I was, my heart turned over and
cracked up inside an' mixed the hatred with love. God, I hated
ya then, Burton – more so because I loved ya. I wanted to slit
yer throat and drink yer blood and then die in yer arms. But
God doesn't make it easy. He likes to make us suffer, Burton.
He likes to test us to the absolute fuckin' limit and that's why
we're here now. I have to wipe the slate clean, Burton. I can't
go on if I don't do that. If I do it, I can't go on anyway, because
I love ya too much. So I'm gonna end it, Burton. For you an' for

me. I'll absolve ya of sin an' relieve ya of guilt an' then I'll pay
for what I've done an' hope to find ya again if there's anything
out there in the beyond that we all hope an' pray for. Oh, fuck
ya, Burton. Fuck ya, I loved ya and now damn ya to hell.' And
she fired the first shot.

Burton felt the bullet's impact, though it caused him no
pain. He was jolted by a burst of electricity and he lit up
inside. A second bullet hit him, then a third, and a fourth,
then he heard the handgun's firing pin clicking on an empty
shell and he felt himself smiling. Teresa threw the handgun
down and it clattered noisily on the floor. There was heat from
the flames still advancing and Burton choked on the smoke.
Teresa sobbed and knelt beside him, materializing like an
angel, and he felt her hands closing around his face as she
pulled him into her breasts. He lost himself in the soothing
warmth of her flesh and let love have dominion. As he rose
out of himself, detached and free, he knew what real joy was.
He stuck to her every inch of that long road that would bring
her back to him. He was there when she finished it.

'Yes,' he managed to whisper before he died. 'You and I – it
was love.'

Teresa sobbed and held him close, pressing his dead lips to
her breasts, then she released him and laid him gently on
the floor and kissed his forehead and walked away. She left
the basement by the side door, forced out by the flames and
smoke, and she entered the dark chill of a night illuminated
by dazzling flames. The whole house was on fire. Flames were
coiling towards a now cloudless sky. There was a full moon and
its light fell on the lake that lay beyond the broad lawn. Teresa
walked towards that lake, shedding tears, breathing heavily,
and she tore at her bruised face with bloody fingers and knew
at last what love was. She kept walking towards the lake, mes-
merized by its glittering stillness, and she heard the snapping
roar of the flames as the big house burnt behind her.

Burton would disappear, consumed by fire. They would not
find his body to desecrate him. He would join her where the
moon met the sun and no pain could intrude. Teresa walked
towards the lake, in the moonlight, under black clouds of
smoke. She walked out with no intention of coming back.
And she never did come back.